DAVID CAUTE

*The Women's Hour*

Flamingo
*An Imprint of* HarperCollins*Publishers*

Flamingo
An Imprint of HarperCollins*Publishers*,
77–85 Fulham Palace Road,
Hammersmith, London W6 8JB

Published by Flamingo 1993
9 8 7 6 5 4 3 2 1

First published in Great Britain by
Paladin 1991

Author photograph by Sophie Baker

ISBN 0 586 09143 2

Set in Meridien

Printed in Great Britain by
HarperCollinsManufacturing Glasgow

# THE
# WOMEN'S
# HOUR

# *One*

Professor Sidney Pyke has a train to catch, essays to mark – enemies to rout. And yet, prey to habitual compulsions, he is to be seen in mid-afternoon scuttling across the campus, with the shortened strides of thickening middle age, to the Benzin Swimming Pool. Seen he always is.

This is no ordinary day – under Samantha's loving guidance he has discarded his standard grimy jeans for clothes worthy of a television pundit. Crumpled into the usual ball, they are duly stuffed into his locker. Contact lenses: careful. Climbing into swimming trunks rotted by chlorine and deformed by gluttony – 'disgusting', Samantha calls them – Sidney trots, cursing, under the obligatory cold-water sprinkler which teases his flesh without improving his personal hygiene.

Emerging into the vast, post-modernist empire of light which is the Benzin Pool, he blinks, pauses in a private chapel of meditation at the poolside, and intently monitors the young legs kicking beneath the rippling, light-enchanted surface of the water. Student buttocks coated in luminous sheens cut away to the hip await his daily pleasure – but without his contact lenses nothing is quite clear.

In mid-afternoon the Benzin Pool is open to any member of the university, male or female. The strictly segregated Women's Hour, engineered by Dr Bess Hooper, comes at six o'clock and fills Sidney Pyke with (he would admit) a nice blend of lust and loathing.

Selecting a target, he dives in pursuit. More of a belly flop these days, but he enjoys the punishing sting. Of the risks he is slyly (un)aware; but a bluff charm has always shielded him (surely) from suspicion. Only once did things get seriously out of hand. There were no consequences and he has stuffed the incident into one of the darker lockers of his subconscious.

Clambering out of the pool ten minutes behind schedule, he showers the stench of chlorine from his hair, beard and skin, towels his several stomachs, then wrestles a crumpled heap of television-pundit clothes on to his still-damp skin. From his '60s suede jacket he extracts the contact lenses: careful. Moments later he is seen galloping back to his office on the first floor of the Media Studies Department.

If seen, he is invariably waylaid. On dry land the roles are reversed – the hunter hunted. Spectacularly approachable, he is a magnet for students begging advice, inspiration, his interpretation of the morning's headlines, or deferment of their essay deadline. (Invariably granted: 'Was it your grandmother who died this time, Kate?' 'Oh *thanks*, Sidney, I – ') According to the Registrar's computer and its satellite video cameras, seventy-three per cent of these 'campus muggings' inflicted on Pyke are perpetrated by females.

'Ragged charm,' is the Vice-Chancellor's verdict.

'But how many of them does he sleep with?'

'Not wishing to know the answer, I decline to hear the question.'

Late for his train, clutching a battered brown briefcase heaped with student essays and pressing departmental crises, plus an angry memo from the Registrar, Sidney Pyke falls into his waiting taxi. Of one thing he's confident: he will enjoy your support – if not approval – throughout the pages ahead.

'I'm late, Joe.'

'You're always late, Sidney. Did I ever let you down?'

'Got to catch the 4.50. "State of the Nation".'

The ancient Mercedes launches itself out of the yard in a cloud of diesel fumes and scattered students, horn blaring.

Though a Londoner by provenance, Joe is definitely a Third World-type driver.

'On telly, are you?' Joe has, as always, only one hand, or forearm, on the wheel. The other pursues this and that, particularly the rhetorical points that Joe wishes to make about blacks, Pakis, women, and 'them'.

'That's been a while, then?' Joe remarks.

'Yes, yes. What has?'

'Since they 'ad you on the box.'

'Oh, these things come and go. Fashion . . .' Sidney notes the pain in the lie – never sure whether he's the centre of the universe or a character in a rejected script. He often makes this point to his more intimate students, but Samantha no longer listens.

'Not like your missus.' (Is Joe a mind-reader?)

'No.'

'I always watch 'er, Friday nights. She isn't shy, your missus.'

'Shy Samantha isn't.'

'I bet she still knows a trick or two.'

Sidney catches Joe's hideous wink in the driving mirror.

'Joe, don't dawdle, please.'

The mirror registers offence taken.

Leaving the brave concrete slabs of the '60s campus, Joe swerves on screeching wheels into the long, quiet avenue which the landscaping architect had lined with poplars as a gesture of blatant francophilia. The poplars shift Sidney's anxieties from his views on child abuse, ozone layers, marital rape, women priests and Tory education policy ('State of the Nation') to his approaching trip to Paris. Live interviews, including en direct (as Chantal says it) radio and television, are scheduled for *Le Rouge et le Vert* par Sidney Pyke – the publicity girl who calls him from Paris says 'Peek', even when corrected. She sounds attractive, petulant, your Françoise Arnoul type; will she be free for dinner? Honesty (wrong word) compels the admission that his spoken French has made modest progress – frankly, negligible – since Chantal began her Tuesday lessons.

9

Down the long, straight Gallic avenue, the taxi is closing on a figure jogging along the grass verge towards them. The taxi slows: Joe's eye has fastened on a slender girl with long, golden hair clad (that's the word, though Joe would probably go for 'poured into' or 'done up') in shiny sea-green stretch-tights. Joe leans across the empty front seat to lower the near-side window, slows to a kerb-crawl, and emits a piercing wolf whistle as he draws level with the girl.

Sidney wraps his face in the *Guardian*.

'Some of them whores are just asking for it if you ask me,' Joe informs his fare while intently studying his mirror to catch the receding rear view. 'Christ — I mean it's blatant, isn't it?' He pauses reflectively: 'Cunts!'

'My train. Joe.'

Joe reluctantly accelerates down the avenue. 'Take some of those hitch-hiking cunts. You know what they're after, don't you.'

Sidney decides that it isn't a question.

But now, ahead of them, lies another rear view. The taxi is overtaking two women cyclists riding side by side. The younger, anorexically thin with a defiant mop of bushy hair, wears a full cotton skirt which billows in the breeze; her older companion, a square, stocky person, sports padded leather shorts almost to the knee, with a protective chamois-leather gusset at the crotch. Joe again slows to a crawl. The window slides down.

'What are you doing tonight, sweetheart?'

The two women turn, fury in their faces.

Sidney groans: Bess and Melanie. 'Joe!' he shouts, but you might as well quote Immanuel Kant to a hound with a rabbit in its jaws. Most of Joe is now in the front passenger seat as he cuts in closer to the cyclists, forcing them to brake, wobble and finally dismount with shrieks of protest. Sinking deeper behind his *Guardian*, Sidney can't avoid Bess Hooper's distinctive granny glasses furiously raking the interior of the taxi.

'Joe!'

The old Mercedes snarls away. 'Cunts! Slags!'

It had to be Bess and Melanie! Of course they'd recognized him — though maybe not. In his briefcase sit two more chapters of Melanie's traumatic thesis on Olive Schreiner and a clutch of explosive curriculum proposals from Bess, one of which he has already glanced at:

Most men are only too happy to benefit from the deeply entrenched inequality of the sexes. Professor Pyke's latest counter-blast, 'Language and Gender', displays the deep vein of misogyny endemic to a patriarchal culture. He continues to refer to the human race as 'he'.

Thank you very much! No recognition here that he, as editor of the *Media Studies Bulletin*, has liberally published Bess Hooper's many 'blasts' and 'counter-counter-blasts' without quibble or amendation. Almost without. 'Abuse of power' has now joined the long line of accusations queuing for a slice of the 'pig'. Did not Bess recently 'indict' him before the full Media Studies Board for putting honesty before fashion?:

It's undeniable [writes Sidney Pyke] that capitalism can turn any liberating movement into a saleable commodity. Feminism is now *the* growth industry. Acres of newsprint are reserved for women journalists, writers, artists and directors. Women reviewing women; women moaning about being women; women chewing their own wombs; women discovering themselves as women; women women women. Bookshops reserve whole walls of shelving for the work of women. In colleges and universities a proliferation of women's studies programmes promote the same racket. It's high time we made our escape from the ghetto of sex and gender.

Leaving the mad architect's avenue, the taxi encounters a thickening tangle of bad-tempered traffic clogging every new dual carriageway and bypass constructed by the pollution-happy District Council of which Sidney Pyke is the only Green member. Defeated streets of Victorian terraced dwellings have been cleared to make space for King Commerce: petrol stations offering 'free' mugs to mugs; vast warehouses; overspilling tips and 'bottle banks' (Sidney's idea); seedy pubs guaranteeing every driver a drunken driver. 'State of the Nation'! Sidney glances at his watch as Joe manoeuvres with blaring horn through the unfinished underpass project which has for months compounded the misery caused by a roundabout with five exits.

'Yeah!' Joe suddenly snarls, studying his mirror. It hasn't occurred to Sidney that the encounter with Bess and Melanie in the avenue was only the hors d'oeuvre, but Joe is beginning to vibrate as the two female cyclists impertinently thread a passage through the constipated lines of stationary cars and trucks, flaunting the advantages of simple technology. Sidney lifts his *Guardian* as Bess's leather shorts pass his window; simultaneously Joe's door shoots open trapping bicycle and rider. A hunk of thigh has entered his hand.

She screams. 'Bastard!'

'Cunt! Slag!' Joe's normally mild and affable features are creased in madness. 'Lesbian cunt!' A gob of spit strikes Bess Hooper full on the cheek and sticks.

'This can't be happening,' Sidney tells himself.

The drivers of neighbouring vehicles, the vast majority of them men, observe the encounter with studied neutrality. In the adjoining lane three young men in a Ford Transit van begin to hoot and honk as Bess Hooper struggles frantically to free her buttock from Joe's manic squeeze and her damaged bicycle from its trapped position between the taxi and the van. Sidney reflects that this geese-like honking, universal at football matches, is now the standard war cry of working-class youth.

'One nil, one nil,' they chant.

But where is Melanie? The thought is scarcely born when the rear door of the taxi opens and a wild-eyed young woman clutches a fair proportion of Sidney's beard. The handlebars of her bicycle, which Sidney sees as the horns of an enraged bison, come with her.

Melanie does not speak. In both love and war, she has always registered the top notes of emotion by intense silence. Samantha regularly bathed in iodine the silent bites on his shoulder, blaming Melanie's anorexia. Sidney notes that his hands are now fastened round Melanie's relentless wrists.

The noise all comes from the front. Joe has met his match in Bess. Her self-defence classes are beginning to make their mark, but it is her power of language which stuns him. The Mercedes lurches forward several yards, dragging both Bess and Melanie along in a tangle of moving metal.

Sidney hurls himself forward over Joe's shoulder and grabs the ignition key. The taxi shudders to a halt, the engine dies.

'Are you completely insane?'

The Ford Transit van has kept abreast. The near-side lad is now leaning out and pinching Bess's chamois-leather gusset. 'One nil, one nil,' he honks. Bess roars like a grounded river tug and Melanie (it must be Melanie) activates a personal alarm, a relentless piercing shriek which attracts a crowd of interested citizens, two police persons among them.

Hauled from the taxi, Sidney recognizes that he will miss his train and never again take part in 'State of the Nation'. Avoiding eye contact with Bess and Melanie as they fill the police notebooks with tales of outrage and injury, he waits for someone in the crowd, some dog-loving Tory, some renegade-hating Labour trade unionist, to identify him. The policeman's lapel radio crackles its routine message of robberies and rapes around the town while the police-woman carefully removes the spittle from Bess's cheek into a tissue for forensic examination.

'This is your spit?' she addresses Joe.

'She opened my door and grabbed my hair.'

'Is it your spit?'

13

'It might be. I'm not going beyond that. Frankly, I was provoked.'

'Did you witness these events?' the policeman asks Sidney.

'Yes but I have a train to catch.'

'Pyke, you're simply contemptible,' Hooper says. 'I know this man,' she tells the thickening crowd. 'He put the driver up to it.'

The crowd assesses Sidney. His eyes are red (chlorine) and shifty. Just the type.

Sidney turns to Joe, whose pleasant, phlegmatic countenance has withdrawn from the world – a study in bored neutrality. Reluctantly Sidney searches Melanie's wild eyes in search of pity, decency, justice – loyalty.

# *Two*

Sidney Pyke stares bleakly at his wife's kitchen notice board. DARLING DUSTBINS *TODAY*. Samantha never takes it down yet expects him to know which 'TODAY' out of seven is the real *TODAY*. 'Your only household chore, Sidney – and you forgot.' He glances at the sand in his egg-timer: Haight Ashbury, 1967, a present for his first wife. The psychedelic paint had worn off by the time Ronald Reagan brought fascism from California to the whole USA.

Sidney pours himself a third Portmeirion cup of coffee, wipes the egg from his sandy beard, finds the book pages of the *Guardian*, and searches sadly for a review of his own latest 'testament', *The Red and the Green*.

Nothing. Nothing again! Betrayal! Professor Pyke barks into the intercom to rouse his wife, while Councillor Pyke begins sifting his hate-mail, an ear open for the first abusive telephone call of the day. He handles the envelopes gingerly: of late, brown envelopes often harboured canine turds.

People – one could generalize – tend to become concerned about threats to the environment very early in the morning. Sidney holds a number of theories about this, which he regularly imposes on Samantha when the TV Queen finally sweeps down into the kitchen, bathed, perfumed and ready to enchant, stimulate – provoke! – 11.5 million Friday-night addicts of enchantment, stimulation, provocation.

Samantha's voice comes through on the intercom, husky

with sleep and dreams. 'Yes, darling. Did you do the dustbins?'

He unlocks the kitchen door and shuffles across the soaking grass of Samantha's carefully cultivated 'wild garden' towards the darling dustbins. For twenty-five years people have been paying his second wife a lot of money to keep the world on its toes. Dear old girl – how long since she last gave him a black eye? He wonders whether the new editor assigned to her at Vampire Books will fill the shoes of that repulsive American fancy man, Jack Lait.

On the frost-wet trail back to the warm kitchen, he allows himself an appraisal of the whitewashed façade of the rather expansive Pyke residence which he and Samantha named Cuba after attending a cultural congress in Havana at which Fidel spoke for ten hours. On bad dustbin days the house reminds Sidney of Dr Johnson's dog walking on its hind legs: not done well, but surprising to have been done at all: post-Bauhaus, neo-Tudor, with a buried debt to William Morris somewhere – the whole thing 'counterpointed' (Samantha's word) by elaborately configured trellises supporting her beloved Tuscan vines. A blot, he concludes, but a beloved blot, on any landscape.

Back in the kitchen with the treacherous *Guardian*, he sullenly studies Prince Charles's latest outburst against the architects.

Sidney reluctantly agrees with the prince. For one who had erected barricades and hurled paving stones in the rue Gay Lussac in May '68 it rather goes against the grain to agree with an unelected Royal, but there you go. After ten years of Thatcher, even the Queen has become a symbol of Republican resistance. Charges of 'lèse majesté' against the monarch are no doubt imminent.


Dr Bess Hooper has got up early to catch a Northern line train to Euston. It's a bitterly cold morning and the Northern line is, as usual, diabolical. Escalators out of order, trains cancelled, incoherent announcements on the platform loudspeakers. Hooper is aware that in this, the eleventh year of Thatcher, half the nation reaches work in a condition of boiling anger – but such knowledge does nothing to assuage her own. If she doesn't make the 8.10 from Euston, if she arrives on campus even five minutes late, a certain MCP – Chair*man* of the Media Studies Department – will joyfully carve another notch against her persistent application for tenure.

Oppression is as simple as that.

Reaching Euston with five minutes to spare, Bess skips her usual dash to the coffee stall and impulsively uses her telephone card to dial a number she knows well.

'Sidney Pyke,' she hears.


Sidney Pyke expects abusive calls. He has as many enemies as the murder victim in an Agatha Christie. Ever since his defection from Labour to the Greens he has held the casting vote on the District Council. The storm of abuse has been unrelenting: a planned campaign of course, blatantly orchestrated: Traitor! Renegade! Sell-out! Stooge of Thatcherism!

He has grown accustomed. Besides, he enjoys the new-model telephones. They are user-friendly and quite ecological. The new chirping tone reminds him of crickets on a tropical night and the sleek miniaturization of the receiver is a heartening response to the global claims of smallness. Post-modernist capitalism is at least responsive.

For no obvious reason this train of thought brings him to Chantal. (Almost everything does.) The silly bitch has deliberately mocked his values by going and buying a big, ugly, black bakelite telephone from a curiosities shop specializing in War Cabinet Room bric-a-brac.

'Typical of the scavenging eclecticism of your generation,' he told her.

'I simply liked it! It's a bargain.'

Chantal's French lessons are carefully scheduled to coincide with Samantha's weekly TV trip to London. Sidney's tongue involuntarily wets his lower lip.


Samantha has descended to the kitchen, gorgeous and regal.

'Don't be silly, darling, you know you love abuse.'

'No one has ever called me a "fucking authoritarian rapist chauvinist pig" before.'

'They must have done. It was probably Bess Hooper. I know how she feels about that little incident in the taxi.'

'I was completely innocent.'

'Well, of course. I wonder why she said "rapist". Bit of a new departure, isn't it?'

Sidney notes with interest that he hasn't passed on to Samantha the whole of Hooper's text: 'Don't forget the swimming pool, you fucking authoritarian rapist chauvinist pig.'

The phone again. Sidney answers, listens, and is about to reply when the caller hangs up.

'Dog lobby?' Samantha murmurs, deep into a little piece she's written for the *Guardian*.

'How often do I have to explain in the Council Chamber, or to the Press, that I am not, repeat not, "anti-dog"!'

'But of course you are, sweetie. Didn't you distribute a Green leaflet likening dog-owners to drunken drivers?'

'Only those who foul parks, pavements and doorsteps. Only those who put our children at risk of intestinal worm eggs, toxocara canis, and blindness.'

The telephone chirps again. He lifts the receiver.

'Sidney Pyke,' he says.

'What about those muggers in the parks, why don't you do something about the muggers? How many muggers are dogs, eh – answer that!'

Sidney thanks the lady for her call. Every vote counts. He assures her he is definitely anti-mugger.

\* \* \*

Swindler House is a much-discussed post-modernist sort of building overlooking St James's Park. Vampire Books occupies the seventh and eighth floors. Ian Davidson shares an office with three other young men of equal status, each occupying an identical swivel chair behind the identical unleathered desk assigned to deputy editorial directors. The only picture allowed on the wall is the standard official photograph of Hans-Dietrich Swindler. Davidson has noticed a certain resemblance to ex-President Ceaucescu of Romania.

Such thoughts are not to be conveyed. Within the Swindler empire loyalties are strictly vertical. Never mentioned is Prince Charles's public condemnation of Swindler House as 'the Martians have landed'. The architect had subsequently jumped from the roof and Swindler's London newspaper had revealed that the prince's unhappy marriage to Princess Di was one of 'Britain's best-guarded secrets'.

Ian Davidson makes a habit of placing a paper cup of Kenyan coffee on a clean napkin on his desktop by 8.20 A.M. Having padlocked his racing bicycle, removed its front wheel, stowed his helmet and thigh-tight black shorts in his locker, showered, chosen a Next jacket from Neue Sachlichkeit Berlin or Surrealist Paris, twiddled the combination, and kicked the coffee machine, he spreads his muscular body behind his desk and snarls at the empty chairs around him. He will be twenty-seven next Tuesday. He plans no festivity; recently he has experienced a shortfall on friends. He doesn't think about it, much.

Lean, athletic, pale, Davidson carries a tidy haircut but not too short – he'd soon learned that middle-aged publishing executives distrust the storm-trooper head-style favoured by his contemporaries making waves in futures, plastic credit and recycled '30s rags (having scrambled out of Silicon chips – a game as greasy as servicing Mexico's debts).

Jack Lait has explained to him that an editor may still encounter authors who are stubbornly sentimental about the obsolete 'special relationship'. Samantha Newman, for example, clearly yearns to run Indian finger-jewels through a young editor's hair.

Three months have passed since Jack Lait last flew in from New York on Concorde. Senior Vice-President of the General Books Division of Swindler-US, with a roving commission of authority as Hans-Dietrich Swindler's trans-atlantic supremo, Lait arrived in the most impressive pair of Italian shoes and complaining of the migraine induced by the supersonic airliner's pencil-fuselage. Advised by fax that he would be lunching at La Cupole, 12.30 sharp, 'with our biggest acquisition', Davidson bought a new psychedelic tie for the occasion.

And how she swept in! Wrapped in the most exotic shawl! Quel bouquet! How she relished the swivelling heads! Lait kissed her five times, Davidson counting, in the French manner. Samantha then held Davidson's hand during a long, grafting appraisal, her mauve glove as fragrant as her mauve pages. He noticed that she had worn well; sleeping with her would be no problem if Mr Lait or Mr Swindler signed the memo. 'Samantha has been thirty-nine for several years,' Lait warned Davidson. 'She's an honest girl and likes to stick to one story.' Then the famous wink. The men's cloakrooms of Swindler House are full of young executives practising the Lait wink, which carries the whole face with it. Like genuine pastrami, it doesn't travel.

'Can she write?' Davidson foolishly asked.

'Write? Listen, Ian, with an 11.5 million rating on BBC1, every Friday 10.45 P.M. she can sell a book. Besides.' Lait had dropped his voice. 'Hans-Dietrich Swindler has been buying up ersatz British Kultur ever since the heir to the throne failed to pronounce his name with his top teeth touching his bottom lip.'

The head waiter of La Cupole held Samantha's chair while she searched Davidson's grudgingly sculpted Presbyterian countenance for evidence of empathy. Finally she relinquished his hand.

'Oh dear, Jack, but he's a mere boy! How can he possibly understand women?'

'How can any of us understand women?' The wink landed on Davidson.

Miss Newman's theatrical distemper lasted until her martini arrived. 'How I hate you conglomerates,' she told them. 'Every human relationship as fickle as the market.'

'Every author deplores us, Samantha, and every author takes our money.'

'Don't be vulgar, Jack.'

After lunch Lait had taken Samantha to Brown's Hotel. 'Service,' he had murmured in Davidson's ear. Then the wink. What followed was mauve pages.

Eleven and a half million viewers or not, Davidson wouldn't have paid £200,000 for *Nature or Nurture*. Or £ anything. Newman writes in short bursts and never seems to remember what she said last time. He takes the mauve pages home to read in bed while watching late-night movies. Newman clearly trades in updated nostalgia but why invest emotion in the past − be it the Spanish Civil War or this "68' thing − when you know the outcome? The only history which excites a spark of genuine interest in Davidson is the history of the future.

Bess Hooper is a bit stunned by what she has done. Fifteen minutes out of Euston, she concludes that she has done what a woman must do. War is declared. Months of rage.

Hooper has travelled to London for the monthly meeting of the Women's Committee of the National Union of Journalists. For once the women have managed to avoid the usual bickering and backbiting: what they have finally achieved is a Strategy for Sisterhood. On the cold winter-morning train − Thatcher herself has banned the use of heaters − Hooper wrestles with a small demon of self-congratulation.

A national network of women will now monitor the media. Every form of sex discrimination will be exposed, including tokenism and harassment: the male hierarchies will no longer be able to exercise their hegemony in smug silence.

Hooper lights another fag, glad (and sad) that Melanie is not on hand to rebuke her. And fuck you, Sidney Pyke: fuck your fucking hegemony over your fucking Media Studies Department. And fuck your painted wife.

Once a heroine to them all, Samantha Newman. But now a classic case of class collaboration.

A man in the seat opposite is looking at Bess. A business type, bloated, self-satisfied: eyeing her. From behind her granny glasses she stares back. Not until women accept the challenge of eye contact with strangers – predators, rapists – will they achieve the confidence required for genuine liberation. That's Melanie's trouble: whenever a young man leers at her over page three of the *Sun* she bursts into tears of frustration.

Thankfully for women, the architecture of trains has improved. They have all heard of the grim days when local trains consisted of rape-trap separate compartments without a connecting corridor.

Of course there's some confusion among the women about what a woman is. The Bulgarian Burgundy faction in the NUJ, led by that smug superstar Samantha Newman and her acolyte Gilly Jones, still contend that women are essentially the same as men – if only men would let them be the same. Newman (much too famous, rich and generally celebrated to attend Committee meetings) still writes and talks on television of 'educating men', as if they were naughty little boys who could be nurtured out of their nature.

Bess stares at the staring businessman. Gilly Jones is a menace all round, an accommodationist in the Peace Movement, wears the same green wellies as Samantha, cosy with the new breed of Labour PR wizards, always showing up at Greenham Common Air Base with prize flowers like Glenys Kinnock – or Samantha Newman. Gilly is also married to Sidney Pyke's great pal in the university Establishment, Bill

Jones, Dean of Studies. Jones is a decent man and they're the worst when it comes down to it. As for the NUJ, Gilly has hung on to her union card although her career as a professional photographer has long been in eclipse – her objective function being to sabotage the Movement on Newman's behalf.

Forgetting to go on staring at the businessman, Bess jots a thought or two in her notebook. 'Judas is male . . . why does hegemonic culture offer no female equivalent? Why are women harlots, spies, never traitors? Because treason indicates grander allegiance. Only members of the ruling class can betray it. The truth, sisters: the history of the female condition is a history of relentless treason.'

And Newman is a traitor – the most prime Judas of the new age – and must be brought down. By any means. There are women in the Movement – Melanie, for example – who still – still! – regard Newman as wonderful but a bit naughty. A phrase proposes itself to Hooper's notebook: 'Camp follower of a demeaning subordination.' Yes! She may well stretch her students across that phrase during every lecture and seminar of the coming week:

– Gender Stereotypes – an Introduction
– 'Daughters of de Beauvoir' (graduate class attended by Melanie)
– Strategies of Male Hegemony
– The Language War – Personal Pronouns.

# *Three*

Samantha Newman occupies a first-class compartment on the fast train travelling south. On the grimy walls of the station waiting room she has noticed a new graffito: PUKE OUT! PUKE TO THE DOGS!

Contentedly she notes that two or three male passengers are studying her with undisguised admiration and lust. That's no problem in first class. A comfort, even. It helps her to concentrate on her notes. She flashes huge smiles at the men staring at her. Instantly they avert their gaze to *The Times*, the *Telegraph*, the latest company sales figures. What she so badly wants to get across to her 11.5 million is that while women are absolutely essentially the same as men they are also absolutely essentially different. In her experience the truly happy men are those who truly understand a woman to be what she truly is.

Men like Sidney. A wild stallion redeemed.

Almost. Is there something going between Sidney and Gilly? If an old flame still splutters, it has to be Gilly's. Samantha has quite forgotten the dinner party at which she brought Gilly and Bill Jones together, but she knows it took place because soon afterwards Sidney had to go to Moss Bros to hire Best Man gear for the wedding. Sidney and Bill got horribly stag-drunk the previous evening (all day if memory serves), what with Bill a confirmed bachelor and Gilly bringing an unknown number of children from her two divorces. Sidney says Bill still doesn't know how many children they have, or which are his own. Anyway it's lovely to have Gilly living 'down the road' – though, quite honestly, best friends stay best at a comfortable distance.

Samantha thinks about Sidney some more.

Of course his bad temper is a problem. And jealousy. Of herself, mainly. Too long since he was invited to lecture in America. Every time he reads a published letter or petition by famous artists and intellectuals, he wants to know why he wasn't invited to sign it. Why do all these young media-trendies who never fought for anything now get their names on the good causes – instead of his? Recently she caught him sulking about not being included in the *Guardian*'s 'Today's Birthdays'.

Why does he regularly arrange for that little slut Chantal to give him 'French lessons' precisely on the one day of the week when Samantha has to be in London? And why does Sidney rather pathetically attempt to keep the Chantal business a secret? Affairs are one thing, secret affairs another. Candid adultery is an essential part of an open marriage – as *Nature or Nurture* would brilliantly explain! When Sidney was screwing little Melanie day and night under the open sky (so to speak), Samantha even lent books to the silly creature. And when Melanie said, 'Oh, Samantha, it's you I really love,' didn't she pretend to believe the anorexic bitch?

Actually, Samantha did believe her.

So why is Melanie now shacked up with that lump of reinforced concrete, Bess Hooper? It must be Sidney's fault. He has always under-estimated Hooper. 'Voilà l'ennemi!' Samantha warned him. He merely smirked. Sidney is of course a complete fool – always has been. 'Twenty years of marriage to a complete fool can't have been easy, darling,' Jack Lait once said, coming out of the shower in Brown's Hotel.

Approaching Euston, Samantha remembers that she is in love with Jack and her thoughts flutter to that lovely bedroom in Brown's – if only his visits to London weren't always so absurdly brief and inhumanly scheduled. Adultery 2.15 to 3.30 P.M. Poor Jack, shackled to that wretched wife in Westchester County – and what use is this dour, silent and badly dressed boy editor that Jack foisted on her? There's really no point in writing books unless one goes to bed with one's editor – or wants to, at least!

Sidney is halfway out of the house when an indignant lady telephones to warn him that his Dog Wardens scheme reminds her of Hitler's Gestapo and that his private life 'warrants urgent investigation'. Sidney knows the woman all too well: Chairman of the local Mothers' Union, and a Tory Councillor.

'Couldn't agree more, madam! Secrecy is our national disease. Freedom of Information and a Bill of Rights [he hopes that the capitals are evident over the phone] are our only weapons against the power elites and the military-industrial establishment. Did I mention Proportional Representation? Rejected out of hand by the Tories and the Labour Party, of course. Kind of you to call, madam. Let me know if I can help!'

The Mothers' Union is not amused. 'And what about your private life?'

'That, of course, is hardly one of the great meta-narratives of modern history.'

Slowly he cycles the three miles to the campus. Pleasant morning. All good stuff. The Mothers' Union's defecating spaniel had been towed away and impounded. It was in the *Examiner* – a scandal. Haynes, the editor, came out with a long leader claiming that Sidney also harboured a secret scheme for clamping the legs of stray dogs. Sidney wrote at once (unpublished as usual) to explain that, alas, the only available Japanese technology for dog-clamping was prohibitively expensive in an age of Thatcherite stringency and rate-capping. For the time being, therefore, Sidney was content to have imposed, by his casting vote, Dog Wardens transported from park to park, playground to playground, in a little Green mini-van.

Wobbling to a halt outside the Media Studies Department, Sidney suddenly remembers why he is so profoundly shaken. Bess Hooper has entered the building a few paces ahead of him, carrying an overnight bag. Voilà l'ennemi! as Samantha said. He glances at his watch: she's two minutes late. By the time she confronts her class she will be at least five minutes late. Ha!

Sidney takes up position in the corridor outside the lecture hall where Hooper's 'Gender Stereotypes' students are congregating. He glances inside, hoping for evidence of a sharp decline in attendance: the room is packed, as usual.

And here she comes. Stops, stares at him frostily from behind granny glasses.

'You're six and a half minutes late, Bess. Writing for *Time Out*, *Spare Rib*, the *New Statesman* – fine, fine, we encourage our staff to practise their craft, but the Vice-Chancellor also expects – '

'I'm applying for tenure. Again. Fifth application.'

She attempts to walk past him. His stomach partially blocks the doorway, barring her passage. Her students keenly observe the next move.

'You're invading my personal space,' she says.

Sidney steps aside. The door closes in his face.


Bess Hooper's concentration keeps lapsing during 'Gender Stereotypes'. The confrontation with Pyke in the corridor, following that historic phone call to him from Euston station, not to mention lack of sleep, have Bess in what she identifies as a 'fizz'. As lecturer in Alternative Journalism, she has convinced herself that the primary battlefield against Department Chairman Pyke lies inside the classroom, but today, aroused by the impelling call of the wider war, she distributes to her mixed class (male students are barred only from 'Daughters of de Beauvoir') a sheet of 'typical' passages harvested from the media by the Women's Committee of the NUJ.

And one of our guests, retired surgeon James Roberts, is going to tell us when a doctor is a Dr and when he is a Mr [BBC Radio 4].

If you're a girl, I hope you'll be beautiful, because a beautiful girl can make somebody very happy . . . If you're a boy, I hope you'll be strong and courageous [from a British Medical Association *Family Doctor* pamphlet, 'The Facts of Life for Children'].

Bess observes her students' reactions keenly from behind the round, wire-framed granny glasses she wears in order not to be – as nature had almost made her – beautiful. She knows that infinite patience is called for when teaching first-year students, yet invariably finds frustrating their inability to transcend instinctive indignation.

Presented to the 'Daughters of de Beauvoir' graduate class, the same quotations had brought from Melanie Rosen an instant analysis: 'Centuries of patriarchal culture have conditioned us to accept Woman as a sex object, and therefore unworthy of "strength and courage", or as a failed sex object, and therefore unfit for anything, even to "make *somebody* very happy".'

Ah, Melanie – and the virulence behind that *somebody*! Let the Movement raise Sidney Pyke in effigy before burning him: for who else transformed Melanie Rosen, the meek, heart-fluttering creature of heterosexism, into the most imaginative, the most intransigent, the most dedicated of Sisters?

With a start Bess realizes that one of her students has her hand up.

'Yes, Chantal?'

Bess isn't yet quite sure what she feels (thinks) about the Poynter girl. Bright as a pin, always attentive, but inclined to deck herself out in the kind of gear liable to bring roadworks and building sites to a howling halt. (Bess of course is in two or three conflicting minds about that – why the hell shouldn't a woman wear what she likes? On the other hand why does she like it?) Nor could it be denied that Chantal Poynter blatantly enjoys the seething attention of male students: moths immolating themselves on molten wax. And Melanie – her instinct is infallible – has informed Bess that the Poynter girl is 'on the make' with S. Pyke – apparently Chantal rather smugly let it out in the cafeteria that she's giving the bugger 'French lessons'.

'Yes, Chantal?' Bess says.

'Centuries of patriarchal culture,' Chantal begins, 'have conditioned us to accept Woman as a sex object . . .'

Bess Hooper's granny glasses are glinting.


Sidney is unburdening his morning's traumas in the Senior Common Room to his closest friend (and tennis partner), Bill Jones, Dean of Students.

'It was outasight, Bill.'

'It was what, old man?'

'You remember Jerry Rubin? "Outasight" Rubin, mad magician of the Yippies? I got to know him during the Pig Convention, Chicago '68 – we both got busted, of course.'

'So?'

'Jerry was a specialist in obscene telephone calls – to the pigs, to judges, to Senators, to the White House. Outasight.'

'Ah.'

' "You fucking authoritarian sexist rapist bastard pig," was the message I received this morning.' Sidney notes that once again he has censored the swimming-pool bit.

Bill Jones guffaws. 'No commas?'

'There were definitely no commas in that sentence, no, none.' Sidney draws on his pipe. 'Rage is the enemy of punctuation. Subverts syntax. She has several available accents, that woman – have you noticed?'

'I try to notice as little of Hooper as possible. It's not easy.'

'Clear socio-semantic indicator of a split personality. Depletion of personal identity. Desperate search for communal validation. In class she's strictly Euston Women

Against Rape – but when she's confronting me what I hear is King's Cross Wages for Lesbians.'

'Really? But surely Euston and King's Cross are barely two hundreds yards apart?'

'That's a long journey in the life of the spoken language.'

Samantha's good humour dies as soon as she is ushered into the hospitality room at the BBC's Wood Lane studios. Lying on the table, beside the bottle of chilled Barsac they always have ready for her, is the latest edition of the *Journalist*, organ of the National Union of Journalists.

EQUALITY COMMITTEE CONDEMNS NEWMAN.

'I'm afraid we can't duck this one, Samantha,' her producer murmurs apologetically.

'Duck it, darling! Did I ever fucking duck anything?'

'Never.'

But the producer is under pressure. Market-leader though she still is, Samantha has recently required frequent repackaging. Originally the 'Samantha Newman Hour' was a surrogate bedroom game – every male viewer imagining himself at her mercy, every female viewer imagining herself to be Samantha. Nowadays Samantha relies more blatantly on the auto-cue and the make-up girls can't quite eliminate the crows' feet under the eyes. Her studio costumes are becoming somewhat desperate. The design people are unhappy. Ratings are static at 10.5 million (officially 11.5) and 'static' is not a good word upstairs. Samantha no longer seems responsive to the escalator clause linking her fee to her ratings. Finding the right celebrity guests – known as the 'victims' in-house – isn't as easy as it was – an awful lot of names are kicked around each week. At any moment Newman may move across the ledger, from the entertainment account to the culture account – turning a market-leader into a loss-leader.

She'd once said 'fuck' on the air. An uproar – but OK. Now she's making a habit of it. And then there's the live music problem: the break. At ease introducing the Stones, or jazz saxophonists, or prize-winners from the Moscow piano competition, she just doesn't sound right when it comes – as it often must – to modern pop. Just not with it.

Oh, she tries. Such a gallant energy. But more and more feeding off that auto-cue.

She doesn't know it, but there have been secret auditions, the search for something much, much younger. One girl, a lovely honeyblonde, barely twenty, with a figure that bombed even the camera crews, instantly walked deep into the BBC management's data-base. Invited to introduce the break, Chantal Poynter responded with the verve of a veteran of pirate radio: 'Let's take a break. An absolute *favourite* of mine is that incredible Los Angeles Funkster, Lenny Ohio. You name it, he can do it – a sophisticated cocktail jazz piece or a light Afro-fusion instrumental. And his three wives all say he's wonderful at that too. Recently Lenny has been in trouble with the LA Drug Squad but now he's back on the EMI label with a massive hit, a real stadium rocker, "Eat Me Alive". Ladies and gentlemen, Lenny Ohio.'

Yep. Chantal Poynter has everything – except the darkest desires and delights of the world in her eyeballs. That takes time. Samantha has it.

The whole thing began (Samantha is explaining to her 'team' at Television Centre) something like this: silly little Melanie Rosen was riding on a Piccadilly line tube train when a man, a perfect stranger, began giving her lecherous winks and leers over his copy of the *Sun* (which was open at the page 3 nude). The man didn't actually say anything but Melanie was frightfully upset and reported the whole incident to Bess Hooper who promptly brought a complaint against the *Sun* under the NUJ's Code of Conduct.

This kind of thing being right up Samantha's street, she'd accorded it five satirical minutes of TV time a month or two ago:

'Well come on and come off it, girls, I mean men have been giving us winks and leers since the Stone Age and quite frankly it's going to be a sad day when it stops happening to me. Honestly, do we women have to defend our dignity by these displays of humourless paranoia?'

The BBC producer and his staff remember. They laugh appreciatively. Samantha is their queen.

'What happened next, my darlings, was a complaint against me – me! – under the same Code of Conduct: "Behaviour demeaning to women and detrimental to the interests of the Union", or some such stuffy nonsense. I was summoned – summoned, yes! – to attend a Hearing! Of course I declined in the rudest possible manner – by postcard, I recall, with a single word: "Poopheads!" And this' – Samantha displays the front page of the *Journalist* – 'is the result: "Samantha Newman censured for conduct likely to intimidate women and women members of the Union into not making such complaints in future."'

Samantha is eyeing the bottle of Barsac. The producer thinks she has drunk enough.

'Give me a drink, darling.'

'I really think – '

'Give me a drink! Don't you realize that these women are fucking illiterates?'

The BBC people – producer, editor, secretary, make-up – laugh nervously but abruptly Samantha relaxes, smiles – television is all about smiling – and kisses the nearest person to hand. In an hour's time she will hold Bess Hooper up to scathing ridicule before 11.5 (or 10.5) million people.

She telephones Sidney.

# *Four*

Lying in the scarlet beanbag at Sidney's feet – Samantha
has an identical one in her study, the pair probably picked
up at Oxfam – Chantal Poynter idly leafs though an old
copy of *Linkeck*. Sidney is wriggling his disgustingly knotted
toes in Sandinista-type liberation sandals and his feet smell
badly of 'a luta continua'! Flipping the large pages of the
vile '60s magazine, Chantal broods about Sidney's detestable self-assurance with women and why she'd actually
enjoyed pinning herself to the bottom line of this jelly-roll
Don Juan's scroll of conquests.

> I have such extensive feelings,
> And love them all,
> And women, who cannot reason,
> Call my good nature conceit.

(Daddy has a subscription at Covent Garden but is always
too busy doing whatever it is he does to go. Maman used
to take Sylvie and herself. Sidney says he hates opera.)

Chantal doesn't read German but the photographs and
cartoons in *Linkeck* are quite disgustingly striking.

'What is this horrible rag?'

'Erste antiautoritare Zeitung – the voice of the '60s
rabble. King Mob.'

'Were you rabble?'

'The police word was Dreck.'

She turns the page. 'Qui est-ce?'

'Rudi Dutschke.'

'Why is he standing on his toes?'

'He always did. He was quite short.'

'What about this bottle?'

'It's a molotov cocktail. We used to make them.'

'Was Molotov a friend of Rudi Dutschke? Did he have to stand on tiptoe as well?'

'No to both questions.'

'Are these Martians?'

'They are members of the CRS storming a barricade in the rue Gay Lussac.'

'Why is this bearded young man masturbating?'

'He didn't want to fight in Vietnam.'

'Why are these people dead?'

'Jews.'

'That wasn't in '68?'

'No, '45. As your paragon, Vice-President Dan Quayle, once remarked, "The Holocaust? Well, er, that was a real tragedy in our history."'

'Is that wrong? Don't smirk! Is it wrong?'

'It's B-plus for effort.'

She turns sullenly back to *Linkeck*. 'Oh look – Mick Jagger!'

'Ah, contact at last.'

'Is this a cartoon of Hans-Dietrich Swindler?'

'He was as bad twenty years ago as he is now.'

'Samantha doesn't mind taking his money.'

'It's not the money, it's Jack Lait.'

'Who's he?'

'Swindler's American end. A gangster. Screws Samantha four times a year in Brown's Hotel.'

'Do you mind?'

'Take your clothes off.'

No compliment, no tenderness, ever passes the lips of King Mob. Wham! Is he any different with Samantha? – that is something Chantal would dearly like to know.

'Oughtn't we to be improving your French?' she objects.

'Vêtements – off!' His accent is appalling.

\* \* \*

Dialling Sidney's office in the Media Studies Department, Samantha is told that he has gone home 'for lunch' – which is bloody odd, since Sidney has a disgusting appetite and couldn't cook himself a carrot. She tries Cuba, gets no answer, and is about to put the phone down when a breathless female voice gasps 'Hold on!' The next thing Samantha hears is Sidney – definitely Sidney – roaring 'Harder! Harder!' – followed by a crash and a scream.

Finally the breathless voice returns. 'Yes, who is it?'

'It's me, darling,' Samantha says.

'Oh gosh. Hullo, Samantha. This is Chantal.'

'I know that, dear.'

'I was just giving Sidney his French lesson.'

'Honi soit qui mal y pense.'


Afterwards Chantal scrubs his hairy back in the bath with a Third World loofah. He always fills the bath to the brim, flooding the floor as soon as he lowers his satiated hulk into the water too hot for her to touch. 'Archimedes would be pleased,' he chortles when she protests. Nudity does not abash Sidney, nothing does. So unlike the 'chaplain', a schoolteacher by the name of James Loftus-Wright, who ended up saying sorry, 'God I'm sorry', after a discreet bistro dinner with a check tablecloth and some hugely mature glances across the dripping candles. 'God I'm sorry.'

A whalelike turbulence in the bath scatters these thoughts. 'Afterwards,' Sidney snorts abruptly, hauling his scalded red flesh to its feet – another flood – and snapping his fingers at her for a hot towel.

'What?'

'"Afterwards" is a cheap literary cliché. The word was in your tiny mind, jumping about, like a marshmallow rabbit. Never begin a post-coital paragraph with "afterwards". And make some coffee.'

'No! I mean – why can't you ask nicely?'

'I pity you your bourgeois upbringing. Clearly hegemonic. De-construct yourself, girl.'

Five minutes later Sidney descends to the kitchen in a Sandinista dressing gown and generously shows her some snapshots from his time at Berkeley.

'Everyone looks so ethnic!' she exclaims.

'That's Sharon.'

'Oh wasn't she beautiful! And who's that hairy bloke holding her hand?'

'That's Allen Ginsberg.'

'Who he?'

'A poet. In fact, the author of the most pirated poem in the English language.'

Sidney waits for his pupil to ask him the name of the poem but she doesn't. He suspects that − cool creature though Chantal is − Samantha's phone call in the middle of it all has shaken her a bit. Chantal is not overawed by Samantha to the point of total evaporation, as Melanie was, but Sidney's wife is a big cat all round, once roused.

'Shouldn't we attempt some French?' Chantal dutifully suggests, curling herself into the scarlet beanbag lying at his feet. 'After all, it's only six weeks before you fly to Paris for publication of *Le Rouge et Le Vert* par Seedny Peek.'

Sidney contemplates her. Such energy; such ambition; straight off the '80s mould; perfect specimen.

'Dialogue should not be used to impart information,' he says.

'Sorry?'

'You sank into the popular-paperback idiom by telling me what I already know, but what the reader does not yet know, but in fact the reader does know.'

'Know what?'

'About my book. In France.'

'Oh really, Sidney! What reader? You and your narrative obsessions!'

'In your case, well justified − biding your time in a minor third-person key, waiting to snatch the stage in chapter eight. I suppose you realize I understand Thatcherite literary strategies.'

She sits up abruptly. 'My dear Sidney: this will be the keynote interview on "France-Culture" at seven-thirty in the morning, with half of Paris forced to listen to you while trapped in traffic – and you're still talking in English.'

'Par-*don*.'

Bess Hooper slams Sidney's office door behind her. On this occasion she arrives by appointment – a convention which Sidney, wedded to informality, has latterly been forced to insist on ('impose' still belongs to the realm of aspiration) since people, mainly Women, began barging in to hector him whenever they felt like it.

'Bess, must you always slam the door?'

'It doesn't close unless it's slammed.'

'That may be because your flying squads and paint-sprayers have so often wrenched it off its hinges.'

Bess is wearing baggy blue dungarees with shoulder straps over a very crisp white blouse, to which a number of metal buttons are pinned, a constellation of brave causes. He motions her to a chair. She remains standing.

'What's the agenda today – Melanie?'

But he knows the agenda. Lying on his desk is Bess's latest teaching project: 'Sexism and Gender Stereotyping in Children's Books'. Sidney studies the table of contents and plays with his pipe and oilskin tobacco pouch (the Hong Kong Boat People trip) while Bess stands over him, revolted by the mess of nicotine and stained pipe-cleaners in, and no longer in, his ashtray. (He has ceased to recognize the habit as a lapse in his ecology, despite Samantha's occasional remonstrances.)

'Well,' he muses, 'fascinating, original, the kind of thing we need here.' He caresses his beard. 'Of course not every member of the Media Studies Board may fully share my enthusiasm.'

'I've been nominated by the Equal Opportunities Commission to work on new Guidelines for Children's Books,' she says.

'Who for?'

'Pardon?'

'Guidelines for whom?'

'For authors, for publishers, for librarians, for educators.'

Sidney has never liked the word 'educators'. Sounds American. Except that Bess Hooper is no bubbling Californian renovator, she belongs to the Roundhead Republic of Camden, that flat, lifeless London voice stretching from Euston to King's Cross, delivering anonymous calls by £2 telephone card.

'Bess, you're also a member of the Committee Against Sexism in Children's Books and an associate of Librarians Against Gender Stereotyping.'

'So?'

'And that's a pressure group demanding "positive discrimination in the acquisition of books for libraries"?'

'Correct.'

He swivels his utilitarian desk chair. 'Of course I admire your commitment. But any course in this department requires a backbone of academic objectivity.'

He experiences the usual helpless surrender to the inevitable brawl. Both are programmed to blow the lid at a certain point on the polemical dial. Foreknowledge is not a prophylactic in this form of congress.

'Should our children read that "The average Englishman drinks his tea with milk", or that "The average English person drinks tea with milk"?' Bess Hooper asks.

'I agree, Bess. I agree!'

'And isn't it time we stopped reading that "John is a brave boy and his sister Mary loves animals"? Isn't it time that our children learned that "Mary is an enterprising girl whose brother John loves animals"?'

Sidney shrugs his leather shoulders. 'Hard to say without meeting John and Mary.'

'The stereotypes mould the children, don't they?'

'Nature or nurture, you mean? I believe Samantha's new book will be taking a large bite out of that question.'

He is flipping the pages of her presentation, reinforcing

the ancient inequality of writer and reader. For her, weeks of careful research and labour; for him, the executive, the disposer, a rapid glance on a desktop cluttered with student essays, timetables, memos, diaries.

'Bess, let's be frank: beyond the yeses and noes of your Guidelines lurks a veritable dictionary of directives.'

'Oh don't let's have any of the usual liberal shit.'

What most revolts her are the buttons stretched across his swollen stomach to show flesh and hair beneath the pink shirt. And when he insists on reading aloud from her memorandum, her words on his sardonic tongue sound like rape.

Men should sometimes be depicted as quiet and passive, or fearful and indecisive, or illogical and immature. Women should sometimes be depicted as tough, aggressive and even insensitive. As for boys and girls, Mary should be first up the tree when the cat needs to be rescued, and first into the water when the dog needs help. Boys should not be shown fighting. Games and sports should be mixed.

Sidney looks up into the eye of a cyclone. 'But boys do fight,' he objects. 'Literature is about life.'

'That's fucking banal,' she says.

'I work hard on my banality.' He turns another page. 'Ah. I see that you also recommend that not only the books, but the authors themselves, hm, should be thoroughly vetted. Well, well. I quote: "1. Are the author's previous publications comparatively free of racist or sexist distortions, bias and omissions? 2. Is the author's bias expressed in more subtle and insidious ways? 3. What is the author's social background?"'

She waits. Why speak to the pig? At this moment she cannot admit, or even inwardly acknowledge, that the passage he has just read has indeed worried her. When she first came to the Media Studies Department, Bess was expecting total support for her radical crusades; it was

Sidney Pyke, after all, who had insisted on her appointment as lecturer despite – as he'd explained in the Peking Duck after her interview and just before he hinted that she'd missed the last train back to London – 'fierce opposition from the Establishment'.

'I wouldn't recommend a witch-hunt to students of this department,' Sidney says, rising and stretching and posing a bit. 'I suppose my generation can never dispose of its libertarian heritage. In Paris, Prague and Berkeley we were in business to bugger the rules, not to impose new ones. L'imagination au pouvoir, hm? . . . whereas you're busily building a new Index Librorum Prohibitorum.'

He offers a small grimace whose apparent diffidence masks (she registers) a vast conceit. She and Melanie have been collecting yellowing pictures of this pig in his prime.

'Is this a formal refusal?' Bess's granny glasses are trained on him.

'I suppose even those hostile to freedom are entitled to it,' he says. 'I suggest we take this discussion to a full meeting of the Department.'

She bangs his desk. '*We* take it? The Department is stuffed with your toadies – seventy per cent of them men! How about convoking the Estates General?'


Chantal is bicycling away from Cuba in a little French Connection outfit when a car travelling in the opposite direction brakes abruptly and a hand waves cheerily out of the window. The woman's smile seems familiar; Chantal notes the middle-aged make-up and the general sense of forgery.

'Hullo, hullo, aren't you Chantal? I'm Gilly Jones. Just on my way to take a few photos of Sidney for his new book.'

Chantal reflects that Sidney has already published his 'new book' and isn't likely to write another just yet – given the reviews.

'That's nice,' she says.

Gilly Jones is now out of her car. 'Samantha up in London today?'

'Yes, I believe so.'

The two women assess each other.

'Of course Samantha and I were at school together. Tremendous pals and comrades all our lives.'

'Oh.'

'Headington School in Oxford. Where did you go?'

'St Faith's.'

'Lovely. I'm a photographer you see.' Gilly Jones gestures towards a camera bag lying on the rear seat.

'Ah.'

'Not a huge success like Samantha, I'm afraid. I try not to call her Sam, she doesn't like it. We all called her Sam at school because she was so tall. But when she got famous she insisted on the whole name. Actually, she always needed to be the centre of attention. Wore outrageous clothes at weekends and broke all the school rules. We had this very ugly uniform they jammed us into. I don't suppose you young girls had to put up with that?'

'At St Faith's we could wear holes in our jeans.'

'We had to do those dreadful Sunday walks, in pairs. One would set out with Samantha and then she'd just vanish. Fifteen minutes later she'd be having tea in some undergrad's digs dressed in existentialist black or whatever the rave was – she adored Left Bank hats. Even at fifteen she was breaking hearts in Trinity and the House. Did you know that Samantha was the first schoolgirl to be elected President of the Oxford Union – in her absence – by acclamation?'

'Heavens!'

'She received the garland in the Blue Boar. Champers in her slipper and all that.'

'Gosh.'

'Of course Sidney's steadied her up a good deal. He's the anchor. I'm afraid she rather despises Sidney – well, not despises but – success, you know, it turns every head.' Gilly Jones pauses. 'So what took you to Cuba, dear?'

'Oh – I'm supposed to be teaching Sidney to speak French.'

'French!' Gilly doesn't look pleased. 'I advise you to keep both eyes open with Sidney. My husband Bill, you know, is Dean of Studies. He and Sidney are frightful old pals. They play tennis.'

'Do they? I'm just a first-year – '

'We don't stand on ceremony here. Are you one of us?'

'Us?'

'On the Left.'

'Oh! Well – '

'You must – really must – come and visit Mauve Gate at Greenham Common. We need more troops! Keep up the good fight! Lawd, I'm late! Sidney will be furious.'

Peddling away, Chantal feels quite sure that Sidney isn't expecting Gilly Jones.

# *Five*

Melanie Rosen goes in to her fateful tutorial with Professor Pyke on an empty stomach. Just a cup of strong herb tea which Bess brewed shortly after dawn following a night of intense, sleepless debate.

All night long Melanie clutched Bess's hand across the small, ugly kitchen table of the tiny maisonette they now occupy, in love, in solidarity, and in Trinity Road. The flat roof over the kitchen extension had lost its guttering, then its felt, and water runs into the largest bucket they can find at such a rate that one or the other has to set the alarm hourly throughout the night, to empty it.

'I'm afraid I may surrender,' Melanie moaned.

Bess's fingers tightened their grip.

When Melanie knocks on the professorial office door at 10.30 a mellow, slightly husky voice bids her enter. The same voice once conducted her through Wordsworth's house in Grasmere – a passionate peroration on romanticism and revolt, on Byron's free spirit and Shelley's hymn to anarchy, on the sad encrustation of the Lakeland poets, Coleridge's distemper, the felon-making polemics of the loathsome laureate, Southey. Later the same husky voice, with its occasional hints of Brando, of Dean, of Beat – though Melanie hadn't a clue about the hints until Bess pointed them out – talked her round Ruskin's house on a shore of Coniston Water enchanted by Swallows and Amazons. They held hands along National Trust nature trails and across bleak, wonderful, fells, and Sidney talked most of the time, though it seemed perfectly natural.

When Melanie enters Professor Pyke's office, Olive Schreiner's *Woman and Labour* (first published in 1911) lies open in his lap. Its author, a progressive woman whose sad but inspirational life was divided between her native South Africa and the more congenial company of liberal London, had brought a fiercely independent intelligence to bear on two major colonial relationships: white and black, men and women. Invariably she spoke for the underdog.

Sidney's office is as usual thick with pipe smoke. Quivering before his desk, Melanie wears the deathly pallor of a Toulouse Lautrec dancer discarded by the Moulin Rouge.

'So,' he begins, 'you want to remove yourself from my supervision into Bess's?'

'Yes.'

'Any good reason?'

'Because female and male rationality are incompatible. And because I'm now a witch.'

He nods. To his credit he says nothing about toads or broomsticks. A number of ragged markers have been inserted in his copy of Schreiner and he promptly reads a short passage aloud.

'Schreiner tells us that "The male and female brains acquire languages, solve mathematical problems, and master scientific detail in a manner wholly indistinguishable . . ."'

Melanie braces herself. Until she met Bess she had never stood up to him, never wanted to. And when his beard had chastened her skin she hadn't understood why her physical passivity in his gorilla grasp made him restless, or what he truly wanted of her; Sidney wouldn't say and, looking up from the pillow, she had always seen her own father's face, subdued by its own unspeakable longings. (At least that's what Bess told her she'd seen.)

'We don't wholly agree with Schreiner, even regarding mathematics,' Melanie tells him.

'We?'

The knuckles of her fingers are knotted white. 'We are learning to think collectively. We . . . we think you are quoting Schreiner out of context. She points out that it's women's experience of childbirth which has put them in the forefront of the struggle against war.'

He has now opened the window though she hasn't dared to ask.

'We feel that you are imposing on me a view of Schreiner that we cannot share. Schreiner predicts that when women finally enter government, the waste and carnage of war will end. "No tinsel of trumpets and flags," she writes, "will ultimately seduce women into the insanity of recklessly destroying life."'

His leather shoulders shrug. 'Well, Melanie, look at the evidence: Mrs Meir, Mrs Gandhi, and Mrs Thatcher. All of them mothers and all of them sent the nation's sons to die.'

'Bess said you'd say that.'

'And what did she say you should say when I said it?'

'Schreiner explains to us that "To the male the giving of life is a laugh; to the female blood, anguish and sometimes death."' Melanie's expression is incandescent. 'Just as you laugh, with your pal Jones, about the birds and chicks you've had – here, in this office.'

Sidney loses his temper. 'That's a lie.'

Melanie responds to this victory with even greater serenity. 'Schreiner tells us that Woman "knows the history of human flesh; she knows its cost; he does not".'

'He?'

'Man. God knows this too; it is woven into Her tapestry.'

'I suppose witches harbour their own secret logicality – which can hardly be mine.'

'Isn't that what I said!'

The tears commence. Melanie is perfectly aware that the sublime, mystical rationality she shares with Bess and the witches must be derided, mocked, scorned, as 'madness'. She feels Bess's presence steadying her – indeed Melanie had wanted her to come, but Bess had said no, no, sweet cunt of mine, you must learn womanly strength. That was at about four A.M., with the bucket beneath the kitchen roof almost full and sweet hot milky tea on the table.

'Please don't cry, Melanie. It's cheating.'

Cheating! How she hates this office! It was always in here, always on this dirty floor – except for those five days in the Lake District, when Samantha and her TV crew were in Somalia, gathering material on female circumcision, or was it her Ethiopian famine-relief trip?

That night Sidney's office is broken into and vandalized. The word WITCHES is spray-painted across his reproduction of Picasso's Guernica. If he could have said, 'The Spanish Civil War changed all our lives,' he would have done so; regrettably, Picasso had never painted a vast, leaping canvas to honour the generation of '68.


It being a dry autumn day, the early-morning chill having yielded to a mellow sun, Sidney feels inclined to shake off the effects of Melanie with a game of tennis. Bill Jones, Dean of Students, is always game for a game; the burdens of his office – as he interprets it – are practically nil. Marriage to Gilly is another matter but by tacit agreement neither man ever mentions her.

'Odd about love,' Jones says, unlocking the padlocked court with his privileged key (there have been at least two student demos, one a sit-in, about the contentious key).

'Love?' Sidney says casually. What does Jones know this time?

Jones chuckles. Anything Sidney says amuses him. 'Yes, old boy. Love fifteen, love thirty – not many people know the derivation. It comes from the French "l'oeuf", as a matter of fact. Consider the shape of the tennis balls sent by the mocking Dauphin to Henry V.'

Jones tosses him a sly glance worthy of Alec Guinness in an Ealing Studios comedy. Given a small twist of fate, Jones would have spent his life not as a lapsed logical positivist but amusing the popcorn crowd in the stalls. Having failed a first-year law course – he passed one subject out of six, a record, his tutors proudly assured him – he switched to philosophy after meeting A. J. Ayer at a Humanists' Prayer Meeting in the Conway Hall. Ayer assured him that minimum application was required in order to become a qualified philosopher with excellent teaching prospects. Ayer was right. The years passed as years should, each one comfortably coupled to its predecessor like indistinguishable wagon-lits – the only setback, and quite a happy one, Sidney assumes, since Jones never refers to it, being his marriage to the twice-divorced Gilly, Samantha's school chum and 'best friend', both of whose divorces had had something to do with Sidney – until abruptly Jones's life of tennis, gardening, exotic travel and occasional forays into philosophy was interrupted by a summons from the Vice-Chancellor.

Bill Jones was to be Dean of Studies. The Vice-Chancellor explained that agitation, militancy and hooligan violence had been dangerously on the increase.

'Really?' Jones said. 'Can't say I've noticed any.'

'Good. I want a Dean of Studies who doesn't notice anything. The Chairman of the Governors agrees that the best tactic is total myopia, until they – the mob, the canaille – grow bored.'

As Dean of Studies, a job traditionally as dangerous as bomb disposal, Bill Jones never fails to wear his MA gown, sports a pair of custom-built spectacles shaped like half-moons, takes care to leave one shoelace untied (to trip over in an emergency) and carefully litters his office with half-empty bottles of claret. He has long since recognized that consistent cartoon characters lie beyond the reach of judgment in this world, if not in the next.

On one occasion Jones's name did surface among the general campus graffiti attacking Sidney Pyke, etc. The 'Situationist-Ubu-Roi-Vandals' urged the Dean to wake up and repress them before they fell asleep. Jones went out that night with his own spray gun and wrote: 'OPPRESSION IS THE OPIUM OF THE UBUS. JONES.' Of course nobody believed that he'd done it. When the Ubus held a mass meeting, their first ever, and all three of them voted Jones an 'Honorary Ubu', they were astonished when he turned up to accept the award, in a clown's hat. A legendary dinner followed – it was Jones's do – during which the inebriated Ubus finally agreed, at the Dean's insistence, that they were adequately oppressed. He then fined each of them twenty pounds for vandalism. Payment was deferred. Jones didn't explain that the Dadaist feast was a way of escaping another CND 'strategy' dinner with Gilly and Glenys – 'strategy' now largely being confined to pretending that unilateral nuclear disarmament and the multi-lateral version were really the same thing. Having lived with the Bomb for forty years, Jones suspected that it was really an Easter egg annually resprayed in holocaust black. True or not, the Bomb seemed to bring out both the best and the worst in women – and once the worst started coming its natural deposits threatened to outlast North Sea oil.

After the first set (six-two to Jones, often to 'l'oeuf') they take a breather. Sidney Pyke and Bill Jones sit in the mellow sun, each in Colonial District Officer shorts, their pre-metal-age racquets – Jones is attached to this spelling, it goes with 'l'oeuf' – strung in good old cat gut, none of your new-fangled nylon, contemplating nothing in particular.

'Your problem, Sidney . . .' Jones pauses.

Sidney barely opens an eye. If Jones were found in his bed Sidney would scarcely notice. There would probably be a good reason for it, or none at all, which is the same thing.

'. . . is your desire to be impressive as well as ridiculous. That's why you serve so many double faults, old man. With you it's either ace or flat on your face.'

'Quite probably.' Sidney believes Jones cheats by calling his best serves out.

'Sidney, bad news, I'm afraid. You're in the shit.'

'So what's new? The V-C again?'

He refers to the Vice-Chancellor. In the days when he was on the American lecture circuit he liked to explain to delighted audiences that the 'Vice' signified corruption rather than subordination. They laughed in Kansas, they laughed in LA, the way Sidney said it, the years peeling from him, the grass passing from mouth to mouth, Sidney back there with Gerry and Abbie (not Tom Hayden, never liked the man) storming the House Un-American Activities Committee dressed as Sitting Bull or Davy Crockett.

But when Jones indicates the colour of the shit he's in, Sidney isn't laughing. Tucking his tennis racket under his sweaty arm, he declines a second set.


Bess Hooper asks her 'Gender Stereotypes' class what they understand by 'sexual harassment'. She also urges them, with the slight smile they adore, to spell the word properly.

As usual, the definitions are disappointing: even the female students seem unable to travel much beyond bottom-pinching and obscene propositions.

'Shall we,' Bess suggests, 'begin within the world of journalism?'

Methodically she leads them on a conducted tour of the real working conditions facing media women: Pirelli calendars on the walls of typesetting firms; blatant propositions from editors enjoying hire-and-fire powers; as for the trade unions, men remain in command, dismissive of women's demands for job-sharing and child-care facilities.

Bess Hooper's khaki dungarees step out from behind the lectern. 'These are not peripheral frills for women, they're make or break in all our working lives.'

Her class is bent over its thirty notepads.

'And secondly,' she says.

Secondly is the confinement of women writers to traditional ghettos: 'If you aspire to write about cars, computers or the coal industry, cocksure male editors will assure you that motor mechanics and coal miners will not talk to a woman reporter.'

Chantal Poynter raises her hand.

'Yes, Chantal?'

Chantal is perfectly clear what she wants to say, and perfectly clear that not saying certain things is what life's about. What she would like to ask Bess Hooper is this: 'But how many women do want to write about cars, computers or the coal industry? It strikes me that what continues to interest them is women's relationship to men. I mean, you have your traditional house-and-garden columnists, and you have your fire-eating feminists, but it's all the same thing really, isn't it? Two sides of the same coin.'

'Yes, Chantal?' Hooper repeats, her granny glasses glinting suspiciously at the first-year dolly-bird who'd been observed making hay with Pyke.

'I just wondered . . . I mean, isn't the first problem for women reporters . . . well, to know something about cars, computers and coal?'

Reading Hooper's expression, Chantal regrets that one tends to say what one thinks even when trying not to say it.


The war between Sidney and the women fascinates Chantal. 'What a story!' (her sister Sylvie says), 'absolutely pure Macbeth, darling, with a hint of Lear, and don't forget Lysistrata.' Chantal notes the names down: must find a reference book of potted drama plots, *The World's Hundred Classics*. Why does Sidney keep referring, when throwing her across his knee, to 'Othello as told by Iago: Iago's Story!' – then the slap on the buttock. Bastard! How self-absorbed, conceited and vain old men are! Completely contemptuous, dismissive, of any generation, any 'time of our time', other than their own. Sidney rambling on about the 'genuine' friendship, loyalty, honour, once shared by his elite commandos of 'comrades'. If Sidney only ever, or ever only, displayed the faintest interest in herself – as a real person, with hopes and fears of her own, not just 'another specimen straight off the Yuppy mould' – well then . . .

Well then, she would never have allowed him to.

Why does she allow it? His breath! Rotting teeth plugged with meat from the Madras meat curries he brews to his own satanic formula and which he disgustingly gouges from the cavities with a fat, dripping finger. Born in 1943, he blames post-war malnutrition for his teeth; is Hitler also responsible for Sidney's habit of excavating his nose like a small boy, then eating the product? Ugh.

Maybe it's his energy. You're alive in his presence and in his arms. No 'chaplain', he; no 'Please undress me', no 'God I'm sorry'. You're alive because he believes the world turns under the force of his tread.

Chantal has lost her sentence. Sitting at her typewriter late into the night, her essay assignments for Sidney and Hooper dutifully completed, she notices that her prose has become breathless, broken-backed. It's getting to me!

She hears Samantha's laughter, then Sylvie whispers in her ear: 'A good journalist is a lonely creature. A motionless hunter of the night.'

Chantal Poynter tears the old page from her typewriter and starts again.

### The Sidney Pyke Story, by Chantal Poynter

Sidney and Samantha were famously married as the climactic event of a decade during which each of them had 'made the revolution' every time they made love. The drug-destructed corpses they had left behind them did not attend the wedding.

It was some event. Emerging from Kensington Register in a scarlet outfit cut from the same cloth as Sidney's, Samantha described the ceremony: not only had she refused to obey Sidney, but also – imagine the Registrar's bafflement – to honour and love him.

The Press asked why she had bothered to marry him.

'To fuck up the institution of marriage, darling.'

An hour later reporters and photographers were admitted to a suite in the Hyde Park Hilton where

Sidney and Samantha were already in bed. Neither revolutionary wore a stitch.

'You're too late.' Sidney grinned.

(It turned out that the Hilton bill was greased by the PR firm hired to promote Sidney's new book, *Up Against the Wall, Motherf*\*\*\*\*\**. In the swinging, hedonistic, utterly liberated '60s, the lawyers still imposed ridiculous asterisks.)

'Is this the first time you've made love in a bed?' a reporter asked Samantha. The man had done his homework and it took the wide-eyed bride a moment or two to remember that when she'd appeared starkers in the Amsterdam Provo-Kabouter pornrag *Suck*, she'd told an awed world that she had screwed on every known horizontal surface except a bed.

'Did you play Italian truck-driver?' Sidney was asked.

The famous Motherfucker, who'd set fire to garbage cans in downtown Manhattan, then stoned the fire fighters, scratched his hairy chest and glanced at his wife for guidance. Evidently the groom had been badly briefed. A real-life Italian truck-driver called Luigi, a good Catholic and father of four, had been dutifully transporting several hundred tons of tomatoes towards the Swiss frontier when Samantha appeared in the middle of a mountain road and demanded a lift.

Within two weeks the tomatoes had rotted, the container truck had been abandoned, Luigi had forgotten about his wife, and Samantha was reporting to a British Sunday paper that educated women who sought out non-violent men would never know what a real orgasm was. (Those were the times when Samantha claimed to have beaten up Mick Jagger for calling her a 'wild chick' or something.)

Anyway, there was Sidney, the fireball who'd stopped the Oakland troop trains by hurling himself across the tracks, propped up on Hyde Park Hilton pink pillows in a storm of flashlights, and a whole Ho Chi Minh Trail away from understanding that he was being asked whether he'd been Greek (or Italian) enough to beat up his Amazonian bride before consummating the marriage.

And Amazonian she was. Tall, broad-shouldered, and with a thigh-lock that had hospitalized the entire leadership of Students for a Democratic Society, Samantha had let off surplus steam as a stuntwoman in a cine citta sexploitation movie about female slave gladiators in the time of the Emperor Trojan. (Hence her famous quip, 'Trojan had a better column than any emperor I've known.') She never got into a Pasolini movie, or a Fellini, but she tried – and when Jean-Luc Godard broke up the Cannes Film Festival in May '68, it was Samantha who got in the first kiss for the cameras.

Sidney's memoirs of life among the New York Motherfuckers turned out to be a nasty blend of boasting and self-flagellation. Condemning himself as a 'phallocrat', he pledged himself never again to call a chick a chick. The Women's Movement was erupting fast and screaming for blood: Sidney had laughed – and been photographed laughing – when Stokely Carmichael told the women that their only appropriate position in the Movement was prone.

This was just one of several reasons why a whole lot of Sisters got a whole lot angry about Samantha's marriage and tried to storm Kensington Register. The Pyke–Newman nuptials were one of the few in that 'angry decade' to require police protection. Newman had ridden too long on the Sisters' shoulders, denouncing the male sex: hadn't she told *Suck* that the only male in the Movement she genuinely respected was Allen Ginsberg, a poet, a genius, and gay as hell? (According to legend Ginsberg had offered her some grass, said a mantra, and asked a friend, 'Who is this huge chick?')

The Pyke–Newman marriage, which both partners

had predicted would last 'a month at most' has meandered on, faute de mieux, for twenty years. Sidney Pyke lapsed into the 'academic gerontocracy' he despised and gradually became – as his recent blurb writers desperately insist – 'increasingly respected'. In short, one of yesterday's men. Pyke talks of big sales for his latest 'testament', *The Red and the Green*, but an inside source admits that the book will be lucky if it offloads a thousand copies.

The breadwinner in the Pyke household is, of course, the built-to-last Samantha Newman. With academic salaries down thirty per cent or is it seventy per cent under Thatcher, it was Samantha who paid the public-school fees for young Emma and Robert. (Newman once stormed the prime-time American TV networks, coast to coast, explaining why she would never have children: 'I wouldn't want my children to have for a father the kind of man I like to sleep with.')

Poor Sidney! When his local branch of the Labour Party discovered that he was sending his kids to private schools, he tried to explain that ten years of Tory misrule had destroyed state education. The comrades didn't buy it. Sidney seized the initiative by expelling himself from the Labour Party and joining the Greens.

Samantha, meanwhile, has fallen in love with love. Love is now back in fashion. She natures-and-nurtures a 'wild' garden and wears big flowery frocks when receiving visiting women columnists – placid ewes, grazing on love. Sidney hides in his study, despite cooing photocalls from the lawn and mimosa petals tossed through his window. Samantha's big, new, £200,000 book for Hans-Dietrich Swindler's Vampire imprint was originally meant to warn the 'Carolingian' '90s that the Love of a Good Man is the only pathway through the minefields of HIV and Aids. Problem is, the Man in question is about to be pulled from his pedestal by enraged Women with scores to settle – not least against Newman.

Prospects for her book: catastrophic at best. But does she know?

One further paragraph – much indebted to her sister Sylvie – lies on her table with a thick blue pencil mark running through it.

The fellow to ask is at this moment turning her mauve pages on the eighth floor of Swindler House. This ambitious Scots boy buys his suits at Next (Contemporary Style jacket, Cambridge 705, double-breasted, one button show, two flips pockets; trousers York 405, four reverse pleats, extension waistband, slant side pockets, turn ups or plain bottoms to order) for a modest two hundred and twenty-five quid.

Ian Davidson casts a glance across the book page of *The Times*, a quick, pragmatic scan programmed to pick up the word 'Vampire' and little else, apart from the hype side. Measuring the ads in column inches, he notices a review of a book by Samantha Newman's husband, Sidney Pyke. Davidson's eye jumps to the concluding paragraph:

Professor Pyke, like others of his media-crazed generation, will do anything to keep a high profile. His mutually self-congratulatory 'interview' with his old 'copain', Danny Cohn-Bendit, the enfant terrible of '68, may remind us that the boy remains father to the man – an impression strongly confirmed by reports of Pyke's recent conduct as Head of Media Studies at the University of Mercia.

Davidson nods. Somewhere on his desk lies a mauve page by Newman in which she announces that Sidney has transformed the Media Studies Department into 'quite simply, unanswerably, the most creative, imaginative and influential in the country!' Those fucking exclamation marks. Like locusts they come. Davidson feels sure that on an earlier page – he cannot lay hand on it – she described her husband as 'not easy to live with, a loyal, cuddly man whose testicles have doubled production in middle age!'

Davidson confines himself to deleting the exclamation marks. His active eye turns to the *Financial Times*, noting that water, gas, British Airways, British Telecom – all privatized since he left school, a revolution of South Korean proportions – are universally up in value. Up and up. Davidson's fingers flick across his calculator. Only the Government's sale of its own holding in British Petroleum caught him (and everyone else) out. Black Monday he won't forget. Three of his Cambridge friends, two merchant bankers and a stockbroker, had jumped from a Thames pleasure boat, sportingly tethered together, after a final acid-house blast-out under the arches of the Westway flyover.

Sunk in gloom, Davidson ponders the latest batch of mauve pages spread across his desk:

I first met Sidney soon after he returned from the Night of the Barricades. I had seen a picture of him seated in the President of Columbia University's leather chair, his boots up on the desk, telling reporters, 'This is the first revolutionary movement that does not covet the power it has overthrown. We have abolished power, period.'

Beautiful! I knew then that I simply had to meet this man. And then he came back to London and tore down the notorious iron gates of the London School of Economics with a crowbar smuggled into the LSE by an anarchist building worker! I was there! I said, 'Right on!' and he looked at me and he said, I shall never forget it, 'Outasight, chick.'

Davidson pushes the pages away. 'Holy cow.' Not for the first time, or the tenth, he reaches into his desk drawer for Newman's original synopsis. *Nature or Nurture* (it invariably informs him) will be about:

– Love as the binding, bonding, building force between woman and man, children and parents. Forging love and making love.

– An updated feminism for the '90s, a generous, imaginative, modern creed for women who wish neither to abandon hard-won victories nor to embrace the sad, self-mutilating, fanatical fundamentalism of the Sister-Ayatollahs who bleakly insist on the Original Sin of Man.

– Recent attacks on me. My enemies.

– Notes on personal hygiene. Is it a sin to look (or smell!) attractive? Do you have a weight problem? Don't ignore it and don't become a slave to the bathroom scales. What to eat. Some delicious recipes. Sidney's bad habits.

– What is Sexism? (a New Look at a tired word). What is true masculinity (Sidney) and true femininity (me)?

– Clothes and accessories. Hers and His. Where to go, what to buy. Don't let your man look a fright (Sidney).

– Should we worry if we are cleverer/more successful/earn more than he is/does? (me and Sidney).

– Nature or Nurture? The Great Debate. What forms a little girl (me) or boy (Sidney) into a mature woman or man? Biology? Genes? Hormones? Culture? Bad luck?

– Career and home: How I Do It. Being a TV star. Planning My Day. Sidney's role. Personal hygiene. My enemies.

– The wonderful modern marriage of Sidney and me, an organic unity based on mutual love, respect, trust and freedom. Doing your own thing and staying together: twenty tips. Sex and sexism. Planning your orgasms.

– Sidney's progress since my last book. From male chauvinist to enlightened husband. Virile, caring, gentle, considerate, wide-angled, imaginative. A man with many critics but no enemies.

– Why Sidney's new book was misunderstood. Sidney's enemies. Sidney and the dogs.

– My Story since my last book. My enemies. What I wear – the whens and the whys. Coping with the fan mail.

– The '60s! A rapid flashback to When It All Began. How we came together for readers unfamiliar with my earlier books (there are always a few). What I wore then.

– My work for charity. The Samantha Newman Day Care Centre. How you can help.

– Famine and female contraception. My journeys to Ethiopia and India. Being tall in Tokyo (getting to know the Japanese).

– Great Issues confronting women today: sex, marriage, contraception (where to go), fidelity, freedom, work, children, abortion, Aids, surrogate mothers, artificial insemination, what to wear, what to eat. More recipes.

– Talking and listening. How to listen to him without paying attention. When to nag and not nag.

– Can't we laugh at ourselves? Why do we have to be so solemn about the oldest war in the world? Women should laugh at men – and laugh at themselves (Sidney and me).


Davidson replaces the synopsis in his drawer. It never gets any better. The only demonstrable link between synopsis and emerging text is the mauve paper. Gloomily he takes himself to the eighth-floor window of 'the Martians have landed'. A huge procession of Muslims – where do they all come from? – is heading across the park towards Penguin Books, chanting anathemas and brandishing hideous effigies of 'Satan Rushdie'. A slim blue file of accompanying PCs and WPCs is turning a deaf ear to incitements to murder.

From the pale face pressed to the smoked glass of Vampire Books comes a chuckle as sweet as salt on porridge.

# *Six*

The Vice-Chancellor's residence has never been inspected by Prince Charles. The Duchess of Kent had laid the foundation stone and not come back. A '60s redbrick lodge done up in pseudo-Georgian pilasters, with a couple of Ionic pillars guarding the front door, Sidney regards it as almost as pretentious as Thomas Jefferson's folly at Monticello. Probably right up the Prince's street.

The Registrar and Bill Jones are already in attendance on the V-C when Sidney arrives. The demeanour of this triptych conveys a static semaphore: This Is Serious.

Sidney pulls off his bicycle clips (having failed, as usual, to chain his precious machine to one of the Ionic pillars) and sinks, without invitation, into a chair. His demeanour is that of a veteran who's engaged in many worthy wars. Among them:

1. Sidney stubbornly fights for continuous assessment against sudden-death exams; the Registrar insists that term papers could be, and usually were, written by 'someone else'.

2. Sidney continues to align himself with student demands for an end to the sexual segregation of hostels; he also supports contraceptive machines in the washrooms. Even without Aids, that's a non-starter: the women students no longer want de-segregated hostels.

3. Sidney demands 'affirmative action' – ten per cent of places to be reserved for black and cultural minority students who fail to meet the normal entrance standards. (The Registrar has invited him to define a black.)

'Frankly, Sidney,' the V-C begins, 'the situation in the Media Studies Department is completely out of hand – '

'Anarchy,' says the Registrar.

Sidney turns a bleak gaze on Jones, poised to 'et tu' him, but his friend is silent.

The V-C consents to sit down. The Registrar copies then stands up again. Because of a dicky heart, the V-C had left the Ministry of Defence with a knighthood and looked for a stress-free academic post: student rioting greeted his appointment and Government rioting in the shape of savage financial cuts followed. The imminent arrival of the Minister of Higher Education, the Iron Lady's latest Hatchet, is all that the V-C needs.

But it's not all he's getting. Yesterday he was visited by Dr Bess Hooper, and without an appointment. The woman just walked in and engaged him in relentless eye contact. In the end he fixed his own eye on the ear of the Duke of Rutland while Hooper flicked cigarette ash (rolls her own) on the rather nice Persian rug he'd picked up in 1977, while bribing one of the Shah's arms procurers on behalf of the MoD. The Hooper woman appeared to be informing him what every senile male judge had ever said about rape.

Now Sidney Pyke is sprawled in a chair without a tie and wearing a disgusting pair of jeans. The Registrar, hands clasped behind his back, does a full circuit of the room:

'Graffiti on the walls – slogans ridiculing Authority; scurrilous attacks on our benefactor, the Benzin Oil Company; vile slogans lampooning the "plutocracy", the "gerontocracy", the "phallocracy". And you do nothing about it, Sidney. Even though I have seen "PUKE MCP" daubed on your own office door.'

'Call it wall newspapers,' Sidney says.

'Call it what?' the V-C asks.

'I defaced a few buildings in my own day,' Sidney says.

'We're not unaware of that,' the Registrar says. 'We're waiting for you to grow up.'

The V-C sighs deeply. Stress. 'Hooper,' he says.

'Hooper? Yes?'

'You appointed her,' the V-C says. 'I know your mistakes are all brave ones, Sidney – presumably Hooper was the bravest of all.'

'I respect her convictions and her right to express them.'

'But she doesn't respect *yours*.'

'I respect her right not to respect mine.'

'I suppose you know she's living with a graduate student in your department, Melanie Rosen, who not only attends Dr Hooper's classes but wishes – one gathers – to transfer her thesis from your supervision to Dr Hooper's.'

'I haven't agreed to that.'

'But how,' demands the Registrar, 'can you possibly condone an affair between a member of staff and a student?'

'Consenting adults,' Sidney says. 'Sorry, I forgot: there are no adults in this university.'

'But you wouldn't do it yourself,' the V-C tells Sidney.

Bill Jones chooses this moment to turn his face towards the Duke of Rutland, shoulders heaving. Jones believes that Sidney's last fling was ten years ago, with a Gilly as yet unredeemed by marriage to Jones.

'I had a visit from Dr Hooper yesterday,' the V-C reports.

Sidney nods. 'Hooper is a Roundhead. We in our time were Cavaliers.'

'Really?'

'Mm. Her militancy is worthy – but dreary, dun-coloured; ours was as colourful as a pope's wedding. And there you go – the Roundheads are now closing the theatres.' Sidney glances up at the Duke of Rutland. 'You may remember the painting by W. F. Yeames, Vice-Chancellor.'

Given the stress he is under, the V-C is pressed to remember any painting, but he nods patiently, his thumbs involuntarily circling one another.

'The young captive Prince is confronted by a panel of grim Puritans,' Sidney goes on. ' "When did you last see your father?" they ask him. Today the panel would consist of the Women's Committee and the question would be, "When did your father last molest you?" '

The Registrar pounces. 'Correction, Sidney. The question

is: "What did you do to Dr Hooper, on 30 September, at 6.58 P.M., in the Benzin Swimming Pool?"'

'Darling, something's happened. I can tell.'

Sweeping in from her taxi, Samantha instantly diagnoses the terminal depression gripping the husband sulking in front of the nine o'clock news. Gently placing a large brown-paper parcel on the floor, she takes his hand and caresses his cheek.

'Tell. Something to do with Bess Hooper?'

'Hooper? I'd sooner screw a Giacometti sculpture buried in the soil to honour the dead.'

'What?' Her hand tests his brow.

'The Benzin Swimming Pool! Ha!'

'Sidney, what the hell are you talking about?'

Samantha is studying him like an archaeologist weary of twenty years' digging on a single site. His expression is a Daumier of dissimulation. At such moments it's quite hard to love him – though loving him has become her major industrial enterprise.

She unwraps the brown-paper parcel. Two pictures emerge and are held up for his morose inspection. 'Eye Contact,' she glows. 'My exhibition, Sidney.'

Sidney sees a woman galloping across what may be the New Forest on a black stallion. Then he sees a photo-montage of the Victoria Falls tinted in screaming blood red.

'Awful,' he says. Samantha has been harvesting this kind of stuff for an exhibition of 'female erotic art' which, he remains happily confident, will never take place.

Samantha turns on her heel, taking herself up to her IBM Fastrite with a strong cup of coffee and loads of new ideas to get her next chapter off the ground. But her jewelled fingers no sooner set the cursor leaping than they are stilled. Perhaps she hears the ruthless beat of Chantal's typewriter in a student hostel three miles away. And why has that sallow boy Davidson not acknowledged her last two chapters? She has a bloody good mind to phone Jack Lait in New York. But she doesn't; instead her eyes fill with tears.

Sidney is now sulking in bed. His thoughts drift in several directions simultaneously. Everyone had his own '68 – British farmers remembered it for foot-and-mouth disease, the V-C had flown to Athens to ascertain the Greek Military Junta's arms requirements, a hush-hush mission for the Ministry of Defence which Sidney had blown in *Black Dwarf* after a tip-off from an inside source who later got three years under the Official Secrets Act . . . Chantal hadn't been born – yet here she was teaching him to pronounce 'oui' as 'weh' when (and if) he was invited by Bernard Pivot to appear on 'Apostrophe'. He'd asked her who this bloke was. 'My God, Sidney, never say that in France, never say "Who's Bernard Pivot?" Forget Mitterrand's name, Rocard, Chirac, Le Pen, Gérard Depardieu, but never Bernard Pivot.'

Chantal reminds him of Sharon – the delicate limbs, the same cool, goading contempt. Like many men of vast self-esteem he finds contempt rousing – Melanie's worshipful moans had done little for him. A mere anorexic interregnum, Melanie. And now that lovely foaming froth of wiry hair has gone, shorn to luminous orange Punk, for night-fighting against Cruise missiles on Salisbury Plain. A self-proclaimed witch.

Melanie! He sits bolt upright in bed. Was this – Hooper's accusation to the V-C – Melanie's revenge?

'There is really no way,' the V-C had told him, 'that we can avoid an internal inquiry. Though we'll try.'


At nineteen, Chantal Poynter is a veteran journalist and broadcaster. Her genial inspiration has been – and remains – her elder sister Sylvie. Beautiful, adorable Sylvie, now deputy Features Editor of a rather big Sunday newspaper, is offering Chantal a lot of money to 'break' the 'Sidney Pyke Story' and thus 'dish' a rival Sunday, owned by Hans-Dietrich Swindler, which has acquired the first-serial rights on Samantha Newman's *Nature or Nurture* from Vampire Books.

It was Sylvie who'd urged Chantal to audition after a secret tip-off about a possible replacement for Samantha Newman at the BBC.

'Some chance, Sylvie!'

'Go. Always apply. It builds contacts. Contacts is it.'

Sylvie had also told her about Samantha's young editor at Vampire Books. Apparently Sylvie had met him in the Zanzibar Club, when going out with one of Davidson's colleagues, later fired. 'The boy's an idiot,' Sylvie reported. 'Got a 2:1 in history at Cambridge. Faintly provincial – Scottish, I believe. Wears the wrong ties. Ambitious.'

Darling Sylvie has a nose for young men and tends to get through more than her share.

As schoolgirls Sylvie and Chantal had set up a pirate radio station called 'Fulham Palace' – which annoyed the Bishop of London, the legal occupant, and immediately earned the clandestine transmitter valuable publicity in the local press. At the age of sixteen, Sylvie specialized in resurrecting stars whose lives had been ruined by the wrong needles. Her proudest coup was to bring back from the dead Bilko Bandung, one-time choppy, edgy, nervy, R'n'R guitarist with Professor Freakout.

To begin with, Fulham Palace's only advertising spot came from Uncle Charles's antique shop on the Broadway. Begging and begging, little Chantal finally persuaded Sylvie to let her do a live commercial for Uncle C.:

Want a genuine hideous Bauhaus settee shaped like a '30s cinema for the price of an hors d'oeuvre at Les Regles de Jeu? Setting up home with someone you've never mentioned to Mum and Dad? – Fulham Palace has the Victorian double bed you've dreamed of. By the way, contrary to legend, Victorians spent a lot of their time in the wrong bed.

So now it's years and years later – three in fact, and Chantal is poised to leap from pirate radio to prime-time television while darling Sylvie is deputy Features Editor of a Sunday newspaper. Chantal and Sylvie both understand (even if their parents don't) that the last thing you need, in order to get an editor by the balls (and balls still bifurcate the legs of seventy-five per cent of editors), is a degree in Media Studies from a third-rate 'rural' university founded in the profligate '60s. But after Chantal more or less buggered up her A-Levels, Sidney Pyke had accepted her on the basis of a C and two Ds, plus a copy of Chantal's school magazine.

Chantal's first foray into notoriety came when she got her bite at editing the St Faith's Girls' School magazine, *Pandora*. Interviews with the teaching staff attained a level of impertinence and invention not even achieved by Sylvie before her. Chantal's prize fabrications were two letters, one from a 'delighted father', the other from a 'disgusted mother'.

Dear Pandora,

I fell off the chair so often while reading your latest issue that I decided it might be wiser to read it lying on the floor. I particularly enjoyed the non-stop insults against boys. Nasty creatures, aren't they? What do girls see in them, one may wonder?

I was particularly impressed by your survey of prevailing attitudes among the eleven-year-olds. One must rejoice that sixty per cent of them intend in future to spend 'less time' in pubs, as compared to fifteen per cent 'more time' and twenty per cent 'about the same'. What a pity you didn't ask the little dears about their drink-and-drive habits, not to mention their heroin addictions. Anyway, keep it up.

A Delighted Father . . .

Dear Editor,

I am referring the current issue of *Pandora* to the Press Council.

The so-called interviews with members of staff are simply libellous. I do not believe the School Chaplain could have said, 'God is merely an option on the religious syllabus at St Faith's.' Nor could Miss Hard-castle possibly have told you, 'Since I began teaching Latin it has become a dead language.' And how did Mr Phillips come to be educated in a convent school, as you claim? He must have been a boy, surely?

Talking of boys, is there not a disproportionate mention of them in your pages? No doubt they have their time and place, but your feature article, 'How to Embrace the Enemy in Five Easy Stages', I found positively obscene. Please remember that *Pandora* is a family magazine.

And I don't want to see the word 'Pill' again in your pages. To list a teacher's engagement under the heading 'Sweetening the Pill' is grossly impertinent.

As for your so-called surveys, graphs and other 'statistics', I have affidavits from the smaller girls of MIV and UIV that they were subjected to torture until they answered 'Yes' to the question, 'You simply *adore* your hateful parents, don't you?'

By the way, I counted the word 'sex' fifty-seven times in eight pages. In my opinion this word should be used only in a decent context, e.g. 'Single-sex school'.

A Disgusted Mother . . .

What 'A Disgusted Mother' didn't know (if she knew anything about anything) was that the sideswipe at the Chaplain was directed not at the real one, a very nice man actually, but at 'God I'm sorry', James Loftus-Wright, Esq, universally dubbed 'the chaplain' by the senior girls, not to mention sex-maniac know-alls in the Lower Fifth, ugh, on account of his divine good looks and dreamy manner of drifting words like 'crucifixion' and 'resurrection' into reflections on the Romantic Poets. A bachelor with a smile for everyone as he crossed the yard, hair flowing, James Loftus-Wright reserved a kind of double-smile, two-for-the-price-of-one, for his pet contributors to *Pandora*, his 'prodigal daughters'. They all hugely despised 'the chaplain' but thought about him quite a lot.

Then he took Chantal to dinner and dripping candles.

'I expect your father keeps an eye on you,' James Loftus-Wright remarked as the salades niçoises landed on the check tablecloth.

'Why shouldn't he?' Chantal replied (she hoped) vampishly.

'Well, quite. But you're discreet?'

'I never lie to my parents,' Chantal lied.

'Quite right. But silence can be divine.'

His flat was super: a real pine-and-leather bachelor pad, sort of a studio, with a spiral iron staircase, and a big etching of Hamlet, or was it Keats, holding a skull.

'Not bad,' she sighed.

'And you, too.' His ringed hand came across the Leather Shop sofa as if inviting to be kissed, then dangled on her thigh. She knew, then, that It was about to Happen (she'd deliberately avoided garlic in the bistro). Up the iron spiral staircase, he with a volume of Byron's letters dripping from his hand − is this how mature men kick off? − and next thing she was slipping things off (and on) in the bathroom, examining every item in his cabinet, boxes of pills, tubes of suspect ointments, sure that a man's identity resided in his toilette and that she would find him stretched, naked, under a silk or at least Irish linen sheet when she emerged.

But James Loftus-Wright was discovered absorbed in Byron. 'Please undress me,' he said languidly, offering the two-for-the-price-of-one smile.

Sidney Pyke never says please.

Chantal's A-Level results were terrible. Even Daddy noticed. (Neither Sylvie nor Chantal quite understood why Maman, a great beauty in her day, and still, had unaccountably abandoned her acting career in France for Daddy, a banker who expected a well-dressed wife at a well-appointed dinner table. Daddy has been something of a chequebook father but quite nice when traced. Besides, you didn't need disgusting Lower Fifth biology lessons to know that if Maman hadn't fallen for Daddy one would have been in no position to wonder why she had.) Anyway, 'appalling' (Daddy said) A-Levels. Then this fearsome, bearded professor scowling at your curriculum vitae. But a copy of *Pandora*, and her persistently insolent (she hoped) gaze during the admissions interview, sufficed for Professor Pyke to bend his normal A-Level requirements.

'So you're a dunce,' he said. And not a ring on his hairy hand.

'Never heard of Sidney Pyke,' Sylvie commented later, 'but if he's really Samantha Newman's husband, darling, pitch in.' Chantal thought that French lessons was her idea, but while she was still hesitating – 'His feet smell vile (ça sent du Roquefort), not to mention rotting teeth and damp stains under his arm-pits by mid-morning,' she reported to Sylvie – Sidney himself made his move. 'You'd better come and teach me to speak French. On Tuesdays.' It was an order. Two sexual carnivores locked jaws; but the French was never quite without tears for Chantal.


First class of the afternoon, Bess Hooper begins by reminding the Daughters of de Beauvoir how *The Second Sex* 'gave us all the courage to *name* our experiences, allowing women to confront their lives and to begin to turn them around'. Bess then moves on to today's subject: the children's classics.

'The untamed or unfettered female must always be chastised. In Grimms' tale the fisherman's wife is guilty of insatiable greed and ambition, while the weak husband fails in his natural duty to curb her . . . Females are admired when passive or obedient – Snow White for example. Spirited tomboys must learn their lesson and be tamed into obedient wives. Destiny is unbending and unforgiving. Women cursed by natural curiosity are punished. For girls it is a sin to look too far, or even to look; Psyche and the wives of Bluebeard paid the penalty for ignoring the prohibition against looking.'

Melanie Rosen, wearing her Botticelli face today, has been gazing out of the window at the graffiti running across the vertical surfaces of the library. FREE NELSON MANDELA. STOP THE TOUR. DEFEND NICARAGUA. CRUISEWATCH. PYKE MUST GO. Sidney himself has pointed out that all these objectives have since been fulfilled, except PYKE MUST GO. Melanie despises the previous incarnation of herself which used to laugh at his jokes.

As she stands up to testify, Botticelli yields (Sidney will later perceive) to Käthe Kollwitz.

'Action must follow analysis – as Sidney Pyke once announced in the courtyard of the Sorbonne. Pyke complains that our Guidelines are illiberal. He calls them censorship. We are not liberals. The oppressed are never liberals. What we demand is academic freedom.'

The Daughters of de Beauvoir bang the desks and drum their thick soles on the floor. Melanie is encouraged.

'Sisters, which of us has not been molested as a child? Grabbed out of our sleep by a father or step-father stinking of beer? Which of us could put a name to our terror and alienation? Which of us does not drop her gaze when a man fixes his predatory eye on her? Which of us has not experienced the asphyxia of finding herself incapable of arguing with a man? Which of us does not feel in her bones that the world, mysteriously, belongs to *them*? Which of us has not consciously suppressed her own intelligence in order to appease a male ego? Which of us has not forced herself to laugh at a man's pathetic jokes?'

Chantal is waiting for Melanie in the corridor as the Daughters of de Beauvoir emerge, elated. Melanie fascinates her: the previous one in the line often does. Or should she say – with Sidney – the several Melanie Rosens: the frail anorexic, the fighting pétroleuse, she of the afro top, the shorn punk, the hetero and the lesbian, she who weeps with Virginia Woolf and Emily Dickinson, she who slays soldiers on Salisbury Plain? Dressed to resemble the autumn compost heap on Monday, she will decorate herself with the dreamy sensuality of an Auguste Renoir on Thursday. Says Sidney. A haggard chalk-white from centuries of male oppression on Wednesday, she skips in and lifts a ballerina's silky leg to Degas on Friday. Says Sidney. Melanie appears to be a detective's nightmare – 'an identikit person capable of reassembling herself at whim' (says Sidney).

Chantal pursues Melanie out of 'Daughters of de Beauvoir' into the concrete wasteland of a winter campus. Wearing a black firing-squad bonnet over wire-wool hair, Melanie clasps a slush-brown Mother Earth cape to her skeletal frame. Chantal trots in pursuit.

Melanie allows herself to be led to the Student Union cafeteria. Passing a group of radicals spray-painting the walls with slogans demanding the overthrow of the ONE-PYKE STATE, Melanie pauses, borrows a paint-gun, and adds POWER TO THE SISTERS! Entering the cafeteria, she recoils from the smoke, the all-enveloping male boisterousness, the screaming juke-box.

Chantal fetches two paper cups of disgusting milky tea and offers Melanie a cube of sugar in a paper wrapper; Melanie pushes it away through pools of fluid and used cups packed with sodden cigarette ends.

'I wanted to ask you about Olive Schreiner,' Chantal says.

'Why?'

'Well, gosh, aren't you writing your PhD thesis about her? She sounds fascinating.'

'Mm.'

Chantal studies Melanie's luminous grey eyes (which Sidney likens to Coniston Water at dusk in mid-winter). Melanie cannot be asked about her trip to the Lake District with Sidney because it has been erased from the witches' calendar, but rumours abound that a pilgrimage to honour Wordsworth (and Dorothy!) and Ruskin became, night and day, a monologue by Sidney about Sidney. Melanie had felt herself 'erased' – and a witch was born.

Surely Melanie's eyes were green yesterday?

'You're staring at me,' Melanie says.

'Oh do please help me understand,' Chantal hastily continues. 'I mean, Schreiner was a pioneer feminist, wasn't she, yet she seems to idealize the love of male and female. All those tiny, singing birds she observed in the African bush, building their nests together, singing their love songs, and generally caring for each other until death did them part.'

'Cock-o-veets,' Melanie says.

'Yes!'

'Cock-o-veets are not human beings.'

'Ah. Jolly good point.'

'Sidney Pyke wants us to believe that they are.'

'Oh – I see.'

'Schreiner denounced male domination and male hegemony, but Pyke is interested only in Schreiner's naïve, pre-feminist faith in the so-called sacred bond between man and woman.'

'Like Samantha Newman?'

A hint of green in Coniston Water.

'Pyke pretends that Schreiner's feminism was what he calls "a healthy escape from gender". He ridicules our own Women's Movement as "morbid, repressed, donor-inseminated".' Melanie's stick-arm shoots out from under the cape and grabs Chantal's wrist. 'Schreiner was writing almost a century ago and we can forgive her. We can't forgive Samantha Newman.'

'How awful, Melanie. How absolutely awful.'

'Bess thinks you use too many adverbs.'

'She – '

'Adverbs are a symptom of female subordination. The male of the species has commandeered the nouns and verbs – the powerhouse of the language.'

'Oh. I really must talk to Bess.'

Melanie nods and tightens her grip on Chantal's wrist. 'Yes. But we think you prefer to talk to "Sidney".'

Chantal notes the quotation marks – as if 'Sidney' was a fraud perpetrated by Professor Pyke; as if 'Sidney' cultivated a sham spirit of 'égalité', encouraging a fraternal 'tu' from his students and then dishing out the hegemonic 'vous'.

'So – '

'So I no longer consent to be supervised by Pyke.' Melanie is wrapping a screaming strand of hair around her forefinger.

Chantal is of course familiar with this dramatic act of rebellion; like most of the witches' secrets, it's as widely reported as the price of lunch in the cafeteria. Sidney's crimes are blazoned on every wall – the entire university now knows how he instructed a taxi-driver to harass, then assault, Bess and Melanie when they were bicycling home.

'Gosh. And what does he say about that?'

Two fierce laser dots of colour have surfaced in Melanie's ashen cheeks. 'You ought to know. Doesn't he tell you everything? Aren't you his current dolly-bird?'


The Vice-Chancellor is lunching in town with the Chairman of the Governors. The venue is the Athenaeum – or perhaps White's, or conceivably the Institute of Directors, but unlikely to be the Garrick or the Reform – and most definitely not the vegetarian cafeteria of the Institute for Contemporary Arts, where Sidney Pyke is today giving a lunchtime lecture on something.

'Frankly,' the V-C says, 'I regard both Pykes, husband and wife, as headline-seeking publicity hounds.'

The Chairman nods. 'Wasn't it Pyke who appointed Hooper in the first place?' He chuckles. 'I must say! Rape in the Benzin Swimming Pool! Ha! Ha ha! Ha ha ha! Ha ha ha ha!'

The Vice-Chancellor frowns. 'I would have thought that you, as Chairman of the Benzin Oil Company – '

'Ha ha. Ha!'

'I'm afraid these charges against Pyke are serious. We cannot avoid an internal inquiry. I don't relish the prospect. That man possesses a unique capacity for treating his own past mistakes as triumphs of high-minded principle.'

'But the two women are bonkers, aren't they?'

The V-C leans further across the table. 'And he regularly seduces his own female students.'

'Is that allowed?'

'Conduct unbecoming – if you can make it stick.'

'Can you?' the Chairman of the Governors asks.

'Pyke has launched a new course on "Government Disinformation".'

'Contradiction in terms, surely. Don't mention it to the Minister.'

'He knows. He wants Pyke fired,' the Vice-Chancellor says.

'Tenure, I suppose. Can't touch him.'

'Not unless the Tribunal of Inquiry – '

'Ah. I might take that one over.'

'It's supposed to be independent.'

'The Chairman of the Governors is independent.'

'Pyke's fully capable of taking us to the European Court . . .'

'We don't want the Benzin Company Swimming Pool dragged into Europe.'

'The Minister's going to demand cuts.'

'Naturally. That's what he's paid to do. It's because he hates Higher Education that she appointed him. Didn't he tell Parliament that the majority of academics are "bums and scroungers"? Quite true, I suppose. Even so, we – '

'They're cutting our grant by fifteen per cent – for starters. I gather the precise "claw-back" expected of us will depend on the Minister's visit. His officials have been drinking my sherry all week, gabbling about axes and dead wood.'

'Well, don't let that man Pyke anywhere near the Minister.'

'The Minister has asked to meet Pyke.'

The Chairman of the Governors pushes away his plate, which naturally bears the crest of the Athenaeum or wherever they are eating.

The Vice-Chancellor continues his meal with a hint of a smile. 'Actually . . .'

'Mm?'

'Given sufficient offence, the Minister might axe the

whole Media Studies Department. That would, er, take the weight off everyone else.'

'Ah.'

The V-C produces a rolled up newspaper and offers it to the Chairman. '*The Examiner*. You might like to scan Haynes's editorial. Mm. On second thoughts, I might take some of that blue Stilton after all.'


'Lies! Damned lies!' Sidney yells.

Samantha has been mildly dreading the moment when Sidney's eye would fall upon the latest diatribe in *The Examiner*. Time had been when Sidney and the paper's editor, Haynes, collided on friendly drinking terms in the saloon bar of the Fox & Goose. Sidney's outrageous campaigns fostered the illusion of a free Press and demonstrably increased circulation. Flagrant bias, lies, misquotation, libel, corruption, pandering to vested interests – Haynes had cheerfully published all such allegations against himself from Pyke so long as the professor remained only a professor and did not accuse Haynes of illiteracy.

But when Sidney was elected the first Green Councillor within a radius of fifty miles, things changed. The Tory majority was gone, the Council was 'hung', Pyke was suddenly in a position to deprive 'the freemen of England' of their historic liberty to befoul their nest.

Sidney had tried to keep his temper (as Samantha later recalled to Chantal – 'though he's not very good at it, darling, or hadn't you noticed? Well, wait until the first infatuation wears off.'). His initial response had been almost frivolous:

To what ancient liberties does your bigoted editorial allude? The right of drunks to smoke on buses? The right of dogs to crap on pavements, parks and children's playgrounds? The ploughing up of our precious and disappearing footpaths by rapacious farmers? The right of industries to dump poisonous effluent into local rivers, or the right of motorists to damage the brains of our growing children by pumping lead from their motor exhausts?

Sidney was well aware that Haynes was a chain-smoking drunk with a string of convictions for dangerous driving and, also, the owner of four large and savage dogs that regularly terrorized a school playground. Haynes was also aware of it. It hadn't stood between them in the Fox & Goose. But now . . .

Now Haynes publishes a report alleging that Sidney is:

. . . nefariously masterminding a callous conspiracy to blackmail the Council into deploying helmeted snatch squads to sequestrate stray dogs, or any best friend of man transitionally off its lead, and to dispense them to an Asiatic company manufacturing gummed labels for Communist China.

Only last weekend Councillor Pyke was discerned by many residents patrolling our parks in the retroactive new Dog Warden vans, hectoring the two Wardens to pursue and dispense with not only stray dogs but any of man's best friend briefly off the lead or whose natural functions its unfortunate owner did not immediately poop-scoop into the desecrated new Dog Bins which have cost our long-suffering ratepayers more than they ever bargained on when they trustingly cast their votes for the Green charlatan.

'That illiterate philistine pedant!' Sidney yells.
'Well, darling, why not complain to the Press Council? That would teach Haynes a lesson.'
'No it wouldn't!'
'I'm sure no one will believe a word of this.'
'They'll all believe it!'

# *Seven*

Melanie Rosen's luminous orange hair moves across Salisbury Plain looking for soldiers and Cruise missiles. The five Women from Yellow Gate march into the cold night wind singing, arm in arm – four witches and one candidate witch. Only the candidate is shivering. Writing for *Pandora* was never like this. Chantal isn't even sure why the women who pitch their survival bags outside Greenham Common Air Base's Yellow Gate are now at war with the other 'Gates'. The byzantine splits which have fractured the peace movement remain obscure to Chantal – nor is she quite sure how the King's Cross Prostitutes Collective comes into it, despite much wordage from Bess and Melanie on the subject.

Bess points. Chantal picks out something black and dense. It seems to move. No, the movement resides in the clouds, scudding across the stormy sky.

'The soldiers will come out of that copse with blackened faces,' Bess advises her. 'They are only boys.'

The Women carry torches which they intend to shine on the boy soldiers. Challenged, the Women will also challenge. Bess and Melanie have made that clear.

Chantal, who never lingers long on the front page of a newspaper, knows that Cruise missiles are phased to destruction as a result of something between Gorbachev and Reagan–Bush. If the super-powers have very sensibly sorted this out, she feels that her own intervention will be superfluous and quite likely counter-productive. But the arms linked through hers belong to powerful women.

Bess is swaddled under layers of padded anorak, an Eskimo. Only the glinting granny glasses distinguish her from the others. Tonight Melanie brandishes leaping fire-sticks of orange hair above a pale, angular face wrapped in mystical delight. Chantal suspects that Cruise missiles, like Canadian seal hunters and Sidney Pyke, are a godsend to Melanie. She needs them like beleaguered Muslim elders need Satan Rushdie. In punishment for her thoughts, Chantal stumbles over a hideous, snakelike tree root, barely stifling a scream.

Melanie grips Chantal's wrist. 'All witches are targeted.'

'Yes?'

'Oh yes. You've met that woman Gilly Jones, cosily married to our Dean of Students, and Samantha Newman's leading acolyte?'

'Have I?' As usual, Chantal opts for discretion.

'Jones belongs to Cruisewatch and Mauve Gate. The women of the Cruisewatch Left Establishment deliberately consort with men and claim credit for "mixed actions" here, on the Plain. The phallocrats of Cruisewatch want to erase us and burn us by grabbing media attention for tracking the Cruise Convoy. The men do this in a deliberately para-military, male way, to prove their male power. They black their faces like the soldiers, they ape the soldiers, they have the souls of soldiers. But we affirm our faith that Women's Power will bring back a Women's Time.'

Bess comfortingly comes up alongside Chantal, like a gallant tugboat.

'The boy soldiers are dangerous because they're vulnerable. They don't possess the rough humour of sergeants or the smooth sarcasm of majors. Most of them come from working-class homes in the North where there are no jobs. Talk to them with friendliness and respect. No jargon. The first rule is to give them your first name. "Hullo, I'm Chantal. You remind me of my brother." Say simple, womanly things: "You'll soon be fathers of children, surely you want to make the world safe for them."'

Bess is a nice person and Chantal would like to tell her

so. But no sooner is Chantal beginning to feel warmed, as if by a tot of rum, than Hooper decides to tighten the screw.

'But the ugliest male aggression lurks close to the deprived, uncertain heart of the young proletarian. We confront the most painful of choices: sex war or class war.'

To Chantal the former sounds more fun than the latter. Bess walks ahead now. Melanie's wind-blistered nose remains.

'Did you ever read the records of the Scottish witch burnings?' She seems to be shouting.

'No,' Chantal whispers.

'Women were killed over and over again,' Melanie yells into the night. 'The witches were powerful women who made a pact with their own power as ♀ ♀. They affirmed their bonding with the Earth, with Nature, with the Goddess. They were healers, herbalists, midwives, farmers. They refused to be dominated or pushed around, they answered men back. Many of them were lesbians, free ♀ ♀. For all this the D/EVIL men burnt and burnt and burnt them . . . through the generations.'

(Since Chantal can only listen, not read, how does she divine this calligraphy? Sidney will later inquire.)

As they approach the dreaded copse, Chantal's strides shorten. The Women's torches rake the undergrowth. Every tree is a camouflaged boy soldier, nervous, trigger-happy: Chantal's heart is hammering somewhere between her knees and her mouth.

Bess gives the command: the Women will now capture the copse.

Suddenly a torch beams back out of the tangled blackness.

'Good god, it's Bess Hooper's gang of loonies,' says a posh woman's voice.

'Shit,' Bess mutters.

'Accommodationists,' Melanie hisses into Chantal's ear. This sounds vaguely like good news to Chantal – better than boy soldiers.

'Hi, Bess.' A woman in green wellies and a point-to-point

78

headscarf emerges from the thicket with a thermos flask of coffee. Chantal recognizes Samantha's notorious pal Gilly Jones, but doesn't say so.

'Let's talk,' proposes Gilly Jones, turning back to summon her Mauve friends. 'Pow-wow time, girls. Grub all round!'

'They burn us by turning their backs,' Melanie hisses in Chantal's ear. 'Last month Angie from Mauve Gate spat and turned her back on me. She and Gilly witch-burn me by saying I'm mad and need ECT treatment.'

The two groups of Peace Women rake each other with torches.

'Who's for coffee and a horrid iced bun?' Gilly Jones calls into the night.

'We're not your guests,' Melanie says, close to tears. 'You have no right to be here.'

'Why, it's Melanie,' says Gilly Jones. 'And you Chantal — fancy you.'

An uncomfortable moment. Samantha will no doubt be fully informed of Chantal's treachery. Fortunately, Bess is too preoccupied by the Battle of the Copse to meditate on that 'fancy you'.

'This is the so-called Peace Movement,' Bess addresses her troops. 'These are the collaborationists who staged an attack on Yellow Gate Women by sending a lynch mob into our sanctuary. They came beating drums — '

'Oh, gawd, Bess, what rubbish,' Gilly Jones says.

' — like a Loyalist march through the Republican spaces of Belfast.'

'All we did was come and sit on one of your tepee poles.'

'And you didn't get off when we asked you to leave.'

'Wanted to pow-wow.'

'We asked you to leave! You invaded our personal space!'

'Sorry,' Gilly Jones says. 'Terribly, terribly sorry, Bess. Even so, was it awfully friendly of Melanie here to take a can of black paint and write SHAME all over one of our vans?'

'Non-violent direct action!' Melanie cries.

'All right, darling.'

But with Melanie all right it is not. She now reminds Gilly Jones how she'd set up, positively orchestrated, a royal flying visit by Samantha Newman and Sidney Pyke to Mauve Gate – television cameras, the lot. Wearing his and hers green wellies. Men everywhere. The celebrity stamp of approval on the anti-Cruise campaign. And then! – then Pyke and Newman had actually dared to approach Yellow Gate in Samantha's Range-Rover and Melanie had screamed and the Women had beaten back the invaders with clods of earth.

'Listen,' Gilly Jones addresses Bess, 'we've just had a tip-off by radio that the Cruise convoy will be heading back to Greenham along the A339. Due to arrive shortly before dawn. Why don't we join forces and see what we can do? No point in hanging about here – nothing but used condoms in this copse.'

The Mauve Women are now de-camping from Condom Copse with a fairly noisy clattering of tin mugs, gas cookers and survival bags. Chantal wishes she could join Gilly Jones's lot. They do seem awfully sensible and rather jolly types. The Mauves chatter and laugh a lot while the Yellows utter medieval Scotch curses between clenched teeth.


Four hours later Chantal is lying on her stomach in a very wet, muddy ditch, sore, cold, exhausted, horribly frightened. The Mauve women are somewhere up the road, Jones's appeals for collaboration having been ignored by Bess and Melanie, who are determined that Yellow Gate shall be the first to hurl slops at the Cruise convoy. But where is it?

There have been two false alerts: a lorry-plus-trailer carrying sheep, and a vast, slow-moving carrier with flashing lights transporting a cabin cruiser.

Daubs of light creep across the sky. The roof of the world seems to be lifting, as in a theatre. Bess stands up and walks out into the middle of the road.

'Fuck,' she says.

An hour later, in full light, the five Women reach the perimeter fence of the United States Air Force base at Greenham Common. Chantal sees her first soldier, patrolling inside the fence. On spotting another bunch of loonies he hastily grinds his fag under his heel. Melanie walks up to the fence, her forks of orange hair now matted in mud, and produces a huge pair of bolt cutters from her knapsack.

'See these?' she challenges the soldier.

He doesn't deign to answer. Perhaps he's thinking.

'These are bolt cutters,' she says. 'I'm going to cut the fence. I'm going to cut a hole big enough for a cow to get through.'

The boy soldier attempts a grin. 'Which of you's the cow then?'

The Women consider this. It bears out just about everything that Bess has just about ever told her students.

'Greenham is common land,' Bess informs the soldier. 'The MoD took it over for the Second World War. After the war they refused to give it back to the people.'

'I am going to cut a hole,' Melanie repeats. 'The cows and the goats and the geese and the horses and the ducks are going to come through the hole and recover their heritage.'

Getting no reaction from the soldier, she fastens the cutter round the wire. Chantal is surprised, fascinated, by the ease and speed with which Melanie's huge clippers go through the strands of wire. Snip snip snip. Snip. The soldier seems mesmerized, as if – this is Chantal's thought – listening to his mum's knitting needles in the small front room of a terraced, back-to-back dwelling after a high tea of bacon, eggs and sliced white bread layered in Flora. Chantal wouldn't particularly want to meet this diffident youth when Manchester United are away to Chelsea – despite her own spectacular seasons as a Spurs football hooligan while at St Faith's.

Snip.

* * *

'Darling!'

Summoned to Cuba for tea, Chantal suffers a rather determined embrace. 'Being kissed on all four cheeks,' is Sidney's description of the experience. Chantal tremendously admires spontaneous affection as calculating as Samantha's. Today – and today is no exception – Samantha smells rather like Liberty's cosmetics department before Christmas. And she always wears a jewel or two – Saxon flint or Aztec silver – which really hurt during the wrestling. (Bess Hooper has warned Chantal to cut down on the 'rathers' and 'reallys'. Apparently they lose wars.)

'Darling what a perfectly lovely little outfit. I simply won't ask where you found it.' (Chantal has indeed discarded her Druid's weeds for this visit; *The Sidney Pyke Story* seems to involve constantly changing clothes.) 'I wanted you to meet me properly,' Samantha explains, leading the way into the drawing room. 'I mean it's perfectly obvious, isn't it, that your affair with Sidney is really an affair with me.'

A Joburg diamond of a smile. An 11.5 million ratings smile. Security men guard it on Tuesdays, which is when the BBC does Friday night. Chantal wonders when Samantha will find out about her own BBC audition for Samantha's job and start hitting her. Samantha is awfully tall.

'So you were out and about all night with the Yellows.'

Chantal is prepared for this. 'Put it down to experience. I now know all about witches and wire-cutters.'

'Well, it's lovely that you should get on with everybody.'

'Do I? Gosh. It's a pity that Bess and Melanie are making these horrible accusations against Sidney.'

Samantha now wears her dried-apricot smile. 'Against me – au fond. You're awfully fond of Sidney, aren't you? Melanie was also awfully fond of Sidney.'

'Well, I'm quite madly in love with him, Samantha.'

Samantha pours the tea.

'I suppose you realize that Sidney is entirely a Platonist at heart?'

'I – '

'It's the *idea* of sex with nymphets that appeals to him. He never really notices who it is.'


'Do Women Chatter?' by Bess Hooper.

Sidney has just finished reading Hooper's latest submission to the Media Studies Bulletin. His temper is not improved by the new graffito on his office door: OVERTHROW THE ONE-PYKE STATE! Jones has also reported to him a mass meeting held the previous evening in the Students' Union. After hearing a moving appeal from Melanie Rosen, the meeting had demanded an immediate Official Inquiry into 'serious personal allegations of sexual harassment against Professor Sidney Pyke'.

Anyway, 'Do Women Chatter?' – Hooper's challenge.

Starting from the 'prevalent, hegemonic assumption' that women never stop talking, gossiping, nagging, grousing, chattering, Hooper cited a recent 'scientific' study published by the University of Wyoming. This apparently demonstrated that in mixed, middle-class company, men talk seventy-eight per cent of the time and women only twenty-two per cent of the time.

Men hold forth [Hooper continued]. They explain the world. They lay down the law. Women are socially conditioned to listen, to smile, to murmur admiringly.

Outside Sidney's window the Women's Committee is forming a phalanx and distributing buckets of slop.

The Wyoming study also shows that men constantly interrupt women in mid-discourse. Sixty-four per cent of statements begun by a woman were interrupted by a man, and usually in a manner calculated to silence the woman.

Sidney glances sideways: Melanie Rosen's face is pressed to the window. He notes that she is bald-headed today and

83

rather beautiful. She appears to be practising the art of window-writing, but without the craft.

Engaging in some research of her own, Bess had applied a stopwatch to meetings of the Media Studies Faculty. The men talked most of the time and Professor Sidney Pyke all of the time. When women lecturers tried to contribute to the discussion, they were ignored, shouted down, slapped, punched and raped.

Between himself and Melanie's manic smile, the word TSIPAR has appeared on his office window.


'So what *do* you know about that Hooper woman and little Melanie?' Samantha asks, twiddling a Thai letter opener, featuring a Shiva in a cute little loincloth. 'What are they up to?'

Chantal is curled into a scarlet beanbag at Samantha's feet, gazing up at a legend. A reporter's notebook lies in her lap.

'I wish I understood,' Chantal says.

'Well, I'll tell you, dear.'

'Oh yes, do.'

'These dotty women have convinced themselves that liberation requires an insane belligerency towards men.' Chantal humbly scribbles in her notebook. 'And it's me they're getting at, not Sidney.'

'Heavens!'

'Have you written that down?'

'Yes!'

'Believe me, genuine liberation is quite simply forgetting that men exist.'

'Gosh. That can't be easy . . .'

'I forget about Sidney all the time.' Swivelling her white leather chair, Samantha flashes her jewelled fingers across the keyboard of her IBM Fastrite. 'And I suggest that you also forget about Sidney.'

'But how can I, Samantha, when he says such dreadful things to me?'

'What dreadful things?'

'He says I was born too late – that I'm floating "outside of history".'

'And that's irresistible? Don't answer, dear. I know.'


When Chantal turns up punctually for Sidney's Tuesday French lesson, he is wearing a pair of clean brown corduroys and seems cheerful.

'There's going to be an official Inquiry. Make some coffee.'

'Ask in French.'

'Why? Do you expect me to go on "France-Culture" and say, "Make some coffee"?'

She half-fills the Habitat electric kettle while Sidney squeezes both her buttocks. 'A crisis always rouses me,' he adds, his beard tickling her neck. 'It was the same in '68 – I screwed one hundred and eighteen chicks that year.'

'Samantha says I should forget about you.'

'Twenty of them in the occupied Sorbonne. Four in the office of the President of Columbia.'

'Hooper is right about you.'

Sidney nods contentedly. 'I hear that Hooper only yesterday informed her "Hegemony" class that Queen Elizabeth I was still on the throne when a certain Thomas Wilson announced that it's natural to place the masculine before the feminine, as in "men and women", "husband and wife", "sons and daughters". Hooper also revealed – I'm told – that an Act of Parliament in 1805 enshrined the word "he" in law, as meaning "he or she".'

Chantal has planted herself mid-floor, stiletto heels wide apart, hands on hips, bosom jutting, in the manner established by '60s magazines. Why does his helpless lust so arouse her?

'What Hooper doesn't know – and what you don't know, Professor Pyke – is that the French language imposes the masculine wherever the subject includes both male and female. A little boy and his sister, for example: "Ils sont beaux".'

'Have I got to know that before I'm interviewed about *The Red and the Green* on "Apostrophe"? What was that bloke's name, by the way – the god?'

'Bernard Pivot. It won't matter what they ask you. You will tell them what you want to tell them. About your spectacular conversion – on the road to Damascus – from the Old Left to the New.'

'My dear girl, my generation of kids utterly failed to question the rules governing our lives. We never challenged the curriculum or the authority of our tutors, or the gulag exam system, or the segregation of the sexes. We marched to Aldermaston – '

'In a duffle beard? With a guitar?'

' – but alpha was the only god we knew. Getting to the top and planting your heel in your rival's neck was it.'

As she pours the coffee from the Habitat percolator Sidney's paws arrive at her breasts.

'And then, you see, it all changed. In 1967. The greatest upheaval in collective consciousness since the Reformation.'

'Such conceit!'

'Quite the contrary: the more we made love, the more we made the revolution. What we finally achieved – almost – was the submergence of the individual ego in the collective consciousness.'

'Drink your coffee.'

'Don't try to imitate Samantha.' But he takes the cup. 'Hm. It's true, of course, by and large, that the struggle against sterile representative government did result, yes, in a cult of personality – as when Danny stood up on the Champs de Mars and declared, "This movement has no leaders . . ."' Sidney sips the hot liquid noisily, smacks his heavy red lips, wipes his beard. 'Well, Danny couldn't help being Danny.'

'Why?'

'Mind you, that raises the whole Sartrean notion of

responsibility. And Rudi was the same – though different. Che, too.'

'Is he the one looking like Jesus in the loo?'

'Chantal, we all loved Che.'

'He got himself bumped off, didn't he?'

'He was murdered by the forces of imperialism.'

'So then it was Ho Ho Ho Chi Minh and the Chinese Cultural Revolution.'

'Yes, we – '

'You ran around smashing windows and waving a little red book?'

'Who told you that?'

'Samantha.'

'We made mistakes. But I think we were right to be wrong about Mao.'

'Oh sure. Mobs beating up people, burning their books, confiscating their homes, making them dig shit on farms – killing them.'

'We discovered that later. It was a terrible blow.'

'Who to: you or the Chinese?'

Sidney drains his coffee and sighs. 'It's obvious that Samantha's been in one of her "Reader, I wish I hadn't married him" moods.'

'Say in French, "I was wrong."'

'She told me you were interviewing her for some Sunday paper.'

'Mm. "I was wrong. On s'est trompé." Go on! Bernard Pivot is waiting to hear it. Better still – "On s'est toujours trompé. I was always wrong."'

'Certainly not! Have you any idea how the imperialist nations behaved in India, in Kenya, in Algeria, in – '

'Hard cheese on the sambos, wogs and chinks.'

She's gone too far; tossed into the scarlet beanbag and flipped on to her stomach, stripped down to the suspenders he always insists on, she is told, at extremely close range: 'Nothing of importance has occurred in your lifetime. History stopped the week before you were born. You're a moral cripple, girl – you remind me of a share-option with an anticipated hundred per cent premium. Frankly' – her buttocks are smarting from non-verbal blows – 'you may be a junk bond.'

'Oh Sidney,' she moans.


Children's books are currently keeping Sidney marginally more sleepless than dogs. He has taken to brewing himself tea and toast at four in the morning.

When he brings the issue before a full departmental meeting, Hooper and all but one of the women are absent. Only stooges, sycophants and place-seekers owing Sidney unconditional allegiance have turned up. Bill Jones, Dean of Studies, representing the V-C, murmurs in Sidney's ear, urging him to exploit the boycott by dropping children's books from the agenda.

But Sidney has been playing with his favourite toy, a kit called Build a Sentence. He's been building sentences day and night, tea and toast. He clearly means to massacre Hooper's proposal and not one of his shirt buttons (Jones notes) is secured through the correct aperture.

'The Equal Opportunities Commission has now got itself into the Guidelines business. Let's not forget that the Commission is a government body set up under the Sex Discrimination Act of 1975. Correct?'

'Correct,' confirms Jones.

'But what is meant by "sexism"? What is a "stereotype"? Those who use words like "sexism" most freely, including the Equal Opportunities Commission, never define them. For the same good reason, McCarthy and the American Inquisition of the 1950s never defined what "Communist" meant.'

Sidney pauses and is astonished not to be heckled. To be heard in respectful silence is by now an experience as fanciful as taking a walk from Cuba to the campus without slipping in dog shit. On he goes.

'When McCarthyism was rampant in the United States, the publishers hastily vetted their schoolbooks and solicited seals of approval from associations of reactionary bigots. Today the pressure groups and vigilantes are notionally "progressive". They want to clean out racism, clean up sexism, ban pornography, boycott all white theatre groups from South Africa – call it Mental Hygiene.'

Again not a whisper of dissent. Sidney glowers suspiciously around the table until his eye comes to rest on Jones's inimitable smirk. It possesses, unlike the run of smirks, gravitas. The Dean of Studies has become a protected tenant in a Gillray cartoon by dedication to self-parody. Doodling his usual Spitfires and Hurricanes across a letterheaded pad, he can't help noticing – and he has trained himself to notice nothing – that an express train, or an avalanche, is roaring along the corridor. The door bursts open and Hooper appears followed by Melanie and the Women – Daughters of de Beauvoir, members of the teaching staff, students, coal-black cleaning ladies, Filipino kitchen staff, the King's Cross Collective. The Women carry a forest of banners and placards.

Sidney stands up and produces the stentorian bellow which had once brought the entire West Berlin police force to a halt near the Adenauer U-Bahn in the Ku'damm.

'Ha! The "Estates General" at last, led by the Communard, Hooper! Also known as the Chairperson of the Campaign to Impede Sexual Stereotyping of the Young. Nice of you to look in.'

Jones, who has never run away from anything, is measuring possible escape routes: there is none. It's like his marriage.

Hooper climbs on to a table, aided by what appear to be crampons.

'Professor Pyke is currently pulling every cheap trick in the book of liberal chauvinism. The self-idolizing phallocracy assumes many disguises.'

'Mob rule not being one of them,' Sidney shouts.

Melanie emits a howl. Her fevered little face is now only inches from Sidney's fevered big one. Remembering the taxi disaster, he clutches his beard.

'Is that what you and your macho chums said in '68 – "no mob rule"? Is this the super-rebel who planted his feet on the President of Columbia's desk for the benefit of the world's photographers?'

'My dear girl – '

Uproar at this. Jones shudders. He had confined his own '60s-thing to attending occasional hip happenings, and reading about beautiful people called Quant, Sassoon and Lennon in colour mags. He had once been to the Arts Lab in Covent Garden and seen Ken Tynan in the flesh, though there wasn't much of it. Jones had never been sure whether Donovan was a man and Biba a shop, or the other way round. Jones had gone through the '60s without really taking them in.

'I'm not a girl!' Melanie shrieks. 'And I'm not "dear". Perhaps you'd like to pinch my arse, while you're about it.'

'Rapist!' screams a Daughter of de Beauvoir.

'Tell me this – ' Sidney yells.

The Women are now slow-handclapping him while drumming their boots on the floor. Some forty people are packed into a room large enough for twenty and when Sidney also climbs on to the same table as Hooper – without crampons – the prospect of imminent physical violence is such that even Jones's perfected myopia is severely taxed.

But Sidney's lungs are the most powerful in the room.

'Tell me this: Does the new generation of vigilantes wish to purge from children's literature all little girls who enjoy frilly dresses and dolls – in short, the vast majority?'

'That's fucking mythology!' screams Bess Hooper.

'The Women's Movement today – '

'Rapist pig!'

'The Movement today,' Sidney's hoarse tenor transcends the barracking, 'makes a great fetish of motherhood – that uniquely female experience.'

(The noise abruptly subsides; Jones notes that 'mother-hood' may be a sacred word.)

'But motherhood,' Sidney drives home his temporary advantage, 'is the culmination of a biological process which involves gaining the attention, and the desire, of the opposite sex. My apologies to the donor-inseminated. A book depicting a woman breast-feeding a child is not condemned as "stereotyped". Why then is a small girl cradling a doll unacceptable? There is, surely, a direct linear connection.'

The room is now spectacularly quiet. Aloft the same sagging table as Sidney, Bess refuses to yield to his advantage in height by looking at him.

'That should be bloody obvious,' she says, 'even to a macho professor. A girl with a doll is receiving a coded programme: you will be wife and mother, nothing else. *Your* programme.'

'Oh come, Bess – '

'Her name isn't Bess!' cries Melanie. 'And she won't "come" either!'

Something has to give and it does – with Sidney reminding the meeting that the women's pages of the quality newspapers are full of anguished letters from educated, liberated mums who simply cannot stop tiny Muriel from hugging dolls and bellicose little Michael from miming Action Man and machine-gunning Muriel, even though the mums have 'tried everything' – including the children's books recommended in the Hooper Guidelines. Under this provocation – Sidney punching the air like Lenin – the fragile platform bearing both Sidney and Bess can take no more. Splitting and sundering at the middle, the cheap utility table, a typical product of cost-cutting Thatcherism, collapses in a V, like a broken-backed ship, the result being that Sidney's thirteen stone land on top of Hooper's nine.

Where (Jones notes) the thirteen stone are happy to stay. Carrying his customarily anodyne, doctored report to the V-C's residence, Jones reflects that, try as she might, Dr Hooper cannot help being an attractive woman. Even Sidney, who has practically no interest in sex, must feel the pull. Odd, really.

\* \* \*

'Samantha, when do you expect to finish *Nature or Nurture*?'

'Darling, these dreadful charges against poor Sidney simply aren't making things easier. I mean where is one?'

'Which of your books do you like best?'

'Oh dear, such a difficult question. I was asked that only recently at the Cheltenham Literary Festival. Or was it in Tokyo – '

'When you did your TV programme on "The Japanese Way of Love"?'

'Oh those futons. So simple and so right. Anyway, I think I said that *Mothers and Daughters* was my favourite book. But afterwards I really began to wonder whether *Woman Awakened* isn't altogether more . . . more beautiful.'

Chantal's pencil flashes in shorthand.

'So you prefer the novel. It's simply amazing to me that you can write fiction and non-fiction with equal brilliance.'

'It's sweet of you to say so. Actually – what I particularly like about *Woman Awakened* is its merciless honesty. The fact is, darling, that women are not allowed to write about . . . you know what.'

'And you did! You showed us how educated women have felt constrained to deny their animal natures!'

Chantal has lifted this from the jacket blurb but Samantha smiles serenely.

'One day I'll tell you about Luigi.'

Practically every book that Samantha has written for the past twenty years has been about Luigi. Luigi, the wild, untamed, driver of an Italian tomato container truck.

Chantal experiences the most delicious of all dilemmas: even at her most calculating, manipulative, mendacious, she suffers a perverse longing to tell the truth. The truth is like an unstoppable belch pressing from within her clenched teeth and urging Chantal to inform Samantha that she could easily – easily! – fight her way out of the mounting *Nature or Nurture* crisis: 'Samantha, forget about Sidney and tell us about muscular, illiterate, lasagna-loving, sun-scorched Luigi all over again.'

But Chantal hasn't said it. This tall, charmante, orna-
mented and quite gutsy lady has had her day; she must fall
in order that Chantal Poynter shall ascend and be anointed
by 11.5 million. Chantal refocuses the interview on the
heroine of *Woman Awakened*, Tina, who was forever taking
off her silk knickers in railway trains between Trieste and
Athens, via Zagreb and Belgrade. After laying every
bronzed animal-boy foolish enough to travel by train, she
fell in love – catastrophically – with a fugitive Armenian
priest who turned out to be pursuing a recovered Dionysus
washed white by the waters of the Aegean . . .

'I did feel sorry for Tina,' Chantal tells the author.

'And that, of course,' (Samantha has lit a roll of cannabis)
'is what all those dried-up, embittered Hoopers and Melan-
ies can't stomach!'

Chantal nods sadly. 'Melanie says you're a pornographer,' she whispers.

'Ugh. The new Puritanism. Roundheads arise . . .'

'Hooper is saying Sidney raped her. In the Benzin Swimming Pool.'

'But Sidney can't swim! We went to St Tropez, and
Corfu, and Sardinia, and he couldn't swim. Oh my God.
The bugger! What am I going to tell Hans-Dietrich Swindler
next week?'

Chantal wonders whether Samantha is absolutely truly
serious – is it possible that she's unaware of Sidney's almost
daily dog-paddle forays into the pool, in pursuit of girls?
Heavens, doesn't she smell the chlorine!

# *Eight*

Sidney's journey from the Red to the Green has been a long spiritual struggle! Twenty years ago Sidney had never heard of the environment! He was at war with the CIA not with ICI! Indeed I myself can take credit for first drawing his attention to the problem of pollution: I begged him to dab a little manly deodorant under his arm-pits! Next I tried to persuade him that his beard is not a tropical rain forest – but that battle is still being fought!

Ian Davidson groans and pushes the mauve pages away. Should he fax a warning to Lait? Other junior editors had made the fatal error of belittling prime acquisitions. Two of the victims had served as Ian's drinking companions at the Zanzibar Club, a third had been a regular squash partner at the Oxford and Cambridge in Pall Mall. A pity about the squash, but Davidson had felt no emotion about their nemesis beyond that experienced by any city motorist who witnesses the cars of others being towed away.

He forces himself back to work – back to this idolized pinko prick who'd indulged in self-serving histrionics god-knows-everywhere, gassed on Berkeley's Sproul Plaza 'by Ronald Reagan', beaten senseless in the Boul' Mich' 'by Charles de Gaulle', water-cannoned in West Berlin 'by Hitler's ghost' . . .

Sidney was a challenge to any woman! He simply couldn't remember how many chicks he'd laid from

Tokyo to Prague. Of course the big bulls of the Counter-Culture were unspeakable chauvinists which made them frightfully exciting. We still have an old-fashioned egg-timer at home which Sidney bought for his first wife in San Francisco during the flower-power era. Her name was Sharon and when she was on acid, which was most of the time, she fucked like an angel. Actually Sidney himself was fairly heavily into grass and crack and stuff at that time and then poor Sharon died but amazingly the egg-timer has survived Johnson, Nixon, Ford, Carter, Reagan and – so far! – Bush. Should I be jealous of an egg-timer?

Alone in his office, Davidson furtively unlocks the one desk drawer that regulations permit him to lock, and grins as he reads again the anonymous leaflet which has been circulating through Swindler House.

### SWINDLER ACQUIRES CATHOLIC CHURCH

Hans-Dietrich Swindler has obtained a majority share-holding in the Catholic Church, according to a joint statement issued in Munich and Rome last night by Swindler GmbH and the Vatican. Two thousand years in the publishing business, and with a subscription list estimated at five hundred million, the Vatican has decided to modernize its marketing. Swindler executives in Munich and New York stress that the Church will maintain its autonomy on all doctrinal matters, with the Pope reporting only to Hans-Dietrich Swindler.

An internal inquiry is now under way. As Jack Lait commented on the phone from New York, 'To get fired by Hans-Dietrich – or by me – no one has to try that hard. It's simpler, if you want out, to say "Swindler" instead of "Sveendler" – like Prince Charles.'

Davidson crunches the leaflet and flushes it down the executive toilet. Back to the Newman salt mines!

Clitoral orgasm, vaginal orgasm, it's all rubbish. A woman feels as good as the man she's with. If it was Socrates you wouldn't even notice what he'd got — if he could take his mind off the boys. Forget 'erogenous zones' and all that pseudo-scientific drivel put out by avaricious Scandinavian 'sexperts'. Show me a man truly capable of love, like Sidney, and I am a continuous erogenous zone from head to toe. What a pity he has to chase girls up and down the Benzin Swimming Pool! What a pity that the Media Studies Department is now a vipers' nest of broken hearts intent on vengeance!

What Davidson can't fathom is this sudden inrush, from the wings, of witches on broomsticks, whom Samantha denounces as 'Sidney's persecutors, my burden, and the enemies of uterine pregnancy'. Who are they? 'The illegitimate daughters of SCUM', she calls them. Who, what, was SCUM? Davidson telephoned the various information services but drew a blank. In despair, he faxed Lait.

Back it came, from the twenty-ninth floor of the Swindler Building on the Avenue of the Americas. 'SCUM: Society for Cutting Up Men. 1968. Samantha is going to pieces. Stick her together again. If too young for this assignment work on your golf handicap.'

Davidson digs into the pocket of his Next double-breasted jacket for a cigarette. His parents don't know he smokes. His father heads a firm of solicitors in Edinburgh and belongs to an uncorrupted splinter of the Scottish Presbyterian Church — 5,600 true believers — which recently expelled Her Majesty's Lord Chancellor for attending the Catholic funeral of a friend. Davidson regards all religions as plain nonsense but he isn't in the habit of parading his convictions and, consequently, has none.

'Stick her together again!'

On impulse he had decided to dial Newman's unlisted number. Must talk to the woman, must. When the call was finally answered, a breathless female voice panted, 'Hold on!' and Davidson heard what sounded like a hoarse male voice roaring 'Don't stop, you bitch!' followed by a crash and the sound of a mirror or heavy, framed picture shattering.

The crocodiles are gathering under Davidson's plank. Colleagues he encounters in the executive cloakroom openly smirk: 'How are the mauve pages, Ian?' You can smell the colour of the water. Swindler, due in town next week, is scheduled to give the Newman woman lunch with Davidson in attendance. No doubt he will 'become' her something special from Munich – the one, famous, lapse in his impeccable English. 'Bekommen': to get. Swindler had once confronted the Managing Director of Vampire: 'Where can I become a decent sausage in London?'

Samantha is on tour – and delighted to take Chantal with her. The girl's brimming admiration is, after all, rather charming, and so unlike little Melanie's imitation of a dead butterfly. And Chantal is always so interested in Samantha's dearest personal charity, the Samantha Newman Day Care Centre. Samantha adores little children, and Chantal adores them too.

While Samantha and her television crew are accommodated in four-star hotels, Chantal feels it appropriate to occupy cold and dingy little rooms with defeated beds, strip lighting over the cracked mirror, and some appalling print of a Highland stag hanging above a dead fireplace boarded up in grained brown vinyl.

The TV crews are forever knocking on her door, lonely and loaded with money. Samantha's producer steers clear of Chantal, alarmed by her surprise arrival, and terrified in case Samantha discovers that Chantal had been auditioned for her job.

'I'm not a fool,' Chantal tells him.

'Girls do chatter,' he mutters.

'I'm not a girl. Buy me a drink and relax.'

Cables, lights and cameras clutter the small halls of targeted towns and villages from London to Edinburgh. Ten minutes into the question-and-answer part of her programme, Samantha is asked why God had allowed the Ethiopian famine. Was it perhaps a punishment? Cradling famished infants in her arms, had she gained any clue as to God's intentions?

'Well, not really.' Samantha assumes her most serious expression. 'The human race must learn to deal with drought, pestilence and plague. I personally wouldn't like to get too far into God's mind – I have an awful feeling there are skeletons in that cupboard.'

The audience laughs rather uneasily. God is still on the agenda: does Samantha find Him a comfort in her daily life?

'Him? Frankly, I've never met *Him*. Whenever I think I'm doing rather well *She* taps me on the shoulder and points out the dirty dishes in the sink.'

How the women love that. Chantal studies the wholemeal faces on either side of her, adoring Samantha's outrageousness. Is she – next question – a feminist?

She feigns surprise. 'Aren't we all? But I do ask myself why we women remain so meek and tongue-tied. Why don't we stop grousing and whining? Bellow like the boys! Scream! And stop playing those nasty little domestic games of attrition and revenge which little girls are schooled to perform against their brute-force brothers. Say what you mean like a man does and stop sulking and nagging and carping and turning your back in bed.'

A collective gasp from the women in the audience. The local vicar is seen to laugh, so everyone does. Samantha is asked whether it's true that she once disrupted the Miss World contest in the Albert Hall, and why, and would she do the same again today?

Chantal studies Samantha's charismatic smile, its glitter softened by those little crows' feet round the eyes which the make-up girl can't quite suppress under the exacting lights.

'Yes, I did. We were all into burning our bras at the time and it seemed wholly important to stop our most glamorous sisters from showing their tits and bums to the men. Heaven knows why. No, I wouldn't do it today – but I do find beauty contests incredibly boring, don't you? And somehow depressing. And let's face it, demeaning for us as women.'

Chantal raises her hand. Although other hands are also up (Samantha insists on 'absolute spontaneity'), to Chantal's mild surprise Samantha's finger-rings flash in her direction and the cameramen who'd been making propositions in the pub an hour earlier swivel towards her.

'Is it true that you were once a member of WITCH – the Women's International Terrorist Conspiracy from Hell?'

'Guilty again. And also of SCUM, the Society for Cutting Up Men.' Pausing for laughter, she gets it. 'We used to invade the Stock Exchange and burn money; or Grand Central Station and turn all the clocks back; and we made a huge thing, I recall, out of Hallowe'en. It all sounds a bit dotty now, but a lot less dotty than circumcising females, or putting girls in purdah, or refusing women the right of abortion.'

His mounting unpopularity among the students bewilders Sidney. Standing (or running) for the joint Staff–Student Council, a body to which he has been elected, virtually unopposed, almost by acclamation, for many years, he finds himself challenged, at the eleventh hour (but the rules have been observed, he checks on that) –

– by Bess Hooper!

'Ha! You appointed the bitch! Such is gratitude!' was Samantha's response when he first reported this news. Sidney refuses to canvass support. 'Quite right, darling, your record stands for itself.'

On this, Hooper's cohorts agree: Pyke's record stands for

itself. Chauvinism, authoritarianism, harassment – rape. Sidney's diurnal existence is now plagued by graffiti, scurrilous leaflets, obscenities discharged by passing students. The campaign is brilliantly orchestrated by Melanie; for the first time Sidney learns that he raped – actually raped, no euphemisms here – Melanie in his office after an angry exchange about the feminism of Olive Schreiner.

Melanie's pamphlets – and she will withstand the bitterest winter wind, at the draughtiest corner of campus, her nose raw with radical virtue – present a glowing profile of Bess Hooper (whose expressionless, passport-type photograph is precisely – Sidney tells Jones during their twice-weekly, weather permitting, game of tennis – what appeals to the British Puritan soul).

'A daunting CV,' Jones admits, extracting a leaflet from his tennis shorts. 'NUJ NEC and Equality Commission; LCS Political Committee; NCCL Exec and Women's Rights Committee; EC of Co-ord and UKIAS; Women Against Rape; Curb Kerb-Crawlers; Working Women's Charter Campaign; Women Against Pornography; Camden Anti-Racist Committee; CND; Journalists Against Nuclear Extinction (JANE); Labour Abortion Rights Campaign; Abortion Law Reform Association (Every child a wanted child. Every mother a willing mother).'

Sidney serves one of his Beckers.

'Fault!' Jones shouts casually, and crouches to receive the second service. Sidney walks forward, slowly, to the net.

'That was in.'

'Sorry, old man. Out. It was out.'

'It was bloody well in. I saw the chalk.'

Jones stops smiling. 'As you wish, McEnroe.'

Nor can Sidney match Hooper in terms of recent victimization – whatever his future prospects in that regard. Melanie Rosen is now up on a table in the cafeteria, reminding a packed audience and piles of dirty brown lunch trays that Bess was fired in her first year as a working journalist by the *West Surrey Gazette and Reporter* for persistently wearing, though warned, a Lesbians Ignite lapel badge.

Melanie tosses Lesbians Ignite lapel badges to her audience.

'An industrial tribunal threw out Bess's appeal against her dismissal. The Chair was a man, of course. He asked Bess – this is true, it's in the transcript – if she was "hell bent on inducting normal young women in the typing pool into a cult of perversion".'

The following day Bess Hooper herself occupies a platform outside the Media Studies Department. Cables run from microphones to loudspeakers illicitly suspended here and there. Hooper reminds the electorate about Sidney Pyke's long-standing, increasingly acrimonious, and 'brazen' opposition to sacred policies of the National Union of Students.

In particular: *no platform for racists, sexists and anti-gays.*

That, the previous year's Big Issue, had sent Sidney into a three-two, first-set lead over Jones on a blustery day when the moulting white lines of a damp court were layered in autumn leaves.

'They've even proscribed the Jewish Union!'

'So I hear, Sidney. Bad show. Good shot.'

'Because it refuses to condemn the existence of the State of Israel.'

'Ridiculous. Out! – bad luck, nice idea.'

'The vote was taken at a barely quorate meeting of Union activists, sixty per cent of whom spoke Arabic as the mother tongue.'

'Yes, but don't put it that way beyond these four tramlines. You're serving, old boy.'

'Am I any friend of Zionism?'

'Let! Two more! Definitely not. In fact I'd say you're a one-man Intifada.'

'I intend to propose to the Academic Senate that all funding be withdrawn from the Student Union until it comes to its democratic senses.'

Which was what he did and how he became a fascist. His

'case' was duly considered, on an 'emergency' motion, by yet another barely quorate meeting of Student Union activists at which it was resolved that anyone advocating the right of racists or sexists to address the Union was him/ herself a racist or sexist or both. The only division of opinion was whether Pyke should be banned from the Student Union building (where he was often found wandering around, smiling and chatting to young people) or merely 'censured'.

Clemency prevailed – on legal advice. But now Sidney is about to be badly humiliated by Hooper in the Staff–Student Council elections. The results give Bess a three-to-one majority.


Sidney is unpadlocking his frequently vandalized machine when a brusque tug on his sleeve and a honking smoker's cackle announces his fellow cyclist, Professor Dame Margery Doughty, a chemist with a Nobel Prize under her belt (shared with an American, unfortunately). Marge wears her invariable green tweed suit, modelled on the wartime WVS uniform, and a soup-plate hat to match.

'Hell hath no fury, Sidney.'

'Hullo, Marge.'

'What a randy boy you are. I hear you jilted little Melanie. Of course I've been jilted more often than I can count. The first was a boy working on DNA, the last thought he was about to discover a mathematical definition of infinity. Can't say I've ever chased a literary bloke.'

The predatory gleam in her bloodshot eye suggests to Sidney that this may be about to happen.

'The V-C called me in yesterday,' she goes on. 'Wants me to sit on this bloody Tribunal to investigate your appalling sex life.'

Sidney cools. 'Naturally you accepted?'

Doughty lights an unfiltered Senior Service with what looks like a Bunsen burner. Her baritone drops to foghorn level.

'Don't be a silly boy, Sidney. You know you're nothing but a fat old liberal who wants to be a juvenile radical for life. Well, here's another fat old liberal – minus the pretensions.' Doughty glances about her conspiratorially – though Sidney knows she would happily denounce Hitler at a Nazi rally. 'Entre nous,' she whispers loud enough to scatter a pride of lions, 'the admin are planning to graft a pair of local bigots on to *your* Tribunal.'

'What! Who?'

'Our retired admiral and the bag who runs the Mothers' Union.'

'That bitch! But she's my most fanatical political opponent on the Council! It's high time I rang my lawyers.'

'Lawyers? Oh, they love a case like this. You could always mortgage Cuba, of course.'

Sidney winces on the shaft: he hates spending money.

'I dare say Samantha could cough up,' Doughty muses. 'Poor girl! She and I had a little natter the other day. I told her that if you tried anything on with me, I'd be delighted.' Doughty guffaws and breaks into a hacking smoker's cough. 'I said to her, "I can imagine a randy man like Sidney having hot pants for little Melanie – but not for that Hooper woman!" Samantha gave me that dried-apricot smile of hers.'

'Of course, she doesn't believe a word of it.'

'Hm. She prefers to believe that Hooper and Rosen are really gunning for *her*. I must say, observing the two of them together, one is rather reminded of Hockney.'

'Hockney! Hardly, Marge.'

'Only a small leap of the imagination is required – we chemists do rather leap about. "We Two Girls Clinging Together", "Two Women in a Shower", and "Two Girls in a Pool".'

Sidney shudders at the word 'pool'.

Dame Marge now mounts a famous ancient bike which is never vandalized. He wants to tell her that he's never been a 'liberal' and never will be, but in Doughty's presence only the naked truth survives.

103

'Anyway, Sidney, next time you feel like harassing some-one, you'll find me in the lab boring myself to death with the problem of endogenous parasites. We Prix Nobels never bring rape charges — unless it's all bark and no bite. Whoof whoof!'

Roaring and whoofing and coughing, Doughty rides away, her front lamp protruding from the pocket of her tweed jacket where she also keeps her cigarettes and the flamethrower she uses to light them.

Finally reaching Edinburgh, Chantal is exhausted — but not Samantha. One of the scheduled stars of the international 'Women Now' conference at the McEwan Hall, she insists on dragging Chantal up to the castle esplanade, where the wind off the Firth of Forth plays havoc with their hair.

'How beautiful!' both women shout into the gale.

Samantha then poses for Chantal's camera beside a kilted bagpiper. 'What's your tartan, dear?' she asks him. The reply is polite but unintelligible. It's not the castle rock which has set Samantha on high, but the news that the Vice-President of Swindler US is on his way to the conference.

Back in the Caledonian Hotel, Chantal (who has found a room in a rather drab boarding house in Morningside) hears Samantha ask the desk clerk for the umpteenth time whether Mr Jack Lait has checked in. He has!

Fifteen minutes later he joins them in the Robert Burns Bar, bringing with him a battered-boxer's face, coarse skin, and awful (Chantal thinks) long silvery hair to the shoulders. All of this belongs not to Jack Lait but to the legendary American feminist writer, Pauline Ochs.

'Swindler US is proud to be publishing Pauline's new book,' Lait announces. Ochs smiles relentlessly.

'Another book — how prolific you are!' Samantha con-gratulates Ochs. 'When is it coming out?'

'This fall,' Lait says. 'A lead title.' Ochs is still smiling.

'Oh.'

'You're all my guests to lunch.' Lait extends his hand to Chantal. 'I don't believe we've met. Jack Lait.'

'Oh forgive me,' Samantha flutters, introducing her protégée, if that's what Chantal is.

'Glad to meet you, Chantal.' His cattle-market eye lingers on her. 'You're also a writer?' His Florentine suit is quite something and he smells a lot nicer than Sidney.

'Oh we're all writers,' Samantha says, close to tears, 'two-a-penny.'

Pauline Ochs takes Chantal's hand. 'Pauline Ochs.' She smiles. 'Such a beautiful city.'

On the first day of the conference Samantha and Ochs are seated side by side on the platform, discussing 'The Present Crisis of Sexual Identity'. Still smiling relentlessly, Ochs explains her own – she started adult life as the wife of a Greek physicist who showed no interest in her opinions. One day she brought home a translation of de Beauvoir's *The Second Sex* from the American Library in Athens. 'And that,' (smiling), 'was that.'

'I'm quite sure I've never had a crisis of identity.' Samantha grips her table microphone. 'Too many of us have been running away from what we are and who we are. I will not say that I am not any of the things that I know I am.'

Samantha seems to be rebuking Ochs for having notoriously done all of these things, but Ochs keeps smiling and nodding while the French women lift their pencilled eyebrows a fraction. An Irish novelist intervenes to recount her tortured convent upbringing, interminably. A person called Sister Mary O'Grady is heavily indicted for everything.

During the lunch interval Ochs and Samantha sign copies of their previous books. The competitive atmosphere is electric. Jack Lait, wearing a spectacular tartan-green golfing jacket with plus-fours from Turnbull & Turnbull, winks at Chantal.

'Bad luck for you it isn't a beauty competition,' he murmurs, a discreet whiff of Highland Stag floating off his emery-paper chin.

Lait takes Ochs off for lunch. Samantha winces, pirouettes, snarls 'She's so ugly!' in Chantal's ear, then circulates among her fans, regal and radiant.

'I really don't understand how Jack can publish Pauline's book in the same month as *Nature or Nurture*,' she tells Chantal in the ladies'. 'I mean you can't have two "lead titles", can you?'

'Certainly not!'

When the afternoon session begins, Ochs's chair is empty. Lait's chair is empty. The atmosphere in the McEwan Hall is now heavy, lugubrious, sleepy; the simultaneous translation headsets begin to hurt. The Russian women writers, as wide as they are tall, and looking like cosmonauts in their earphones, remain inscrutable, a carbohydrated buffer zone between the mysteries of the world and of the word. Samantha, whose flickering eye continually returns to Lait's empty chair, distracts herself – or reclaims attention – Chantal is by now quite bored – by congratulating the Russians on perestroika, glasnost and 'your wonderful President'.

'I feel ashamed,' she announces. 'Yes, ashamed! Not of the freedoms we enjoy, but of how frivolously we have taken them for granted and converted them to trivial pursuits.' (This provokes huge applause from everyone except the Russians, who don't understand – and the French, who never applaud.)

At the tea break Jack Lait reappears in the company of the prettiest of the Soviet writers. 'Svetlana writes wonderful, just wonderful, children's stories,' he announces. 'We believe her stories are universal – they'll travel. Svetlana, welcome to Swindler.'

Arriving back at the Caledonian Hotel in search of 'the scene', Chantal finds a note inviting her to dine with Jack Lait at a new French restaurant in a quiet part of town. This needs thought, but not much, and whatever it needs carries her to Lait's third-floor suite which, he has told her, boasts 'a nice view of that lump of rock'. Reaching his door she pauses; voices within are raised.

'Jack, I won't be made a fool of.'

'Samantha, your book and Pauline's book have nothing, repeat nothing, in common.'

'You mean hers is brilliant, as usual, and mine isn't even finished.'

'Pauline is an intellectual. You're mass-market.'

'What a horrible thing to say!'

'You didn't complain about the up-front money.'

'I just knew we'd get to that. Oh you smug bastard!'

Discernible dialogue then blurs, merging into a furry moan with four legs. Chantal could sketch the embrace and the exact angle of Lait's plus-fours.

'Oh Jack, take me to bed. It's been such a long time.'

He sounds as sincere as a cobra signing a peace treaty with a mongoose. Chantal steals away down the thickly carpeted corridor. Poor Samantha. Rich, attractive, powerful men are detestable. Overcome by loyalty, Chantal decides to spend the evening penitentially writing up her notes in her dingy boarding house. Sleeping with Sidney is one thing; dining alone with Lait quite another.

Out in Princes Street, she looks for a bus and takes a taxi. The driver doesn't know the new French restaurant but threads stoically among tall granite tenements until eventually he nails it near the Leith docks. He refuses to charge her the fare on the meter.

'I'm dense,' he says. She gives him a huge tip – the Scotch are quite hugely lovely.

A waiter shows her to a corner table and lights the candle. A picture on the wall depicts Mary of Scotland's betrothal to the Dauphin of France, the one who didn't last long, like all the men in Mary's life. Chantal sips Perrier water, studies the day's notes, and tries not to nibble bread. After an hour she is summoned to the telephone.

'Chantal? This is Jack. Oh my God, what can I say? I was just setting out when one of my authors decided to have a nervous breakdown. Not anyone you know but quite a precious property. A real crack-up. Look, how about lunch in London next month? It's five-to-three I'll be passing

107

through London on my way to Paris and Milan. Where can I reach you?'

'You can leave a message with Samantha.'

'Well, frankly – '

Chantal puts the receiver down. Humiliated in front of the restaurant staff, she commands them to phone for a taxi.

The following morning Chantal meets Samantha by pre-arrangement at the airport. Scheduled to lunch with Hans-Dietrich Swindler in London, she has bought Chantal a first-class seat out of her own pocket.

'Would you describe Sidney as a generous man, Samantha?'

'Must we talk about Sidney?' Samantha looks quite sick as the plane banks over the Forth Bridge.

'Oh . . . no.'

'What I will say for Sidney is that he's as mean to his various women as to his wife. Sidney has never bought any woman a dress, a dressing gown, a pair of slippers even. No flowers, no chocolates – sweet nothing.'

'Yet you still love him.'

'Officially.'

'Mr Lait seems very nice,' Chantal says. 'It must be comforting to have *Nature or Nurture* under his wing.'

Samantha orders her third vodka. When it comes she kicks off her shoes: 'He's entertaining in his own dreary fashion. But not an original mind. Adept at regurgitating other people's ideas and making them sound like his own. I wouldn't dream of mentioning this to a living soul, but even in the '60s the *New Left Review* turned down everything he wrote.'

'You don't mean Jack Lait wrote for the *New Left Review*?'

Slowly Samantha's red eyes reach for focus, the pupils floating around the irises like drugged goldfish.

'Sidney. You should learn to listen. Where was I?'

Chantal tells her where she was. Samantha squeezes her hand in contrition.

'Hm. Finally the editor sent Sidney a simply awful letter

by bicycle. "You can't make up your mind whether you're Henry Miller, Frantz Fanon, Norman Mailer, Kropotkin, Malcolm X or Régis Debray. On the evidence available to me, you are none of them." Awful! I may have got some of the names wrong.'

Chantal's notepad lies across her thigh. Sidney will be happy to spell the names for her next Tuesday. Poor Samantha! – fancy arriving dead drunk for lunch with Hans-Dietrich Swindler!

# *Nine*

'Grants Yes, Loans No! Government Out Out Out!'

The Minister's black limousine sweeps up to the Vice-Chancellor's neo-Georgian residence on time, to the minute, its gleaming surfaces splattered with rotten eggs, flour, spray paint, and one or two bullet holes. Emerging from their cars, the Minister's officials flinch, duck — then sprint towards the Senior Common Room. Once inside, they will continually dust down their suits, as if insult could be dry-cleaned.

'Grants Yes, Loans No! Government Out Out Out!'

Crossing from the Media Studies Department to the Senior Common Room, Sidney notes that the police are back on the campus. Arms linked, they are attempting to corral and contain a seething, yelling mob of banner-waving students, some of whom are wearing stocking-masks. Sidney experiences a twinge of nostalgia. In the old days, of course, there hadn't been so many WPCs. These cheery little creatures, with their chess-board hats, rather spoil the fun. Recognizing the one who'd wiped Taxi Joe's spittle from Bess's cheek, he remembers the missed train and the terminal contempt in the voice of the Editor of 'State of the Nation' when Sidney had called him from a police station.

For the first time in weeks he himself is not the prime target for student hostility. Working his way through the mob virtually unnoticed and unabused, the politician in him is not entirely pleased. Reaching the Senior Common

Room, he finds the Chairman of the Governors, the V-C, and the Registrar are all fussing solicitously around the Minister of State for Higher Education. The Minister has received only one direct hit, but his temper is up. He likes a fight. He snarls wolfishly.

'Ha! If Loans No, then Grants No. Clean out this scum.'

He looks to his officials as if expecting them to shovel the ranting students into wheelbarrows. The officials, who know the score, make a close study of the ceiling and floor; under this Government their own pay, as senior civil servants, has kept ahead of inflation while that of professors and lecturers has fallen, in real terms, by forty per cent. The genteel fury of the dons gathered round them is faintly oppressive, yet understandable; they'd feel the same if the boot were on the other foot. Fortunately, it isn't. Ever since the dons of Oxford refused to give Her an honorary degree – a unique insult – Her boot has been up the academic arse.

Coffee is served.

The Minister embarks on a justification of Government policy and a rout of its critics. Although trained (like other members of HMG) by public-relations consultants to coat the irrational in layers of sweet reason, his nature cannot be curbed and his tone, like his familiar expression, is frankly abrasive, contemptuous. What's more, he was once a don himself, of sorts.

'The arguments put forward by your profession are shamelessly dishonest. For example, on comparative government spending in different countries. American statistics include courses for beauticians. The Japs bung in correspondence courses. I could go on.'

He probably will. The Minister has placed himself close to a table groaning with canapes, sandwiches and supermarket claret. Crunching a huge spring onion, he reminds his audience about the unstoppable laws of economics: unit costs, delegated managerial accountability, productivity. He sounds bored: the universal stupidity of the intelligent classes is hugely boring.

'Where's Pyke?' he snaps.

The Vice-Chancellor shudders and prays that Pyke can't be found. It's not likely. The Chairman of the Media Studies Department is discovered lurking around the food table in a faded combat jacket, no tie, and blue jeans threadbare at the knees. The Minister looks him up and down like a disgusted adjutant.

'"Media Studies" – what the hell are they? I hear that you've assembled a team of research students who are currently blotting out their brains by recording hour after hour of television on expensive video-recording equipment.'

'The nation watches television,' Sidney says. 'Popular consciousness is moulded, informed and disinformed by television.'

'We certainly don't need you to tell us there's too much sex and violence on the screen.'

Sidney strokes his beard and asks the Minister how many blind, deaf, dyslexic and epileptic people appear on the four main channels during an average evening.

The Minister winches up his eyebrows. 'You want dyslexic newsreaders?'

The civil servants titter.

'How often does a character in a soap opera refuse a drink?' Sidney asks the Minister.

'And you call *that* academic research?'

'How often do characters in drama and films discuss contraception before climbing into bed?'

'Ha! It might take the lustre off the lust, eh?' The Minister reaches towards the laden table and extracts several sandwiches. Then he looks towards the Vice-Chancellor.

'I gather that the Head of your Media Studies Department is accused of raping his entire staff.'

The civil servants accord the ceiling further study.

'Minister, we are holding an internal inquiry,' the V-C murmurs.

'Well, Pyke,' the Minister says, 'you're probably regretting you packed your department with the monstrous regiment of "Peace Women", eh? The hens have come home to roost, eh?'

The Minister grabs another spring onion. No one else has dared reach for a morsel of food. Dean Jones places a glass of wine in the Minister's hand. Sidney is reminded of a medieval court; the noblesse de robe and the noblesse d'épée will watch the monarch eat. Only the poison taster is missing.

'I gather you're also in politics, Professor Pyke,' the Minister says. 'Time on your hands? Friends of the Earth, Greenpeace, CND, Voluntary Euthanasia Society, Repeal Obscene Publications Act, Campaign for Racial Equality, Anti-Apartheid, Decriminalize Incest, Dogwatch. Anything I've forgotten?'

'Yours is the worst government in living memory,' Sidney says.

'Well it's the one you've got.'

'Lords of misrule. Bullying philistines.'

The tense circle of officials discover specks of dust on their collars. The faces of the V-C, the Chairman of the Governors and the Registrar are studies in misery. But the Minister is clearly enjoying himself.

'So what are your Greens advocating this week, Professor Pyke? Instant disarmament, unfettered immigration, a ban on all industrial investment, euthanasia on demand, probation for terrorists?'

'Merely the survival of the human race,' Sidney says. 'Your Government not included.'

The Vice-Chancellor takes a tentative half-step forward, like a boxing referee expecting to be struck by both contestants.

'Minister, we hoped Professor Pyke would tell you about the work of our Media Studies Department.'

'Work?' says the Minister, snatching another spring onion. 'Work? Is that what your department does, Pyke?'

'I have just launched,' says Sidney, 'a course on Government Disinformation. Your own speeches figure prominently in the curriculum.'

The Minister wears his most wolfish smile.

'If we're the fascists you say we are, naturally we'll close you down. You're still living in the spendthrift '60s, Pyke. The bottomless handout and no questions asked. Now we're telling you people to cut down on waste, to put your operations on a genuinely competitive basis, and to deliver the goods. Frankly, we have too many universities and too many redundant departments. Too many small, second-rate, jerked-up, pseudo-academic departments.'

Sidney has been lighting his pipe.

'Presumably that's why you don't pay us a living wage. And force us into early redundancy.'

'The dead wood – certainly. There's plenty of it. And don't talk to me about tenure or academic freedom.'

'I'm glad you've heard of them.'

'Academic freedom is a red herring. The real purpose of tenure is to provide idle teachers with a lifetime's immunity from work-assessment. Frankly, this profession suffers from sluggish corporate mendacity.'

'Abolish us,' Sidney advises. 'So long as we're using our brains your dark ages will be in jeopardy.'

'What we want – and what we're going to have – is a lean, virile university in cut-throat competition with every other university for the best staff and the best students.'

'And the money nexus will govern all human relations,' Sidney says. 'The result being a collapse of research, low teaching morale, and the virtual exclusion of working-class kids from higher education.'

The Minister grins satanically at the Chairman and Vice-Chancellor. 'Not for me to tell you gentlemen how to achieve genuine cost-effectiveness – but you might not be a million miles adrift if you amalgamated Media Studies, English, History, Philosophy and Social Studies into a single Department of Humanities. That's how many tenured professors?'

These words are greeted with a collective gasp. The Minister repeats his question, slowly, as if addressing disabled children incapable of making an inventory of their own toy cupboard.

'There are approximately eighteen professors in the departments you mentioned, Minister,' the Vice-Chancellor says, after a whispered consultation with the Registrar and Dean of Studies.

The Minister scans the ranks of petrified dons as if hunting for the redundancy victims.

'Eighteen! Fire sixteen of them, abolish their chairs, establish four new posts of "Coordinator", head-hunt the right young men in the market, hire them on short-term contracts, pay them what you need to pay them, the going price, link their careers to productivity – and you may find yourself burdened with a university which actually works instead of agitates.'

'It must be a grief to you that you've failed to privatize our universities,' Sidney says, his mouth crammed with salmon sandwich. (Everyone is now eating like mad, reaching, grabbing, stuffing, as if to assuage anxiety.)

'We may have to try harder,' the Minister snarls at Sidney. 'Frankly, the fact that this country still has only one private university is an absolute disaster. Our middle classes want something for nothing. What you don't pay for you don't value.'

This is received in shocked silence. Even the Chairman of the Governors, who has laid the foundation stones of the Benzin Theatre and the Benzin Swimming Pool – that pool! – looks aghast.

Sidney laughs grimly. 'So the middle classes desperately want what they can't possibly value. Is that the lesson in logic you bring us, Minister? If so, you certainly ought to begin by closing down our Philosophy Department.'

A few dons are emboldened to titter. The Minister drains his glass and holds it out for more.

'In my view the way to learn about print journalism and television is to get out and do them – not to unscrew your head with pretentious nonsense about "consciousness and ideology" or "patriarchal language".'

'I may still be living in the 1960s,' Sidney says, 'but I

have a distinct impression that you have escaped from the 1850s.'

The Minister grabs two spring onions.

'I'll give you credit for guts, Pyke. Most of the people standing round me in this room hate mine but daren't say so. Wish I could give you credit for anything else.'

'You're a turd,' Sidney says.

The Minister and his entourage abruptly turn their backs on him. The V-C and Registrar fuss frantically: a planned visit to the new GEC engineering complex has been suspended in view of a student occupation of the building. An alternative schedule involving the Sanyo Computer Studies block is hastily substituted – then cancelled when the same difficulty is found to prevail.

'He may have to leave by helicopter,' Sidney remarks to anyone ready to listen, but by a subtle shift of shoulders he is now shunned. His bravado could lose them all their jobs – nor do they have prime-time wives to cushion the calamity. Only Jones gives him a friendly dig in the ribs.

The assembled dons are left to pick at the remains of the food like furtive mice awaiting the exterminator.

Threading his way back across a devastated campus to his office, virtually unnoticed, Sidney sadly reflects that words are the armoury of the powerless. Besides, the Minister had done most of the talking. Another defeat.


Swindler House's nine hundred employees have been herded into the Odeon, Leicester Square, to hear Hans-Dietrich Swindler. Every seat is numbered – by rank. Davidson is alarmed (and hurt!) to find himself in row P, beside a couple of janitors and a motorcycle messenger. Preceded by a posse of dreadlocked Rasta security guards, evidently hired at short notice and carrying walkie-talkies relaying the top Euro-song on the Swindler label, the great man mounts the platform – small head on a long neck – accompanied by a massive Bavarian male secretary in a murder-black body-stocking.

Swindler delicately lays his notes, bound in tooled leather, on the lectern.

'Perhaps Sveendler is not understood,' Swindler begins, 'by the English. Sveendler is not Bismarck. Sveendler's late Aunt Mathilda advised him that one cannot sing in every courtyard. So Sveendler delegates his precious trust because Aunt Mathilda was a wise woman.'

He pauses in case anyone wants to challenge this.

'Sveendler seeks "aziendisti", as does his dear friend Agnelli – loyal devotees of the company. Sveendler Enterprises will be your father, like his dear friend Mitsubishi. But Sveendler cherishes no satraps or pawns, he seeks Knights Templar capable of bold thrusts towards Jerusalem!'

In Row P, Davidson simply wants to try his hand at publishing.

'Sveendler is not a "Media Mogul" or a "Media Mongol". His name does not begin with "M".' (Nervous laughter.)

'So! Situation report. Sveendler has many desks in many capitals but until recently no desk in East Berlin, Prague, Warsaw, Budapest, Leningrad, Moscow and Beijing. This is where logic now leads him, ladies and gentlemen.'

For a moment Davidson visualizes himself inducting Slavs into satellite dishes and user-friendly software but that might be quite a leap from Row P and the President-Chairman is now reporting on his recent trip to Beijing, where he received Deng Hsiao-Ping, officially in retirement but unable to resist running his small country in between siestas. Deng explained that pluralist democracy is incompatible with the ancient Chinese emphasis on discipline and consensus.

'Sveendler informed Deng Hsiao-Ping that we employ the same rule in Vampire Books: discipline and consensus. Deng was impressed. Sveendler Enterprises will establish an office in Beijing.'

The Bavarian male secretary breaks into applause. The nine hundred British employees clap in a ragged manner.

The Bavarian's expression above his body-stocking indicates that they should try harder.

'Stopping off in Moscow on his return flight, Sveendler
granted half an hour to Mikhail Gorbachev. The two leaders
talked for ninety minutes until Sveendler agreed to buy the
Baltic States. Sveendler explained to the President that
Europe has reinvented itself as the centre of the universe.
We, the Caucasians, have created a magnetic field of
spiritual possibilities: the democratic soul is capable of
infinite potential growth. President Gorbachev emphati-
cally agreed with Sveendler – and he is a man who becomes
what he wants.'

Those members of the audience determined to keep their
jobs break into spontaneous applause. Only a suicidal
minority, Davidson among them, laugh at the famous
Swindler 'become'. The latter are herded out into Leicester
Square and messily beaten to death with Swindler satellite
dishes by the Rastas.

Death! Davidson wakes up from this nightmare in a
Presbyterian panic – Dad, I didn't mean to let you down! –
sheer anxiety has sent him to sleep. Guiltily he glances at
the two janitors to his left: both sound asleep.


An hour later Mr Swindler is behind his desk in the
presidential suite. Having rushed back to Swindler House
by taxi, tube and bus, those who have been summoned
form a silent queue of terror and ambition in the corridor
outside, the senior executives desperately avoiding eye
contact with the junior editors whom they only yesterday
'Swindlered'.

The intercom brings the voice of the Bavarian male
secretary.

'Davidson, Ian. Step forward, please.'

A grained oak door hums open. Davidson steps through
it and hesitates – he has never been inside Buchenwald
before. An assistant motions him to a further door which
in turn hums. Davidson walks.

The Bavarian secretary is standing behind Mr Swindler's chair, his arms so rigidly clasped behind his back that he appears to be trying to pull his shoulders out of their sockets. On the richly tooled red leather surface of the Chairman-President's Chippendale desk lies a pile of mauve pages. Swindler's hands are folded across them. The same small head still perches on the same long neck, with the inert attentiveness of a sated vulture.

'Become me a black coffee, Fritz.' His neutral gaze settles on Davidson, who is not invited to sit down.

'What does work mean to you, Mr Davidson?'

'Work, sir?'

'Work.'

'I love it, sir.'

'But what is it?'

'I arrive an hour early every morning, sir. Normally I leave an hour or two late.'

'Mr Davidson, your work is editing books. Once in your hands, a book is your book. If it is good you are good, if it is not good you are not good.'

Judging his accent at uncomfortably close quarters, it remains a puzzle whether Swindler attended Trinity College, Oxford, before or after he graduated from the Gestapo. According to rumour, he later bought the one and asset-stripped the other.

'Frankly, Mr Davidson, this manuscript is Dreck. Hysteria. Yellow Gate witches everywhere! What is a Yellow Gate witch, please? And why should they be persecuting tSwindler's Frau-Author and her ridiculous leftist husband with allegations of rape? Rape! *Nature or Nurture* is supposed to be about the ideal modern marriage! The TV Queen of Happiness is now as serene as Medea. And a great deal less coherent!'

Davidson's throat is clogged. 'That's a problem, sir. Miss Newman's contract expressly forbids alterations to the text without her consent.'

'Contract!' Swindler shouts. 'Contract! And have you

ever attempted to obtain Miss Newman's consent to such alterations?'

'Certainly, sir. I regularly send back her pages with suggested amendments.'

'Ja? And what happens next?'

'Well . . . she ignores them. Usually. I'd say invariably.'

'So. She ignores them. And what do you do?'

'I consult Mr Lait, sir.'

'I stand to lose more than a trivial sum of money, Mr Davidson – I shall get a laughing stock!'

Davidson is also tempted to explain the ongoing problem of 'bekommen': to get. Might he not earn the great man's grudging gratitude? Davidson will never know, for this is the moment that Swindler chooses to sweep the offending mauve pages off his desk with the back of his hand. The Bavarian secretary bends to pick them up. Davidson does not bend. Who won the last war anyway?

'Miss Newman is due to have lunch with both of us, Mr Swindler. I'm confident that you – '

'You are not confident! That's your problem, Mr Davidson. Los, Mr Davidson.'

'Sorry?'

'Los!' shouts the Bavarian male secretary. 'Become lost!'

Leaving the outer office, Davidson turns his face from the mute queue of waiting victims. They know and he knows they know. This is the first fall on the wall chart of his life and he feels no resentment at all, merely the unanswerable indictment of the emperor of modern multinational merchandizing.

Reaching his own office, he finds his colleagues' desks empty. Without pause he empties the mauve pages and the floppy disks which accompany them into his briefcase, grabs his address book and portable telephone, snatches his personal comb and deodorant from the executive cloakroom – and is out of the building five minutes after Swindler's dismissal. He almost forgets his precious racing bicycle.

Once on the street, he knows not where to go. Confronting him are a fifteen per cent Abbey National mortgage, with a top-up loan from the National Westminster and a back-up top-up loan from the Black Horse. Fifteen hundred in debt on his plastic cards, paying APR nineteen per cent on his Audi, he's confronted by the unthinkable prospect of missing his annual skiing holiday in Val d'Isère. Wandering up Piccadilly, blindfolded in misery, he clutches at one comfort: this year there has been no snow.

Spotting a cash dispenser, he decides to check his current account. But he can't remember his account number. Four digits, surely! An impatient line forms behind him.


At 12.45, as Samantha sweeps into La Cupole, a storm of nervy celebrity, Davidson is sitting on a bench in St James's Park, a sandwich in his lap, pigeons clustered at his feet. Fired! Not even moved sideways! Jack Lait would have moved him sideways, but Swindler . . .

'I'm on the job market,' he would be saying all afternoon. But why? And in what tone of voice? No one hires a young executive shaken by anxiety. Confidence is the name and the number. 'I have an hour to rebuild my confidence, an hour to believe in myself,' he informs the filthy pigeons pecking at the detritus of his lunch. 'I thought you'd want to be the first to know . . .'


Swindler rises stiffly – he is not pleased and is not in the habit of concealing his displeasure. He also knows that the Newman woman wishes he were Jack Lait with his flashy cocktails, his Manhattan wit and wink, and the afternoon in Brown's Hotel. Swindler lifts her gloved and perfumed hand to his clamped mouth as the waiter whips away all trace of the cancelled third place at the table.

For ten minutes Samantha rattles on about the Edinburgh conference, desperately nervous, fending off the moment of truth. Noting her anxiety as further evidence of guilt, Swindler nods politely while ordering the wine, the food, the world.

Draining her bloody mary, she suddenly smiles radiantly. 'And how are you, Hans-Dietrich?'

'I have problems with your book, Miss Newman.'

'So do I! Doesn't every author! Could I possibly have another bloody mary?'

It's clear to him that the woman has been drinking like a fish all the way from Edinburgh. He flicks his fingers at the waiter.

'A bloody mary and schnell.'

A grateful hand touches his sleeve. 'I really do feel that the war between the sexes is terribly passé, I mean we women have simply eaten you men alive, it was never a contest, and now the intelligent women are desperately searching for a man who has real authority, who believes in himself, which of course enrages all these fat dykes in denims, unisex drudges wrapped in canvas, big bums . . .'

Observing that his lady author is close to tears, that her incoherent rubbish signifies terror of his verdict, Swindler merely nods. Her glass is again empty, thickly rimmed in lipstick. He doesn't order another.

'What is your view of the Aids epidemic?' he asks. 'Sveendler finds nothing in your books about Aids.'

'Swindler finds . . .?'

'Finds nothing.'

'Oh − oh, I see. Well . . . Aids is the best excuse for establishment puritanism since − ' Her hand shakes. 'But you're quite right, I really will make a statement about Aids.'

'And about promiscuity.'

'Yes, I − '

'And about abortion. Sveendler finds abortion in your synopsis, on the basis of which your book was commissioned − but nothing in your text. As yet. But your text is already very long. Too long.'

'I'm . . .'

'You must have an opinion about abortion, Miss

122

Newman. The Book of the Month Club requires an opinion. Sveendler is, you understand, a Catholic – a Believer.' Swindler smiles like one of the Viennese crooks in Harry Lime's penicillin racket – 'Veenkle' – and says: 'It's *your* book, of course, Miss Newman.'

Samantha is not eating her smoked salmon. 'Couldn't you call me Samantha, Hans-Dietrich? Jack always does. I do feel that Jack could help with – ' She reaches into her bag for a paper handkerchief. 'Jack is always so sympathique.'

'He has many corporate responsibilities.'

She dabs her eyes. 'Yes.'

'And your husband,' Swindler says. 'What is happening to this oddball?'

Samantha blinks. 'Well of course it's terribly terribly difficult for poor Sidney to be married to someone more famous than he is.'

'Ja?'

'Sidney is the kind of man who steps out of a jam-packed tube train in the rush hour, to let the other passengers off – and then never manages to get back on again.'

'And he has raped, we gather, most of his female faculty?'

'Oh no! Not really!'

'Maybe your husband is merely a sheep in wolf's clothing?'

Samantha's eyes flash defiantly: 'Don't you believe it! Sidney can still bring a university to his knees. Two years ago he forced the Governors to disinvest in South Africa.'

'Sveendler has investments worth eight million in South Africa. What, in your own opinion, is *Nature or Nurture* about? Sveendler asks because Sveendler does not know what it is about.'

Her eyes are brimming again. 'What happened to that Davidson boy? Wasn't he – '

'Sveendler fired him this morning.'

Samantha's hand shoots out towards Swindler's sleeve then withdraws, as if electrocuted. 'He was too young,' she whispers. 'If only Jack could . . .'

'Edit your book? Sveendler will edit your book.'

'Oh. Oh how wonderful, Hans-Dietrich. I really thought, just for a moment, that you were about to – '

'Cancel it? Believe him, it never crossed Sveendler's mind. So tell him what *Nature or Nurture* is about, please.'

'Well – it's really saying that any woman can do it.'

'Ja. Do what?'

'We women really have to refeminize ourselves, don't we, without abandoning our rights, our dignity, our new communal strength . . . Which brings me to marriage and . . .' An onrush of tears. Keenly observed by the clientele of the Cupole, Samantha hurries to the ladies'. Hans-Dietrich Swindler stares rigidly at no one.

Chantal is on her way to confer with Sylvie about *The Sidney Pyke Story*. On the train she rebuffs the usual lecherous advances then tosses off a piece about 'Working-class London Today' for Sidney's undergraduate journalism class:

I'd heard about people on housing estates tossing their garbage out of the window in the medieval manner. I didn't believe it until I visited a third-floor flat in Hackney and saw a filled nappy fly past the window.

Chantal writes the piece in ten minutes flat. Sidney will give her an 'A' whatever she writes. More of a problem – Chantal's pencil rests pensively in her beautiful mouth – is Bess Hooper's latest essay title: 'How Can We Conquer Male Chauvinism Unless We Can Confront Our Own Colonized Regions?'

Davidson has followed Mrs Thatcher's advice to the unemployed and 'got on his bike'. He has been on his bike for three days, cycling through the Enterprise Zone which stretches from South Kensington to Ludgate Circus. As for the City, its streets are crawling with unemployed bankers, brokers, market analysts and ad men, most of them fired for fashionable crimes such as insider dealing, takeover fraud, and foisting junk bonds on the public.

Davidson has also discovered that no worthwhile job is still available by the time it's advertised in a newspaper.

This is Ian Davidson thank you for calling back about the job sorry I am not available right now but please leave a message and count on me to call you within the hour . . .

And how do you get a job without a reference?

Lying on his kitchen table, next to a pile of unwashed dishes and Chinese takeaway cartons, is a letter from the legal department of Swindler Enterprises (Vampire), demanding the immediate return of certain properties allegedly in the illicit possession of Mr Ian Davidson:

– one cordless telephone;
– one company address book;
– one copy of *Nature or Nurture* by Samantha Newman (unfinished text) plus floppy disks of same.

Trawling among the mega-conglomerates of the multi-national carnivores, Davidson stoically takes the world as he finds it. (There is no other.) Wandering around Bloomsbury Square and Bedford Square, along Great Russell Street and down to Long Acre, he is quite unaware of yesterday's brass nameplates, of vanished publishers and dead imprints, mawed into aspic preserve, jawed into extinction by the conglomerates. Nothing has more confirmed his contempt for Sidney Pyke than Newman's proud insistence that her husband cherishes the names of all the extinguished publishers.

That must have delighted Swindler when he read it! Davidson bitterly regrets that he'd lacked the nerve to delete the offending passage – and everything else.

The only nostalgia for vanished species felt by Davidson is for cars. Wolseley, Austin-Healey, Morgan-MG, Talbot, Hillman, Bentley, Daimler, Lagonda, Riley – unfortunately collecting old cars is less easy than collecting old books.

Davidson no longer believes his own sludged voice when

he informs some sceptical employer that he decided to leave Vampire after being 'moved sideways'. No longer can he bring himself to begin with, 'Naturally, you're the first person I've called.' Impossible, now, brazenly to assert, 'I've had three offers close to forty K but, frankly, it's quality I'm interested in.' Not having read Balzac's *Lost Illusions*, he can take no comfort from the soothing embrace of ancient misfortunes and parallel tragedies. When still a rising and ruthless executive, he had rejoiced in his own solitude; now he wilts under a paralysing loneliness. Eats not, sleeps not.

# *Ten*

After two weeks of humiliating rejections, Davidson is reduced to soliciting fringes of publishing whose existence he never suspected: sinister pressure groups, fanatical religious sects, fixated lobbyists, vendors of aphrodisiac potions, retired generals determined to alert the Nation before it is too late.

Increasingly he is to be found, collar turned up, eyes closed, in the back row of some seedy Soho cinema in mid-afternoon – the hour of maximum Guilt for Presbyterians.

The young woman who slips into the empty seat next to his, forty minutes into *Revenge of the Vienna Vixens*, carries the crisp black suit and briefcase of those who work.

'Remember me? Met you in the Zanzibar once.'

'Oh . . . aye.' Having been asleep, he suspects he may be dreaming. Is she a Vienna Vixen?

'I bet you pump iron.' She squeezes his arm above the elbow – but dispassionately, without intimacy or inference.

'I play squash,' he says.

A man in the row in front, distracted from the pressing task of trying to pull off his penis under an anorak, hisses at them. Davidson follows the girl out of the cinema, deeply ashamed to have been found there, the more so that he has begun to suspect that he's met her before. Led to a pub, he allows her to buy the drinks.

'I'm Sylvie Poynter, by the way.'

'Ah – the journalist? Wait . . . didn't I read something by you last Sunday . . . about . . . ah . . .'

'About the Isle of Dogs.'

'Aye. That was it. A fashionable new Enterprise Zone.'

In the heady excitement of converting dead wasteland into living money [writes Sylvie Poynter], the boring old demands of human sanity go by the board. The smartest new restaurant may dispense salmonella food poisoning to the Yuppy couples able to afford £250,000 apartments with post-modernist balconies overlooking the river. The latest office tower equipped with state-of-the-art air conditioning can kill off its upwardly mobile staff with Legionnaire's Disease. Young bankers earning more than Cabinet ministers may be blasted off their waterbeds every morning by pneumatic drills. In short, life on the Isle of Dogs isn't worth living but everyone who is anyone wants to live there anyway.

'Actually,' Davidson tells the writer of this sparkling report, 'I need a job.'

'Yes. I know.'

'You do?'

'There are two people you must meet. My sister Chantal and Mr Al Sabah Al Masri Al Fatah.'

'Why?'

'Because both are expecting you.'

'Secret Service, are you?' Sidney Pyke asks casually.

'As I said, sir, I'm in publishing,' Davidson replies.

Pyke chuckles. 'Well of course that's the oldest cover-story in the business.'

Davidson's Audi has found its way to Cuba with the aid of a brilliant sketch map by Chantal, delivered by Sylvie, complete with compass points, gale-force cherubs, and local dog-free zones. Davidson is now intently observing the beautiful cartographer perched on the arm of the professor's armchair, while its swollen occupant, still wearing his '70s sideburns, massages her black-stockinged knee.

'I believe I could obtain for you a substantial advance, Professor Pyke, if – '

'MI6 come in all shapes and sizes,' Sidney tells Chantal. 'The only constant factor is the "substantial advance". I met enough of these CIA types when I went on that mission to Vietnam for Bertie Russell to co-ordinate resistance among conscript soldiers. I no sooner arrived than Thieu and Ky began to crack down on the Buddhists.'

'Yes, Sidney, but I think Mr Davidson is really just a publisher.'

Sidney looks disappointed. 'As Byron said, "Barabbas was a publisher." Ever heard of Byron? Ever heard of Barabbas? Bukharin? Bakunin? Barishnikov? Blake?'

'And let's admit it, Sidney, they did stop tapping your phone twenty years ago.' Chantal gently twists Sidney's dried-fig ear.

'Who told you that?'

'Samantha.'

Davidson is beginning to realize why Samantha Newman's mauve pages have failed to sustain a viable portrait of this bloated lunatic. Fancy living in a house called Cuba bang in the middle of a suburb girdled in rhododendron bushes and golf courses. And a Che Guevara door knocker. Garden gnomes modelled on Fidel Castro.

'You have enemies, sir,' Davidson says sombrely.

Sidney's expression brightens. 'Women, mainly.'

Davidson nods. 'One in particular. Hm.'

'She's mad, of course.'

This surprises Davidson. 'Well – '

'It's frustration, you understand. The bitch really wants to sleep with me.'

Davidson gapes. 'Doesn't she? I mean – '

'Are you out of your mind, young man? Would I go to bed with a punchbag? She'd demand tenure all night long.'

'Tenure? Your wife wants tenure?'

'What? Samantha? No no no no. I'm talking about Hooper.' Sidney guffaws and Chantal smiles mockingly, showing Davidson an extra inch of stocking by way of punishment for his stupidity.

The unemployed young visitor braces himself: 'Professor Pyke, I really believe the nation awaits *The Sidney Pyke Story*. You must develop first-strike capability.'

'No need. Samantha's got it all under control. She'll put the bitches and witches to rout.'

Not a penny in the world, Davidson remembers that the name of the game is confidence. Believe in yourself. Acquire the right property and the money will turn up.

'One hundred thousand pounds, a third on signature, a third on delivery – acceptance – a third on publication. Ten per cent royalty escalating to seventeen point five. Paperback split sixty–forty, rising by agreement to seventy–thirty. US rights ninety, translation rights eighty, first serial ninety, bookclub by agreement, TV, radio, film and theatre, seventy-five, digests, anthologies, strip cartoon, braille – '

'Who's paying for all this, Mr, er . . .'

'Davidson.'

'Davidson's paying? Who's he?'

'Me, sir.'

'Ah – so you're an independent publisher. Did you know my old friend Allen Lane? Victor Gollancz?'

Chantal rises from the arm of Sidney's chair and proposes to make coffee. Passing Davidson, she whispers, urgently, in his ear: 'Paving stones, idiot!'

Alone with the young man, Sidney's shifty expression returns. He is silent. Clearly he needs an audience. Davidson ponders the girl's baffling message: 'Paving stones, idiot!' Ah!

'Of course, you've had a most remarkable life, professor. Do tell me one thing I've never understood – how does one actually throw a paving stone at the police? I mean, it must be extremely heavy even to lift . . .'

'Ha!' Sidney leaps up, delighted. 'You're a bright fellow! Most members of your generation never give it a thought! Well, actually, as a matter of fact, the French "pavé" is a cobblestone. Not what we call a paving stone. Of course

130

after '68 the Gaullists simply removed the "pavés" from the Latin Quarter and covered the streets round the Sorbonne in tarmac. Pity. The tyres of a Renault 4 or a Deux Chevaux sound quite different on cobbles.'

'Fascinating. Fascinating.' Davidson knows how to release his more Scottish vowels when simulating solemn admiration. 'Sir, all this needs writing down.'

Sidney examines the young stranger whom Chantal has produced inexplicably and, worse, without explanation. Clean-cut type. Well born, badly educated. Father probably a minister of the Scotch Reformed Tabernacles. Yuppy. Already lusting after Chantal. Clearly undergoing ill-concealed nervous breakdown. Probably works for Murdoch, Maxwell or Moloch in some post-modernist imitation of a Sunset Boulevard motel, the desks too low to accommodate a middle drawer, no sandwiches and no live plants allowed . . .

'As a matter of fact,' Sidney says, 'I've begun to dream about all the women I've ever known.'

Davidson leans forward intently. 'Aye?'

'It's a bit like a TV serial – but more surreal. Definitely post-Dada. We used to ridicule psychoanalysis as bourgeois escapism. A racket. Wrong, of course. Only your dreams can reveal who you really are. Do you know who you really are?'

Davidson solemnly rotates his head. 'No.' He sighs. 'Yes.'

'Honest answer. Of course there's the physical dimension as well – a dialectical tension, you see, both spatial and temporal.'

Davidson nods. 'Aye.'

'The struggle to extend the libidinal cordon sanitaire.'

Fortunately Chantal returns at this delicate juncture, with coffee, brandy and small biscuits layered in bright red caviar. Her ravishing smile invades Davidson's Calvinist soul like Mediterranean sunlight flooding a January grouse moor.

Sidney drains his brandy in a single gulp. 'A writer must watch his mind like a pianist watches his hands,' he announces. 'Dreams are the front line, the forward trenches, of praxis. In the Sorbonne we obliterated the dichotomy between illusion and reality, between the pleasure principle and – '

'Oh do shut up, Sidney,' Chantal says. She turns to Davidson. 'Haven't I seen you somewhere before? Wait a mo' – Harrods! The staff canteen of Harrods!'

Davidson smiles at last. 'China department.'

'And I was in books! Christmas hols! Then we suffered a state visit from a woman who'd written a book about otters. We stocked fifty copies for the occasion. She brought the otters with her. One of the smelly little beasts dived under my blouse and bit my left nipple. I stank of fish and had to be sent home.'

Sidney has meanwhile helped himself to a second brandy, and a third. Then he points to three framed colour photographs leaning against the coal scuttle. 'Wha'isit, eh?'

Davidson wonders whether this is some kind of test. 'Looks like three tulips.'

Sidney snorts. 'It's a triptych of a tulip in three stages of ecstasy, my boy. It's a work of genius! Hm. By Gilly Jones. Samantha's pal.'

He burps and falls asleep. Chantal folds his dangling arms across his stomach. Can this really be, Davidson marvels, the virile, explosive, all-leather, anarchic hipster whose exploits Samantha Newman had insisted on spreading across Davidson's desk? Sidney with the Stones in Hyde Park. Sidney with John and Yoko during their famous bed-in for peace (which Sidney and Samantha had blatantly imitated at their own, subsequent, wedding). Sidney the New York Motherfucker. The Oxford anarchist. The LSE Maoist. Sidney in High Noon boots being dragged into Bow Street Magistrates Court by a posse of burnt-out cops . . .

Chantal walks Ian Davidson to his Audi. 'Expect to keep it long?' she asks.

'What?'

'The flash car. Out of a job, aren't you? Pushy youth,

currently driving on three wheels and scarcely charismatic,
I'd say.'

'Miss Poynter, if I may – '

'Only one person can keep you out of the credit company's dog pound.'

'Pyke? But can he write?'

'No. I can.'


An hour later, trapped in an M1 tail-back between Exits 18 and 16, but resisting his natural inclination to play shark and steal up the soft shoulder into the blinking blue arms of the police, Davidson finds himself absorbed in:


### *The Sidney Pyke Story* by Chantal Poynter

Twenty years ago, Newman and Pyke were celebrities of the Sixties counter-culture. Name any big demo, sit-in, pop concert or porn festival, and they were there. No star of the radical male circus could escape Newman's embrace; the dagger sank in the next day, when she went to press. She fought the men punch for punch, a strikingly handsome, raunchy, swinging, super-intelligent gal, shouting for attention, stuffing their cocks down their throats – though most of them were too spellbound by their own crowing to notice.

Her proclaimed mission was to take the sadism (male) and masochism (female) out of heterosex. To rescue man from his primeval fear of that 'magical orifice', the vagina, and to rid woman of her post-Reformation image as chaste, long-suffering, non-erotic and subservient. Her message to women: don't hate your cunt. Don't panic over its bloodstreams and its natural odours; don't listen to the admen and stop deodorizing yourself.

Thanks to Samantha, the true potential of cunt was at last revealed. That slack and passive tunnel sprang to life, elastic and gymnastic, ready to grip and pulse and pleasure itself. Newman advised women that they could masturbate without even touching themselves: 'Picture someone nice and contract the buttocks rhythmically. Keep it up until you come.' Newman also advised that women could develop self-servicing erogenous power by picking up bottle tops in their vaginas. (She found literary precedents – there was always a cultured gloss to her obscenity.)

Some eager disciples became puzzled. How were women to forge out into the world, climbing and commanding, if they spent half an hour every day contracting their buttocks? Newman reassured them whenever she returned to the subject, which was often: these muscular exercises could time-savingly be performed in trains, buses, offices and – she couldn't resist it – churches. (A scandalous writer is like a junkie; each time the dose has to be increased or immunity creeps in with boredom.)

Like other middle-class women of that liberated era, Newman picked up a few physical complications on the way. She demanded that the medical profession constantly inspect her troubled private parts with the utmost love and appreciation. Physicians who didn't hate cunt, she lamented, were rare – but keep searching, sisters.

Twenty years ago, Newman sternly admonished her devotees to abandon the hated nuclear family. She had travelled to poor, arid, trapped, peasant societies where she discovered a 'primitive' culture much wiser and more humane than the neurotic, hyper-individualist frenzy of the Western metropolis. The extended family, the multi-woman family, where babies were passed from loving hand to loving hand, provided the answer to the neuroses of possessive individualism.

Inspired by Samantha, hundreds of eager pilgrims set out for Sicily, India, Tahiti in search of wholemeal brown women weaving a new humanism out of an old, arcadian wisdom.

Simultaneously, Newman achieved an even higher profile in the glossy mags. Breaking the balls of the Western radical phallocracy, she released a stream of four-letter words, advising her breathless clientele that the run of male intellectuals made poor studs. Strongly recommended were Sicilian peasants or truck-drivers with no hang-ups about educated woman.

The editors of the mass-circulation newspapers hesitated to take on board a woman writer whose trademark was an outbreak of genitalia in the first paragraph. This obsessional quality is of course very often a winner in showbiz. People like to know where they are, even if it's below the belt ninety per cent of the time. When the editors panicked and dropped her she felt, of course, horribly betrayed. There's capitalism for you!

Today, mellower (and richer), she muses about Eros and Art, Nature and Nurture as she tends the vegetable beds of her £300,000 home, Cuba, with organic manure. The foul-mouthed virago has become the high priestess of Tenderness. Her knickers – and how she walked up Fifth Avenue without any – are no longer a global issue. The four-letter words, at one time the fibre of her literary diet, have now yielded to caring, sharing, feeling, loving. Making a go of 'modern marriage' is what it's all about.

Which brings her (and us) to Sidney Pyke.

(to follow)

# *Eleven*

Sidney awakes to find his garden occupied by Women.

His addled brain initially interprets the foreign sounds as possibly to do with dustbins. He has been dreaming, thickly, a scotch broth of a dream, about a manic demolition contractor who closely resembles the Minister of State for Higher Education. Seething with indignation, Sidney is unable to reason the exterminator and his helmeted Visigoths out of ramming bulldozers against the Media Studies Department until it crumbles to its foundations. Shrieking harpies, also wearing steel helmets, emerge from the ruins and squat to pee on Sidney's work-in-progress.

Dogs are soon on the scene.

Drawing the bedroom curtain, and slowly wiping the condensation from the pane, he seems to see one of his better apple trees keel over. He becomes aware that the thud-thud of the bulldozers in his dream has its provenance in the axing down, only an hour after first light, of his 'orchard'. (Even Sidney yields it to quotation marks.)

At first glance, the person wielding the axe resembles an Eskimo of short stature.

'The garden is full of Eskimos,' Sidney announces.

Samantha opens one eye and yawns. 'Yes, dear.'

'They've lit a bonfire in the middle of the lawn!'

'Eskimos always do that. Why not offer them some coffee, darling? Or make me some.'

Sidney can distinctly discern a thin coil of grudging smoke rising from the sappy ruins of several apple trees. A number of Eskimos are plodding round the 'fire', on which a black kettle is hopefully perched.

Sidney swears, zieht sich an (German he taught himself, to read Brecht in the original), and descends to the garden, still swearing. The Eskimos close ranks at his approach; they now resemble women swaddled in anoraks as thick as eiderdowns. One or two of the small, frosted faces glowering at him are recognizable.

'Good morning, Bess. Good morning, Melanie.'

No response. He counts nine quilted warriors. The Eskimo holding the axe is Bess Hooper.

He counts his fruit trees. Two have fallen, two out of five. Forty per cent of his orchard – in his rage he removes the quotation marks – vandalized. He has never done so much counting so early in the day. It occurs to him that 'Eskimo' is probably a sexist term. He wonders about its etymology and its semiology.

It's a cold morning, he now notices. The women's breath hangs just offshore their open mouths, like cartoon balloons. Sidney is reminded of the plucky little coal-fired shunting engines he used to monitor as a boy living near Didcot. (Not even Samantha knows he grew up near Didcot and that his late mother worked in the junction canteen for twenty years. Twenty years! Or that his father . . .) Anyway, the shunting engines never cut down his apple trees. Nor did they arrive in his garden at dawn and – he is now beginning to absorb the wider decor – pitch tents and survival bags on his lawn. Nor did they bring prams; or pin posters to his garden fence.

Padlocking his rage, he reaches for the universal language of rational discourse.

'Why are you here? Now. Why?'

'We demand a Tribunal of Inquiry,' Bess shouts. 'Your pals in the oligarchy are stalling.'

'Why don't you occupy the V-C's garden?'

At a sign from Eskimo Hooper, they turn their backs on him and form a circle round the fire. Sidney withdraws to the kitchen and speaks into the intercom connecting the kitchen to the master bedroom.

'I think you'd better come down and talk to them.'

'Don't fuss, darling. Just offer them coffee.'

Sidney knows that civilization has collapsed. The Liberation Front has seized the armouries and that's that. Bess Hooper has commanded his grudging respect by spending freezing winter nights camped outside the perimeter fence of Greenham Air Base, taunted by soldiers, assaulted by Ministry of Defence Police, harassed by local vigilantes fearful for the value of their properties. But the garden of Cuba harbours no missiles.

'And a boiled egg, darling.' Samantha on the intercom. 'And do bring me *The Times*.'

Sidney wipes the steamed-up window – the Women seem to be practising Morris dancing but that can't be the case; it takes him an idiot's minute to realize that by jumping up and down they are fanning the still-feeble flames.

'Get your broad arse out of bed and come down here,' he tells the wife at the end of the intercom. He regrets that he is increasingly adopting this tone with Samantha – and how gallantly she masks her pain with lacquered urbanity. Dear old thing.

'I'm getting up,' she says. 'Never mind the coffee. Never mind the egg.'

Sidney and Samantha, of course, are fully committed to unilateral nuclear disarmament. It's in the Green Manifesto. The Labour Party has abandoned it and Sidney has abandoned the Labour Party. Samantha's approach to these matters is naturally more sophisticated than Hooper's. When Samantha sweeps down to Greenham with her TV crew and continuity girls, some of the porcupines quiver their quills, resenting the flash of fame, the flaunted filigree of talent. Samantha has told the *Sunday Times* colour mag how completely vital it is to convince the nation that Peace Women don't have to look like their own survival bags –

indeed Hooper later claimed that Samantha bought her survival bag at Fortnum and Mason's.

'We women have to civilize men,' Samantha assured her television audience. 'What are nuclear missiles but penises concreted into permanent erections by rage?'

Anyway. In recent times Samantha has slightly dropped out of the Greenham scene. The mountain, however, has come to Muhammad. Pulling on a pair of denim trousers, a Hebridean seamen's turtle-neck jersey, and her Millett's Mountain Ranger boots, Samantha appraises the garden scenario and puts a call through to her friend Gilly Jones.

'Gilly, you've just got to mobilize the Mauves.'

No need to inform Sidney. She feels he deserves some punishment for the ruin of her organic vegetable beds. Ignoring his questions, pleas and fulminations, Samantha spends the morning bashing her IBM Fastrite with flying fingers.

Jack Lait has cabled from New York to say her new pages are a whole lot better. Apparently Swindler himself is pleased with them. Samantha feels quite sure that the invasion of her garden is really another attempt to sabotage her book.

By mid-morning the garden fence is festooned with posters, banners, cartoons and – most oddly – nappies and knickers.

> WOMEN AGAINST RAPE
> WAGES FOR HOUSEWORK
> WAGES DUE LESBIANS
> MALE WATCH

On top of which the garden gate has been painted bright yellow. A subdued Sidney takes a cup of coffee up to Samantha and asks her why.

'Why yellow? Heavens, don't you men know anything?'

Dutifully Sidney lays out lunch on the kitchen table – a rectangular job in pine, with fitted benches, like the sort they use in pub gardens. Plates, salad, cheese, Samantha's fat-free yoghurt. After much agonizing he draws the curtains closed.

Samantha sweeps down and undraws them. 'Heavens, darling! We're not hiding in our own home.'

'Perhaps I should make a statement?' he suggests. 'Issue a denial . . .'

'Mm?' She bites into a weightless Ryvita, scooping a slice of Brie off Sidney's overflowing plate. 'Deny what?'

'The four-letter word now suspended, in letters a foot high, from the raspberry canes to the Victoria plum tree.'

'Oh rape, you mean? Oh. Oh I see. Well, I would certainly have welcomed some kind of denial myself . . .'

He draws breath. 'Very well. I can assure you that – '

'I thought you were a fighter, Sidney. A streetfightin' man.'

A call comes from Gilly Jones, now buzzing around Greenham Common and Newbury, tracking down Mauves with time on their hands. The Ansafone also records urgent messages from the Press, various dog-owners, and BBC television. Sidney handles all of these, with consummate skill, while Samantha writes the day's events on to mauve paper.

'I think I might try fetching some firewood from the shed,' he announces on the intercom.

'Brave boy.'

'Sort of test the water . . .'

'Do it.'

He does it and nothing happens. He walks out of the kitchen door and right through their 'camp' to the wood shed without suffering a single assault, physical or verbal. The Women ignore him. On his second trip it occurs to him that he has already conditioned himself to accept the Women's presence in his garden and to accord it a rudimentary legitimacy – he is fascinated to observe himself not walking into their tents, or treading on their survival bags, or kicking over their water buckets. Nor, even more fascinating, does he pull down their abusive placards.

And he has an uncanny sense – not deigning to glance

up – that Samantha is observing him observe himself. Might his own silence not be construed as some kind of admission of guilt – or defeat – by his wife?

Action he must take.

At 2.30 Sidney wheels out his bicycle with the brazen intention of pedalling in to the university to service his mail or confer with Jones – or maybe take a swim. As soon as the Women spot his plan there's a commotion in the 'camp', followed by a scurrying and rushing to fill the gate. Swaddled figures lumber to block his path.

Observing these manoeuvres from her window, Samantha is reminded of a lame old polar bear confronting its destiny. This image duly appears on the screen of the IBM Fastrite.

'Excuse me,' Sidney says, but they don't.

Sidney pushes gently forward; the Women link arms and shove him back. Sidney is familiar with the rules of non-violent violence. No hands are allowed. The heaving scrummage remains more or less silent so long as Sidney keeps both hands on his bicycle, but as soon as, exasperated, he raises an arm to support his exit project, he is deafened by shrieks.

'I have a lecture,' he lies.

'Rapist!' Hooper says.

By now the Press agencies have been alerted and photographers are recording this new version of the Eton wall game. The journalists call out to Sidney from the other side of the garden fence, soliciting a comment.

'I have raped all these women in my time,' he explains. 'You can't really blame them. I have also succeeded in blocking their careers, whenever possible.'

Why hasn't he called the police?

'Because this is an argument among progressive people.'

'Rapist pig!' shouts Hooper, hurling herself at his chest and, supported by a mesh of sustaining bodies, driving him back a full yard. Sidney rediscovers the excitement of direct combat with Hooper. Wrestling with her in what is now the large puddle of mud surrounding the gate is, all in all, a diverting way to spend a winter afternoon. The swimming-pool incident comes back to him with an almost delicious clarity – Bess surfacing beside him in the deep end with a single demand: 'Tenure.' Firm-fleshed and strong. 'Tenure, you bastard.' At that moment the pool was empty of other women and not yet filled with men. Just one of each.

Could he really have grabbed her by the buttocks and squeezed? He isn't sure: the pleasure of that long, slow squeeze would remain with him long after he was dead but he may have dreamed it.

When Samantha emerges from the house at three o'clock, wearing a long leather coat and high heels, Sidney has been pushing for thirty minutes and is still some six inches inside Yellow Gate. Abruptly the Women lose all interest in Sidney. They now converge on Samantha Newman, seething with animosity yet fascinated by a legendary figure possessing a kind of complex complete-ness, as if a brilliant, mature, radical woman's life is a delicate architecture of rooms and compartments, of fine principles and romantic passions, of working dungarees and beautiful clothes, of liberation and necklaces, of gender solidarity and dildoes, of confrontation and cosmetics, of public positions and (very) private positions. Utterly mys-terious and wonderfully open, secretive and candid, chaste and lustful, ugly and beautiful, naïve and knowing – the women confronting her feel like clods of earth.

Samantha's powerful chemistry has a particularly decon-structional effect on Melanie, whose witch's weeds visibly wither in the presence of the perfumed queen bee. The small, pale face framed by its anorak hood is abruptly drained of resolve. But Bess is made of coarser fibre and saves the day by bringing up the inflammatory issue of 'Guidelines to Children's Books', which –

' – which I rubbished,' Samantha cuts in. 'On television. Unforgivable.'

'"Despicable" was the word we used,' Bess says. 'You mocked your sisters as "sinister zealots and vigilantes" –

wasn't that the phrase? — "intent on purging all our libraries".'

'So you are,' Samantha says. 'And, sadly, not my "sisters" either.'

'And then you refused us the right of reply,' Melanie says timidly.

'Nothing to do with me, Melanie. The producers make their own decisions.'

'And she's content to squeeze cash and fame out of such a corrupt system!' Hooper triumphantly tells the sisters.

For a moment Samantha wears her wobbly look but her regal nature rapidly reasserts itself.

'Literature — need I remind you, Bess — must reflect the conflicting aims and ideals which are constantly at war within all of us. The sad truth is that the children's books you promote reek of deodorant. Frankly, what we don't need is a new generation of Young Pioneers spoon-fed in one-dimensional virtue.'

Back on top, Samantha drives away in her little red Renault 5, wisely leaving her Range-Rover out of sight in the garage. Sidney's relief is tempered only by the realization that her brilliant riposte has been lifted, word-perfect, from his own desktop. Evidently his new lecture course is going straight into *Nature or Nurture*. Sidney pedals off thoughtfully on what remains of his often vandalized bicycle.


**THE EXAMINER**
University of Shame!
— Criminal Assault by Students on Minister —
— Pyke Insults Minister of State —

Sipping sherry while hiding from the roaming student mobs in his neo-Georgian mansion, the Vice-Chancellor notes that Pyke has once again been whipped to death by Haynes, the drunken editor of the local *Examiner*. Under a two-column headline, the editorial deplores the reception accorded to 'our distinguished guest, the Minister of State for Higher Education' by a 'student mob who could teach our local football hooligans a trick or two'. Haynes goes on to inform 'the entire local community' that it is 'revolted by the arrogant antics of conceited youths whose brazen contempt for civilized behaviour is subsidized by the long-suffering taxpayer'.

And more. Reaching for the sherry decanter, the V-C allows his reading spectacles to shift a millimetre down his nose:

> The fact that Professor Sidney Pyke, the head of a Media Studies Department whose disgusting goings-on are now notorious, has encouraged the leftist yobbos by reportedly calling the Minister a word impossible to print in a family newspaper, merely reminds the local community that a Tribunal of Inquiry will soon be investigating the gravest charges of personal misconduct against Professor Pyke. Innocent until proved guilty is of course the watchword of British Justice, which is second to none, but readers are advised that the charges against the dog-hating Green Councillor, although made by two women of known sexual tendencies, carry a guarded credence.

The Vice-Chancellor groans at this last phrase. With the gist of Haynes's editorial he rather agrees. Normally he does rather agree with Haynes. Both are active supporters of the local Conservative Association – the natural alliance of horse and hound – and on this occasion the V-C has personally dictated the editorial over the telephone. It pains him, therefore, that Haynes's congenital illiteracy should have intervened to substitute 'guarded credence' for 'provisional credibility'.

The Registrar calls in.

'Sherry?'

'Yes.'

'How's the mob?'

'Most of them have gone off to see the football match.'

'What about the Pyke Inquiry?'

'Cuba has been invaded.'

'Cuba invaded? By the Americans? More sherry?'

'Yes to the sherry. His garden.'

'Pyke's garden we're talking about – not Cuba?'

The Registrar sighs a bit. 'Pyke's garden invaded.'

'By grey squirrels?'

'By women disguised as grey squirrels. Or so Jones reports. Apparently his wife's in the thick of it. He went up there to have a look-see. Didn't like what he saw. Came away fairly fast, I gather. Covered in gloop.'

'In glue?'

'Gloop. It's a mixture of wallpaper paste, water and food colouring customarily hurled at Cruise missile support vehicles.'

'Is it a legal substance?'

'Probably.'

The V-C thinks about all this. Finally one question forces its way over and above all others: 'By women disguised as grey squirrels, you say?'


'You Jew?' is Mr Al Sabah's first question to Davidson.

As soon as Davidson enters the Bond Street headquarters of Al Sabah Enterprises the smell of real money causes his nostrils to pump like bellows. That ostentatious spread of marble stretching on and on; the wide walnut staircase sweeping up and up in a regal curve; the menacing chandeliers and the many, many 'priceless' rugs; the receiving line of decorative assistants, doe-eyed Middle Eastern beauties subtly positioned before huge gilded mirrors so that there are two of each; the motionless janissaries poised to become unmotionless at some secret oriental signal; the soft-soled slave-servants obsequiously drugging him on cup after cup of Turkish coffee.

Clearly a Presbyterian soul is in peril here.

Davidson is eventually received by a kind of priest, a guru or fakir, a Hindu or Hindoo or Buddhist, a lama, imam or mullah. The man wears a saffron robe; the benign soft face of a eunuch; the head is tonsured in the Benedictine monkish mode – but also, by some Korean optical illusion, polished clean of hair. Presently he introduces himself as Maharishi Swamiji.

'You are doubtless asking your good self who is this priest?' the Swamiji smiles. 'I am pantheist. If anybody call me Hindu or Sikh then nobody have more faith in Islam than Swamiji. Nobody more faith in Christian.'

Davidson nods reverentially. 'Aye.'

'When Almighty God gave us birth he never stamped our buttocks Muslim Boy, Christian Boy. We all breathing the same divine air, Mr Davidson.'

Davidson inhales some more divine air.

After further passages of oriental prevarication punctuated by interminable silences, meditations and counting of banknotes, the Swamiji finally gestures to Davidson to rise from the rush mat on which he has been – painfully – forced to squat.

'We ascending,' says the Swamiji.

They ascend. The lift is perfumed, lined with marble, not onyx, and it exudes heavenly music. Released from this divine cell by a veiled Bedouin beauty, Davidson is cordially invited to squat in yet another ante-room and to begin the process of waiting all over again. Silken cords of cordiality strangle him.

Then! A choreographed commotion. Servants scurry, secretaries scamper, the Swamiji breaks into a double-shuffle. A split second later Davidson finds himself within the throne-room. The opulence of the great man's office is just incredible. It puts Swindler House straight into the flea market. The frieze is done in high relief and seems to represent Saladin putting the Crusaders to the sword. You could spend a million just by blinking.

'You Jew?' Mr Al Sabah Al Masri Al Fatah asks. Just how small he is will not become apparent until he stands up. He will not stand up. 'Youjoo?'

Davidson wonders whether there's a short version of Al Sabah Al Masri Al Fatah (the name, not the man) which is also polite. He isn't entirely clear whether Arabs, like Chinese, put their christian names at the end – or whether, if you think about it, they have christian names.

'I am not a Jew.' Davidson immediately feels ashamed.

Mr Al Sabah explains that recently he has been 'thwarted' in his legitimate ambitions to own a publishing house. 'Thwarted' despite the 'billions' he has brought into this country; 'thwarted' despite the high esteem in which he is held by the Confederation of British Industries, by the Chairman of the BBC – and by the Prime Minister. 'Thwarted by certain Jew interests, you see.'

'Jewish interests,' the Swamiji nods gravely.

'International Zionism,' says Mr Al Sabah. 'So you recently working for Swindler?'

'Yes, sir. Recently.'

'What you thinking him?'

'Sorry?'

'What you thinking Swindler? This Swindler Jew thwarting Al Sabah Al Masri Al Fatah.'

(Active in Bavarian right-wing politics, and a rather nasty variety of Catholic, Swindler has published several veiled apologies for the Third Reich. But here in Mr Al Sabah's Xanadu, Swindler is a Jew.)

'He speaking Yiddish – for a fact,' Mr Al Sabah tells Davidson. The Swamiji's polished head nods in confirmation. Slowly it emerges that Swindler has not only frustrated Mr Al Sabah's legitimate publishing expectations, he has also 'thwarted' him of several hotels, gambling casinos, office towers and more.

'Mr Al Sabah needing your loving confidence,' the Swamiji explains. 'Otherwise things being just materialistic and mortal.'

At this juncture Mr Al Sabah presses a button hidden in his desk and the tambour door of an antique cabinet rolls silently back to reveal a television screen.

'Mr Al Sabah watching news,' the Swamiji whispers. In the event Mr Al Sabah flicks from channel to channel as if

147

searching for news of himself. No luck: another conspiracy. His brow furrows.

'You having friends? References?' he abruptly asks Davidson.

Davidson knows that the answer must be yes, but he can't, at the drop of a hat or turban or dishcloth, think of a single friend. Or reference.

'I always say a few honest friends are worth a lot of dishonest ones,' he says. It sounds sort of Arabic-folkloric. Mr Al Sabah beams appreciatively – as, no doubt, when he buys a horse at Newmarket or a castle in Scotland or a department store in Oxford Street.

'You not bringing reference, eh?'

A ghastly decision to make, fraught with dangers, but Davidson reaches into his pockets and hands Mr Al Sabah the increasingly threatening letters received from Swindler's lawyers. The Arab reads them slowly and with intense concentration.

'True?' he scowls. 'This true?'

'Yes, sir.'

'You cheating employer? You stealing address books and manuscript?' Davidson trembles but the Arab smiles, showing touches of gold. 'Swindler being crook. People saying Al Sabah wicked man, wicked Arab. People saying Al Sabah wanting buy *Times* and making Arabic paper it. All lies. Swindler bribing journalists for making big lies against Al Sabah. That Jew.'

'All lies,' adds the Swamiji.

'Yeah. But this being rumours, see, all rumours, who making rumours? Last time I buying publishing outfit in New York I losing million dollars in one year. Whole hog. Gone with wind. You knowing why?' Davidson waits attentively. 'Swindler why, Mr Davidson.'

Davidson clears his throat and caresses his briefcase. 'I've brought you a number of interesting projects, Mr Al Sabah.'

'Yeah?'

'Prestige projects. We urgently need a big book on all the mosques you are building, sir. And all your many charities.

Lots of pictures, beautiful art work, top designers, best writers.'

Mr Al Sabah nods sombrely. 'Yeah. Good idea. Brainwave.'

'I can guarantee major review coverage on all the main literary pages, the quality newspapers, the *TLS* – '

'*TLS*? What that?'

'You buying it soon,' the Swamiji tells him.

Mr Al Sabah lights a cigar – or the Swamiji lights it, whipping a lighter out of his saffron robe. Davidson gets his own lighter to the cigar seconds too late.

'That Pindah girl telling me you having big scandal up sleeve.'

'Pindah, sir?'

'Sylvie Pindah. Big scandal concerning Samba woman.'

'Samba, sir?'

'Samba Newman.'

Davidson hears himself trying to explain about Samantha Newman and Sidney Pyke – the 'literary showdown of the year, the ultimate battle of the sexes'. Hoping that the Arab will instinctively align himself with battered husbands everywhere, it gradually dawns on him that the monarch of a harem, and owner of half the hotels in London, might not understand a husband's inescapable need to write a book in order to keep his one wife in her place.

'Wait wait wait,' Mr Al Sabah intervenes. 'You saying this Samba woman – '

'Samantha.'

' – this Samba woman praising husband in book? Why he complaining?'

A good point. Davidson desperately tries to remember why Sidney is complaining. The conclusion is inescapable – he isn't. Fortunately, the Swamiji comes to Davidson's rescue.

'Not fitting that wife writing about husband,' the Buddhist-Christian-Islamic priest snorts. 'He should divorcing she.'

'Shut up.' Mr Al Sabah's eyes have narrowed. 'I asking Mr Davidson.'

'According to the wife's version,' Davidson explains, 'the husband is now her poodle and – '

'Is dog?'

'Is silly dog for women,' the Swamiji says, clearly anxious to recover his authority.

'Meanwhile,' says Davidson, 'the wife is having an affair with Swindler's New York executive, Jack Lait. The husband is furious, you understand and – '

'Aaah. So.' Mr Al Sabah smiles and rubs his hands. 'That Jew Lait. Ach. Aaah.'

(Lait is a WASP if ever there was one but Davidson has by now abandoned all ethnographic pretensions.)

'Yes, sir – Swindler and Lait are planning a huge promotion.'

'Yeah,' Mr Al Sabah is musing, calculating. 'OK, we publishing this Sidney Pyke. You showing me he book.'

'Oh, he's . . . still writing it. He'll need a commission.'

'How much costing?'

'Swindler is paying the woman two hundred thousand. She's a famous feminist.'

'Yeah? All this feminist destroying Western civilization.'

'I couldn't agree more, sir.'

'Yeah? But where your references?'

'I can hardly obtain a reference from Swindler . . .'

'Yeah. Problem.'

'Problem,' says the Swamiji.

An uncomfortable pause.

'No problem,' Mr Al Sabah announces.

'No problem,' confirms the Swamiji, clasping both of Davidson's hands. 'Whatever we do there is nothing can keep us safe in the eyes of God except the goodness we make for ourselves and not for ourselves only.'

'OK, OK,' says Mr Al Sabah. 'We launching publishing house. We calling it Buckingham Palace Press.'

'I think there might be objections,' murmurs the elated Davidson. 'Why not name it after your castle in Scotland – I happen to be Scottish myself.'

But it turns out that the Al Sabah castle is called

Lochauchterarder, which lacks instant marketability. After a quick tour of the obvious historical and social landmarks, during which Davidson is very much in the driver's seat, the short list is down to Trafalgar and Wellington.

'Yeah, OK, Wellington,' decides Mr Al Sabah. 'I liking.'

Ian Davidson, Esq is hired as managing director of the Wellington Press, at a modest probationary salary fifty per cent above Swindler's pittance. Suitable premises will be 'no problem' – Mr Al Sabah is the owner of thousands of square yards of unoccupied office space and employs numberless bailiffs, stewards, and security guards to eject homeless squatters.

Staggering out into Bond Street, Davidson is tempted to buy himself a silk tie and to embrace the first passing stranger. By coincidence this just happens to be Sylvie Poynter, spilling out of a taxi and hustling Ian into a pub where they both get very drunk – he for real, she pretending.

'Chantal will be over the moon,' Sylvie says. 'Maybe you're not as thick as you look.'

'We could go to bed and find out,' he says.

'Careful, Ian, or I'll write to your daddy.'


The following day, still in a manic state of elation, Davidson telephones the Pyke household, ostensibly to congratulate the author of *The Sidney Pyke Story*, but really to congratulate himself. At this juncture, despite the flattering attentions of Sylvie and Chantal, Davidson rather stubbornly persists in identifying old man Pyke himself as the most plausible author of Pyke's autobiography.

A recorded message on the Cuba Ansafone greets him:

'This is the fucking authoritarian male chauvinist rapist pig Sidney Pyke speaking. I'm sorry I'm not available as of now due to an invasion of my garden by creatures from outer space. If you wish to be raped, or to have your dog turned into glue, kindly leave your name and number.'

Davidson groans. 'Holy cow.'

# *Twelve*

The following morning Sidney is again awoken by a commotion in the garden. On this occasion it's not the thump of axe on wood which disrupts a sleep weighted with whisky, but a dawn chorus of shrieking. Furious stuff. Cautiously drawing the curtain, he wipes the condensation from the window and observes two groups of Eskimos lumbering in clumsy circles and throwing mud pies at each other.

'There's a development,' he informs Samantha. 'More Eskimos from Greenham Common. Mud pies.'

'Good for Gilly,' she murmurs, stretching her long arms above the duvet.

'It doesn't look good.'

'Is it Mauve Gate or Orange Gate?'

'Is it what?' He understands perfectly well.

'Sidney, go and make a dozen mugs of coffee.'

All the Eskimos look the same to Sidney, although the battle formations suggest that the Women know who's who. Opening the window a fraction, he hears: 'Fuck off you racist bitch!'

He also hears the CIA mentioned, then the KGB. The two factions of quilted Women didn't look like the CIA and the KGB, but Sidney's generation of radicals, let it never be forgotten, has taught the world to look beyond the surface for hidden agendas.

One of the Yellow Gate Women – it's surely Hooper – has advanced on the newcomers, who are milling nervously about in Samantha's organic strawberry beds with the uncertain truculence of gang kids facing defeat.

'Lackeys of the Soviet war machine!' Hooper yells.

'That's a new twist,' Sidney comments at the bedroom window.

Samantha, having rapidly brushed some life into her hair, pushes him aside and thrusts her head out of the window.

'Hullo, hullo, Mauves, hullo, Gilly!'

Hugely heartened, the Mauves raise a cheer, wave back and rush two yards towards Hooper, who doesn't move.

'What the hell is Mauve Gate?' he asks.

'You visited it last year. Just make the coffee. Bloody Hooper has brought in overnight reinforcements from the King's Cross Women's Collective.'

'Who?'

'Oh Gawd, Sidney.'

Later that morning the Mauve Gate Women chop down part of his fence in the friendliest possible spirit to create a new gate, through which Sidney is assured free passage. When he brings out the coffee and biscuits they are awfully nice and tell him about their husbands and partners. Gilly Jones even steals a kiss, her first on Sidney in some time.

The garden of Cuba is now rigidly divided into separate zones, each with its own democratic, non-bureaucratic administration and infrastructure: tents, survival bags, chemical latrines, bonfires, pamphlets, posters, spray-paint, printing presses. Only a few yards separate the frontier posts but the mud-throwing has stopped and both factions are determined to demonstrate their greater devotion to womanly strategies of non-violent confrontation.

Shouting is allowed. Yellow Gate and King's Cross frequently explain, by megaphone, that the 'split' has deepened their consciousness, hardened their resolve, and exposed the 'network' of the media-pandering Left establishment. Bess and Melanie constantly use the megaphone to taunt the opposition.

'The Molesworth Peace Camp rapes,' announces Hooper,

'prove that the mixed peace movement protects men who rape. When the raped women took action to bring the truth out into the open, they, not the rapists, were accused of being violent. The elitist women's peace movement said these rapes weren't rapes.'

While Samantha's fingers fly for Swindler across her keyboard, Sidney once again finds concentration impossible.

'What was all that about?' he asks on the intercom connecting his study to hers.

'You, darling. Au fond.'

'But I've never been near Molesworth.'

'That's nothing to be proud of, Sidney.'

Now Melanie has the megaphone. Astride two fallen apple trees and ripping off her khaki balaclava to release the full energies of her green-punk hairdo, she describes her most recent encounter with a soldier at Greenham Common.

'HE: Do you recognize these bolt cutters?

ME: These are my bolt cutters.

HE: Did you cut the perimeter fence with these bolt cutters earlier this evening?

ME: I was cutting a hole big enough for a cow to get through. There are about forty-eight cows and twenty-odd horses and say twelve goats it might be five goats and two geese and two ducks. All these creatures could be grazed on Greenham Common but for the fact that quite illegally the Ministry of Defence erected a perimeter fence and handed over the Common to missiles.'

Sidney is back on the intercom: 'Is this some kind of code, the animals I mean?'

'I'm trying to work!'

It becomes clear to Sidney that the Mauve Women are no match for the Yellows at shouting. It doesn't surprise him. Gilly never bellowed, even when he kept going back to Samantha. Worse, the Yellows have the better words. They enjoy a clear semantic ascendancy. For a moment he experiences a flush of pride in having appointed Bess

Hooper, who is now taunting the Mauves with another report from the front line.

'In the early hours of the morning the Greenham convoy was returning to base after an exercise on Salisbury Plain. Melanie, me and three other ♀ ♀ ♀ were standing along the A339, near to Green Gate, waiting to throw our slop. We saw the convoy coming and attempted to run towards it. Immediately we were all thrown to the ground and pinned down. We started screaming "Blood on your hands!" and "Murderers!" until the soldiers pushed our faces into the mud. The women of Mauve Gate did nothing to help. This is what happens to Yellow Gate Women. When did it last happen to Mauve Gate or Orange Gate? When did it last happen to *you*? Power to the Sisters!'

From his window Sidney notices that the Press corps gathered in his garden is expanding. Reporters from *Sanity*, *Time Out* and *City Limits* are lovingly entertained by Mauve Gate but abused as the 'Left Establishment' by Yellow. The Yellow Women and their King's Cross allies seem to take bitter satisfaction in their own isolation. Only when two women from *Spare Rib* arrive do Hooper's troops unbend a bit.

Later, at nightfall, a flushed Gilly Jones comes into the house – by now most of the Mauves, softies, are preparing to cook delicious omelettes and quiches in Samantha's super-kitchen and to spend the night under Sidney's roof – to report on what really happened between Hooper and the *Spare Ribs*.

'Bess offered them photographs of the scrummage yesterday but she insisted that the caption should read: "Yellow Gate Women Confront the Rapist Pyke".'

Samantha arches her carefully situated eyebrows. Gathered in her kitchen, the Mauve Women sip Sidney's mulled wine with cloves, and offer him knowing little smiles. He shrouds himself in pipe smoke while eyeing a lively little number called Pam or Pat or possibly Veronica.

'And then,' says Gilly, loving her story, 'guess what.'

'What, darling?' (This is Samantha, not Sidney.)

Gilly's performance becomes quite flamboyant and Expressionist – 'Woman on the Potsdamer Platz, 1926' – and also a bit dreamy and Impressionist – 'The Opera Box, 1884'. Or so Sidney concludes, calculating that his last fling with Gilly may have occurred after they went to see *Last Tango in Paris* when Samantha was in Italy (again) but he isn't sure. It's ten to one that Gilly is sure. Perhaps that's why Bill Jones regularly cheats at tennis.

'The *Rib* women,' Gilly is reporting, 'decided they wanted the caption to read: "Peace Women Confront the Chauvinist Pyke". But Hooper insisted on "Yellow Gate Women". The *Rib* dears so desperately want unity, you see. Then Melanie announced that the only true Peace Women are Yellow Gate Women. Well!' Gilly rolls her eyes like a silent movie queen. 'A spy in the enemy camp tells me that negotiations have broken down!'

Sidney pours more mulled wine while Samantha runs out into the muddy garden, though in the wrong shoes, to invite the two beleaguered *Spare Ribs* in for wine and supper. Soon everyone in the cosy house is asking after everyone else's natural, adopted and artificially inseminated babies. Samantha knows the names of all the babies.


'How the hell did you get in here?'

Ian Davidson scowls at the ravishing creature in a short mauve mohair skirt who has sidled into his office.

'Nice view you've got,' Chantal drawls, indicating the dome of St Paul's crouching below the executive eyeline of the managing director of the Wellington Press.

In common with most of his squash partners, Davidson believes that the only way to deal with very attractive women is to be as rude as possible. But belief is hardly the issue here. The ten days since Davidson first encountered Chantal at Cuba have seemed like . . . well, a lot longer. So the bellicosity of his greeting has more in common with that of the anxious mother who has suffered agonies for a missing child, only to express her relief with a scolding. Not that Davidson's anyone's mother.

'Where's the professor, then?' (as curtly as possible).

'Sidney couldn't make it. Pressure of work. The Minister's visit. The Tribunal of Inquiry. And now they've occupied his garden.'

'Who has – the Tribunal of Inquiry?'

'Sylvie says you're as thick as a chamber pot. The Women.'

'But he was due to sign a contract!'

Chantal perches herself on the edge of his desk. He notes that she's your perching type of girl. Thick!

'I suppose,' she says, 'you'll cancel the posh restaurant reservation and take me to a wine bar. Or will it be McDonald's?'

In fact expense-account lunches are 'no problem' for Davidson so long as Mr Al Masri Al Fatah Al Sabah (Davidson still has difficulties with the word order) remains cocooned in his long sabbath of the vanities. Which is fortunate, since Chantal turns out to have – despite her eight-and-a-half-stone and pre-Raphaelite ethereality – an appetite for oysters, avocado, fresh salmon and Muscadet worthy of a 'lady author' (a phrase which insists on fastening itself awkwardly, like a cactus in a tweed skirt, to the walls of Davidson's mind).

'Do you always do that?' she asks in the restaurant.

'Do what?'

'Cut your meat into squares before eating it.'

Davidson's normally sallow complexion resembles a poppadom pulled too late from under the grill.

'Since I'm buying the lunch, perhaps I could ask the questions.'

'I suppose you realize you're fairly graceless, Ian. I've seen faces like yours at Young Conservative conferences. Sylvie's right about that.'

'I'm not political. Why should you be?' he adds resentfully.

Her lovely mouth forms into a mocking bud.

'Drive up to Southport to the annual YC marriage mart and you find no end of feckless Davidsons playing charades and the game called "dead beetle". When the wet candidate for YC president appears, the Davidsons wave balloons and stamp their feet to their idea of an acid-house beat, then sneak across to the dry camp discotheque and cheer some more when a baby accountant from Surrey calls for the abolition of child benefit and free education, not to mention lethal injections for murderers. Every time I attend those YC dos I swear never to go again – but when the next year comes round I fear I may be missing the heartbeat of the age. Sidney calls me a Yuppy.'

'What Tribunal of Inquiry?'

'Pardon?'

'You referred earlier – in my office – to a Tribunal of Inquiry.'

'Oh – of course you don't know about that!'

If there's one thing that rouses Davidson's indignation, it's the imputation that he doesn't know something he doesn't know.

'Pyke is conducting some kind of Inquiry into what?'

'And they let you into Cambridge! Sidney's in deep trouble. A real stink. The Media Studies Department resembles Romania the day before they shot Ceaucescu.'

'Holy cow.'

'Oh yes, strikes, boycotts, even violence – Sidney's bike's regularly vandalized by "enragés" and "sans-culottes". Of course I know all the parties involved.' Chantal dabs at her mouth with a paper napkin – and waits.

'What are the charges against Pyke?'

'Rape.'

'Holy mackerel! A professor!'

'And a Green councillor. A nice case of hubris and nemesis.' Chantal glances at the passing trolley. 'Does your new Arab master run to dessert? That chocolate mousse looks eatable.'

'I might join you,' Davidson grunts.

'Not awfully good for your squash.'

He manages a smile of sorts, flattered that Sylvie should have passed on that bit of information. Maybe both sisters are in love with him. Bound to be.

'Clever girl.' He winks like Lait, or tries to.

'Girl? Girl! Do I address you as "boy"?'

'Tell me – do the Pykes have any notion of what you're up to?'

'None at all.'

'What *are* you up to?'

'I'm writing a book, aren't I?'

'What does Samantha make of your, er, relationship with – '

'Well I expect sexual life is rather less complicated up there in Scotland. It's disaster time for poor Samantha – what with Sidney's ongoing crisis and the increasingly vehement attacks on her from Hooper and the Women, not to mention Samantha's own long-planned and now imminent exhibition of female erotic art . . .'

'Good grief.'

'I've been making copies of her floppy disks, by the way – the ones she's used since Swindler fired you.'

'I was moved sideways.'

'You were fired.' Chantal snaps her fingers under his nose. 'And I want forty thousand pounds from Mr Al Sabah.'

'Ha ha. What for?'

'What do you mean ha ha? For *The Sidney Pyke Story* by Chantal Poynter. Damn it, you were offering Sidney one hundred K.'

'I didn't mean it.'

'Tell me – does your daddy know you're a crook?'

Davidson lets this one sink home. He has to.

'Tell *me*, Miss Poynter, why would a young woman like you want to roll in the hay with a senile, self-deluding old ass like Pyke?'

Chantal throws her napkin at him. 'Fuck you! Listen Davidson, with the backing of Sylvie's newspaper I can take this project to any major publisher in London – '

'Except those controlled by Swindler, except those controlled by corporation lawyers sensitive to libel, except those with a lingering sense of decency – '

'Decency! From you!'

Chantal is stung. 'A senile, self-deluding old ass like Pyke.' It might be time to find a nice young man. Twenty minutes after James Loftus-Wright, the 'chaplain', said, 'Please undress me,' he said, 'God I'm sorry.' She'd thought: why apologize to Him? Have you let Him down by not getting it up? She can understand now why secular Sidney's roaring 'Get 'em off!' had appealed to her – and also the knowledge that nothing, not guilt, not drink, not his current crisis, could diminish his seignorial appetite. Chantal can't (quite) get over the frisson of being taken for granted.

What's the matter with me? She studies Davidson, a brash young man double-folded in doubt. Hm.

Davidson is trying to calculate how he can explain to Mr Al Sabah that he's offered forty thousand pounds to a beautiful young woman who's never written a book. Then, with profound relief, he remembers that the best books are invariably written by people who can't write. But Chantal can write. The pages she's shown him are good. That's a problem. No, it's 'no problem'. If Chantal gets too pretentious, too waspish, too infatuated with her own sardonic gifts, he can always turn her rapier prose into ploughshares – made-to-measure, single-sentence paragraphs.

'OK,' he growls, 'one third on signature, one third on *acceptance*, one third on publication.'

'Half on signature, half on delivery.'

Davidson experiences a bad bout of sexual jealousy. 'So what's the form on Tuesdays with these French lessons?'

Her smile slices him. 'Don't worry, it'll all be in the book.' She pauses reverentially, placing herself in the gap between pulpit and prayer. 'He's a brute,' she whispers. 'He even writes Sorbonne graffiti on my buttocks with a felt-tipped pen.'

'He does!'

Chantal leans across the remains of her chocolate mousse. 'I adore armagnac,' she murmurs.

Davidson orders an armagnac and a cognac. Amazing how both the Poynter girls get him drunk while staying sober themselves.

'Frankly,' she sighs, sipping her liqueur, 'Sidney's a monster. Quite horribly depraved. Oh yes. The things he calls me! I simply can't repeat them.'

'For forty thousand – '

'He calls me his "little wannabee".'

'His what?'

'"My little wannabee famous, wannabee rich, wannabee successful, wannabee courted, admired, wannabee recognized in restaurants, parties, theatres, flashy little wine bars. My little wannatake the world as she finds it. Not love ever after for my little wannabee but power and wealth until the candle of infamous youth splutters, dies."'

Davidson's mouth had opened wide enough to serve as a napkin ring.

'Holy smoke. He says all this to you while – '

Chantal nods. 'Normally in the missionary position.'

'He's quite mad, this old – '

'Not at all! Sidney's the most potent man I've ever had. He can even make me cry. No one else can.'

'Cry? You?' Davidson's expression is incredulous.

'Yes. When he says, "Post coitum omnis animal tristis est."'

After a long silence Davidson is forced to ask her what it means.

Chantal gives him a small, pitying pout. 'I'm sure it wouldn't apply to you. Sidney becomes sad when he remembers that the power of his penis has outlasted the power of his pen.'

'It must be a lot of fun being Chantal Poynter,' Davidson says bitterly.

'It's not bad. But women in general still have a hard time. I mean impoverished mothers, abandoned mothers, black women on social security, peasant women in the

Third World, sick women, battered women.' Davidson notes that she is counting her fingers as she runs through the obligatory check list. 'Their lot is grim and awful. Sidney says so.'

'Wait a moment, this doesn't sound like you. Maybe you're in with the lesbian ayatollahs as well?'

'Of course. But Samantha has also taught *me* that life is what you make of it – and that no longer means communes, drugs, squatting, sabotaging flyovers, or poking flowers into soldiers' gun barrels. It no longer means cavorting around Greenham Common with Hooper and Rosen.'

So deeply in agreement are Chantal and Ian Davidson that their noses are almost touching.

'So what does it mean?' he asks, banging the table with excitement. 'It means making money. It means making more money. It fucking means treading on the necks of Sidney Pyke, Samantha Newman and all the other flower children and Che children and Ho Chi Minh children of yesteryear. Yes?'

'Possibly. Do you have a fag?'

He lights her cigarette with an unsteady hand. 'Want to play squash?'

'Are you very good or just good?'

'Just very good.'

'Well not today, dear. I'd like to have your signature on that contract before we play squash.'

Chantal spends the afternoon shopping before catching her train. For Samantha she chooses a huge box of weight-building Turkish Delight from Fortnum's. Only a hundred steps down the road in Hatchard's she finds the complete works of Virginia Woolf for Melanie and Bess. Happily it has emerged that VW was sexually abused as a child. For Sidney something special – it's his story, after all, she's writing. Her crisp footsteps pursue Shaftesbury Avenue until, at the Queen's Theatre, she makes the necessary turning into Wardour Street and Soho.

By which time Davidson has St Paul's below his executive eyeline and Chantal's latest pages on his desk.

### The Sidney Pyke Story, by Chantal Poynter

Jetting across the world in a whirlwind of publicity, Samantha Newman played ducks and drakes with her knickers and told TV audiences that it was fine to burn your bra and equally fine not to burn it. The commercial might intervene between the two halves of that single thought.

Inspired by Samantha's message that cunt-power could defeat the war culture of the death-dealing phallocracy, the sisters sought universal peace by licking, sniffing and feeling each other's orifices.

But while the true believers were attempting her prescribed contortions, stretching in agony to lick their own privates, a feat impossible for vertebrates, Newman herself was nightriding some of the wealthiest male impresarios of the great media honeypot which stretches from Hollywood to Madison Avenue.

Worse, she went on to marry the randiest phallocrat of the Radical racket, Sidney Pyke. Worse still, she was soon gloating in print about their wonderful, sharing, caring nuclear love affair.

And when the children came the only loving, extended hands that received them belonged to hired nannies and au pairs. Having forgotten to shack up with a working-class male and put her cunt where her Marxism was – to quote another memorable Newman nostrum – Samantha had remembered that working-class women are good for cleaning floors and ironing shirts.

Her faithful, tamed husband, meanwhile, stopped burning down universities and devoted his energies to seducing his prettier female pupils . . .

Other meanwhiles . . .

The lesbian legions were meanwhile planning and

163

planting a darker theology of sex. Gathering in secret conventicles, they composed satanic prayers and lit candles for matriarchy. Man – the eternal enemy – was to be phased out. Science would take care of the technical details, the plumbing angle – if in need of a child, apply to the sperm bank. Human society would ascend to the patterns of grazing cattle – many cows and a single, isolated pedigree bull – except that he would do his thing by draining his procreative powers into a test tube.

Some lesbians, having mistaken Samantha Newman for an ally, subsequently embraced the fury of betrayal, the storm that now threatens her family and career.

Yet Newman has never betrayed herself. On inspection, there is nothing to betray. Every sentence and every sentiment found its own denial within her writings, sometimes in the same sentence. Masturbation was great and energizing; masturbation was also a metaphor for helpless passivity. Self-service was the solution, self-service was slumming.

Newman no more betrayed herself than Sidney Pyke betrayed his own ideals. Yesterday's Red, today's Green, no contradiction at all. The consistency lies in the deeper personal project. Just as Pyke once subsumed the tremors of global society, including the Vietnam War, into his own effervescent ego, so Newman, a woman first and last, expropriated the territory between the legs of one hundred billion women. Neither Pyke, Mr or Mrs, has ever stopped telling the human race what to do next.

Prophets are inconstant people. In abruptly changing direction they shrug off thousands of angry followers; after all, the religion is wherever the messiah is. When they lose Asia Minor, they head for Gaul. If the Alps prove impassable, they march their elephants over the Pyrenees. The route is immaterial so long as the divine profile remains at high altitude. The ego

164

will lead its legions anywhere in search of the sun. Every retreat is an advance.

The wailers and backsliders are contemptuously put down. All opposition and criticism is mendacious, hypocritical, 'political'. Critics are always serving some vested interest, invariably sinister, inherently insincere.

Which brings us, without more ado, to Dr Bess Hooper and Ms Melanie Rosen. Are the charges they have brought against Sidney Pyke true? Or should we believe Sidney and Samantha, both of whom insist that she, not he, is the real target of the wild Women?

Sidney has achieved safe exit and entrance through Mauve Gate whenever 'the arrogant bastard [this is Hooper, with megaphone] feels like flaunting his so-called "civil liberties" and "human rights" – Human Rights for Rapists!'

The Yellow Gate ♀ ♀ retaliate by throwing gloop at him. He disdains to duck – a lifelong failing. It sticks, it stains, but it doesn't count as 'malicious damage' (Melanie tells him through the small cell-window of her anorak cowl, her delicate features surprisingly close to his. Indeed, only now does he grasp her reincarnation: Käthe Kollwitz! Melanie has joined Bess as a woodcut in the great Protestant-Humanist lament against the World, the Flesh and the Devil, which runs from Cranach and Dürer to Käthe Kollwitz and Anna Seghers. But neither Melanie nor Bess is familiar with this tradition, which is why he settles for it.)

'Interesting. Thank you.' Sidney scoops up the foulest wad of mud he can find – there's no shortage – and lovingly applies it to Melanie's face. She does not – the approaching Samantha notes – recoil, flinch or scream. Melanie stands as still and acquiescent as an actress having cosmetic clay lovingly applied to her precious skin. ('Spellbound,' Samantha thinks. 'Fuck you, Sidney. Who next?')

All the Women are watching: Yellows, Mauves, the lot.

They are watching Sidney's chin and bits of his beard reaching into Melanie's cowl to kiss the mud on Melanie's nose. Or the nose beneath the mud. They all await the witch's shriek, the howl for vengeance, but nothing much is heard beyond the occasional slurp of Sidney eating his own mud off the nose of Melanie.

All of this is no good at all. Bess Hooper walks slowly forward in her Cruisewatch boots and kicks Sidney's shins. This hurts.

'I'm calling the police,' he tells her.

'It's not kosher, darling.' Samantha intervenes. She's wearing green wellies and a harmonizing point-to-point jacket and a silk scarf tied round her head like the Queen. Most probably she's heading for her new gas-guzzling Range-Rover, but Sidney eating Melanie's nose has diverted her. 'Besides,' she muses, 'it really is time some woman beat you up, Sidney. Go on, Bess, kick him again, once for every woman here who loves and admires my husband. And once more for every woman here who thinks you're really kicking me.' She flashes Bess Hooper her nicest smile. 'Simply because I invented the phrase "post-feminism".'

Hooper says 'Did you?' then walks away to confer with the sisters. After a brief conference she comes back.

'You also invented *!*,' she accuses Samantha. (Sidney hears this *!* as Expletive Exclamation Expletive.)

'Oh that! My little strip-cartoon for Sidney's *Media Studies Bulletin*.'

Bess turns to her platoon. 'You all heard that. The *Bulletin* is Sidney's.'

'He edits it, dear,' Samantha says easily.

Bess is frowning beneath her cowl. '*!* is demeaning to women. Consistently. Its half-naked heroine is a dumb dolly-bird forever discovering the facts of life by making herself available to whatever Top Man happens to be passing.'

'I think it's extremely political and radical.'

'It brazenly perpetuates the image of women as silly, trivial and weak-minded.'

'Oh how humourless your cohorts are.'

'*!* is clearly in breach of the anti-sexist provisions of the NUJ's Code of Conduct. And to call women humourless is simply another chauvinist attack on women.'

'Bye. I have work to do. Sort it out with Sidney.'

Sidney has been hovering on the fringe of the tight, attentive circle of women, Yellows and Mauves. As Samantha vanishes into the house, Gilly Jones tosses him the warmest of smiles, which sends him scuttling upstairs to his study, where he concludes that the dynamic, diachronic dimension of things is impossible. Any 'soixante-huitard' – my god, those impending French radio interviews, and Chantal nowhere to be seen! – would recognize the vital moment when the life of the theatre yields to the theatre of life. And yet, observing the garden scenario from his first-floor window, Sidney finds himself anchored in stasis. He jots the phrase down.

Likewise 'putting one's finger in the dike' – his immediate verdict on seeing Gilly Jones, clearly hyped-up, having a go at the Yellows. Sidney leans out of the window, 'au dessus de la mêlée' – a phrase drilled into him by Chantal, who hasn't been seen since the occupation began.

'This is supposed to be a united women's peace movement, Bess, but you're intent on fucking us all up.'

'That's fucking outrageous,' Hooper says.

Gilly reaches out to touch Bess's arm. 'Sisterhood, Bess.'

'Don't touch me, Gilly, just don't touch me.' Bess turns away but Gilly follows, still plucking at her sleeve.

Melanie screams. 'Don't touch her! You're violating her personal space. I just can't believe this is happening.'

All the Yellow Gate and King's Cross Women are screaming. Gloop flies. Some of it, aimed at Sidney, strikes Samantha's study window.

Samantha descends. Like naughty girls apprehended by the headmistress, the Women drop their gloop and assume pious poses.

'Enough is really enough,' Samantha tells Bess. 'Sidney never laid a finger on you. Why should he need to? I mean you're hardly crêpes en grand Marnier, Dr Hooper. You made it up. To get at me. You don't give a fig about Sidney. It's me you're after.' Samantha picks Melanie out of the crowd. 'Isn't that right, darling? It's *my* new book and *my* art exhibition that you're determined to rubbish. D'accord?'

Melanie's eyes, white marbles a moment ago, now resemble roasted chestnuts.

(Sidney is not at ease with the rising paramountcy, to employ a colonial term he's attached to, of the noun. To rubbish, to critique, to foreground, to finesse, ugh. Ugh! And just as the sensitive verb has yielded to the brute force of the noun, so also the supple adjectival adverb has opened its orifices to hard little pushy hybrid prepositions: one-man, up-front, one-off, on-air . . .)

In the mud pond beneath his window Bess Hooper is making her last stand.

'You may not know the truth,' she concedes to Samantha. 'Don't forget the policewoman who was married for seven years to the notorious Putney rapist and never knew.'

'But she wasn't married to Sidney,' Samantha drawls. 'If she was married to Sidney, she would know. She would know everything all the time. Believe me, it's quite tiring.'

Sidney, whose head still protrudes from his study window, is stung by his wife's words. They rouse the animal cunning in the man, the predatory prospects of prowling his own garden by night, seizing his prey, deaf to entreaties, foreign to compassion. He will have them all: Hooper, Melanie, the entire King's Cross collective – he will rape any woman who accuses him of being a rapist. Groucho as well as macho.

But Samantha swiftly brings down the curtain on the scheduled rape-in.

'Now, Sisters, the game is over and I've had enough. Get out of my garden and stay out. Mauves are invited to tea.'

By last light the fierce Yellows have gone. The Mauve Gate Women, meanwhile, celebrate their 'victory' by moving into the house, by cooking Sidney cordon mauve meals to atone for his ordeal, by drinking lots of his wine, and by borrowing Samantha's TV costumes. Vaguely hoping to find the one who calls herself Pat, Pam or Veronica in the warm laundry room, where the girls have been hanging up their steaming battle fatigues, Sidney stumbles across Gilly Jones in her underclothes.

'Why, Sidney! You mustn't look!'

He upends her with the utmost brutality, in and out in under a minute.

'For old times' sake,' he tells her.

'You bastard,' she moans happily.

'Care to bring charges?'

'Oh dear,' Samantha says, arriving in the laundry room with her inspired sense of timing, 'what a bad bear you are, Sidney.'

# *Thirteen*

'What the hell is this?' Chantal asks, indicating a framed picture hanging in the front hall.

'Who knows?' Sidney grunts. 'It appears to be a Blitz photo taken from inside a darkened tube tunnel and showing tightly packed rows of children asleep on the platform. Samantha's planning some bloody exhibition of "female erotic art".'

'Erotic!' Chantal laughs, leading Sidney upstairs and showing him the gift she has carefully chosen in a Soho theatrical-costume shop after tying up a contract with Ian Davidson and purchasing Turkish Delight for Samantha and Virginia Woolf for Melanie and Bess.

She has heard Sidney reminisce often enough about some old '60s show called *Marat/Sade* to anticipate the pleasure that the radical tribune Marat would derive from being whipped to death in his bath by the hand of a blue-stockinged Charlotte Corday. In Soho you can find more or less anything.

The bathroom of Cuba is soon full of steam and hoarse, exultant cries.


A day later and here is Davidson, 'working out' at lunch-time in the Barbican Health Clinic, surrounded by gleaming chrome bars, pulleys and gorgeous girl athletes in tiger and zebra leotards – one of them being Chantal Poynter. Grinding his limbs, pumping iron, pushing himself through the anaerobic pain barrier on a mainly carbohydrate diet, Davidson realizes that he is being deliberately humiliated by Mr Al Sabah because he – Davidson – is a Christian (though he isn't anything).

Getting the ear of Mr Al Sabah Al Masri Al Fatah is a problem. So many aides, secretaries, social secretaries, bodyguards, servants, swamijis surround him. Entourages, constellations, holy men, dogs. Davidson is not convinced that he has been accorded the respect and the access due to the Managing Director of the Wellington Press. With the rich and the powerful, access is the key. With the very rich and very powerful, it is the very key.

The Swamiji is about as far as Davidson normally gets. He is quite helpful or, as the Swamiji himself puts it, 'quite confidential'. 'You and me, confidential friends,' he telephones to say. Evidently Mr Al Sabah Al Masri Al Fatah is currently (and confidentially) busy having his short legs fitted under the dinner table at 10, Downing Street, where he is wallpapering the lounge in £100 notes, and from which he periodically walks backwards, head inclined, turban doffed, his purpose achieved – suppression of a Trade and Industry report into his fraudulent acquisition of the United Kingdom.

Chantal, clad in a psychedelic leotard with black tights, is completing her routine fifteen minutes on a Tunturi Ergometer W3 exercise bike. Beside her the Flying Scotsman labours at his rowing machine, stroking a winning Cambridge crew from Putney to Mortlake, thus conquering Chantal's heart and converting her infuriating resistance into moaning submission. Davidson's fever rises as Chantal stretches her gorgeous, supple limbs from one futuristic chrome contraption to the next, but the girl's mind is firmly focused on her next piece for Sylvie's weekly 'Living' page:

So the royal fitness secrets are out. Diana's passion is jazz dancing and tennis, while hubby does daily Canadian Air Force exercises in between breaking the necks of architects. But which of them will take part in next year's London Marathon (it couldn't really be Fergie, could it)? Or might Olympian Auntie Anne come off her high horse and trot from Greenwich to the Tower for Save the Children?

If so, the commercial sponsors will be fighting to cover every inch of royal flesh with their logos and brand-names. Does a princess lose her amateur status if she wears Puma across her thirty-eight-inch chest?

By the way, don't let the Health Ayatollahs tell you how to look. Everywoman's Running Guide urges you to pin to your training chart a photo of yourself at your fattest, spottiest and generally most hideous. Watch out for that old sexist agenda: a fit man is how he feels, a fit woman is how she looks.

Balls to that.

Done. Hard at it on the rowing machine, her shoulders pleasantly gleaming through the string straps of her new Berlin Wall workout vest, Chantal turns her attention to Samantha. The evidence of stolen floppy disks and mauve pages indicates that *Nature or Nurture* is again picking up steam and style, thriving on adversity. The invasion of her garden seems to have galvanized Samantha. All quite worrying.

Chantal finds Samantha gallantly bent over her devastated garden, naturing and nurturing the survivors, binding, bandaging and generally badgering them back to health. The famous author carries a traditional vegetable basket on her arm, from which dead and irreparably maimed friends will soon be laid to rest on the (organic) compost heap.

Chantal notes Samantha's really big, voluminous skirt, and a charming rainhat. She concludes that while the hat is voluntary the skirt belongs to force majeure.

'Ah,' Samantha drawls, ' a fair-weather friend.'

'I adore your skirt, Samantha.'

'Hm? Do tell me where I bought it – and when.'

Chantal takes this with the sweetest of smiles – only the queen bee carries a licence to sting.

'I think your figure is just wonderful,' she says. 'Here – I've brought you some Turkish Delight.'

'My dear child, you know I can't resist the stuff. Hm. Mmmm! There goes my "wonderful figure" – I'm sure you never thought of that.'

'And you're so incredibly versatile,' Chantal sighs. 'How on earth do you do it all?'

'Darling, that's the kind of question that matrons with four children ask. Not your kind of question at all.'

'Oh do tell me about "Eye Contact"! Will it be a great success? I really do feel that an exhibition of female erotic art is most urgently needed.'

'You do? Of course we'll be massacred. Criticism today is simply the revenge of mediocrity against talent.'

Chantal dutifully writes this in her notebook. A notebook does help, tremendously, with Samantha's temper.

Chantal decides not to tell Samantha about the recent women-only cycling picnic in the Charlebury hills – not unless Samantha shows signs of knowing about it. The picnic was to celebrate Bess's victory over Sidney in the Staff–Student Council elections. Melanie's bony blue hand held Chantal's from Bradbury Rings to the Roman fort.

'We intend to destroy Newman's exhibition,' she whispered, the hot tip of her tongue lubricating Chantal's ear.

'Gosh – how?'

'By semiotics and deconstruction.'

Melanie always made these sound like witchcraft.

Chantal is studying Samantha: 'What are semiotics and deconstruction, Samantha?'

'Heavens, child! Ask Sidney.'

Chantal is on the verge of citing Melanie but notices a stalk trapped between the blades of Samantha's secateurs, like an eel in a puffin's beak.

'How's Sidney?' she asks.

'Isn't that the question *I'm* supposed to ask *you*? I have no idea how he is. Never have had. He rogered Gilly Jones,

173

by the way, in the laundry room. I let them off, of course. One does. But Gilly looked frightfully disappointed later. I tried to commiserate with her. "Darling," I said, "the engine no longer fires on all cylinders. Never again that engorging rush of spermatozoa which once made him mate to Shakespeare's Sonnet CXXIX." I'm not sure that Gilly knows her Shakespeare. You do, of course. What was your question? Oh yes. "How's Sidney?" which means "Where's Sidney?" Sidney's in town seeing his lawyers. About this ridiculous Inquiry. It sounds so good in the plural, doesn't it – talking to one's bankers or consulting one's doctors.'

'I've got awfully bad news about Sidney,' Chantal says.

Samantha straightens up from her ruined sunflowers: 'Don't tell me, let me guess. He passed a well-filled miniskirt in the street and hurt his neck? I always try to remind him nowadays: "Sidney, dear, at your age you really must turn your whole body." Hm . . .? Not that? Don't tell me he's run away to Australia with Hooper? I suppose you would be the first to know, dear, having as many feet as there are camps.'

Chantal experiences a moment's doubt. Does Samantha know, like the heroine Tina in *Woman Awakened*, 'more than she should'? Has she discovered that Chantal is poised to make her fortune with *The Sidney Pyke Story*? Or is it merely Chantal's convenient absence during the recent Battle of the Garden that rankles?

'Sidney isn't with any lawyers,' Chantal says.

'I sometimes feel, Chantal, that you're one little mistress too many. And not good for Sidney.'

'Oh, Samantha, what a horrible word!'

'"Mistress"? My dear, mistresses enjoy real power and loot, whereas the lot of a modern lover – or partner, ugh! – is a laconic lament. One would hardly call Madame de Pompadour the "partner" of Louis XV.'

'I thought you were just being nasty.'

'I was *trying*. Not awfully good at it.'

Following Samantha from the garden into the kitchen, Chantal has tucked a little frown into her seamless brow.

'I don't think it would help your book if Sidney burst into print, Samantha.'

'About what? Sidney may well burst at some point below the Equator line, but into print burst he will most definitely not.' She smashes the handsome copper kettle on to the stove and lights the gas with a roar. '"How I Drove the Witches from My Garden", by Sidney Pyke.'

'About your . . . marriage.'

'My dear, male intellectuals do not notice their marriages, let alone write about them.' Samantha is hurling tea cups at saucers. 'Sidney has never, never, acknowledged my existence in print. It's a matter of male honour, you see. One doesn't mention the wife. One doesn't have one. Ha!'

'But now they've offered him pots of money to come clean about everything.'

'Everything? What's everything?'

'Well . . . you . . . Bess Hooper . . . Melanie . . . me . . . all the others . . . oh it's horrible! They want his version of the whole story.'

'A newspaper, you mean? How do you know so much?'

'Oh Samantha, don't ask me that but I swear, I really do . . . I just hope all this won't hurt your book for Vampire.'

Samantha suddenly looks defeated. As if the relapse had been biding its time, in her liver, waiting. But she won't express her defeat to this creature. And Chantal isn't quite satisfied.

'Oh, Samantha, there's something else you ought to know.'

'Don't tell me you're preggers!'

Actually, Chantal hasn't thought of that. But it sounds just the job. Trust Samantha.

'The awful thing is,' Chantal sobs, 'I'm so happy! Not only for the baby – and myself – but for Sidney as well.'

'For Sidney!'

'Is that ridiculous? I know how he loves children!'

Crows' feet surface round Samantha's drawn mouth. 'Loves them? If Emma or Robert ever enjoyed five minutes of their father's undivided attention, it's news to me – and to them. No doubt that's why one married a New Zealand sheep farmer and the other is in and out of loony bins.'

'Oh Samantha . . . I'm so sorry. I didn't know.'

'Sidney never speaks of his children. They were a considerable disappointment to him. Anyway, what makes you think the baby's Sidney's?'

'Samantha! There is no one else!'

Samantha digs into her bag for her diary. 'I know a very good man at University College Hospital. He did me lots of times. I just hate those coil things and the pill destroys one's entire character, doesn't it.'

She scribbles the name on to a pad, then pours scalding water out of the copper kettle into a flowery teapot from Uzbekistan.

Chantal gives abortion the statutory twenty seconds' reflection. 'Oh, I don't think I could!'

Samantha holds the Uzbek pot in one hand, its lid in the other. 'Couldn't what, Chantal?'

'Murder my child!'

'Murder!'

'Oh yes. That's what I believe.'

'But you're not a Catholic!'

'Well I am. I mean my mother had us baptized and confirmed. I've been to mass more often than I've been to Paris.'

'Heavens, girl, surely you lapsed like everyone else?'

'I thought I did. I mean I suppose I believe in God but not all the time. Really more on special occasions. Being pregnant is a special occasion, isn't it?'

'But a woman has the right to control her own body!'

'Oh yes. I agree.'

'Which means you must get rid of it, sensibly and safely – without delay.'

Chantal is now weeping copiously. She looks (she hopes) a mess. She has a train to catch.

Sidney will be talking to his editors.

Neurotically early for appointments, he has killed time

by visiting a Turkish barber off Charlotte Street who regularly briefs him on human-rights violations in Cyprus. Each delicate sweep of the razor brings another atrocity.

Oiled and perfumed, Sidney makes his way by taxi to Wapping where hi-tech national newspapers now loom over the Thames in bullying façades of green glass, the whole conceit crowned in the standard post-modernist pediment, challenging the Prince and the bemused waters below to deny its classical provenance. Not many years ago – how many? memory going again – Sidney took himself on Saturday nights past Tower Bridge to the bleak streets where phalanxes of incensed printers raged against mass dismissal. The classic confrontation between the bosses and the unionized working class was played out beneath faceless warehouse walls, their windows long ago bricked-in. Rocks and ball bearings hammered against the 'scab' delivery vans running the gauntlet of the picket lines under police escort. Sidney knew that a man must do what a man must do. Solidarity did not begin in Poland.

Clubbed senseless in Paris and Chicago, great days – but to be confronted in London twenty years later by police brutality on this scale – the mounted charges, the flailing batons, the sadistic pursuit of those who fled, the rabid gangsterism of the beatings: he was shocked. He'd always claimed that Britain was no better than anywhere else, but obviously his subconscious had believed otherwise. It was to be Sidney's last stand under the Red Flag.

Arriving early, Sidney finds himself in the white stone church of St George-in-the-East, raised by Nicholas Hawksmoor almost three centuries ago, blitzed to ruin in May 1941, and now raised again. Recalling the almost religious awe evoked by Grotowski's production of *Acropolis* in the restored crypt – did he take Samantha on that occasion, or the chick from the Arts lab? – Sidney lights a votive candle and places 10p in the wall safe – make it 50p.

Still early, he ambles down Artichoke Hill to the prettified tourist arcade known as Tobacco Dock, with its fancy trellises, craft shops and walk-on schooners at anchor;

Enterprise Zones are clearly dedicated to the destruction of history by heart-massaging olde tymes.

And here I am, he reflects, scanned by electronic screens, reporting at the gatehouse, reeking of Turkish pomade, prefacing my name with 'Professor', the politest of traitors. At a certain juncture, evidently, a man ceases to do what a man must do.

Sidney is conducted through a vast, windowless fortress in whose strip-lit bowels rows of journalists are arranged in front of direct-input word processors which feed computerized typesetting machines and automated presses. Dressed in uniform white shirts, with ties, these young journalists remind him of foreign-exchange dealers in the City. Shocking. Junk-bond merchants.

On principle he never reads Sunday newspapers – except on Mondays, in the Senior Common Room. Samantha buys all the Sunday papers and deliberately leaves them lying about, each one dismantled into its separate sections, sensational headlines and sexy supplements beckoning his attention like uninvited guests determined to stay for every meal. Samantha wouldn't dream of saying so, but the Sunday newspapers do tend to contain articles by, or about, herself – rather than by or about Sidney.

The rather attractive young woman who is waiting for Sidney as he emerges from the lift uncannily resembles Chantal. He wonders what she's doing for dinner.

'I'm Sylvie Poynter.'

Sidney instantly forgets her second name. He subscribes to a general understanding within his own generation, that young people, like butlers, children and dogs, have only one name. He follows Sylvie – nice rear view – to the office of the Features Editor, who rises respectfully.

'You probably don't remember me. Jack Gillespie. I was a pupil of yours twelve years ago.'

'Forgive me, I – ' Sidney has already forgotten both of Features' names.

'Obviously you've met Sylvie.'

'Who? Ah, yes – '

'And you know her sister Chantal.'

'Chantal?'

'She's standing behind you. She'll be ghosting your autobiography.'

As Sidney turns his slow turn, Chantal's soft cheek touches his.

'You've met Ian Davidson too, I believe,' Features continues with his introductions.

Sidney vaguely recognizes the dour young man in the good suit who offers his hand.

'I shall be publishing the book,' Davidson explains with slow deliberation, each word enunciated as if for a mental defective. Sidney is glad to play the part.

'Really? What book?'

'*The Sidney Pyke Story* by Sidney Pyke and Chantal Poynter twelve pounds ninety-five.'

'Isn't it wonderful?' Chantal says. 'Does all this surprise you, Sidney?'

'Not one bit,' Sidney lies, having guessed that to be surprised by anything in this company involves fatal loss of face. 'In mature middle age one learns not to be surprised by surprises – one shoves them back into the revolving drum of random probability, from which they duly emerge as immaculate predictabilities. Like, for example, finding oneself reincarnated as Sidney Pyke and Chantal Poynter.'

'It was just an idea, Sidney,' Chantal says hastily. 'I don't at all mind doing the work while you take the credit.'

Noting with anger the bored expressions of his young companions, he lights his pipe. Sylvie grimaces and recoils. His eye is gradually coming to terms with batteries of silently winking telephones, bleeping computer screens, fax machines and other hardware suggestive of the command console of a nuclear submarine. Not a scrap of paper in sight. Indeed what is perched on Sylvie's engaging knee appears to be a very miniature tape recorder. (Sidney is no fool.)

(But he is. Their game – to tie him up contractually, morally and generally, while Chantal sets about destroying

179

his reputation in a book entirely her own – this he cannot guess. Probably he never will. The crocodile is creeping up behind our hero and all we can do to help him is to shout. Shout now!)

'Brandy? coffee? whisky?' Features asks him.

'That of course was Marx's great world-trick,' Sidney continues, 'the claim that everything that happened was inscribed on the undeciphered wax tablet of History.'

'Is that your image or Marx's?' Sylvie asks.

'Yes, I'll have a brandy,' Sidney tells Features, ignoring her. 'As a matter of fact, I couldn't help remembering, outside in the streets of Wapping, the picket lines.'

'Before my time,' Features says.

'Thank God that's all over,' Sylvie says.

'I stood with the printers,' Sidney announces. 'Week after week.'

This news produces expressions of polite disdain. Davidson, for whom Pyke is of no account beyond his capacity to dish his wife and Hans-Dietrich Swindler, making the Wellington Press a tidy profit in the process, digs his fists deep into the pockets of his Next trousers.

'For years the printers held all the great newspapers to ransom,' he tells Sidney. 'The proprietors grovelled and begged for the privilege of getting their papers to the public.'

Part of Sidney recognizes the truth of this, but truth demands a legitimate voice. 'Balls,' he says, draining his cognac. 'So who owns your bodies and souls this week?'

'Al Sabah,' Features says. 'We all pray five times a day. Mecca lies at 129 degrees from Wapping. You point your head at that potted cactus.'

'Never heard of him,' Sidney says.

Davidson looks sullen. 'Mr Al Sabah is merely the second wealthiest media proprietor in the world. He also employs me to run the Wellington Press.'

'Never heard of it,' Sidney repeats himself.

Features refills Sidney's glass while Davidson presents him with two copies of a book contract, inviting him to sign the last page. Sidney ignores it.

'So how are the rape charges against you?' Sylvie inquires cheerfully, pouring everyone freshly brewed coffee in real china cups. 'What really happened in the Benzin Swimming Pool? We all long to know.'

Sidney studies Chantal, who is shyly perched on the edge of Features' desk; beyond her, as if set up by Joseph Losey, is a vast open-plan office full of reflecting surfaces and bounded by big, plate-glass windows with a daytime view (Sidney guesses) commanding the river. The heat is oppressive; Sidney removes his Marks & Spencer green anorak, then his Harris tweed jacket with its carefully worn leather elbow patches, then his Shetland pullover.

'Chantal thinks you're innocent,' Sylvie says. The word sounds faintly demeaning. This is clearly not the place to be innocent.

'Sidney had no idea that Bess Hooper was still in the pool,' Chantal says loyally.

'Really?' Sylvie lights a cigarette. 'And are we really to believe that Hooper was lurking in the slow, turquoise coils of the deep end, waiting to mug her victim?'

'Our readers would very much like to hear your side of the story,' Features affably assures Sidney. 'May I be perfectly frank? Our main rival has bought first-serial rights in your wife's book. We need a come-back.'

'You expect me to cut my wife's throat?'

'A confidential source inside Vampire Books assures us that she's now intent on cutting yours.'

Sidney experiences a sharp depression.

'And we admire your work,' Sylvie adds.

His depression deepens. 'Oh yes? Name me one book I've written.'

Sylvie turns to Chantal. 'My God, he certainly doesn't make things easy, does he?'

'Why should he? – he's a mensch. He once raised the Pentagon two feet off the ground with an incense stick and a Ginsberg mantra. And he regards us all by a single name: Yuppy. Only our breasts and bums are identifiably human.'

Et tu . . .? But Chantal is smiling affectionately at him

181

and he knows that she would say as much when lying beside him on the futon, their bodies coiled in the comforting silence of a Samantha-free Cuba.

'Explain to us,' Sylvie asks, 'why you appointed Bess Hooper in the first place.'

'She sounded like the cutting edge of the Zeitgeist.'

'And is that why you took her out to dinner after the interview?'

Sidney does not ask her how she knows. 'I try to form a portrait of a person in depth – that is to say, in the totality of their – '

'Can we avoid words like that?' Davidson says. 'Big money, short words.'

'Did you find Hooper attractive – as a woman?' Sylvie asks.

'An energized intelligence and a passionate commitment tend to be attractive,' Sidney says.

'Did you invite Hooper to spend the night with you in the Crown Hotel after the tête-à-tête?'

Sidney studies Chantal. 'I see you've been talking to Hooper.'

'To Melanie. She claims that you promised Hooper the job if she slept with you.'

'You believe that?'

Sylvie cuts in. 'No. Just inviting your comment.'

The neon strip-lighting is oppressive. Headache. 'You want me to write an autobiography – I thought. I didn't come to this slab of concrete for an interrogation.' The youngsters look chastened but tenacious. He sighs. 'Bess took the night train back to London and she got the job. That's my comment.'

'Try again,' Sylvie snaps.

What follows between Chantal and Sylvie is an energetic exchange in colloquial French, impossible to follow for a man who has not only drunk too much but has not yet mastered Cassette 1 of the BBC series, 'France Encore', and who is unaware that his French publishers have cancelled

182

his projected visit to Paris following threats from the ultra-radical group, Les Pétroleuses, to burn both book and author. Sidney doesn't know this because his French publishers haven't informed him. They haven't informed him because they have just been acquired by Hans-Dietrich Swindler and promptly closed down.

Sylvie is walking round his chair – legs identical to Chantal's. 'Tell me, Sidney, would you say that your fame works as an aphrodisiac on younger women?'

'Fame?' Sidney snorts. 'Are you confusing me with my wife?'

'No,' Davidson says gloomily.

'Perhaps "reputation" is what I meant,' Sylvie says. 'Chantal, you must tell us what attracted you to him.'

'That's easy,' Sidney cuts in prophylactically. 'Bad breath, yellowing teeth, '70s sideburns and a stomach worthy of a Rowlandson wheelbarrow.'

'You enjoy power, don't you?' Sylvie asks. 'And women do tend to take men at their own valuation – whereas we measure ourselves by your valuation.'

'The language of the market isn't mine.'

'Men are what they do, women are what they are? Correct?'

'Not in my book.'

Chantal refills Sidney's glass. 'Are we being utterly horrible to you, darling?'

'The intention is merely to fill in a few gaps in our knowledge,' Features says.

Chantal is flipping the pages of her notebook. 'Melanie quoted me some lines from Emily Dickinson. "He put the Belt around my Life/I heard the Buckle snap/And turned away, imperial/My Lifetime folding up."'

'Self-pity makes poor poetry,' Sidney says. '"He stuns you by degrees." That's also Emily Dickinson – quite a nice pun on a professor's relationship with his pupil?'

Chantal yields a flicker of annoyance. 'Melanie told me you made her feel that the attention you bestowed on her was a unique gift, reserved for her alone.'

'You do rather sleep around, don't you?' Sylvie says.

Sidney snorts. 'I have more respect for the language.'

'How many pupils have you laid?' Sylvie asks.

'The notches are on the leg of my desk.'

'I do wish you'd be serious, Professor Pyke,' Davidson says.

'And all of this will no doubt emerge as if it was my own confession, freely offered, without prompting?'

'I – '

'Sidney,' Chantal cuts in quickly, 'you once told me that in the days of your youth you felt a strong sense of personal destiny – of making history. Then it ebbed away, the newspapers were full of younger faces, new names – and you discovered that you were just going through the motions of life.'

'True.'

'That won't sell any copies,' Sylvie says.

'Who's writing this fucking story?' Chantal says.

'Yes, shut up, Sylvie,' Features says. 'Sidney, could it be said that you've sought compensation for your, er, sense of disappointment by screw – , er, by having younger women? Some sort of revenge on youth in general?'

Watching the tiny red light glowing in the miniature tape recorder, Sidney makes as if to reply – not unlike the scrum half who dummies a pass out of the ruck to put the opposition off-side. The image fades; Jones would chuckle but only one side is now permanently off-side.

'Yes, revenge,' Sidney confirms. 'I'm a Platonist at heart. The Idea is compelling, the practice less so.'

'And would you say,' Sylvie asks in a tone of studied neutrality, 'that nowadays the penis speaks louder than the pen?'

He nods. 'Omnis animal . . . et cetera.'

'Latin now!' Clearly she does not like Pyke.

'Post coitum omnis animal tristis est,' Chantal completes the quotation. 'It's not unlike post-natal depression, I suppose.'

'Jesus,' mutters Davidson.

'He's not a nut, Ian,' Chantal rebukes him. 'He happens to be a man of quite extraordinary talent.'

'That's agreed,' Features says. 'And a brilliant teacher, if I may say so. I've never forgotten your course on "Media Monopolies".'

But Sylvie's hostility refuses to lie down. Chantal knows its source. 'One hears,' Sylvie acidly addresses Sidney, 'that you like to play bedroom games.'

Sidney looks at Chantal. 'No doubt you'd sell your own Jewish grandma to the Gestapo for a byline on page ten of *Nazi News*. Where do I pee?' he asks Features.

Features politely accompanies him, carrying courtesy to the point of peeing alongside, which Sidney could do without, his bladder tending to take its time. Returning (finally), he addresses everyone and no one.

'Things can only get worse before they get worse still. Yes, yes, I'm easily bored, irredeemably a child of the '60s, essentially theatrical, not very serious, playful if you like, and much drawn to alternative identities.'

'A masochist?' Sylvie suggests.

Sidney appraises her. 'What does that mean?' Receiving no answer, he feels happier. 'Genuine masochists are rare. Most of us are really sadists wrapped in guilt. Quite lightly wrapped.'

'But what do you feel guilty about?' Davidson asks cannily, as Sylvie makes an exasperated exit.

'About? The most abused word in the language. One *is* guilty – ontology of existence.'

'Aye, but – '

'Things are too easy,' Sidney continues. 'Talk to Malraux about that.'

'Isn't he dead?' Features objects. 'When I was in your class you told us he was dead.'

'An author "dead"? Is the habit of reading beyond the horizon of the Wapping newspaper world? If so, try an acid trip. It solved most of our ontological problems.'

'Didn't your first wife die of an overdose?' Davidson asks.

'Certainly. It's no secret.' Sidney now deigns to pick up Davidson's contract but the small print of the clauses makes no sense at all. 'Where do you come into all this?' he asks Chantal.

'Well, we like the "as told to" formula,' Davidson says hurriedly. 'You tell the story, she writes it.'

'Hm. I believe I can lift a pen.'

'It's entirely in your own interest,' Davidson says.

'What about the money side?' Sidney grunts.

Davidson politely turns the pages of the contract and shows him the relevant clause. 'That's a generous advance, Professor Pyke.'

'If it were, you wouldn't have made it. Not on the first throw.' A belch escapes. 'Double it.'

Features and Davidson exchange glances.

'And tell this Al Sabah that I want to speak to him,' Sidney adds. 'Tell him – ' (the first hiccup), 'tell him, he should come and inspect my wife's art exhibition.'

A stunned silence.

'"Eye Contact". Hugely significant stuff. It litters my house.' Sidney begins to struggle back into his Shetland jersey and his Harris tweed jacket, hiccuping.

'What are you doing for dinner?' he growls at Chantal.

'Oh damn it, Sidney darling, Sylvie simply won't let me out of here until I've written my piece for her. My sister's a tyrant.'

'Sister?' Sulking, he feigns ignorance of what he's recently been told.

They all escort him to the post-modernist lift. The two young men cordially shake his hand. A taxi will be waiting for him below. As the lift doors close, Chantal blows him a kiss and Sidney observes Davidson's arm enfolding her waist. The reader must decide whether Sidney has pocketed the book contract or not.

As the taxi carries him away through dark, deserted urban corridors, he hears the printers' rocks and ball bearings battering the doors and windows, the final storm of hot metal and cockney craft. He shrinks into himself.

# *Fourteen*

Samantha isn't talking to Sidney so he decides to complain about the obscene 'Eye Contact' paintings littering the hallway and upstairs corridors. He has just stumbled across a new one on the landing: it seems to be a blow-up photo of a long container truck entering a tunnel in what he strongly suspects is the Italian Alps.

'I see Luigi is back,' he says.

Hard at work on her IBM Fastrite, she does not deign to turn her head.

'It's high time I recognized that I'm married to an ageing, ridiculous, philandering rapist.'

'What's that got to do with the pictures?'

'It's perfectly obvious that you raped poor Bess. And Melanie too. In fact I had a little chat with Melanie yesterday. Quite like old times. A woman can tell when a woman's telling the truth.'

'It doesn't happen often.'

'I've suspected it for weeks, of course. And Chantal will *kindly* not cross the threshold of this house again. Perhaps French lessons, haha ha ha ha, haha, can be conducted in future in the deep end of the Benzin Swimming Pool.'

Sidney grins. 'When Beatrix made a similar speech to Benedict, he knew she loved him.'

Samantha identifies this as the ultimate test of strength.

'I'm not aware that Beatrix accused Benedict of making a fool of himself in the Benzin Swimming Pool. Nor am I aware that your shabby secrets have received the attention

187

of a Shakespeare or a Berlioz. My dear Sidney, what you do – even something as pathetically comic as removing Gilly Jones's knickers in the laundry room – leaves me utterly indifferent. The only question for me is whether my career can survive what I must laughingly call my marriage. Clearly, it can't. My solicitor agrees.'

Sidney is stung. 'Tax,' he says automatically.

'What?'

'Hate to mention it yet again, but you still owe me the forty per cent tax I paid on your income last year.'

'Really? Shall I write you a cheque now?'

'Yes.'

'Find my chequebook!'

'It's lying in front of you.'

'That's an old one. All used up on supporting a feckless husband whose income is less than a quarter of my own. No, I insist. If money means so much to you, find my chequebook.'

'No hurry at all.'

'Talking of hurries, Sidney – Chantal is proudly carrying your baby. And intends to have it. And to marry you. And kindly use the spare room.'


Jones insists on 'representing' Sidney at the Inquiry. It's almost thirty years since Jones failed five out of six first-year law exams but the dream of advocacy persists. He reads the law reports even before he loses himself in the sports pages.

'Always wanted to win a hopeless case,' he confides to Sidney in the Fox & Goose. 'Basically, old man, the tactic is this: we put them into bat on a sticky wicket and bowl to a length. Let the occasional one turn from the back of the hand.'

'What's your fee for that kind of advice?'

'One bottle of malt whisky per diem. That should cost you a crate or two.' Jones lays his non-drinking hand on Sidney's sleeve. 'This isn't limited-over stuff, Sidney. We may have to dig in at the crease. I don't want you swinging your bat at every bouncer.'

'Hm.'

'Now what about Samantha?'

'Keep her out of it.'

'I recall she appeared as a witness in a road-accident case at the Crown Court. When was it? Last year?'

'God knows. Probably after the scandal of Somalian female circumcision and possibly before the scandal of Indian child marriage in Bradford . . .'

'The gal simply swept the jury off its feet. The evidence all pointed in one direction, your missus pointed in the other. The evidence stood no chance.'

'Perhaps you ought to know that my "missus" wants a divorce.'

'Really? Who from?'

'Am I speaking to the greatest defence counsel since Marshall Hall?'

'Good grief. From you? Why?'

'Because I'm writing my autobiography.'

'Not before the Tribunal reaches its verdict, I hope. I'm sure Samantha feels the same.'

'You've never understood women, have you?'

'I've understood them well enough to steer clear of them.'


The Chairman of the Governors has summoned the Vice-Chancellor and the Registrar to a secret conference at the Athenaeum, or maybe the Reform Club – but once again not the vegetarian soup kitchen of the ICA. Secrecy is dear to all of them. Separately alighting from taxis in Pall Mall, each stiffly swivels a thickening neck at the prospect of a student picket line, or a mob of loony women, or Sidney Pyke, gathered on the club's imposing steps. But no alien presence disturbs the normal atmosphere of sleepy exclusivity.

Over lobster soup and a not-bad bottle of St Julien –

still a bit chilly, perhaps – the Chairman unveils his coup d'état: the Inquiry will be held not within the university, a perilous place, but within the boardroom of the Benzin Oil Company, whose guard dogs have been trained to identify a student as reliably as an Afrikaaner alsatian knows a kaffir.

'What if they refuse?' the Registrar says.

'Hm?'

'Either side, Pyke or the women, or both, might refuse to attend an off-campus inquiry.'

The Chairman keeps forgetting that the university is a hotbed of refusal. No employee of the Benzin Oil Company ever refuses. Refuseniks are all very commendable in the Soviet Union but serve no purpose at all locally.

'Will they,' he asks the Registrar sharply, 'refuse?'

'Pyke will go through the motions of a protest but will be secretly relieved. All current student demos are anti-Pyke and anti-men.'

'Anti-what!'

'Anti-men, Chairman.'

'I'm sorry. Please explain. How can anyone be "anti-men"?'

'In fairness, we're sitting in a men-only club,' the V-C murmurs.

'Well? I don't see how that's "anti-men".'

'It isn't.'

'So what's your point?'

'It's anti-women.'

'Not officially. We have ladies' evenings. To exclude women from membership isn't "anti-women". Heaven knows, they wouldn't enjoy themselves in an all-male club.'

'If they were eligible for membership, it wouldn't be an all-male club, Chairman.'

'My dear Robert, you sound like a Beirut kidnap victim who's just been released after a year's incarceration by Muslim fanatics.'

'I'm not aware that Muslim fanatics are pressing for the

admission of women to this club,' the V-C says, offended. 'Nor, of course, am I.'

'A Muslim? Glad to hear it. So what's your point?'

'Merely that my life is currently haunted, plagued, by women who are anti-men. And so is Sidney Pyke's – though in his case they are anti-Sidney as well. And – therefore – Pyke – may – welcome – an inquiry – held off-campus.'

'Thank you, Robert. I'm not an idiot. And what about that woman – Hopkins?'

'Hooper. Actually, it's now Hooper and Rosen.'

'Another woman?'

'A graduate student of Pyke's. Possibly an ex-mistress as well.'

'You mean he . . . this girl . . .'

'Possibly. She's now Hooper's lover.'

'Wait a minute. First she was in the sack with Pyke, now with this woman Hopkins?'

'Hooper.'

'The Head of our Media Studies Department has raped two women? When does he find time to teach?'

'Pyke denies it.'

'That he finds time to teach?'

'He denies the charges, Chairman.'

'You mean he claims they said No when they meant Yes? It happens all the time. Even so, once might be bad luck but twice – '

'Pyke's position, I must admit, is obscure to me.'

'To all of us,' adds the Registrar. 'Even to Jones, who insists on representing him. Pyke believes it's all to do with some kind of argument about children's books, a strip-cartoon, a person called Olive Schreiner, and, as he puts it, the "Zeitgeist". He also throws his wife into the pot.'

The Chairman chuckles. 'I wonder what la belle Samantha makes of it all. Of course she's quite a girl. I sometimes catch a glimpse of her on television. Still well built, one notices – though no doubt there's concealed scaffolding. One might imagine that with a wife like that . . .'

'There wouldn't be much energy left over for raping the entire university?' The V-C nods in weary agreement.


The conference table of the Benzin boardroom is a splendid affair – several rain forests gone, Sidney notes – and quite long enough to keep the opposing parties at shouting distance. The Tribunal, which occupies the chairs in between, consists of:
– The Chairman of the Governors
– The Vice-Chancellor
– The Registrar
– Professor Dame Margery Doughty (Prix Nobel)
– The Retired Admiral
– The Chairman (as she prefers) of the local Mothers' Union.

Dame Doughty opens the proceedings by complaining, in her mildest stentorian roar, that she has found nowhere to chain her bike. Hence its presence in the boardroom.

'Your security guards weren't tremendously helpful, Mr Chairman. They kept asking me if I was a student. I said, "Of course, my boy, of life." At which I was sniffed all over by one of your bigger dogs.'

All eyes come to rest on Professor Doughty's bicycle. Although both wheels are of roughly equal size, it clearly broke out of its factory before the Japanese invaded Manchuria. The warning bell it carries appears to have been filched from a Norman church tower. The only modern touch is a warning arm in luminous plastic which extends more than halfway across the average main road. No one, to Sidney's knowledge, has ever knocked Marge off her bike, though she has often enough forced container trucks deep into the saloon bars of public houses bordering the narrowest streets of the old town. Sidney wonders whether the Chairman remembers how Marge's Nobel-winning discovery – that forgotten cigarette ends can destroy not only a chemistry lab, but an entire science block – had resulted in the withdrawal of a massive grant by the nation's leading tobacco company.

The Chairman assures her that his own chauffeur will in future take personal responsibility for the bicycle. He then explains that the parties to the dispute are entitled to one legal representative each.

Jones rises in a shiny black suit not worn for several decades, over which tumbles a soup-stained MA gown, and bows with what Sidney feels is unnecessary obsequiousness.

'I have that honour,' Jones says, barely stifling a 'M'lud.'

Hooper too is up, dressed in the army-surplus combat fatigues which arouse Sidney's darkest desires.

'Ms Rosen and I will be represented by the National Union of Journalists,' she tells the Tribunal.

The Chairman bridles. 'Oh? So where is he, then?'

'She. As it happens, she's having a baby today.'

'Couldn't you have found someone who isn't having a baby today, Dr Hooper?'

'Women have babies when they have them. Men can hardly disclaim responsibility.'

'Chairman,' the Admiral says. 'Frankly, I think we should keep the unions out of this. And the Civil Liberties people. And anyone else.'

Dangerous lights refract off Hooper's granny lenses. Sidney notices that she has further butchered her hair without, of course, dying it. It splays out in short, electric tufts.

'No unions, no Inquiry,' Bess says.

'The Tribunal lays down the rules, Dr Hooper.'

Bess Hooper gathers her papers. Melanie, who is wearing her cropped, punk hair waist-length today (witchcraft), under a little blue bonnet, also rises. The sight of her evokes an immense, paternal sadness in Sidney. A lost daughter.

At this juncture Jones leans to Sidney's ear. 'Just keep your trap shut, old man, and we'll win this thing by default.'

Bess is clearly hesitant about walking out. Perhaps she can read Jones's lips. She and Melanie remain standing.

The Chairman nods to the V-C, who clears his throat.

'All proceedings of this Tribunal will be strictly confidential, including the membership of the panel, the rules governing the proceedings, and the precise nature of the allegations.'

'Everyone knows the allegations,' Hooper cuts in.

The V-C ignores her. 'Any ruling determination recommendation or steps taken as a result of this Inquiry will not be made known and will therefore not be subject to appeal to any court industrial tribunal or ombudsman.'

'That's absurd,' Sidney mutters to Jones.

'Quod principi placet, legis vigorem habet, old man.'

'If you don't object to this nonsense, I will.'

Jones rises. 'Mr Chairman, my client is not happy.'

'Nor would any of us be – in his place,' the Chairman snaps.

Jones quivers, sits down, half-rises and remains in that posture, crouched over the table, neither up nor down.

Bess is whispering urgently to Melanie.

'We have decided to represent ourselves,' she announces. 'We have to point out that the rules and composition of this Tribunal are patently medieval and misogynist. Four men and only two women, one of them a token woman.'

'A what!' cries the Mothers' Union. Dame Doughty murmurs into her ear. The Mothers' Union registers increasing perplexity.

'Chairman, may I ask what a "token woman" means? Professor Doughty tells me it means a woman well disposed towards men, which was really no kind of crime when I was a gel.'

'No, no, dear,' rasps Dame Doughty through her smoker's cough. 'A token woman is the current jargon for some harmless old bag like me or you who the chaps pluck out of a hat for purposes of window dressing. If you follow.'

'I honestly can't say I do,' the Mothers' Union bridles. 'I

happen to have been a lay magistrate for the past ten years. And a District Councillor. Nor am I harmless.'

Jones is up. 'Chairman, my client wishes to go on record as deploring Dr Hooper's demeaning reference to a lady who has earned the respect of the entire local community – '

'Oh balls!' Sidney finally explodes. 'This woman owns six large dogs, regularly harasses me by letter and telephone, and has been out to "have my hide", as she puts it, ever since I was elected as the first Green Councillor within a radius of – '

' – fifty miles,' say the V-C and Registrar in unison. 'Objection overruled.'

Jones is tugging at Sidney's jacket but his client declines to sit down.

'As for the Admiral, he happens to be Vice-Chairman of the local Conservative Association. At a full Council meeting last month he described me as "a menace to society" and "a wanker". Towards the end of the debate, which concerned my proposal to spend a mere fifty thousand a year on a motorized pooper-scooper, the Admiral called me "a fart", "a pansy in corduroys", and a "banana muncher".'

All eyes are now on the Admiral. Clearly he is toying with the notion that a denial would be beneath his dignity.

'Pyke's a born liar,' he says finally. 'What's more, he always has been. Personally, I have no prejudice against the man.'

Sidney is about to subject these sentences to internal logical scrutiny, but Jones finally succeeds in pulling him down into his chair.

'Perhaps we can get on,' the Chairman sighs.

'There are libel laws,' the Admiral growls, 'in this country.'

Jones says: 'I'm sure the Admiral has been struck by the occasional bouncer in his time, without appealing to the umpire.'

'Objection!' Hooper shouts, exultant. 'These are chauvinist metaphors. They assume that the members of the panel share male values and play Sunday cricket with Pyke and Jones.'

'Well, I don't,' the Mothers' Union says.

'You make the sandwiches,' Hooper says contemptuously.

'What a horrible woman you are!' cries the Mothers' Union.

'You're not supposed to pre-judge that, dear,' Margery Doughty says. 'That's the fun of the whole show. We know nothing when we begin and even less when we finish.'

Jones rises, at last, with all the gravitas he has long rehearsed. 'Mr Chairman, what we find – *apparently* – are two quite separate charges against my client, hm. Not one, but two. Two charges look – could look – may very well look – yet may very well not be – more serious than one.'

The Tribunal have assumed precisely the puzzled expressions that Jones has joyfully imagined in his bath.

'That is to say, Mr Chairman, that each charge may appear to reinforce – should I say "substantiate" – the other. Or the contrary, hm.'

'The contrary?' The Chairman is drumming the table.

'Chairman, I ask the Tribunal to conclude that each of these deplorable, utterly unconvincing, allegations cancels the other out. In short – an ugly case, an unprecedented case, of criminal collusion and conspiracy.'

Wrapping his tattered gown round his groin, Jones smiles happily.

The Admiral's back has been stiffening. 'Dr Jones, we're not inviting you to run rings round us, you know.'

'I quite agree with the Admiral,' the Mothers' Union says. 'Why don't we hear what the two ladies have to say?'

'We're not ladies,' Melanie says – her first intervention. 'We're women. And witches.' Her cheeks turn bright red.

Jones is up. 'May I ask whether Dr Hooper and Ms Rosen – the two "witches" – co-habit?'

'Objection!' cries Bess.

'Objection not sustained,' the Chairman rules. 'Just answer Dr Jones's question. Which is also mine.'

'I'd like to know what Dr Jones means by "co-habit",' says Dame Doughty.

'Whatever he means, we won't answer,' Hooper says. 'As victims of rape, we reject any attack on our sexuality.'

'Their what?' the Admiral looks about him for enlightenment.

Margery Doughty whispers in his ear, every word audible across the room, then concludes with a broad grin: 'But they won't tell us whether they enjoy pinching each other's bottoms, of course – nor would I.'

The Admiral nods. 'Lesbians, are they?'

'Objection!' cry Bess and Melanie.

'I suppose it's the fashion nowadays,' the Admiral tells the Mothers' Union.

Bess is gripped by mounting rage. 'Dr Jones's question is an invasion of privacy and clearly discriminatory. Its sole purpose is to excite heterosexist prejudice and chauvinism.'

'Mr Chairman,' Jones says, 'can we not safely conclude that if Dr Hooper and Ms Rosen were not, repeat not, lesbian lovers – they would deny it?'

'You smug bastard!' shouts Bess. She turns to the Chairman. 'Are you now, or have you ever been, a member of the Communist Party?'

'What?'

'So you decline to answer? So a Communist you must be.'

'I don't think any of us believe that the Chairman is a Communist,' says the Mothers' Union.

'One can never be too sure,' the Admiral advises her. 'Take that Blunt fellow. He used to clean the Queen's pictures.' He turns to the Chairman. 'Frankly, the air has to be cleared – yes or no?'

'No,' the Chairman says icily.

'Well, you would say that, wouldn't you? If you were a spy, I mean. Imagine: a Red spy at the head of the Benzin Oil Company! Consider the defence contracts ...'

'Admiral, we're now very friendly with the Soviet Union,' Doughty says. 'I was there only last year, at

Novosibirsk. Such lovely blue eyes those men have. Frankly, the more spies they send us, the more fun all round.'

'What about Professor Pyke's "sexuality" or whatever she called it?' the Admiral asks. 'Isn't that the issue?' He peers at the documents in front of him. ' "Sexual chauvinist" . . . "phallic autocrat" . . . "hegemonic cock-power" – frankly, this is what we've got to get to the bottom of.'

Hooper now seems to be upset that everyone has lost interest in pursuing her relationship with Melanie.

'Doesn't it strike the Tribunal that Pyke attacked and raped both of us precisely because he resents our relationship?'

'Yes, yes, dear,' the Mothers' Union says, 'but why should he, why should he mind at all? A man, I mean, a married man.'

Sidney is now studying his adversaries intently. They have been at it for an hour and this is the first time, in his view, that skin has been broken. Both he and Melanie – and therefore Bess as well – are trapped in a conspiracy of silence. Neither can reveal that Sidney and Melanie have been lovers – Sidney because such conduct with a pupil would be held against him; Melanie because an embittered mistress is notoriously motivated by anything but the truth.

Sidney is longing to say all sorts of things: that no one should be prejudiced against lesbians, only against militant, Sidney-hating lesbians. But his mind veers off to Samantha's imminent, unstoppable, exhibition of female erotic art, 'Eye Contact'. 'Of course I'll be massacred,' she keeps saying, even though she's not supposed to be talking to him any more. She has now developed a style of projecting her remarks away from him, as if he weren't there. It transpires that Sidney is expected – required! – even while banished to the spare room – to attend the dreadful occasion.

Jones casually tosses an off-break out of the back of his hand while no one is looking.

'Dr Hooper, did you apply to Professor Pyke to turn your

academic post as lecturer into a job-sharing post with Ms Rosen?'

'Yes.'

'What was Professor Pyke's response?'

'Dismissive, scornful, wholly negative.'

'Did he not point out that Ms Rosen, still a graduate student without a higher degree, was scarcely qualified to apply for a post which she had in any case not applied for, and which in any case does not exist?'

'Pyke has shown himself consistently hostile to the basic right to job-sharing because he is hostile to women's rights. Only thirty per cent of academic posts in this university are held by women. What we need but don't get is affirmative action.'

'What's that?' the Admiral asks everyone.

'It's a policy of discrimination,' the V-C tells him, 'designed to ensure that jobs are filled by unqualified candidates.'

'Good grief. Is that the university's policy?'

'No, Admiral – not yet.'

'What's it got to do with ungentlemanly conduct in the swimming pool, eh?'

The V-C turns to Jones with raised eyebrows.

Jones rises. 'Mr Chairman, I earlier asked whether Dr Hooper and Ms Rosen were co-habiting lesbian lovers. I got no answer. In my view, the job-sharing incident confirms that they indeed are. And if they are – '

'Objection!' cries Bess Hooper. 'This is just a standard smear tactic by the phallocracy!'

'By the what?' the Admiral wants to know.

'If they are co-habiting lesbian lovers,' Jones persists, 'we discover that both these women are colluding to revenge themselves on Professor Pyke for many imagined injustices which have nothing to do with rape. In short . . .' Jones pauses dramatically, 'we are confronted by a twin-headed calumny!'

Swishing his gown beneath his LX arse, Jones sits down with such palpable self-satisfaction that the boy in Sidney is tempted to remove his friend's chair during the descent. And there's also Jones's habit of cheating at tennis to consider.

All eyes have turned to the other end of the table, where Bess is on her feet, seething.

'If the job-sharing incident is at all relevant, we may discover that Professor Pyke is not a man who likes to have his authority challenged by women. For Pyke, females are for laying, not for arguing. We may also discover that he exacts retribution in his own way.'

Yes, the more Sidney thinks about it, the more he is sure that Jones calls his own ace services out when he knows they are in.

# *Fifteen*

'I thought you might like to see this,' Chantal says demurely. 'I'm afraid it's quite horrible.'

'This' is a copy of Melanie Rosen's latest attack on Samantha, scheduled for release to students and the Press to coincide with the opening of Samantha's labour of love, 'Eye Contact'. Chantal has come to Cuba to 'warn' Samantha, who is writing cheques, slightly smaller amounts than usual, for her various personal charities, including the local Samantha Newman Day Care Centre. Gazing up into that spirited, ravaged face, Chantal knows that 11.5 million viewers will soon be hers.

But she does also feel a twinge of pity. If only there had been another way.

Samantha refuses even to glance at Melanie's thing. But it's in her hand, like a writ:

Newman [writes M. Rosen] is a pornographer. And now, a patron of the same. Pornography is the terminal disease of male hegemony. Like male artists, Newman and her acolytes 'fix' women as sex objects. Every initiative she takes is poisoned by self-hatred and by slavish acquiescence in a patriarchal culture which is predatory, imperialistic, inhuman.

Newman's work reinforces the stereotype of woman as vamp, seductress, parasite. Men – notably her husband Sidney Pyke – are invariably depicted as sensitive, scrupulous 'victims' of female unreason. We must love our oppressors. That is the message of 'Eye Contact'.

Newman is telling us that twenty years of struggle by the Women's Movement has been a zero. An illusion. We are what men always said we were: the whores of biology. Newman's sordid prose style, and her jazzy, modish art exhibition, are clearly at the service of the counter-revolution. Sex, she insists, is rooted in fantasy and sadism rather than in humane, caring relationships – and for Newman that means, must mean, the biological necessity of being dominated and maltreated by a man.

In short, Newman has accorded men a new rapist's charter. Not that they need one. But the ruling Phallocracy, seriously threatened by the Women's Movement, now desperately requires Quislings and agents in the camp of the oppressed. Newman is already well known for her defence of pornographic art and literature. She has also made it an issue of loyalty to her husband, Professor Sidney Pyke, who was once co-editor of the porn magazine *Up* and contributed a sketch to *Oh! Calcutta* which had to be removed from even that sexploitationist show.

'Eye Contact' is Newman's final fling – a vulgar, voyeuristic and artistically pretentious porn show dressed up as an 'art exhibition'. No doubt Newman will be richly rewarded. Her neo-Nazi German patron, Hans-Dietrich Swindler, will buy the lot.

The struggle continues. A luta continua!

Although Samantha ignores Melanie's pamphlet, Chantal knows that she will devour it as soon as she herself has run down the stairs and across the lawn of Cuba, in her demure little Laura Ashley frock, the wind tugging at the black satin bow in her ash-blonde hair.

Behind her she leaves, in an envelope, on the kitchen table, a cheque for one hundred pounds written out to 'The Samantha Newman Day Care Centre'.

\* \* \*

When the Tribunal reconvenes, the Chairman politely inquires after Dame Doughty's bicycle.

'I handed it over to a most gorgeous brute.' She winks.

'Man or dog?' Sidney inquires.

Doughty chuckles but no one else does.

'We all know that Professor Pyke hates man's best friend,' the Mothers' Union says.

'Idiot,' Jones mutters in Sidney's ear.

The Chairman now invites Dr Hooper to describe what happened in the Benzin Swimming Pool. Bess stands up and stares down the table at Sidney. He thinks: tricoteuse. But no, that was a passive role. This one works the guillotine.

'The assault took place a minute or two before the end of the "Women's Hour", when Pyke had no right to be in the pool and I was completing my normal exercise routine of thirty lengths.'

The language she uses sounds to Sidney like a police report.

'Might one ask what is the "Woman's Hour"?' inquires the Mothers' Union. 'Does she mean the radio programme?'

'The "Women's Hour",' the V-C says bitterly, 'is the result of a great deal of protracted agitation which I, for one, have regarded with profound misgivings.'

'We know that,' Hooper says. 'It's a matter of history and herstory.'

'Of what?' asks the Admiral, whom Sidney judges to have been dead since the Dutch sailed up the Thames Estuary. But Sidney knows all about history and herstory – he can't help remembering, twenty-five years ago, bursting into the dining hall of All Souls College, Oxford (where the gowned dons were feasting, free of charge, on the ill-gotten gains of rackrenting landlordism – as the Anarchist Student Front leaflet which he scattered across tables loaded with caviar and prime beef put it) to demand that women students be admitted to the college within the coming week. The dons laughed while the Mancipal summoned the police.

'Oxford,' Sidney was goaded to inform his audience, 'is a place where nothing ever happens, for which you are proud and grateful.'

After a quick spurt of paint-pot vandalism around the Hawksmoor quadrangle, and a night in a police cell, followed by a savage fine, Sidney took himself back to the LSE where he and his Maoist comrades roughed up the senior common room before tearing down the iron 'emergency' gates installed by a Director dedicated to Hegemonic Repression. Dragged from the building (the bar, actually) into a police van, Sidney was incarcerated for ten days, on remand – Samantha always said that was the moment she decided to marry him.

As a don, Sidney remained dedicated to integrated cafeterias and common rooms – despite the noise, the juke-boxes, the drunkenness, the litter of beer cans, the grimy sneakers up on the chairs. It came as a bit of a shock when the students of the '80s began demanding separate facilities. The right-wing students, who carried copies of the *Salisbury Review* under their arms, and rode motorbikes in imitation of Roger Scruton, said they wanted 'to raise the tone' by expelling 'scruffy, smelly socialist lecturers'. The Left, not to be outdone, demanded the expulsion of 'Establishment collaborators and spies'. Either way, the teaching staff gratefully withdrew to their own common room and restaurant. Soon afterwards, following Bess Hooper's arrival, the women, both students and some staff, demanded separate tables for women who felt unable to speak freely, or 'put down', or 'patronized', or generally raped when forced to eat next to men. The Black students responded with a table of their own, and the Black Women with yet another. Sidney Pyke had made weak Swiftian jokes about High Heels and Low Heels, Big Enders and Little Enders, which no one understood, except for Dame Margery Doughty, who called it all 'the Ayatollah's Revenge' and sat herself at any table, always welcome, always loved.

Marge, who adored Cumberland sausages with lots of mustard, took delight in consoling her white male colleagues about the shock-waves of ostracism that had struck them.

'Oh you poor dears, the rulers of the world, and no one wants to sit with you. And you can't think of any demands of your own!'

What was good for the dining and common rooms was naturally even better for the university's sports hall and swimming pool. The Women demanded an hour or two of their own every evening of the week. Sidney earned himself odium by campaigning against this, by calling it 'apartheid', by distributing chadors – and by invoking his own generation's vision of an integrated humanity. When the Administration finally capitulated and granted the daily 'Women's Hour', Sidney put through anguished phone calls to Jane Fonda, Vanessa Redgrave, Glenda Jackson, Joan Baez, Julie Christie and Germaine Greer. On each occasion he got no further than an Ansafone inviting him to leave his message after the bleep.

Only Samantha responded positively. 'Aren't men the only reason for suffering all that chlorine?'

The Women jealously guarded their segregated hours, pursuing aerobics, yoga, dance, multigym, self-defence, 'aggression', 'self-confidence therapy', shouting and screaming techniques, plus general rapping, the accepted antidote to raping. Sidney remarked to Samantha and Marge Doughty that despite all this exercise they generally put on weight. Often they would sit cross-legged on mats, babies at their breasts, eating their toddlers' crisps and Mars Bars, for hours at a time – long past their allocated convent hour.

Sixty minutes of Benzin Swimming Pool time (Bess Hooper is reminding the Tribunal) are strictly reserved every evening for females. The allocated hour runs from six to seven. And yet, on that fateful Thursday evening, Sidney Pyke had entered the pool five minutes before he, as a male person, was entitled to.

'You're sure of that, Dr Hooper?' Jones cut in. 'Exactly five minutes, hm?'

Bess is sure. 'I was the only other person in the pool at the time. As soon as I saw him I looked at the wall clock.'

'Supposing the clock was in fact five minutes slow? It does happen – with clocks.' Jones beams.

'The rule is that you obey that wall clock.'

'The clock is the referee,' Marge Doughty booms.

'Never mind the clock,' the Chairman says testily.

But Bess minds it. 'Pyke deliberately entered the pool early – because I was alone in the water. He dived into the deep end, more of a belly flop really, just as I was turning for my final length. He hit the water only a few feet from me. A moment later I felt hands gripping me by the arm and ankle, I was dragged under water towards the diving boards, then he pressed me against the side of the pool, squeezed my buttocks, and said: "You want tenure, you bitch? You want job-sharing with little Melanie? I'll give your pussy a taste of tenure."'

Hooper pauses, removes her granny glasses, and wipes them on a clean handkerchief provided by Melanie. Not a sound is to be heard in the boardroom of the Benzin Oil Company. But the Mothers' Union abhors any vacuum.

'You have a cat, dear?'

Bess puts on her glasses. 'What?'

'You and Melanie have a pet cat that he wanted to drown?'

'Pussy is a rather '60s word,' Doughty roars confidentially. 'It means you know what.'

'It's a sexist term much in vogue among phallocrats,' Hooper informs the Mothers' Union.

'Oh.'

Jones is up. 'With respect, the Tribunal should not forget that Professor Pyke has described nuclear warheads as . . . er, the revenge of a . . . genitally frustrated . . . er, erotically repressed . . . gerontocracy.'

Another silence.

'I don't follow,' the Admiral says.

'No one does,' the Vice-Chancellor reassures him.

'Oh but I do,' says the Mothers' Union. 'Mr Jones means that both Dr Hooper and Professor Pyke are peaceniks. And of course this is what happens.'

Here Melanie intervenes, quivering.

'Pyke's writings are saturated with such phrases as "release of libidinal energies" and "the politics of joy". He has also described revolution as "the festival of wet dreams", though this didn't quite match his wife's famous phrase' – Melanie leaves them guessing for a moment – '"the carnival of cock and cunt".'

'"Cunt" and "pussy" are the same,' Doughty advises the Mothers' Union.

'Perhaps,' suggests the Registrar, 'we can get back to the swimming pool.'

'Please continue, Dr Hooper,' the Chairman says.

'I noticed that his breath stank of Dutch courage. I am of course quite used to his habitual verbal abuse – in faculty meetings he rarely misses an opportunity to demean and humiliate me. But this was the first time he had assaulted me physically. I resisted, of course, but he repeatedly dragged me under until I was choking and helpless.'

Listening to Hooper's vivid report, Sidney finds himself horribly aroused by the word 'helpless'. He wonders whether the Tribunal would be interested in witnessing a re-enactment of the whole thing. To rape Bess in front of an audience would certainly be quite a trip.

'Did you say anything, Dr Hooper?' Jones asks casually.

'I tried to scream but my lungs were full of water. I was choking. Go on, tell me that he interpreted my silence as consent. Why don't you ask me whether I enjoyed it?'

'No need for that, Dr Hooper,' the Chairman says. 'Just continue.'

'At some stage during the struggle I became aware of Pyke's erect penis pressing against my thigh. The shoulder straps of my bathing suit were snapped, my breasts were mauled, and his hand wrenched at the material covering my crotch until it ripped along the seam. Bent backwards

207

against the side of the pool, I finally had to suffer penetration.'

Silence.

'There was definitely penetration?' Dame Doughty finally inquires.

Hooper nods. 'And orgasm. His. Just in case that's in doubt.'

Jones rises solemnly. 'Dr Hooper – I do believe you have enjoyed telling your tale. If, as they say, recounting the ordeal is almost as bad as the experience, one has to congratulate you on your courage.'

'Questions not statements, Dr Jones,' the Chairman says.

'M'lud.' Jones bows, delighted to have fulfilled the old legal gambit of earning a rebuke while making one's point. 'So tell us, Dr Hooper: how many hands did Professor Pyke possess on that occasion?'

'Two.'

'Two! Given the fact that all this took place in the deep end, as you tell us, I got the impression that you were up against a marine creature with the multi-manual capability of an octopus. Rather than, if he will forgive me, a fat and breathless academic in late middle age whose highest aquatic achievement is the dog-paddle.'

Even the Mothers' Union is irritated by Jones's smug tone.

'Tell me, dear,' she asks Bess, 'did you fear for your life?'

'I did. I was half drowned. I found, as so many women have done, that it is not a fate worse than death.'

'And how did you make your escape?'

'When he'd done with me, he clambered out of the pool and kind of loped away.'

'And you're sure there were no witnesses? No swimming-bath attendant?' the Admiral asks.

'The cuts.'

The Admiral cups a hand over his ear. 'Pardon?'

'The Thatcher cuts.'

'Well, I'm sure we don't have to get into politics,' the Mothers' Union says. 'What I really can't understand is

208

why you didn't make a complaint against Professor Pyke at the time. Why the delay?'

'Complain? Who to? The police? "Hysterical woman syndrome". To the university? "Over-ambitious female lecturer syndrome". Besides.'

'Besides?'

'A woman's first instinct is always to bury her shame. To avoid a scandal – the protracted humiliation of autopsy and inquisition. Particularly when she knows the man well. When he bestrides the departmental hierarchy several significant rungs above her. When he holds her future in his hands.'

'A question,' Jones addresses Hooper down the table. 'If you were so reluctant, initially, to report this, er, allegation, why did you subsequently decide to raise a hue and cry about it?'

'Because of what Pyke later did to Melanie. He raped Melanie too! We discussed the situation with our friends and decided that other women had to be protected.'

The Chairman turns and squints down the table. 'Professor Pyke, a yes or no question. Did you rape Dr Hooper?'

Sidney ponders this. A man of the theatre (and of everything else), he enjoys the rising graph of astonishment created by his silence.

'Yes and no. More accurately, no and yes.'

Were a three-legged rhinoceros with the Mona Lisa stamped on its rump and a dozen eggs balanced on its head to walk into the room in ballet shoes, the impact of this reply could not be more dramatic. Glancing at Jones, Sidney observes the mouth which has imbibed so many gallons of claret in his company sagging. But a great barrister is never down for long.

'Mr Chairman, this has been something of an ordeal for my client and I really – '

The Chairman is implacable. 'Professor Pyke, either you did or you didn't.'

'Precisely,' says the Admiral.

'Well,' Sidney muses, 'I believe I may have entertained

the thought. There's a delicate, precarious, point of balance in the war of the sexes. On the other hand, as Sartre pointed out – '

With a huge guffaw, Dame Marge slides halfway out of her chair and under the table. If the Chairman could strip her of her Prix Nobel, he would do so; given her libidinous nature (Sidney fondly reflects) she would be glad to be stripped of anything.

Jones, now recovered, takes up the questioning.

'Professor Pyke, did you enter the swimming pool on that Thursday evening?'

'I did. My usual bellyflop – painful but bracing.'

Dame Marge, back in her seat, goes under again with a howl.

'What was the time of evening?' Jones asks.

'The "Women's Hour" was over.'

'Might it have been a minute or two earlier?'

'Without my contact lenses I can't read wall clocks.'

'Who else was in the pool at that moment?'

'As far as I was aware, no one. But I am short-sighted. I began my routine dog-paddle – as you kindly described it. Possibly it is the only common ground I share with dogs – my manner of swimming.'

'This is a serious business.' The Chairman rebukes him.

'On reaching the deep end I encountered an unexpected object with which I became somewhat entangled and which kicked me hard. It turned out to be Dr Hooper.'

'Did either of you say anything?' Jones asks.

'I think I said – "Hullo, Bess, fancy finding you here." She told me to "fuck off". I noticed that her eyes were red with chlorine and, presumably, animosity.'

'And then?'

'Dr Hooper then asked me for tenure.'

'She had asked you for tenure before?'

'At least once a week.'

'What was your response? To the tenure business, I mean.'

'I asked her what was on offer.'

The Mothers' Union gasps. 'Bounder!' snaps the Admiral.

Jones's jaw sags and his chins multiply. '. . . Sorry . . .?'

'It was of course an unforgivable remark. Dr Hooper has provoked me unrelentingly for months. Only in my own home can I see the back of her – until the anonymous telephone calls began and – '

'Objection!' cries Bess. 'There is no evidence to link me to any anonymous telephone calls.'

'Regretting my remark, I immediately swam away. Or tried to. But my leg was caught. By Dr Hooper. She then tried to drown me.'

Dame Doughty howls. The Mothers' Union is giving her increasingly nasty looks.

'You say she tried to drown you?' the Admiral asks Sidney. 'How tall is Dr Hooper, and how heavy?'

'You must weigh and measure her. She is however, an adept swimmer and I am not. She is also trained in the martial arts. It's called self-defence but doesn't at all feel like that when you're on the receiving end. I had a hard time. I was of course hugely aroused, in every sense, by this humiliating experience – the prospect of yielding tenure on one's knees to a triumphant feminist at the bottom of twelve feet of over-chlorinated water . . . need I say more?'

'Yes,' says the Chairman. 'You need.'

'It was then that thoughts of rape surfaced. I entered the realm of yes and no.'

'But you told us you were getting the worst of it,' the Admiral objects, his hand shaking with excitement.

'I believe a certain juncture was arrived at when, purely out of self-protection, I had Dr Hooper flat up against the wall of the pool, her wrists pinioned, and quite possibly my leg between hers.'

'While your other hand was making merry with her bare breasts?' Dame Marge inquires.

'I recall nothing of that.'

'He doesn't deny it,' Hooper says.

'I believe my other hand must have been employed in

grabbing the edge of the pool,' Sidney says. 'We were in twelve feet of water.'

'Exactly my point,' Jones mutters, clearly much distempered by Sidney's love of oratory.

'However,' Sidney adds, 'I do remember saying, when the advantage was clearly mine, "I'll give you tenure, you bitch."'

'Hm,' muses Dame Marge. 'Tenure is becoming rather a naughty word. It could mean more.'

'Ask him whether he squeezed my buttocks,' Bess shouts. Doughty nods. 'Did you?'

Sidney thinks about this. 'Yes.'

'Dr Hooper has claimed that you, er, suffered an erection,' the Registrar intervenes.

'Suffered – yes. Entirely involuntary.'

'But then you broke off the engagement?' the Admiral asks.

The Mothers' Union touches his arm. 'They weren't ever engaged, Admiral. Professor Pyke is married.'

'And did you,' the Registrar perseveres, 'then penetrate Dr Hooper – whether voluntarily or involuntarily?'

'No. No coitus. That she has invented.'

'You bloody liar!' Hooper yells. 'I had your fucking spunk all over my thigh!'

'Oh!' protests the Mothers' Union.

Sidney sighs theatrically.

'Would the Tribunal consider, for a moment, what I must call the strategies of narrative? I am habitually recorded as "saying" things, whereas Dr Hooper "yells", "shouts" or "screams". In addition I am permitted to "think" or "ponder", whereas Dr Hooper is allowed no inner life at all – she is known by her actions alone. I am, accordingly, the "darling of the report", attracting a voltage called empathy.' Sidney smiles with deep self-satisfaction. 'Call it "Iago's Version".'

Clearly no one has understood a word of this – except Melanie Rosen, whose eyes switch from grey to green.

'Iago is not a party to this case,' the V-C says. 'Mr

Chairman, I suggest it's time we heard Miss Rosen's version.'

The Chairman nods. 'The Tribunal is adjourned.'

Melanie's version must wait.

Melanie is the only person in whom Bess has ever fully confided. Melanie wears her life on her sleeve, but not Bess – she distrusts the weeping heart as a symptom of female subordination. Men act, women complain. And besides . . . although Bess's ideology predicates inevitable conflict with men (not least the 'progressive' ones), she's invariably shaken when it occurs at a personal level. To protect herself, Bess has developed a second, armoured, skin, a guardedness, to seal off her vulnerable nature from hurt. 'Like tanking the cellar,' is Melanie's image of it.

As for Sidney Pyke – when Bess applied for the post of lecturer, she'd rather liked the man: wide-angled, anti-authoritarian, a rebel himself. His subsequent belligerence wounded her deeply.

Bess's mother had been a nurse and midwife all her working life – finally retiring as a nursing sister in St Bartholomew's Hospital. Bess describes her mother as a 'closet feminist' with instinctively socialist views which she never expressed when her husband was around. Deference was her rule. Mr Hooper was a withdrawn introvert, liable to fits of self-pitying temper, whose work as an insurance salesman left him exhausted and distracted. His main devotion was to his car; he lay beneath it for long stretches of the weekend, mending punctures and defective gear boxes; the merest glance at Bess and she knew that her very existence was a trial to him.

Bess went up the fast stream of the local comprehensive and passed eight O-Levels, sustained by her mother's passionate commitment to her education. Her father said, 'You've done well then. I can't see what need a girl has of more schooling.'

His opinions, rarely expressed, came straight out of the

*Express*, daily and Sunday, whereas Bess's mother read papers like the *News Chronicle*, *Reynold's News* and the *Mirror*. He hated unions – 'Reds' – yet Mrs Hooper had once led a file of nurses out of the no-strike Royal College of Nursing into one of the militant health unions. She didn't tell him; her rule was never to argue with her husband. She let him 'carry on'. Men, she told Bess, don't like to be contradicted.

She was fond of classical music, radio plays, and discussion programmes about current affairs; Bess's father could sit for an hour, staring into space, smoking, silent. As a girl Bess never suspected that her dad's thoughts were invariably lodged in some seedy hotel bedroom in a northern industrial town. When Bess was sixteen he took off with a new woman and was not seen again. Her mother then told her about all the others.

Bess's accumulated resentment burst out: 'But why did you put up with it? Why the hell did you let him treat you like a doormat?'

'I just did. The first time is when you either do or don't. If you do, it becomes a habit.'

The lesson was clear: to love, or suffer, a man is to get hurt. But Bess denies that her conscious feminism was born so early. As a student she had two heterosexual affairs and an abortion. 'Rather than running away from men,' she told Melanie, 'I was probably trying to form the kind of relationship denied to my mum.' Bess insists that her conversion began when she first read de Beauvoir and Adrienne Rich. For Melanie, light comes from the heart. That heart once belonged to Sidney Pyke – until, one night in a Lake District hotel, jealous of her deepening admiration for Bess, he launched the vilest diatribe against the new 'Roundheads' – horrible word! – and their pleasure-hating, womb-centred, obsession with gender conflict.

It was the way he said it. To hurt and destroy. Drunk, too.

Later she confided in Bess. Bess is a good listener, thoughtful, caring, supportive. Melanie remembers her brewing some herb tea in the tiny kitchen in Trinity Road, then running her kind hand through Melanie's wiry hair, bringing an electric charge to her scalp.

'Make war, not love,' Bess said.

By the time she joined the new Women's Committee, Melanie would tolerate no criticism of Bess. Women who complained that Bess was friendly and supportive only if you endorsed her line, one hundred per cent, on every issue – such women didn't understand the personal price that Bess constantly paid for her courage, her militancy. Sidney's brutal response to Melanie's altered perspective on Olive Schreiner taught her that Bess was right, so right: the war of the sexes is deadly serious. And if Bess did indeed sometimes generate a tense atmosphere during discussions, with brusque dismissals of even the most timid challenge, that was because the objective situation itself was tense. It was Bess's unblinking objectivity that certain other women couldn't stomach.

Besides: making war is Bess's way of harvesting love – Melanie is sure of that.


Sidney is only fifteen minutes late for the District Council meeting, which convenes in the Town Hall at 7.00 P.M. Stuck in lead-gushing, brain-destroying traffic, he contemplates a world of polluted beaches and rivers, aerosol cans punching holes in the ozone layer, vanishing shales, radiated sperm and infant leukaemia, melting ice caps, forests destroyed by acid rain. Turning the traffic jam to advantage, he finds 'France-Inter' on the radio and is heartened to learn that Paris is locked in a political crisis about dog shit. The capital's canine population produces twenty tons of crotte a day. He understands most of it – Chantal will be proud of her pupil.

The Councillors' car park at the Town Hall is full. The Tories briefly heckle his arrival, then revert to barracking the Labour woman who is moving 'Composite 11' which, Sidney gathers, would require every employee of the Council to sign an affidavit in support of single-parent families, black people, gays and the disabled.

'Point of information,' Sidney rises.

'Sit down,' the Chairman says.

'The dogs of Paris produce twenty tons of . . .' (Sidney gropes for the French word) '. . . of crap a day. Is this Council aware that dogs now outnumber human beings three-to-one?'

'Out of order!' barks the Chairman, who is accompanied by two mature alsatians, temporarily leashed to his throne. 'Anyway,' he adds, exchanging smiles with the Tory benches, 'dogs were born free and are everywhere on the lead.'

The Mothers' Union, fresh from the Tribunal, is filing her nails. 'Hear hear. The dogs of this Borough wag their own tails. Mr Chairman, I move that any person found loitering in the street without a dog be put on a lead.'

'Dog licences yes, people licences no!' roar Labour's benches.

Sidney is up again. Since he holds the casting vote in the 'hung' Council, he can safely disregard the Chairman's rulings.

'As Charles Dana remarked in 1882, "When a dog bites a man that is not news, but when a man bites a dog that is news."'

'Rubbish!'

Sidney contentedly lets the abuse flow over him. 'This is the way the world ends, not with a bang but a bark.'

One or two former pals from the Labour side suppress a laugh. Encouraged, Sidney tosses out another old favourite: 'The ruling class exposes itself every day in our public parks.' He smirks in anticipation of laughter. Councillor Blood, leader of the Labour Group, and a Keir Hardie fundamentalist, can take no more of the renegade's vanity.

'Is this Council aware that eighty-five per cent of dogs in this Borough occupy low-rent Council accommodation in urgent need of improving?'

Barking from the Tory benches. 'Whoof!'

'And now our working-class dogs are faced with the criminal Poll Tax!' roars Councillor Blood.

'Order order,' murmurs the Chairman. 'Whoof. As the Latin poet Terence wrote, "Nothing canine is alien to me." Anyway, no dog will be required to pay the Community Charge if unemployed, a student, or a senior citizen.'

'How many dogs have been excluded from the Electoral Register?' Blood demands to know. 'Ha! Gotcha!'

The smallest gesture by the Mothers' Union commands the receptive eye of the Chairman, who is also her husband.

'Mr Chairman . . .' (she relishes the propriety), 'is the Council aware that Councillor Pyke has plans to snatch and sell man's best friend to an animal laboratory?' Her Yorkshire terrier barks furiously at Sidney, straining at its leash and rousing the forty to fifty other dogs in the Council Chamber. Sidney's protests are not heeded. 'Oh yes,' she continues, 'Professor Pyke is not content with abusing our respected Minister for Higher Education in the coarsest terms. He is not content with raping the women lecturers he appoints – '

Uproar. Sidney is apoplectic with rage. Even the Labour ranks think this is a bit much, until a word from the Whip reminds them that nothing is too much for Pyke.

'I can now reveal,' the Mothers' Union raises her voice above the male barking, 'that our Green has met with our Reds in secret caucus to hatch a diabolical plot to purchase – '

'Rubbish!'

' – to purchase, at exorbitant cost to the community, an extermination van – '

'Lies! Rubbish! Sit down!'

' – an extermination van which will prowl our streets and parks, the mad Professor Pyke at the wheel, turning our beloved pets into glue!'

Unleashed, the Tory dogs come for Sidney. Driving home, he falls into a sulk about the recent dearth of American lecture invitations – ages since he's tasted a real brownie or an imperial club sandwich. Washed up on the shores of Promise by the waves of Time – nicely put, though he says

217

so himself. And the Media Studies Department will be abolished: the whole Tribunal-thing is blatantly a plot, Bess and Melanie tools of a Thatcherite conspiracy. Gone are the days when Sidney believed that knowledge liberates and absolute knowledge liberates absolutely. Gone, also, the days when he could follow his own train of thought.

Samantha spends the evening alone, at her IBM Fastrite, crying, hating husbands, and trying to write them out of her system. Melanie Rosen's poisonous blast against 'Eye Contact', so thoughtfully, so very thoughtfully, messengered by dearest Chantal, hasn't exactly lifted Samantha's spirits. The blinking cursor on her screen, normally the slave-genie of her diamond-flashing fingers, now mocks, torments, her. Blink blink. But her regular, 'My Week', column for Hans-Dietrich Swindler's Sunday newspaper finally emerges from her ongoing irritation about Gilly Jones's behaviour in the laundry room of Cuba.

When Gilly [change name later] comes for a tête-à-tête, it's always the same story. I thank her for the wine, or the flowers, pour her a drink, we exchange compliments of the 'You're looking younger every day' variety – and then it happens. No sooner are we tuning each other in to the old girls-together wavelength (before marriage turned us into guilt-ridden bores), than Gilly begins to look far-away. I always know what's coming.

'Mind if I just ring Bill?'

Bill is her husband. [Change name.] For the record, he's ugly, pompous and frequently smug. [Call him Sidney.] Poor Gilly hasn't seen him for five or six hours. Almost anything could have happened to him.

What gets me about all this married smugness [word repeated] is how out of date it is. A prayer for the '90s: the abolition of marriage.

Samantha doesn't bother to print this off on mauve paper. The gin bottle stands half-empty beside the IBM Fastrite. Tottering into the master bedroom, the inner sanctum of *Nature or Nurture*, she empties the contents of Sidney's wardrobe and drawers on to the floor, kicks his shirts, shoes and trousers around the room, smashes a few framed photographs of Old Times, then telephones Gilly Jones, not merely her best friend, but – when it comes down to it, and down it has come – her only one.

'Gilly? . . . 'T's me. Mm. I'm leaving Sidney.'

'Darling, you're not!'

'Mm . . . You can have him. All yours . . . at long last.'

'Could I possibly ring you back, Samantha darling? Bill and I are in the middle of this silly little dinner party for Glenys. Oh, do come round for coffee, she'd adore to meet you.'

# *Sixteen*

'Melanie, this may be an ordeal for you,' Marge Doughty booms. 'Quite sure you want to go through with it, dear?'

'Oh yes.' Melanie bravely tosses her small sleepless head, one hand twined into Bess's, a black shawl offsetting the faintest of anticipatory smiles, a Degas dancer before the performance (Sidney concludes).

'And you're a graduate student working on an MA thesis under the supervision of Professor Pyke,' the Chairman tells her.

'I was. I can no longer tolerate his – ' The last word is lost, though Sidney lip-reads something which begins as 'supervision' and mutates into 'oppression'.

'Please speak up, Miss Rosen.'

'Men have louder voices,' Bess Hooper says. 'Try listening to any so-called debate in the House of Commons.'

'It's no use if we can't hear,' the Admiral says, cupping his hand over his ear as if about to trap Melanie's faint testimony.

Melanie stands, lifting high her precious, annotated copy of Olive Schreiner's *Woman and Labour*, now bristling with angrily torn fingers of paper.

'I shall read,' she announces.

'Must you?' the Chairman asks in a tone of weariness.

'Yes,' says Melanie. 'I must.' She reads: ' "The male and female brains acquire languages, solve mathematical problems, and master scientific detail in a manner wholly indistinguishable . . ." '

Laying the book down, Melanie stares the length of the table. 'Professor Pyke, did you instruct me to accept that passage as true – without qualification?'

'No.'

Melanie releases a small but beautiful smile, then moves on to the next angry marker. Momentarily enraptured, Sidney detects a hint of Vermeer as a braver light filters through the high windows.

'Schreiner predicts that when women finally enter government, the waste and carnage of war will end. "No tinsel of trumpets and flags," she wrote, "will ultimately seduce women into the insanity of recklessly destroying life."' Melanie again accords Sidney a long, slow appraisal: 'Did you instruct me to disregard this passage as "sentimental nonsense"?'

Racked by regret and love for Melanie, Sidney laughs (mainly to annoy Jones). 'I don't "instruct" my pupils what to think. I merely reminded you about the awkward cases of Mrs Meir, Mrs Gandhi, and Mrs Thatcher, each of whom conducted a rather spirited war.'

'Did I not reply that according to Schreiner "woman knows the history of human flesh; she knows its cost; he does not"?'

'"He"?' inquires the Mothers' Union, breaking off her search for something in her huge handbag. 'Who's "he"? And who's Schreiner? I really can't see what all this has to do with – '

'Man,' Melanie explains patiently, as if their ages were reversed. 'Schreiner writes: "To the male the giving of life is a laugh; to the female blood, anguish and sometimes death."'

Melanie turns again to Sidney. 'Is it not your laugh she describes? Did you dismiss her words as mere "sentimental rhetoric"?'

Far more desirable than Chantal – always was.

'That happens to be my view,' Sidney says. 'I believe it was also yours – until Dr Hooper began to fill your notebooks with your "own" opinions.'

'Oh no! Oh no! It was your arrogance, Professor Pyke, and your contempt, which finally dispelled my false consciousness. Bess explained to me that your interpretation of Schreiner is a deeply chauvinist and hostile one. Hostile to us.'

'Sidney's a frightful old liberal at heart,' guffaws Dame Marge. 'But he doesn't know it.'

'Patriotic, you mean,' the Admiral suggests.

'Do I?'

'Schreiner was patriotic?' the Mothers' Union asks him.

'No, no. Pyke. The girl's accusing him of being "chauvinist". I take that to mean ultra-patriotic. It's their language you know. One has to interpret them.' He smiles kindly at the bafflement of the ladies. 'The truth of the matter is that Pyke wants to leave this country defenceless, but pretended to Miss Rosen that he's a patriot because the man's a bounder and – '

'I suppose I'm out of date,' the Mothers' Union says, 'but one might think professors are paid to know what they're talking about.'

'But not to threaten me!' exclaims Melanie. The Tribunal sits up. 'Not to refuse to recommend my thesis to the examiners.'

'Did you do that?' Jones asks Sidney.

'Of course. It was a warning, a legitimate exercise of judgment.' Jones attempts to mask his surprise; Sidney has done no such thing.

Bess Hooper cuts in, her arm extended in accusation: 'That man cannot tolerate any challenge to his authority, especially by women.'

Sidney senses that Jones is growing anxious and is about to bowl a bouncer.

'Miss Rosen, are you a witch?' Jones asks.

'I say! – that's a bit hard, isn't it,' mutters the Admiral.

'Yes,' Melanie replies, radiant. 'I am proud to be a witch.'

Jones contentedly twirls the ends of his gown while the Admiral and the Mothers' Union exchange meaningful nods: no fool he, that Dr Jones.

'And what is a witch, Miss Rosen?'

'A man can never understand.'

Jones wears his most benign expression. 'He can try.' (Sidney attempts to recall the TV-soap model for this, the mellow, avuncular Jones QC.)

Melanie clasps her head, a long, thin hand pressing on either side, and closes her eyes.

'We Women set off . . . in the freezing night . . . arm in arm . . . across Salisbury Plain . . . Satan's terrain . . . Then we hear it . . . this loud, weird, droning sound from the wood ahead of us – the evil genocidal whine of the generators . . . which provide the power . . . to launch the missiles. And when the soldiers find us and abuse us and drag us through the cold mud . . . we sing.'

Melanie sings.

' "We are the witches and we'll never be burnt

We are the witches and we know what it is to be free." '

'Is that in *Macbeth*?' the Admiral inquires, anxious to be helpful.

'No. That play is a work of gynocide. We witches hear God weeping on Salisbury Plain. Weeping because the tapestry of creation that She has woven with joy is now torn into shreds. But we know! We know that She will soon begin Her work anew and the hum of Her loom will drown out the evil droning of the missile generators.'

The Tribunal could pass for monks of Lindisfarne who've just sighted Viking ships. Melanie's eye have closed. Clear case of trance. But then they pop open, steel grey, and she shrieks: 'That man raped me!'

'You mean metaphorically,' Jones adopts his most benign tone. 'I fear that witches harbour their own secret knowledge, and their own language which is not ours. That, at least, is the kindest interpretation.'

'Balls to that,' snaps Bess Hooper,' – to use the language that you and Pyke understand best.'

'Mr Chairman, when *are* we going to get to the rape?' the Mothers' Union asks. 'Isn't that why we're here?'

'Now,' Melanie says. 'Now. Pyke summoned me to his

office at eight in the evening. This was four weeks after he attacked Bess in the swimming pool. He told me to sit down. Then, with a sickening smirk, he produced a fabricated "confession" by Olive Schreiner!'

'Schreiner again!' laments the Admiral. 'That woman has a lot to answer for, if you ask me.'

'Schreiner's sexual feelings were directed towards men,' Sidney intervenes with professorial assurance. 'A romantic woman, but things didn't always go well. Of her current lover she once said, "I would like *him* to tread on me and stamp me fine into powder." This, of course, was precisely the nature of Melanie's own suppressed feelings.'

'Who for?' the Registrar snaps.

Sidney's leather shoulders shrug diffidently. 'For me.' Patiently he suffers the vituperative screams from Bess and Melanie with his gravest expression.

'But what did he *do* to you, child?' cries the exasperated Mothers' Union. 'No more quotations, please!'

Melanie struggles to collect herself. 'He said I'd turned my thesis "inside out" as a way of simultaneously signalling and suppressing my jealous claims on him as a woman.'

'More verbal "rape"?' Jones feigns exasperation.

'He reached across his desk and took my hand. He wouldn't let go of it. I remember my feet beating on the floor to get free and he was grinning as if . . . as if I was a caged gerbil on a treadmill. Then he came round his desk and seized me by my hair and – '

'Not much of it to seize,' Jones interjects, doodling Spitfires and Hurricanes on his lined pad.

'It was long then! It was very long.'

'Miss Rosen, are you implying that you'd previously had a sexual relationship with Professor Pyke?'

'No!'

'But you're telling the Tribunal that he not only pursued such relationships – but freely confessed as much?'

'Confessed, you say? Boasted. Anyway, everyone knew.'

Jones raises his chins. 'If "everyone knew", Miss Rosen, can you produce any witnesses to that effect?'

Melanie looks to Bess while Sidney's mind reverts to early retirement.

'Such women are frightened to speak,' Bess says.

'Frightened of what, precisely?' storms Jones, now authentically angry. 'Of *what*!?' he yells.

'Of retribution,' Melanie whispers.

Jones has marched halfway down the table like a defence lawyer in an American B movie.

'You are telling us that women who have been boycotting Professor Pyke's classes since you first made your foul accusations against him, women who have been openly picketing his lectures, are *frightened* women?'

Melanie nods calmly. 'We're all frightened of him.'

Jones points histrionically at Sidney. 'Does the Tribunal find that man "frightening"?' The object of this inquiry remains slumped in his chair, dished by a long haul through the Fox & Goose in Jones's company during the lunch hour, his streetfightin' scowl barely visible above the table.

No one finds him frightening. Not even Bess and Melanie. Having scored, Jones then proceeds to run the ball the full length of the pitch into his own goal (i.e. Sidney's).

'Name one woman!' Jones roars, 'just one, with whom Professor Jones has committed adultery!'

Sidney hears a clock ticking in the silence – it turns out to be under his own rib-cage. Melanie is shaking her head: loyalty, decency, sisterhood, all forbid disclosure. But evidently Bess has come round to a different equation. (Sidney notes the 'evidently' – his speech at the previous session has not alleviated the prevailing narrative injustice.)

'The current mistress,' Bess announces, 'is Chantal Poynter. A first-year student. The younger, the better.'

'Oh Bess, oh Bess,' cries Melanie, appalled, 'how could you? That poor girl!'

The Registrar is writing 'Chantal Poynter' on his pad. 'Any comment, Professor Pyke?'

'None. One crime at a time, please.'

'Well quite!' Dame Marge booms. 'I seem to recall that Ms Rosen had been seized by the hair and was about to be raped – when Dr Jones shunted us into a siding.' Briskly she extracts a man's watch from the pocket of her tweed jacket. 'I am neglecting my chemistry pupils. Well, Melanie?'

'He grabbed me and told me not to be "a little fool". Then he began to tear off my clothes. I tried to scream but no sound came out. No sound at all. It's terrible what fear does to you. He kept saying, "You know you want this as much as I do." I tried to resist him but he was very strong and I felt as if my nerves had been severed.'

Weeping now, Melanie seeks shelter in Bess's arms.

'He forced me . . . down . . . to the floor. He was breathing heavily, like an old man labouring up a hill, and his breath stank of gin and tobacco – and garlic as well.'

Sidney has been brooding about anonymous phone calls, graffiti on his walls, his defeat in the Staff-Student Council elections, the occupation of his garden . . . His miraculously renewed love for Melanie has now evaporated. After all, there are decent lies and indecent ones.

'It was a pasta dish I invariably indulge in before raping my graduate students. A splendid aphrodisiac when washed down with a bottle of chilled Frascati. Correction: half a bottle. I don't drink gin by the way.'

Jones kicks him hard under the table.

'And he forced himself into you?' Bess coaxes Melanie, holding her right hand in both of her own.

'I thought I would choke. I really thought I would die of disgust and shame. He kept saying, "You know you want this."'

'Either the girl's a damned good actress,' mutters the Admiral, 'or – '

' – or she and Dr Hooper are damned good liars,' Jones roars. 'Tell me, Miss Rosen: the floor of Professor Pyke's small office, a mere four metres by five as it happens, is normally piled with books, magazines and periodicals. Visitors complain that it's difficult to thread a passage from the door to the desk. Presumably this "rape" was achieved amid a cascade of falling volumes?'

Melanie glances at Bess.

'Waiting to be prompted – again – by Dr Hooper?' Jones presses. Not staying for an answer he turns to Sidney: 'Do you recognize the incident – in your office – late in the evening – that Ms Rosen refers to?'

'Yes and no.'

'Again?' says the Registrar. 'You seem quite attached to that answer.'

'It's probably the response you gave the Minister of Higher Education when he asked you whether you could contrive to close down the Media Studies as a result of this Tribunal – which is of course its primary purpose – though, I must add, not that of Dr Hooper and Ms Rosen.'

The Registrar and the Vice-Chancellor catapult out of their seats; only the thinnest of elastic holds the Chairman in his.

'That is an outrageous calumny!' the Vice-Chancellor declares.

'My client – ' stutters Jones, ' – very much of an ordeal, Mr Chairman – any of us in his position – '

'Nonsense, Bill,' Dame Doughty says. 'Everyone knows Sidney was the only one of us who had the guts to stand up to that hatchet-faced philistine, the Minister of Lower Education.'

At the sound of that famous stentorian voice – the only voice from this university which has won a Nobel Prize and delivered the Reith Lectures, the Vice-Chancellor and the Registrar are back in their chairs.

'May I speak?' Hooper says quietly. The Tribunal being too shaken to deny a voice to Kermit the Frog, she continues unchallenged into the vacuum. 'Pyke has guts – he's not only a rampant bully, he stands up to bullies. One habit offers perfect training for the other. Sidney's charm is real; likewise his snarl when pulled off his perch. His outside track in the Establishment makes him an uncomfortable critic of the inside track. The clubs he doesn't belong to are the ones he's decided not to join – *we* are excluded. If our allegations against him have been

227

exploited by a calculating male cabal with its own scores to settle – fine! No woman is taken in by Pyke's mock-self-deprecating "yes and no" responses to our allegations. He says "yes" because lies wound his pride; he says "no" because only lies can save him. He says "yes and no" because it charms the pants off the thinking classes – Nobel Prize-winners included. So let's have his answer: did he rape Melanie Rosen in his office? And since we are unrepresented in this case, it might be a good idea if Dr Jones aborted his dismal imitation of an overpaid Queen's Counsel and took himself off to the saloon bar, where he belongs.'

Silence. Not a murmur from the QC.

'I endorse,' says Dame Marge. 'Speak, Sidney, and cut the fancy footwork. My pants are back on.'

Reaching under the boardroom table, Sidney produces what appears to be – it is – a black plastic dustbin bag, out of which he empties a mound of shredded paper.

'Melanie's Schreiner thesis. First draft. As returned to me on the evening my pupil barged into my office, unheralded, picked up a pile of *Media Studies Bulletins*, and proceeded to hurl them at me. During the ensuing challenge I lost both contact lenses. That I kept my eyes is the only happy side of the story.'

'You might have reported it,' the V-C grumbles sceptically. 'Assault, after all – '

'Ha! I'm assaulted virtually every day. Did any of you pay a visit when they occupied my garden for three days and nights? Besides.'

'Besides, Professor Pyke?'

'I don't rat.'

'Hear hear,' says the Admiral, no doubt sighting female privateers of his own sailing up the Channel. He then bolts for the Gents', the Tribunal adjourns, and Marge Doughty, still shaken by Hooper's scorn, plants an uncertain hand on Sidney's shoulder.

'The Roundheads will always get the Cavaliers in the end, you naughty boy.'

Sidney is determined to have no friends. 'Make your peace with the powers, Marge.'

She's not pleased. 'Is Chantal Poynter that gorgeous honey-bun who teaches you French, by the way?'

Dame Marge's words loom large in Sidney's fragmented consciousness throughout the ordeal of 'Eye Contact – Female Erotic Art Twenty Years On'. Samantha has insisted that Sidney 'escort' her to the Press Show.

'I thought you were divorcing me. What do I wear?'

'Something psychedelic, darling – a splash of '60s in a drab age dominated by the Japanese compact camera.'

The exhibition is held in the crypt of St Michael and All Angels. Samantha knows the vicar, a wide-angled man who has appeared on her television show with the message that Christianity, Islam and atheism are 'facets of the deeply felt urge we all experience to know the unknowable'. Sidney likes the vicar because he, too, doesn't believe in God and drinks Frascati immoderately.

At noon Samantha sweeps into the crypt on Sidney's arm – a twin-headed riot of rainbow coalitions. Sidney has unearthed an off-white John Michael suit with absurdly flared trousers which he hasn't worn for eighteen years and which he assumed had long since found its way, via Oxfam, to those parts of the world where it was really needed. The waistband now has to be fastened with a safety pin. A ruffled purple shirt from a Jermyn Street sale and a satin bow tie set the seal on Sidney's reincarnation as a friend of John, Paul, George and Ringo.

Digging himself into a dark corner beside the drinks table, Sidney is confronted by the photo-montage of the Victoria Falls tinted in screaming blood-red. Only the caption is news: 'Menstruation'. Alongside it a woman uncannily resembling his wife sweeps ecstatically across the New Forest on a black stallion. Sidney recalls Samantha's exhortation to 11.5 million fans to 'discover freedom' through

Dorothea Brooke's passionate gallops across the pages of *Middlemarch*.

The journalists are drifting into the crypt with the affected weariness of professionals whose job it is to travel too far to see too little. They both admire and despise themselves, a 'condition humaine' which Sidney understands. He recognizes a few of them and hopes to remain invisible, a psychedelic marker-buoy anchored to the wine table. Embracing each in turn, Samantha announces that the human spirit is breaking its chains, springing its cage, and casting off its shackles.

'Sidney, stop hiding!' she calls. 'My husband is a reconstructed man,' she explains. 'He's very shy but his energies are beautiful and life-enhancing.'

A woman from the *Daily Mail* closes on him and asks where and when he acquired 'the suit'.

'It's an exhibit,' he tells her. She's quite attractive.

'Which of these paintings turn you on?' she asks.

'Me? I believe they're aimed at women. What are you doing for dinner?'

'I'm not crazy about those tulips.' She indicates Gilly Jones's triptych of a tulip in three stages of ecstasy: petals closed, half open, abandoned to the sun. Sidney bleakly peers at a notice pinned to the wall beside the tulips, which informs him that Gilly Jones's art depicts women as both powerful and subjugated. Fertility symbols are explored as 'myth, madness and fantasy from a broad feminist point of view'. Sidney would have classified Gilly as a very occasional once-was photographer married to a tennis cheat and with time on her hands, time evenly divided between standing bail before the Newbury magistrates on behalf of arrested Mauves, and lurking in the laundry room of Cuba.

'Well, that must be it,' he murmurs.

'I prefer the copulating Longleat lions,' the *Daily Mail* says, nodding towards the blow-up that has latterly dominated the staircase of Cuba. At this a no-make-up woman in blue dungarees with *Spare Rib* written on her lapel card

230

snorts scornfully. Sidney vaguely identifies her with the occupation of his garden.

'Oh come on, Fiona,' *Spare Rib* rebukes the *Mail*, 'you know bloody well that lionesses and their cubs can survive only by forming a collective against predatory males. The male lion is the perfect egoist: lives alone, rapes what he can, then scavenges off the females' kill. He'll even eat his own cubs.'

Tail between his legs, Sidney shuffles away towards a satiated paintbrush at rest in a slender jam jar. (Caption: 'Afterwards'.)

'Brave of you to show up,' murmurs a man with a Bomber Command moustache and a *Daily Telegraph* lapel card, trailing him to the Blitz photo taken from inside a darkened tube tunnel showing tightly packed rows of children asleep on the platform. (Caption: 'Womb'.) 'Off the record, old chap, do you find this stuff erotic?'

'I'm not a woman.'

The *Daily Telegraph* ponders this insight. 'How's the rape case going?'

Sidney is now pinned to 'Conception' by a knot of quotation-hungry journalists but fortunately Samantha's ecstatic voice diverts them. Holding court in front of the famous blown-up photograph of a long container truck entering a tunnel in the Italian Alps (Caption: 'Trip'), she is explaining its provenance.

'This one I have lived with for twenty-one years. It was the ultimate trip.'

'You mean you were on drugs?' the *Telegraph* asks.

'Who wasn't, darling? I'd been commissioned to write a series of articles for an American travel magazine. "The Female Hitch-hiker's Guide to Survival. From Ploughkeepsie to Peking".'

'How old were you then?' the *Daily Mail* asks.

'Twenty-one years younger, darling.'

'Weren't you rather asking for it?' the *Telegraph* persists.

'Chauvinist bastard,' says *Spare Rib* who has been simmering on the fringe of the group.

'Oh, I was totally innocent and naïve,' Samantha responds. 'I had no idea that vans and commercial travellers spend entire days cruising and kerb-crawling, hunting crumpet. But the blokes on motorbikes are lovely, crazy boys and a lot of fun. The big lorries and container trucks are the safest bet. The drivers are terribly lonely but absolutely trustworthy.'

For the fiftieth time since he won her heart by smashing the iron gates at the LSE, Sidney now hears how Samantha fell in love with a container truck transporting two tons of tomatoes from Sicily to Milan in the era of the Red Brigades.

'His name was Luigi. The poor man was going in quite the wrong direction. He was heading north but I really had to go south. He simply turned his tomatoes round. Luigi was a Communist, born in the Po Valley, and straight out of Rossellini's film *Paisa*. Somewhere between Turin and Florence I knew I had to fuck Luigi. So I told him. Of course he was quite terrified because Catholic influence remains strong even among Communists – especially for a married man with three children.'

'Four,' Sidney corrects her, 'at the last count.'

'When we got to Florence we drove the tomatoes up into the hills near Fiesole – have you *ever* seen that view? – and screwed one another after dark in the grounds of an old Roman amphitheatre. After that Luigi's wife took a back seat, so to speak.'

Samantha is radiant, her eyes restless.

'And his children also took a back seat?' *Spare Rib* asks.

'Oh Harriet, darling, don't be tedious.'

'That was your idea of sisterhood?' *Spare Rib* persists. 'Wrecking the life of a working-class mother?'

'This Luigi, was he handsome?' the *Daily Mail* asks.

'He had the muscles of a Mathias, the beauty of a Mastroanni, and the brains of a Moravia.'

The *Daily Telegraph* guffaws. 'And presumably this truck and this tunnel – '

'Yes, Freddy – but art is symbolic, isn't it? And in the end satisfied desire becomes a source of despondency. Alone

232

with Luigi, night and day, in the abandoned cottage of some Tuscan shepherd, I began to notice that I was drying my wings and examining the sky. I also realized that Luigi had gone mad and taken me prisoner. You must all know the sonnet. Sidney, darling, recite it.'

'No.' He grins at *Spare Rib*. 'When I say "no" I mean "yes". What about you?'

'God, I do pray that Bess and Melanie nail you.'

Driven by the clamouring hacks, he takes care to mock his own recital by waving his hands in the extravagant gestures of a second-rate Italian tenor:

'Enjoy'd no sooner but despised straight;
Past reason hunted; and no sooner had,
Past reason hated, as a swallow'd bait,
On purpose laid to make the taker mad;
Mad in pursuit and in possession so;
Had, having, and in quest to have, extreme.
A bliss in proof, and proved, a very woe;
Before, a joy proposed; behind, a dream.
    All this the world well knows; yet none knows well
    To shun the heaven that leads men to this hell.'

'Thank you, Sidney,' Samantha says. 'Of course my two weeks with Luigi taught me so much.'

'About what?' demands *Spare Rib*.

'About myself. About love and desire. About male hegemony and capitalism. About the Women's Movement. About the futility of censorship. That sort of thing.'

*Spare Rib* turns a baleful stare on the walls of the crypt.

'What you're peddling here is a kind of mixed economy of the sexes. The men sell off a few shares in the porn market, elect token women like yourself to the board of directors, and generally co-opt the mass of women into their own exploitation.'

'I'm afraid Harriet always ends up interviewing herself,' the *Daily Mail* says. 'Samantha, do you still believe in free love?'

'Love is never free.'

Sidney has decided *Spare Rib* is a better bet for dinner than the *Daily Mail*.

'What about promiscuity in the age of Aids?' the *Telegraph* wants to know.

'Freddie, that word was invented to frighten women. It's only women who are "promiscuous". You men sow your "wild oats", don't you – it sounds so much more forgivable. Believe me – men have also suffered from their own convenient double standards. They have created generations of nagging, possessive wives: pure hell.'

'Do you encourage your husband to have affairs with his students?' the *Daily Mail* woman asks casually.

'Or to rape them?' *Spare Rib* adds.

Sidney awards the *Rib* a medal for letting Samantha off the *Mail*'s sharper hook. Samantha has assumed her saddest expression.

'That remark, Harriet, just makes me terribly, terribly sorry for you. The malevolence behind it. The rage, the violence. My book will tell you that Sidney is a loving, spontaneous person, on easy terms with Eros – a naturally *generous* man. And a wonderful teacher. Of course he doesn't always take account of the amount of repression, of Thanatos, around him. His crime is innocence.'

Half an hour later, as Sidney makes his escape, nervously fingering the safety pin holding up his trousers, he hears the *Telegraph* inviting Samantha to comment on rumours that plans to publish *Nature or Nurture* have been postponed by Vampire Books. Samantha ignores the question by embracing a bemused newcomer from *Le Monde*. At the entrance to the crypt Sidney encounters a beaming sentinel, the vicar, with Gilly Jones.

'Everyone having fun, Sidney?' the vicar beams.

'Huge fun.'

'Oh Sidney,' Gilly moans, 'I so want to go in but I've got the most horrible feeling that Samantha wants to kill me.'

The vicar pretends not to hear this. So does Sidney.

Outside, in the market square, a light drizzle is falling.

Casting about for transport, he feels an arm slipping round his own.

'Doing a bunk, professor? Share a taxi?'

He studies Chantal's stomach.

'What's this about a baby?'

'A baby? Oh! False alarm.'

'I could do with a few more of those.'

'Well what shall I wear?' Samantha asks Sidney and Jones.

'Anything black,' Sidney says.

'Wear that Swiss-muesli carpet thing of yours,' Jones suggests.

'My what, Bill!'

'The one you wore when you gave out the prizes at that girls' school. It reeks of integrity and family values.'

Learning from Sidney that Samantha has dragged him to the Press showing of 'Eye Contact', the great barrister has decided that one favour deserves another. Samantha alone can save the Pyke bacon.

'Though I must add that I'm as baffled as Gilly is to comprehend how a man who's never looked at another woman can have got himself into this kind of mess.'

'Isn't it odd,' Samantha murmurs. 'What a pity that Gilly couldn't join us.'

Patiently working his way through canard à l'orange in their favourite bistro, Jones is consuming the greasy bird with disgusting relish, wiping gravy from his mouth and slurping more than his share of the 'rather good' Beaujolais Villages – the house wine since the bistro came under new management and changed its name from Pot Luck to A La Recherche du Temps Perdu. Ever since the 'case' began, Sidney has found himself lining his 'lawyer's' stomach.

'Well I can't wear the "muesli", as you call it,' Samantha says. 'That prize-giving was on television and one simply must never, never, repeat oneself. Besides.'

Samantha is toying with an artichoke salad.

'Besides what?' Sidney growls, jealous of his own rhetorical trick.

'Well . . . I mean isn't it always better to be oneself?'

'Not in your case.'

'I might wear that little chaste number I picked up for a song from that Uzbek market woman in Samarkand. Or was she Armenian?'

'I wasn't there, was I?' Sidney says. 'You travelled alone – with a crew of thirty assembled by the roaming executive producer of the book–TV tie-in, the versatile Jack Lait, who – if memory serves – bought you "the little chaste number".'

Samantha's eyelashes blaze but Jones doesn't notice.

'Nothing blatantly Oriental, please,' he advises, draining the last of the Villages into his own glass, as usual, and holding up the empty bottle to the waitress. 'Marriage, home, children, the good name of your family – all in peril.'

'Of course I'll have to tell the Tribunal I'm divorcing Sidney,' Samantha says icily. 'And why.'

Jones gapes. 'But you – I thought . . .'

'And don't either of you men forget who's the real target of these women's disgusting campaign. It's not Sidney Pyke, it's Samantha Newman.'

'Ha,' Sidney says, 'ha.'

'Oh yes it is, Sidney. If they could accuse me of raping them they would.'

Jones nervously takes the new bottle out of the waitress's hand. 'I suppose we might pursue that line,' he muses.

'What line?' Sidney says. 'That it was really Samantha who raped them? Don't worry, she'll steal the show.'

'Tell me, Bill darling – ' Samantha leans intimately across to Jones ' – is it true you cheat at tennis? Sidney says it's your only way of keeping your end up.'

236

# Seventeen

Davidson has smuggled himself aboard the Boss's private Boeing 747, under the Swamiji's wing, en route to Geneva, Kuwait, Hong Kong, Brunei. It's the only way to gain an audience. The Swamiji turns out to have a passion for South African crystallized fruit as well as boys under a certain age. The latter being difficult to obtain, it is sugar-coated figs and plums and enticing little slices of orange which enable Davidson to work his way from the status of stowaway in a rear toilet to the curtained cubicle where Mr Al Sabah closets himself, drinking whisky, nibbling Peking duck, watching Danish movies, chuckling over Batman comics, and reading (or not-reading) the Koran.

And yet, when Davidson is granted Access to Mr Al Sabah, the great man seems utterly affable, relaxed, unpretentious. His magic is his lack of magic; his hypnotic charisma resides in its absence. He sits in his quite ordinary leather chair in his quite ordinary business suit looking quite ordinary.

'The problem is, sir,' Davidson begins nervously, 'that we – '

'Problem?' Mr Al Sabah cuts in. 'I liking problem. Problem no problem.' He laughs. His aides laugh, Davidson has learned to smile, almost. Chantal and Sylvie are working on it.

'We have commissioned only one book so far.'

'Book?' Mr Al Sabah clearly can't remember who Davidson is, exactly.

'*The Sidney Pyke Story* by Chantal Poynter.'

'Ah, Shendah Pindah. Is good?'

'Sensational. Worth every penny.'

'You Ian Davidduhn sleeping this Shendah?'

'Sorry? Oh – no, certainly not. That would be unprofessional.'

'Yeah?' Mr Al Sabah's head is still full of Danish movie. 'You wanting buying more book?'

'Well, sir . . . it's partly a question of prestige – to say the least. A Spring List, let alone an Autumn List, may not impress the trade if it announces only one title.'

'Yeah?'

'We need more contemporary books, sir.'

'Temporary book?'

'Con-temporary.'

'OK, OK.' Mr Al Sabah waves his hands somewhere over the Persian (careful! – Arabian) Gulf. 'OK, you getting on exposing of Zionist world conspiracy and Christians child abusing.'

'Ah – yes. Yes. Of course traditional history books also sell very well.'

'Yeah. King and Queen book. Pictures of Princess Di.'

'Actually, I have here a list of potential market-leaders for your consideration, sir. Maybe we could kick some ideas around.'

'Yeah.' Mr Al Sabah kicks the seat in front of him experimentally.

'We should definitely acquire at least one occult title. Devils. Exorcism. The Americans love it.'

'Is good.'

'Good clean stuff.'

'Yeah. Clean.'

'And also a blockbuster. We need a blockbuster.'

'Big one.'

'A brilliant idea, sir. Something for the supermarket chains. Quick return on product. Low unit costs. Mega-merchandizing.'

'Yeah. Big is beautiful, like they saying. You bright boy.'

He reaches up to pinch Davidson's cheek. A Scottish cheek is not an Arab cheek, no flesh to speak of, and it hurts. Davidson likes the pain. It also indicates how drunk Mr Al Sabah is.

'Of course we need to beef up our promotions and marketing department. Bring in one or two topline number crunchers. That's if we mean to climb on to the big board and stay there. High growth potential and good monopoly positioning, Mr Al Sabah. Marry the hardware to the software. But what we most need is market-leaders, big names for super-release, backup with television and radio advertising, Granada, Yorkshire, Capital, Forth, Solent. Display bin available with header, counterpack, poster, streamer, sticker and showcard. Shrinkwrap pack available to wholesalers.'

'Yeah?' Mr Al Sabah nods to his chain of charm-beads and snaps his fingers for another whisky, dreaming of all the companies he has turned around and turned over; all the assets he's stripped and all the strips he's asseted. Davidson changes tack.

'Mr Al Sabah, when I go to cocktail parties, Swindler's men sneer at me.'

'Swindler! That Jew crook!' Mr Al Sabah is out of his seat and back in it all in one motion.

'They tell me the Wellington Press won't last six months. What they don't know is that Chantal's book – that is to say, your book – will torpedo Swindler's big investment in Pyke's wife.'

'Phut.' Grinning, Mr Al Sabah uses his hands expressively to indicate a phut.

'As a matter of fact, sir, I have it on the grapevine that Samantha Newman is to be given the full media treatment by Swindler at the Frankfurt Book Fair.'

'Which hotel that Jew putting Samba woman?'

'The Hessischer Hof.' Davidson makes this up but it seems a reasonable guess, subject to subsequent amendment. Facts are negotiable, like everything else.

'We putting Shendah Pintah also in Hessischer Hof,' Mr Al Sabah announces.

'Thank you. If I may so, that's a brilliant business move. Of course you'll want me to accompany her . . .'

'Yeah. But not sleeping her. Not like that Jew Lait sleeping Samba woman.'

At this moment Davidson can imagine himself the highest-profiled buccaneer of London publishing, escorting a radiant Chantal from Tramp to Annabel's to Groucho's, the handsome couple the toast of the Fourth Estate, pursued – better, hounded! Davidson wants to be hounded! – by photographers and frenetic gossip columnists. This euphoric prospect, combined with the thin air at 30,000 feet, leaves him feeling both elated and lonely – yet lonely is surely the thing for a young wannabee to be – all the banking and credit-card ads make that perfectly clear.

Below, the Earth stretches submissively as the shadow of the drink-laden, Islamic Boeing 747 caresses its many lands, many peoples.


Jones hoists his belly out of his chair, eyes bloodshot. Sidney notices that the distinguished QC's hands shake so badly early in the day that his papers simply fall out of them. Nervousness it isn't. And before Jones chooses to call his famous witness, he's determined to show that he's his own man.

'Dr Hooper, I put it to you that your allegation against Professor Pyke is a fantasy, an invention, sustained by a fanatical hostility to men in general.'

Bess flies straight into the sky. 'You sound exactly like generations of male policemen, judges and magistrates. Go on, tell me that I led him on, that I really *wanted* to be raped? "Lucky girl", eh?'

'I didn't say that, Dr Hooper.'

'The implication is clear to any woman. This is what we are up against. The physical rape is not enough. The victim must subsequently suffer verbal and psychological rape.'

240

Jones smiles his special smile. 'You are clearly not a person who can distinguish between hyperbole and reality, Dr Hooper.' Now he turns to Samantha. 'Ah, ehm . . . Mrs Pyke, please tell the Panel what effect these deplorable allegations have had on your ah, ehm . . . marriage.'

Rising majestically in an oatmeal convent-cloak adorned by an austere Afghan brooch, pits of sleepless grief discreetly painted beneath her eyes, Samantha fixes her stricken gaze on the Mothers' Union.

'Devastating, of course. Two months ago I counted myself a happy woman. Since that time we have suffered anonymous phone calls at any hour of the day or night, our house has been besieged by reporters, our garden occupied by Dr Hooper and her friends, our fences and apple trees cut down, my beloved plants destroyed. As for my husband, he has been traduced, colleagues cut him dead in the common room, students picket his classes, scurrilous leaflets flood the campus, and the honest life of a devoted servant of this university has been reduced to a degrading public spectacle. All in all, a wonderful display of guilty until proved innocent.'

Samantha dabs at her moist eyes with a little embroidered hanky (probably Azerbaijani, Sidney guesses). During this performance Sidney has been studying Melanie. Her gaze is fastened on Samantha by threads of silk. Small burners glow in her cheeks. Her half-bared teeth are perfect; Sidney's rump seethes in memory of their cruellest bite – the truth is, the glamorous Chantal is quite without sexual originality – Soho's her limit – whereas flat-chested Melanie had been transformed by his ministrations into a priestess of delicious occult practices. Where she dug them up he'd never know.

Jones's voice is greased in tenderness: 'Mrs Pyke, from your knowledge – your intimate knowledge – of your husband over twenty years, could these allegations be true?'

'No. Not Sidney. Never.'

Hooper's granny glasses glint. 'She would say that, wouldn't she?'

Jones assumes an expression of innocence. This – as Sidney has been continuously informed the previous evening, carafe after carafe – is 'It': the master trap.

'Would the Tribunal kindly note that Dr Hooper appears to believe that co-habitation must inevitably result in mendacious collusion in the case of the Pykes – but not in the case of Dr Hooper and Ms Rosen.'

'Exactly,' declares the Mothers' Union. 'I wanted to say that myself.'

Jones beams at everyone indulgently. 'It is odd that a natural relationship, sanctified by God, should produce lies – whereas a perverse, deformed relationship – '

Sidney is studying the opposition. He expects an outburst of obscenities from Bess, tears – or a trance – from Melanie, but both women merely make an entry in the notebooks spread before them. (Bess frequently studies her notes; Melanie never.)

Jones, meanwhile, is bending over Samantha like a horticulturalist nursing a prize orchid at the Chelsea Flower Show. She certainly smells the part.

'Mrs Pyke, if you were permitted to cross-examine Dr Hooper, what would you ask her?'

'I would ask her whether she regularly attends keep-fit and self-defence classes. I would ask her whether she has struggled with armed soldiers at Greenham Air Base, torn down wire fences, and left the MoD police who arrested her severely bruised.'

Jones's sombre frown of interrogation is now directed down the table. 'That is my question to you, Dr Hooper.'

'The questions are tendentious,' Bess says calmly.

'What does that mean?' asks the Mothers' Union.

'My experience of being raped was no different from that of hundreds of other women,' Bess says.

Jones plays with his gown. 'Dr Hooper, we are talking about a highly personal experience. Yet you seem to regard yourself with rather chilling detachment as a kind of case history; a statistic almost? And raping a fighting-fit woman without a weapon can't be *all that* easy, particularly in twelve feet of water.'

'And Sidney is scarcely King Kong,' Samantha adds. 'I should know.'

Jones chuckles, Sidney scowls. He always knew it was a mistake to bring Samantha into the act. A split-second later he has to wonder.

'Do Dr Hooper and Ms Rosen not regard all men as rapists?' she asks.

'Do they?' The Admiral is aghast.

'Do you?' Jones obediently asks the two women.

'Do you?' the Chairman also wants to know.

Bess hesitates. Then she points to each of the four male members of the Tribunal in turn.

'Typical tactic of the male ruling class – and its female collaborators. A blatant provocation to offend our judges. At every turn the inner truth that women hold is confronted by the power that men exercise over their lives.'

'But that is itself an answer,' Samantha says sweetly. 'You would not offend them unless your answer to my questions was yes.'

'Wait a minute,' says the Admiral. 'What was the question?'

'Whether you're a rapist, dear,' Marge Doughty booms.

Bess explodes. 'You – ' she points at the elderly chemist, Prix Nobel, 'should be ashamed.'

Dame Doughty looks aghast. 'I'm sorry. I take your point – utterly. I do beg your pardon, Dr Hooper.'

But Bess doesn't enjoy contrition or appeasement. 'Here we go,' she says, 'the paranoid females.'

'No one said that,' the Chairman interjects mildly.

'What *she* meant – ' a finger jabbing down the table at Samantha, 'is that our paranoia leads us – drives us – to interpret potential rapists as rapists.'

Sidney glances at Samantha. Can she come back from that?

'And let me tell you all,' Bess rubs it in, 'that those who

express a fear of persecution are all the more inevitably persecuted. Ask any Czech dissident. Ask any South African freedom fighter.'

Sidney reflects that 'inevitable' is like 'unique'; it doesn't permit of qualification. Things cannot be 'all the more inevitable' or 'all the more unique'. From Jones he receives the ghost of a confirming wink. Further downstream, however, the Admiral and the Mothers' Union are blinking rather than winking. It is they who will decide whether Professor Pyke is to be unfrocked, disgraced, dismissed.

The Chairman sighs. 'Mrs Pyke, a question to you. A practical one, I hope.'

'Of course.' Samantha tosses charm like confetti.

'When Professor Pyke arrived home on that particular Thursday evening, did he say anything about the incident in the swimming pool?'

Samantha's voice is pure marzipan. 'Sidney merely told me that Dr Hooper had asked for tenure again – then tried to drown him.'

'But you didn't advise him to bring a complaint against Dr Hooper?'

'Good gracious, no. I've often wanted to drown him myself. Men can be awfully arrogant you know, and Sidney is no exception.'

Jones leans into Sidney's ear. 'Hooked to the boundary.' But the V-C's ensuing bouncer sends the snoozing pigeons fluttering around the pavilion.

'Mrs Pyke, has your husband ever had affairs with any of his female colleagues or students?'

Samantha rolls her eyes in an established gesture of comic ignorance. 'Would I know? You must ask him.'

'The name of Miss Chantal Poynter has been mentioned. Any comment, Mrs Pyke?'

Jones miserably offers a routine objection to the question while Sidney licks his lips (contrary to general belief, it is fear, not the predatory prospect of pleasure, which normally provokes this response to dehydrating tension).

'No more legal rigmaroles, please, Dr Jones,' says the Chairman. 'The fact is, Mrs Pyke, that – '

Samantha cuts him off. 'I know. I understand. Sidney has always been a sexually fulfilled man. As the French say, "un homme couvert de femmes". But he isn't awfully interested. From time to time some passionate young girl will seek revenge for his lack of interest. Melanie, for example, was never out of our house for the best part of a year. I used to tell her that nothing could ever come of her hopeless passion for Sidney – and here we are.'

The Admiral and the Mothers' Union are nodding while Jones happily drums his fingers on the table, no doubt counting bottles of malt whisky.

'Need we go on?' Samantha drawls. 'So absurd.'

Bess Hooper is halfway down the table in her slush-green overalls before Marge Doughty bars her path with a massively tweeded presence.

'You servile opportunist!' Hooper screams at Samantha. 'You are stamping on your own kind, degrading your sisters, demeaning yourself, playing the old dolly game of nod and wink. Every subordinated class produces its own self-hating Quislings! You are guilty of gynocide!'

'Of what?' ask the Admiral and the Mothers' Union simultaneously.

'Let me speak!' Melanie cries.

'Speak,' the Chairman sighs.

'When he'd had his fill he lay on top of me, like a sack stuffed with bricks, panting, his lungs like bellows, his breath foul, and then he said, "Post coitum omnis animal tristis est."'

Samantha emits a long, low groan. Everyone hears it.

'Would someone translate?' the Admiral demands.

'"After coitus every animal is sad,"' Melanie obliges.

'Sidney doesn't know a word of Latin,' Samantha desperately assures the Tribunal. 'Or any language.'

The exultant laughter from Bess and Melanie reaches Sidney like a 'Happy Hallowe'en' by Hogarth. Melanie puts the boot deeper yet.

'And then, when he'd climbed off me, I noticed a large scar on his scrotum.'

The gaze of the unified boardroom swivels towards Sidney with the slow deliberation of a tank gun turret.

He shrugs. 'A war wound. It's common knowledge.'

'Is it?' the Chairman asks bleakly.

'I acquired that scar in Chicago during the Democratic Convention of 1968. Two cops tossed me through the plate-glass window of the Hilton. I was bleeding so badly that they gave me a transfusion in the ambulance. My injuries were on the front page of the *New York Times* the following morning. Obviously I have been lecturing on that annus mirabilis for the past twenty years . . .'

'And you put your scrotum on display, you naughty boy?' inquires Dame Marge.

Sidney accords her a modest glance which sends Melanie's mercury higher up the tube.

'That man there abused me physically for six months before he raped me! And she – she – knew it. Connived at it! And currently she's at it again – with – with another girl. She's nothing but a . . . a . . . madame!'

'My dear child,' purrs Samantha, 'everyone knows you're madly in love with Sidney, who simply can't interest himself in the silly infatuations of star-struck infants.'

'He screwed me every week! It was "post coitum omnis animal tristis est" every week!'

Samantha's little grimace is of the sweet-and-sour variety. Her elbow digs into Jones's ribs.

'Ah,' says Jones. 'Hm. Mr Chairman . . . naturally we do not accept Ms Rosen's claim but I'm sure the Tribunal recognizes that it totally undermines her contention that she knows what she knows uniquely as a result of rape.'

Melanie clutches her head in both hands and screams.

'Adjourned!' declares the Chairman.

\* \* \*

Leaving the boardroom of Benzin Oil, Samantha heads for the car with longer legs than usual and her Uzbek handbag swinging wildly.

'I'll drive,' she announces – always a bad sign. Sidney takes refuge in the rear seat beside Jones. The car lurches forward, across the Benzin yard, in a series of sickening shudders.

'Try releasing the handbrake,' Sidney advises.

'"Post coitum omnis animal tristis est" indeed!'

'A clever touch, that,' Jones says uneasily. 'Melanie's a bright girl. Not that Sidney's any kind of classicist. Entirely implausible . . .'

Samantha blasts her Range-Rover through the Benzin gates and out into the main road, looking neither to right nor to left.

'Idiot! That's what Sidney says *to me*! And I was stupid enough, naïve enough – bastard! – swine! – to believe it was only to me! I wanted him to be "sad" only with me, but we now learn – oh wonderful, oh ho oh oh ho, that this monster is "sad" with every little bit-part chance nymphet!'

'Samantha, that was a red light,' Sidney says.

'Sidney, I want a divorce. This time I fucking mean it. To hell with *Nature or Nurture*. Who cares whether I become a national laughing stock?'

'No one will notice,' Sidney agrees.

'Your little bitch Chantal will have the run of the field.'

'We're in the speed-limit zone, you know.'

'She'll make a fucking fortune, of course. And take you for a ride. As for the baby! Your baby! ha ha ha ha – she took me in!'

'You're having a baby?' Jones politely inquires.

'Sidney is.'

'I'm in my seventh month,' Sidney explains.

'Don't imagine you can hang on to anything as prime time as Chantal, you stinking, lecherous, pathetic – '

Sidney decides to be offended.

'Frankly, Chantal's no more than my amanuensis.

Another young slave of passion. I have to give her something to do. They can't make a move until I sign a contract with the Arab.'

'What fucking Arab?'

'He happens to be the most powerful media proprietor in the world.'

'Ha! I'm sure that will be news to Hans-Dietrich Swindler. What's this fucking Arab's name, anyway?'

'Al Something.'

'Al Something! All right, I'll burn *Nature or Nurture* – will that satisfy you?'

'Samantha, that was a container truck you tried to ram,' Jones groans, his eyes tight shut.

# *Eighteen*

Hans-Dietrich Swindler's silver Rolls-Royce Corniche glides down the motorway, sporting its unique licence plate: S1. Coils of rich cigar smoke drift across the rear seat.

'We give Samantha total support,' Swindler reminds Jack Lait yet again. 'Total, ja?'

'Even if we have to buy every painting.'

'Even if her exhibition stinks of permissive decadence, every Sveendler newspaper from Munich to Montana will hail Samantha's genius.'

Lait is wrapped in gloom and migraine. He wants to drop Newman and her fucking book. If he has to live without three or four steamy afternoons a year in Brown's Hotel, so be it. Samantha's perfumes, stronger each time, tempt him to remind her that chemical warfare is banned by international convention. On the last occasion, in the Caledonian Hotel, with that great lump of Edinburgh rock outside the window, and the Poynter girl cooling her pretty ass in a downtown restaurant, he'd heard the giveaway woosh of a vaginal deodorant can from the bathroom.

'All the business indicators are negative,' he says.

'I make my own indicators.' (Only to Lait does Swindler refer to himself as 'I'.)

'Frankly, Hans-Dietrich, the Sidney Pyke scandal has finally got to her. Alternate sentences defend her wonderful husband and denounce the bastard's treachery. Italics and exclamation marks like pepper and salt. And now this "post coitum omnis animal tristis est" business. I tell you, these women who are gunning for Sidney – '

'Ach – women.'

'Samantha herself is a paid-up member of the species. There's no escape from destiny – I thought you were pretty hot on destiny, Hans-Dietrich.'

'I'm having the book rewritten in Munich.'

'But do you understand? Samantha has now "discovered" that seventy per cent of rape charges are malicious fabrications by women.'

'So? Call it ninety-five per cent.'

'Jesus. Listen: no feminist can survive stuff like that. She even accuses Pyke's victims of having "asked for it". That phrase is death.'

'We cut the phrase – no problem.'

'In the next breath she accuses her husband of a lifetime of deception. Then she calls me in New York and reports that poltergeists are moving her floppy disks about. Davidson and that Poynter girl have us by the short hairs.' (Al Sabah's name is never to be spoken in Mr Swindler's presence.)

'Eliminate Davidson and the girl.'

'Hans-Dietrich, this is England. Publishing ethics here are still quite backward.'

'Ja, perhaps.' Swindler's small head has pointed itself to the smoked-glass windows. The overt sums of money involved in the Newman affair are of course risible; but a loss of face, a humiliation by Al Sabah, cannot be countenanced on the eve of the crazy Arab's bid, part-financed by the Sultan of Qishar, for the entire Swindler empire. About this Lait does not as yet know because he does not as yet need to know. Swindler knows because the Swamiji told him. Putting the Swamiji in spiritual charge of three Bavarian orphanages has been enough. Al Sabah's orphanages are located exclusively in the Arab world and the Swamiji is growing bored of brown skins.

'Hans-Dietrich,' Lait makes a final plea, 'let that crazy

250

Arab rub the skin off his hands. Samantha Newman isn't Stalingrad.'

'It is.'

Lait absorbs the 'it'. OK, all Germans are crazy, where does that get you? OK, Swindler never checks into an airline under his own name, and never flies on any plane he's checked into, including his own private fleet of Boeings. It's legendary that as a young officer in Rommel's army, he'd killed a camel merely because it farted as he mounted it. Where did that get the camel? As for the prospect of 'Eye Contact' in some damp Olde English crypt, it's almost as depressing as the prospect of Samantha's ethnic jewellery biting into his Bermuda tan. English county towns look best in travel brochures.

Turning off the motorway, Rolls Corniche S1 passes a nasty accident involving two cars and an overturned container truck. One of the cars is crushed under the cabin of the truck. Shattered bodies lie unattended in the road. No one has stopped to help and the emergency services have not yet arrived. Swindler's massive, black-coated Bavarian secretary-chauffeur sounds his horn in a long, furious warning, a remonstrance.

'We ought to stop,' Lait says.

'You mentioned Stalingrad,' Swindler says.

'Sorry?'

'My uncle lay on the frozen earth at Stalingrad. None of the democratic nations of the West lifted him from the ground.'


Al Sabah Al Masri Al Fatah's silver Rolls-Royce Corniche glides down the motorway, sporting its unique licence plate: AS1. (He had wanted ASAMAF1, until his aides explained that distinction lay in brevity.) Davidson, nauseated by the reek of incense and the reek of Swamiji within the closed windows, is trying to calm his boss's stretched nerves.

'Almost there, sir.'

251

'You keeping saying so!'

'I'm sure you won't regret the journey, sir.'

'I already regretting. Who being this Pyke man to summoning Al Sabah Al Masri Al Fatah to filthy art exhibition?'

'And you'll also be meeting his co-author, Chantal Poynter.'

'Yeah, Shendah Pintah.' Mr Al Sabah keeps tapping his knee like a drum, and sometimes the Swamiji's knee, and occasionally Davidson's. 'Yeah, Shendah book sinking Samba book and sinking that Jew Swindler.'

'That Jew,' the Swamiji sighs.

'You reading again Shendah pages,' Mr Al Sabah commands Davidson. 'I liking.'

Davidson has already read him Chantal's latest chapter three times. He doesn't like to admit that reading in the rear seats of well-sprung luxury cars makes him sick, for is it not precisely such quirks of physiology that separate the winners from the wannabees? A publishing executive who can't read in his boss's car enjoys no brighter future than a stockbroker with a stutter. You might as well confess to suffering from computer-screen migraines.

'I waiting,' Mr Al Sabah growls.

'I reading,' Davidson says.


In April 1967 [writes Chantal] Sidney Pyke visited West Berlin's notorious Kommune 1, located in an old warehouse at 60 Stephanstrasse. The previous year, during the famous San Francisco Be-In, when hundreds of kids worshipping Ken Kesey had gone into a protracted psychedelic trance (five, including Pyke's first wife, Sharon, never woke up), Pyke had been introduced to Berlin's infamous porn merchant, Klaus Rainer Rohl, at that time still the husband of Ulrike Meinhof, the woman who was to give her name to Germany's murderous Red Army Faction in the 1970s. Rohl, who edited a corrupting mag aimed at schoolchildren called *Politporn*, immediately embraced Pyke as a kindred spirit and invited him to Berlin.

By Pyke's own account, hidden for years in his private papers, his visit to Kommune 1 was a revelation. The drugged atmosphere in the loft of 60 Stephanstrasse, the day-and-night television, the constant swapping of sexual partners, the open love-making in full view of anyone who cared to watch, all this, noted Pyke in his journal, "turned me on". He had found Sodom at last.

Pyke was excited to learn that the Kommunards had recently peddled photographs of themselves copulating to bookstores, as an under-the-counter inducement to prospective buyers of Kommune 1's notorious pamphlet, 'Burn'. Celebrating the recent deaths of three hundred people in a Brussels department store fire, the Kommunards openly incited German radicals to light fires of their own. Sidney Pyke loudly applauded this gesture as a 'deeply relevant' response to America's use of napalm against Vietnamese peasants.

Pyke adored the panache with which the male Kommunards 'fucked their chicks' on grimy mattresses. 'Groovy', also, was a series of porn photos peddled by the Kommunards in return for LSD, cocaine, marijuana and, occasionally, the despised substance called money. In Pyke's own words, these glossy pics showed 'two huge spades stud-fucking the archetypal superblonde in the ass and the cunt at the same time'.

What the superblondes really felt about it he did not speculate. Probably the question never occurred to the young radical who later became a prime mover of Amsterdam's 'Wet Dream Film Festival'. To explain his attitude towards women as typical of a whole generation of radicals might be uncharitable to a whole generation of radicals. Pyke was in a class of his own.

A friend of the theatre critic and sybarite, Ken Tynan, he frequently took time off from making the revolution in order to make sado-mas 8mm movies in which his own parts and his own prowess were massively on display. Pyke's sojourns among the hippies and Diggers of Berlin and San Francisco confirm that here was a Napoleon among male chauvinist pigs. Co-author of a pamphlet celebrating the promiscuity of the anarchist scavengers who called themselves Diggers, he wrote: 'They're beautiful people. Their men are tough. They have style, guile, balls, imagination and autonomy. Their women are soft, skilled, fuck like angels . . .'

Whether Sharon Pyke felt the same way we shall never know. Abandoned by Sidney, she died in obscure squalor. All that remains of her is an egg-timer.

What kind of a man was, and is, Sidney Pyke? More especially, how does he regard women today? Even if he has jettisoned the grosser terms of his youth, like 'pussypower', has the beast fled from the professor? Has age quelled the heroic chauvinist at the centre of a non-stop media storm whose urgent desires it is the duty of the chosen 'sisters' to service? Or does the strutting rooster of the '60s still inhabit his own Phallic Universe? What happens to a junior colleague or a female student who says no to Sidney Pyke?

In short, what did happen to Bess Hooper and Melanie Rosen? In short, they got raped. Whatever he did to them, no other word fits. In private, Sidney is honest enough to admit as much. You can't help liking the man.


Davidson closes his eyes. He feels seriously sick. The Swamiji's perfumes and Al Sabah's cigar smoke have finally got to him.

'Yeah,' says Mr Al Sabah. 'Is good, this *Sidney Pyke Story*. Market-leader, eh?'

'Let's hope the University Tribunal confronts its moral duty, sir.'

Mr Al Sabah gives this some thought. 'How much it costing buying university?'

'Not for sale, sir.'

'Everything for sale, young man.'

'As a matter of fact, sir, you might be interested to know that Vampire Books is in trouble. High interest rates, spiralling manufacturing costs, rising overheads, persistent negative investment and a Managing Director who warehouses titles he believes have literary value. Call it incurable tunnel vision. The Samantha Newman book will finish Vampire.'

'Yeah, Samba.'

'You could buy the outfit for only twice the value of current turnover. Slash the editorial staff and eliminate all titles not moving at the rate of one thousand a month. Chop the poetry list entirely.'

'Yeah.'

'Yeah,' murmurs the Swamiji, dozing. But not dozing. Never dozing in this big game of life. Davidson doesn't yet know of Mr Al Sabah's elaborate plans to launch a billion-dollar bid for the entire Swindler empire. The Swamiji knows, Swindler knows, Al Sabah doesn't know Swindler knows, all those pretty Bavarian boys. Al Sabah's American lawyers, Roth, McCoy, Cohn and Stein, are secretly preparing papers to be filed with the Securities and Exchange Commission. The initial offer of seventeen dollars a share will of course be rejected by the Swindler Board, who will immediately appeal to the Federal Communications Commission, pleading that Al Sabah is not a fit person to control thirteen American and two British TV stations or to own parts of orbiting satellites. Swindler will attempt to mobilize the Jewish lobby in support of Swindler's inevitable rejection of the Al Sabah bid as 'unsolicited, unwelcome, improper and alien' – yeah. But Messrs Roth, McCoy, Cohn and Stein, they taking care of Jewish lobby: big donations to Israel. No problem.

Mr Al Sabah no fool. Swindler no fool either. Maybe

time for the Swamiji to retreat to Himalayan monastery . . . nice holiday for Bavarian orphan boys.

Turning off the motorway, Rolls-Royce AS1 passes a nasty accident involving two cars and an overturned container truck. One of the cars is crushed under the cabin of the truck. Shattered bodies lie unattended in the road. No one has stopped to help and the emergency services have not yet arrived. Al Sabah's chauffeur sounds his horn in a long, furious warning, a remonstrance.

'We ought to stop,' Davidson says.

'Intifada,' Mr Al Sabah says.

'Sorry?'

'West Bank Intifada massacre by Israeli. Nobody stopping for those dead brothers of mine.'

# *Nineteen*

On the Saturday 'Eye Contact' opens to the public.

Descending to the kitchen, Sidney gives DARLING DUST-BINS the evil eye, then reads the uniformly awful Press notices with deepening anxiety – Samantha's mood since the 'omnis animal tristis est' business has convinced him that the Sartrean duty of the hour is guilt. Thought and action being dialectically interdependent, to say the least, Sidney has accordingly entered the marital bed in the middle of the night and raped his wife, his sensitive purpose being, of course, to say nothing, in Latin or any other language, after the event.

Mission accomplished. But now the venomously derisive columns of the *Mail*, the *Telegraph* and everyone else threaten to undo his healing gesture.

Samantha descends at nine radiant in a 'bombe glacée', or is it 'bombe surprise', peach outfit of silk and organdie. Pouring her coffee, Sidney takes note of his own profound understanding of women.

'Just had a fax from Jack, darling. He and Hans-Dietrich are on their way!'

Sidney stops pouring the coffee. 'Don't forget your breath fresheners.' She beams happily. 'And don't read the reviews of your exhibition.'

'Oh.' With rising terror she surveys the papers spread on the table. 'Are they utterly beastly?'

'As you often say, criticism is the revenge of mediocrity against talent.'

Nervously she skims the surface vibes of the *Daily Mail* review, ending with a howl.

'That bitch Fiona! And I went to her horrible little brat's christening! Even though it had the wrong father!'

'Pure jealousy, of course.'

'Sidney, don't treat me like a fool. And I really don't think you should wear that same comic-opera suit again today. You're not the leader of a failed Latin American coup d'état.'

'Today? Today! I'm going nowhere today.'

'Don't be so silly, Hans-Dietrich wants to meet you. It's in the fax.'

'He does? And the divorce can wait until Monday?'

'Sidney, don't be tedious.'

Driving into the town square, Mr Al Sabah's chauffeur finds a double yellow line to park on. Davidson's first impression is of some kind of fancy-dress carnival – the square is packed with female Eskimos. Not ten paces from AS1, one of them is burning a bra, observed by a group of sceptical firemen. Davidson wonders whether Muslims burning books is worse, or better, than Eskimos burning bras.

'I'm a working-class lesbian mother,' the Eskimo suddenly shrieks to the crowd, 'and I don't feel confident about confronting authority.'

Mr Al Sabah wears an expression of profound incredulity. Neither he nor the Swamiji displays any inclination to leave the car.

Rolls Corniche S1, meanwhile, has also found a double yellow line worthy of it.

'Anarchy,' Swindler tells Lait. 'Typical of England.'

'You're sure this is England? When did the Eskimos get here? They're not in the travel brochures.'

From the safety of the car, Swindler and Lait observe a crowd of Eskimos and townspeople gathered round a transit van bearing the inscription 'Yellow Gate ♀ ♀' in somewhat irregular lettering. A woman in granny glasses and green battle fatigues stands astride the bonnet of the van, orating into a megaphone.

'What does the woman say?' Swindler asks Lait, whose dangerous duty it is to lean out of the car.

'Hard to tell. Sounds like a lecture on Virginia Woolf. From what I can gather, Woolf was abused as a girl then demanded a money wage for the unpaid houseworker . . . stressing the link between low pay and . . . rape. Virginia also realized . . . that the war machine thrives only because women lack the economic power to . . . destroy it.'

'Red scum.'

Jack Lait climbs out of the car. 'Is that the famous Bess Hooper?' he asks the Eskimo who has been burning her bra. She turns and looks him over. 'Fuck off, MCP.'

'And cold turkey to you, madam. I'd like you to know that my daddy served in Korea. I can call him collect any time.'

At this moment Lait catches sight of Ian Davidson alighting from Al Sabah's Rolls.

'The Sheikh is with us,' Lait informs Swindler.

'Ja?' Swindler is out of the car even before the Bavarian secretary-chauffeur can open the door. 'Where is the woman's exhibition?'

Lait asks several non-Eskimos the way to the exhibition, but the advice he receives, adamant on each occasion, is wildly contradictory.

'We must become a map!' Swindler snaps.

Finally, an indignant woman in a hat, accompanied by an indignant dog wearing tartan pants, points them towards the parish church of St Michael and All Angels.

'Every loony antic takes place there. The vicar's a Communist vegetarian.'

'That must be the place.' Lait thanks her.

Approaching the church, Lait and Swindler stop short at the spectacle of local youths jeering at a banner held by angry Eskimos: LESBIANS AND PROSTITUTES COLLECTIVE.

'Women do two-thirds of the world's work and get five

per cent of world income. Menials Unite!' a furious Eskimo shouts back at the youths. She then sets fire to a grotesque effigy. The youths barrack and throw empty beer cans at her.

'Who is that creature burning?' Swindler wants to know.

'I'd give odds of five-to-one it's Professor Sidney Pyke.'

'This could never happen in Germany.'

'I guess you burn books in Germany, Hans-Dietrich.'

Two policemen are pushing through the crowd of jeering youths with water buckets, which they hurl at the smouldering Pyke effigy. They then seize the Eskimo woman, who resists furiously.

'Which end do you want?' Lait hears one of the policemen. 'The end that bites or the end that stinks?'

At the moment Davidson catches sight of Swindler and Lait staring at a burning effigy, he suffers a sharp bite in his calf – the two unpleasant experiences make instant symbiotic sense. Davidson finds himself engulfed by a demonstration of Angry Dog Owners hunting for Councillor Sidney Pyke. The dogs themselves, all off the lead and barking for blood, pause for a special crap-in on the steps of a pretty, Georgian façade on whose handsome stonework is neatly inscribed: 'The Samantha Newman Day Care Centre'.

An arm, a nice arm, threads into Davidson's. Even so, he jumps. The atmosphere is distinctly jumpy.

'So there you are,' Chantal says. 'If intestinal worm eggs didn't finish off Samantha's toddlers, then toxocara canis infection will surely lead to blindness. A good subject for a book?'

Davidson emits a sceptical grunt. The Swamiji has advised him that Mr Al Sabah owns some two hundred dogs, here and there, besides 'many many' orphans.

'Well, what do you think of my outfit?' Chantal says.

'Splendid.'

'Some gallant, you. Isn't that Swindler with Lait over there?'

'Aye. How come you recognize Lait?'

'He's quite handsome, isn't he?'

'You didn't answer my question.'

'Want to introduce me to Swindler?'

'No.'

Chantal points to the church entrance into which Bess Hooper and Melanie Rosen are leading a posse of Eskimo women.

'Out out out!' they scream.

Davidson registers disgust. 'The Left has two big ideas these days: Stop and Out.'

'You mean you didn't engineer the whole thing?'

'What?'

'God, you're thick, Ian. I'm going to tell Mr Al Sabah that you masterminded the entire riot. He'll double your salary. What *is* your salary, by the way?'

Chantal pulls Davidson through the seething crowd towards the church.


Inside the crypt Sidney gallantly places himself between Samantha and the oncoming stormtroopers. Hooper rips the copulating lions of Longleat off the wall for starters, smashes the tulip tryptich, then heads for Samantha's Italian truck-driver's truck and its tunnel. But Samantha, brushing her husband's slow-acting frame aside, gets there first.

'Just try!' she hisses. 'Just you try!'

The women don't try. Spotting Sidney cowering in a corner, they surround him with cries of 'Rape!' Melanie Rosen silently goes for his beard – never more dangerous than when silent. At this moment Samantha's attention is diverted by the arrival of Lait and Swindler.

'Welcome, welcome,' Samantha, cries, flinging her arms round Lait's neck. 'Jack darling, darling.' As anticipated, the ethnic earrings hurt.

Swindler stiffly suffers her next embrace. 'So very, very, very kind of you to come, Hans-Dietrich. Isn't it all marvellous?' Samantha is incandescent.

'Is it?' Lait asks.

'It's happening at last, it's really happening! Doesn't this prove, at last, that art *matters*?'

Not five feet away from these embraces, Sidney and Melanie are both on their knees, locked in struggle for possession of Sidney's beard.

'The girl adores him,' Samantha confides to her guests. 'And of course you know Sidney: a man who can't admit what a sweet teddy bear he really is.'

'That is your husband?' Swindler asks, incredulous.

Samantha aims a slap at Melanie, who shies away. 'Women should never hit women,' she gasps.

'Oh poor Sidney – ' Samantha fondles him, 'at least half your beard gone. Again.' She flashes a gorgeous smile at Swindler, who isn't smiling. 'Sidney, do meet Mr Swindler.'

'Sveendler,' says Swindler.

'Sidney,' says Sidney.

Jack Lait extends his hand to Sidney. 'You deserve a medal, old man.' He winks.

'A scotch would do.'

'Sveendler buys all these magnificent pictures,' Swindler announces, thrusting a wad of notes into Sidney's hand. 'And become yourself a scotch.'


Frustrated in their attempt to penetrate the church by the frantic surge of an increasingly hysterical crowd, Chantal and Davidson observe Hooper, Rosen, Virginia Woolf, Emily Dickinson and other Yellow Gate ♀ ♀ being dragged from the crypt and loaded into police vans. The standard technique is to bump their backs on the ground – Hooper is accorded the extra bumps reserved for ringleaders, and the pain of it is manifest on her fighting features. Faithful to their principles, the Women offer no violent resistance beyond tearing off the policemen's lapel numbers as evidence. The sticklike Melanie is clearly the hardest to handle – a policeman punches her in the mouth. Blood pours from her teeth.

262

'Oh Melanie!' Chantal cries. 'I saw that!' She rushes to the policeman and shouts his lapel number to Davidson. 'Write it down.' Davidson hesitates: writing down policeman's numbers is not, on the whole, sensible business practice – a point well illustrated by what happens next to Chantal. In a flash she's in the van, shrieking.

Davidson sums up the situation: his prize author, his only author, is in the van. His eye searches for silver braid and finds it.

'She was a witness not a demonstrator,' Davidson tells it.

'Obstructing the police in the course of their duty.'

'In the course of their brutality – as the jury will no doubt decide. I'll come along, too.'

The braided Superintendent is clearly impressed by Davidson's smart business suit and by the word 'jury'. His tone changes to the confidential, man-to-man: 'Frankly, sir, I'd rather arrest an IRA bomb squad than this lot. Breach of the peace, aggravated assault, malicious damage, arson and witchcraft – and what will we get? Lectures about Habeas Corpus, the European Convention on Human Rights, Veganism – Vega being, as Dr Hooper has more than once reminded me, the brightest star in the constellation Lyra, whatever that is – readings from Sappho and Emily Dickinson – I now know her entire work by heart – perorations on genocide not to be confused with gynocide, pornography and matriarchy not to mention appeals to the Police Complaints Authority. And when they appear before the magistrates on Monday, having been fed vegetarian meals all weekend, we, sir, will not oppose bail despite – at a guess – thirty-three previous convictions spread unevenly among the nine defendants. Bail not contested, they never go far,' he concludes gloomily.

A moment later a somewhat stunned Chantal emerges from the police van.

'Now kindly go about your business, miss, and leave us to ours.'

'But he punched her! – your man punched Melanie in the mouth!'

'In a general mêlée, the eye can be easily deceived. The untrained eye, miss. Probably she tried to bite the officer's hand – it's one of their standard tactics.'

Chantal and Davidson watch the police van threading through the dense, curious crowd, its blue light rotating, its siren demanding passage.

Samantha now emerges from the church, radiant in peach silk and organdie, half-supporting Sidney and less than half of his beard. The *Examiner*'s photographer, who is having the afternoon of his life, with the prospect of fat fees from the national newspapers before sundown, douses the Pykes in flashlight.

'How did you get the black eye, Professor?'

The crowd parts respectfully for Samantha; even the dog owners fall back in deference to this famous television face.

'Oh Samantha, you have such charisma,' Chantal sighs, threading her arm through Sidney's.

Davidson concludes that this is the moment of make-or-break. At all costs he must take control of Pyke and lead him to Rolls-Royce AS1. Swindler and Lait are closing in.

'Who the hell,' Sidney asks Davidson, 'are you?'

'Yes, who is this nastily handsome young man?' Samantha demands of Chantal. 'I'm sure I've seen him before.'

It is Chantal who in the nick of time detaches the dazed Sidney from his wife and leads him through the jeering throng of dog-owners towards the double yellow lines where (Davidson swears) AS1 is parked. But no car, no Mr Al Sabah, no Swamiji.

'I bet they've fled to the Lebanon,' Chantal taunts Davidson. 'You dolt.'

Fortunately Davidson is tall. Above the heads of the crowd he glimpses the slowly departing Rolls, its gleaming silver bonnet now covered with Women Against Rape stickers. Charging forward with the strength of daily visits to the Barbican Health Clinic, he pulls open the door as the car gathers speed and is seized by helpful hands.

Davidson realizes his mistake too late – or too Lait.

'Welcome aboard,' Jack Lait says.


Chantal, meanwhile, has lost Sidney and found Samantha.

'Where's Sidney?' Chantal cries in alarm.

'Where are Jack and Hans-Dietrich?' moans Samantha.

Whatever the answers, the two women know one thing: they don't want each other. However, lacking their several men, they can only cling together.


Where Sidney is can be explained. At the moment the tall young Presbyterian lout started charging away god knows where, Chantal's grip on Sidney's arm had been loosened by the arrival of the Dogs. Snarling, snapping, maddened, their teeth pulling him down and across the square, he listened to the steady snapping of his bones, ligaments and joints.

According to the police doctor's report to the Coroner's court, Sidney Pyke probably lived for 'four or five minutes' before two rottweilers belonging to the Tory Chairman of the Council and his wife, the Mothers' Union, got to him.

('But this version,' the Coroner warned, 'is strictly optional. The deceased is likely to contest it, a trouble-maker even in the mortuary.')


Discovering by purest chance a Rolls-Royce parked in majestic indifference to the rioting around it, with both Mr Al Sabah and the Swamiji (must be them) pretending to be fast asleep inside, Chantal can think of no solution other than to bundle both herself and Samantha inside it.

'Where's Ian?' Chantal asks, breathless.

Mr Al Sabah is instantly out of his 'sleep'. 'Welcome, Shendah Pindah. Welcome also Mrs Samba. Al Sabah Al Masri Al Fatah at your servicing.'

'Oh what a lovely aroma of incense,' Samantha sighs, admiring the smiling Swamiji's saffron robe.

'Where's Ian?' Chantal repeats.

'Ach, that traitor. He just getting into Swindler's car. He thinking he can thwarting Allah's purpose. Death awaiting him.'

'Swindler's car! Oh Lord.'

'Isn't that where I should be?' Samantha asks.

'Well – '

'Never mind, dear. How's your baby? Still with us? Sidney will be so pleased. Where is Sidney, by the way?'

'He eaten by dogs,' the Swamiji smiles.

'Eaten!' Samantha and Chantal cry in unison.

'Yeah.'

'You seeing my licence plate, Mrs Samba,' Al Sabah says proudly.

'Your what?'

'Yeah. Infidels can calling my mother whore but not my licence plate. Koran saying avenging insult.'

Samantha and Chantal exchange glances, though they hate doing it. The car, meanwhile, glides out of the market square, its horn blaring continuously.

'Where are you taking us?' Samantha wants to know.

Al Sabah does not deign to answer this. 'OK, Mrs Samba, when you finishing nature book for Swindler?'

'Do you mean *Nature or Nurture*?' Samantha's tone carries all the condescension of which she is capable. 'Hans-Dietrich assures me it will be his lead title in the autumn. I do of course finds these worldwide promotional tours quite exhausting.'


S1 is now parked somewhere very quiet except for the sudden, neurotic flapping of wood pigeons. The blindfolded Davidson makes the mental note of a trained Boy Scout: there must be trees around. There is also an uncomfortable smell of rotting leaves or is it corpses. Davidson imagines tomorrow's headlines: 'Corpse in Copse'.

If they ever find his remains. The expensive shoes softly crunching round him in tightening circles must be Jack Lait's. In his youth Lait had made his mark publishing downtown crime novels with a faint social sting in the tail: the rotten cop had fixed the evidence against the black kid. Lait had then begun to climb toward the executive wash-room and books about Rasputin.

'Ian, you're in trouble,' Lait announces.

'You mean I've got something you want.'

'Exactly. You've got it, I want it, and you're in trouble.'

'I may have been the wrong person to fire.'

'We want the Chantal Poynter manuscript for a start – by which I mean every file disk, every backup, every print-off, every proof from Holland. Understood?'

'Very modest. Don't you want the young lady as well?'

'Why not? – a slice of her cute ass by tomorrow night. Mr Swindler is not pleased about the systematic theft of his property. Not to mention all those phoney expenses invoices you signed while working for Vampire Books.'

'Business on the downturn, I hear.'

The expensive shoes halt. 'Straight down the elevator shaft is what you deserve, you Scotch prick.'

'Scotch is whisky.'

A nasty pause. More wood pigeons. They make Davidson jump, rather. 'How would you like to receive a slice of your uncle's ear through the post from Edinburgh?' Lait inquires.

'It depends which uncle.'

'You've got guts, Davidson – and I'll have them.'

'I hope I've got higher principles than a Yankee carpet bagger.'

'On Monday we launch injunctions against Al Sabah in the sixteen printing capitals of the world. Your name will figure prominently. Even Zambia won't offer you a fried-banana stall.'

Davidson manages a broken chuckle. 'I'm sure your rewrite boys are working hard on Newman's book.'

'Listen, kid, this isn't some soft line business like oil, or armaments, or nuclear waste, or drug running, or the protection business. This is the hard end, boy – this is publishing.'

A short silence and then Davidson detects the car door of S1 open, followed by footsteps on the leaves. With the antennae of the blind, he divines shoes still more expensive than Lait's approaching. Even the wood pigeons fall silent.

'Ja, this is publishing and this is Hans-Dietrich Sveendler,' Davidson hears the dreaded voice. 'The big Mafia bosses attend all of the christenings, weddings and funerals of the Sveendler family. Only recently, in New York, Vittorio Cappuccino, the godfather of godfathers, approached Sveendler, hat in hand, following the funeral of Sveendler's American Aunt Mathilda. "Mr Sveendler," said Vittorio, "I only wish all the members of my family died so peacefully as yours."'

Davidson has to concede that the royal 'he' may be a step up from the royal 'we'. To confirm the point, Lait takes a fistful of Davidson's lapels.

'Don't you know that His Holiness the Pope invited Mr Swindler to stand beside him on the balcony of St Peter's while blessing all the people at Easter? One of the pilgrims, an old lady who'd come all the way from Spain, was heard to ask, "Who's that up there on the balcony with Mr Swindler?"' A pause. '*Did* you know that, Ian?'

'If you say so.'

'Swindler says so,' comes the other voice.

The two smart blows across Davidson's face come from a hand bearing a heavy signet ring. Only later, examining the scar on his smooth, hollow cheek, will Ian Davidson identify the crooked claws of the swastika.


Mr Al Sabah is taking tea with Samantha in the drawing room of Cuba when a Mercedes taxi covered with Women Against Rape stickers grinds to a halt. Samantha and Chantal rush to the bay window. After a long pause, taxi-driver Joe – it is he – emerges, opens the rear door, and hauls out bits and pieces of what may be Sidney.

'Oh darling!' Samantha stifles a scream and runs out to the taxi, Chantal hot on her heels.

It's not a pretty sight. Clothes ripped, caked in mud, the black eye burgeoning, the beard shredded, marks of tooth and claw across the neck and hands. Drunk on top of it.

Joe winks insolently as he takes Samantha's money. 'The prof musta been givin' a lecture.'

Sidney chuckles. 'Today Joe spotted only one girl cyclist in provocative clothing on the way out of town but succeeded in forcing her into a ditch.'

As the Mercedes guns away on screeching tyres, Samantha and Chantal carry Sidney into the drawing room and gently lower him into an armchair. Grinning nastily, he surveys the scene through one eye.

'You all thought I was savaged to death by two rottweilers, eh? Bad luck – alternative ending. May as well post-modern the post-moderns.' Finally he deigns to take in his guests. 'You must be Al Something. Who's the guru?'

Mr Al Sabah rises with dignity and introduces himself. 'Pleased to meeting you, Professor Sidney.'

'Swamiji,' smiles the Swamiji.

Sidney nods. 'Glad you decided to come. No come, no contract.'

Samantha's exhibition eyebrows are up.

'Oh gosh,' murmurs Chantal, stretching her black-stockinged legs towards Sidney's functioning eye. 'I do hope you're not going to be silly, Sidney.'

Sidney settles into a smug smile. 'Loyalty, you see, Mr Al Salaam. I've never understood why I inspire it – call it chemistry – symbiosis between the generations – heuristic energy – the Sartrean pour soi – you either have it or you don't. What about a brandy?'

'You've had enough,' Samantha says.

Chantal fetches him a brandy.

Mr Al Sabah and the Swamiji are observing these minor transactions keenly.

'Professor what I wanting from you being few words endorsing Shendah book.'

269

'Wait a minute,' Sidney says. 'Wait a minute.' Everyone waits. 'I thought it was to be a joint venture.'

'Yeah, yeah, joint venture. But bird in hand worth two in bush. She writing, you endorsing, I paying.'

'Sidney, I wanting a divorce.' Samantha walks to the door.

'Good idea,' says Mr Al Sabah. 'Swamiji can fixing it here and now.'

'Yes, and marry Sidney to Chantal in the same ceremony. And christen their child on the Koran or whatever you use.'

Mr Al Sabah's eye is fevered with the complexities of English family life. Magnificently back in the middle of the room, Samantha allows anger to drown in sorrow.

'Really, Sidney, to write a preface for a mistress but not for a wife!'

'Yeah, but you divorcing him,' Al Sabah informs her. 'And Shendah having he baby. You not having any he baby, Mrs Samba.'

'Do stop calling me that, you horrible Arab!'

Sidney stretches his legs towards his wife. 'Can't recall your ever having asked me to write a preface.'

'Well, I'm asking you now, you swine!'

'Not very nicely,' Chantal says, prettily repossessing her perch on the arm of Sidney's chair. 'It may be time, Samantha, that you saw the light.'

Samantha quivers speechless but Sidney doesn't. No one insults his wife in his presence, no one. 'What is a head-lock?' he asks Chantal.

'A what?'

'A headlock is an infallible submission hold. Marat would have survived to rule Jacobin France if he'd managed to climb out of his bath and put Charlotte Corday in a classic headlock. Trotsky invariably forgot, at Central Committee meetings, to fasten Stalin in a headlock. I remember shouting "Uncle!" to a copper's headlock in Grosvenor Square.'

Mr Al Sabah and the Swamiji exchange glances. Mad.

Sidney strikes. Chantal is off her perch and across his

knee, squealing and squirming like the heroine of the infamous strip cartoon, *!*, as the flat of his hand descends on her buttocks.

'This one for loyalty! This for vanishing values! This a gift to Yuppies everywhere!'

Chantal howls.

'Sidney, stop that!' Samantha protests. 'This isn't the Media Studies Department!'

'This one for May '68, this for the sacked printers of Wapping!'

'Spanking for God!' the Swamiji whoops. Mr Al Sabah's small feet are drumming on the floor. 'Sparing rod spoiling child to be coining phase,' he pants.

'No, no, you don't understand,' Samantha cries. 'It's really me he's striking!'

Sidney desists, out of breath. 'Ha! Did you hear what she said? Women are all the same. When they say no they mean yes. They're all asking for it, each in her own way.'


A gentle evening sunlight caresses the eclectic façade of Cuba, as if offering tribute to the stubborn autumn of the patriarch. Tonight the nation will put its clocks forward an hour while Sidney, as is his custom, puts his egg-timer an hour (or two) back.

But not before he has taken a stroll in his garden, where all his apple trees flourish as if Bess's ♀ ♀ never arrived to cut them down. (Obviously they didn't.) Follow on his halting heel and you will catch him talking aloud, confident that he has retained – as predicted in the first chapter – your entire sympathy. Iago's Version.

Circumambulating Samantha's organic compost heap, he is weighed down by your desire to know more. What will be the Tribunal's verdict? Will Professor Pyke be publicly disgraced and dismissed? Will Melanie and Bess be condemned as malicious liars and sent packing? The fate of Samantha's book? Ah. And of Chantal's? Ah. Must Samantha yield her hour of prime time to her ruthless young rival?

271

And will Samantha Newman remain Mrs Sidney Pyke?

Arriving at Yellow Gate, where he and the Women – strictly in his own imagination, let it be understood – famously (he believes) scrummaged in the mud, he can no longer evade your cardinal question: Did I rape Bess? Did I rape Melanie? Well, I'll tell you:

– The Large Copper butterfly is now extinct in East Anglia, along with the wolf, the boar and the bear.

– Half the Earth's 8,000 extant species of bird are now in peril. The Barbados racoon and the Australian numbat are on their way out.

– Samuel Beckett is dead. Never cared for his work but that's not the point.

– Dogs on the increase, Thatcherism throughout Eastern Europe.

– As the Russian poet Brodsky said, 'Tomorrow is just less attractive than yesterday. For some reason, the past doesn't radiate such immense monotony as the future.'

# David Caute

won the Authors' Club Award and the John Llewellyn Rhys Memorial Prize for his first novel *At Fever Pitch*. His other novels include *The K-Factor, The Occupation, The Decline of the West, Veronica or The Two Nations* and *Comrade Jacob*, which was the basis for the film *Winstanley*. His non-fiction publications include *'68: The Year of the Barricades*, and *Under the Skin: The Death of White Rhodesia*. He has been a Fellow of All Souls College and literary editor of the *New Statesman*.

# WHOA!
## I SPY A
## WEREWOLF

FOR SHEILA MUM